THE ITCHES
OF
BEASWICK

GERALD DESHAYES

 www.trafford.com

North America & international
toll-free: 1 888 232 4444 (USA & Canada)
fax: 812 355 4082

The author would like to acknowledge **Random House Publications-1986** and **John Updike** (*The Witches of Eastwick*), along with **Jack Nicholson** and **Cher**.

Thank you, **Robert Daniel**, for your support and countless hours of hard work in editing. You are my second set of eyes. Also thanks goes out to **Tony Koenen**, my multi-talented friend, for allowing me to use his lyrics from *The Hey Hey Song* and *Promise Land*. More importantly, I want to thank you, **Tony** (tonykoenenmusic.com), for *The Itch of a Rose*, a song written about Rose, the lead character in this story. Please visit **www.geralddeshayes.com** for a free download and also for more information on my first novel, *Gene*.

Also, a thank-you goes to author, **Cadence Trites,** for her suggestions and support (ferrisfarnsworth.com) and **Wes Van** for his valued input. Special mention goes to **Don Burnett (**thegardenexpert.com) and **Don Mutter** (anymalhouse.com).

Cover photo: **Angie Bonten (**angelabonten.com), **Tony Koenen** (tonykoenenmusic.com)

This book is dedicated to my grandchildren, Scarlett, Noah and Chynna

The Itch of a Rose

Excerpt used with permission. Tony Koenen-socan- Sept. 2013

She is just another girl with dreams of a better day
The line is fine between right and wrong
"I am righteous," she would say
Oh, she loved this place, in another time,
But the love has died now she can't stay

There's a better way, but the line gets blurred
Hell the law ain't right all the time
So she worked it out, the weeds they grew high
That magic forever, changed her world
In her wildest dreams she never saw people die
Now we live our lives wondering, "Why?"

For the complete lyrics and song, please visit **geralddeshayes/music.com**.

I

The tree branch exploded inches above her head. Thousands of tiny wood fragments rocketed in all directions—some lodging in her long, red hair. The sharp crack from the high powered rifle followed milliseconds later, slicing through the cool autumn air.

Dropping to the dusty ground on her stomach, she lay motionless in the middle of the deer path. Her mind raced. *Jen and Carla! Are they okay?* Her two partners had been several feet behind her. Rose prayed that they hadn't been struck by the bullet.

A twig snapped from above. *He's on the move!* She squeezed the soft earth in her outstretched hands, needing to get a fix on where the shooter was. Sounds in the mountains sometimes played tricks.

Pulling in several shallow breaths, she tried not to sneeze from the pine dust that hung in the air. *Whoever you are, please go back up the mountain. Leave us—*

BOOM! Another deafening gun blast slammed into her, making her ears ring even more. The bullet tore through dense bush several feet to her right, clipping branches before hitting a small tree dead-on. The sapling reeled, almost splitting in two from the impact.

She burrowed into the dirt, trying to make herself as small a target as possible. *If he gets any closer I'll yell. I'll let him know that—*

More branches and twigs snapped as he clumsily pushed his way closer toward her and her friends.

Rose slowly raised her head, ready to yell out to him. A peculiar sound stopped her. *Is that ... water running?* She tried putting it together. *Did he shoot one of our pipes? It must have sprung a—?*

"Did ya get one?" It was a male voice and it came from farther up the slope.

There are two of them! Her nerves were on overload. *I've got to let them know that—*

"I'm not sure." The shooter was no more than a hundred feet from her.

Is he ready to shoot—?

"Did you hit it or what?" The voice from farther away sounded impatient.

Rose waited for a reply. There was none.

Louder, and with an angry edge to it, he tried again. "Eddy! Damn it! Answer me! What's goin' on down there?"

"Just takin' a piss. This beer's goin' straight through me."

"Jeeze. Did you shoot it or *what*?" Al wanted answers from his hunting partner several hundred feet below him.

Ignoring his irate buddy, Eddy zipped up. With his right arm cradling his rifle, he eyed a partially exposed stone. It was no more than eight feet away.

Deciding that it would make a challenging target, he worked his jaw for the perfect mix before spewing out a wad of tobacco coupled with a healthy combination of spit and beer.

The stone didn't stand a chance. He hit it smack in the middle—the slimy gob splattering across its exposed face.

Pleased with his spitting skills, he made an attempt at wiping his mouth. A string of brown saliva stuck to the back of his hand. Eddy smeared the mess on his pants before getting back to his hunting.

"What's goin' on? Did you hit it?" Al was anxious. Dusk was approaching and the wind was picking up.

"Uh? I'm not sure. I thought I saw somethin' move. It's hard to tell from up here. There's lots of trees in the way. I'm gonna take a closer look." He moved closer to the three women.

Rose was ready to shout out to him. It was time to let him know that she and her two companions were nearby and not to do any more shooting. *I will not—*

Al shouted out instead. "You see anything?" Peering in Eddy's direction, he waited for an answer before trying again, this time with a much harder voice.

"Answer me!"

Rose's heart raced as she pictured the nearby hunter taking aim at her and her friends.

"Eddy?"

Annoyed with the nagging, his friend hollered back. "Jeeze, Al! What's your friggin' problem?"

"What's my problem? What's my problem? I'll tell you what my problem is. It'll be dark in a few minutes and the wind's pickin' up. Might be a storm comin'. Leave the fuckin' thing. I ain't haulin' it up this cliff. Besides, it could be long gone by now." As an afterthought, he added, "If you ever *did* hit it."

Al did not want to drag game through bush, especially up a steep incline. He hunted mostly for the sport and shot at easy prey—preferably from the driver's side of his pickup with the heater on and a cold beer between his legs.

It was late October and a chill was in the air. Wanting nothing more than to head back to their warm cabin, his mind drifted to the steaks that they had brought and how he liked his done—medium-rare. Besides, it was Friday and the weekend was here. It was time to do some serious drinking.

Eddy knew that his buddy was right. It would be hard work lugging a deer back to their truck. In the fading light, he studied the dense bush, doubting if he had hit anything.

A raucous caw grabbed his attention. Jerking his head toward a stand of dead fir, the bird was perched on a limb. *At least I can get me a crow.*

Pain stabbed at his stomach as he raised his Browning Mark II. His ulcer was acting up—the result of several cans of beer.

"Are you headin' back up here or what?" Al was frustrated. *What's he doin' down there? He's startin' ta piss me off!*

His buddy lowered the .30-30, his mid-section on fire. In a weak voice he mumbled, "Relax. I'm comin'."

Rose gulped in a lungful of air. She had been holding her breath for what seemed like an eternity. *Just go back to your partner. There's nothing for you here.*

With his mind on the roll of Tums in Al's glove box, Eddy pushed his way back, toward his friend. He planned on swallowing at least half a dozen. Branches snapped and cracked as he bulldozed through a jungle of dry trees and brush, moving away from her and her friends.

The little relief that Rose was beginning to feel quickly faded. *Carla and Jen! Are they okay?* Shifting on her side, she turned in their direction.

They were on their stomachs in the middle of the deer path no more than twenty feet behind her. Outside of being terrified, they seemed to be fine. She gave them a weak smile before turning back to the hunter, catching a glimpse of his red, plaid hat as he noisily retreated up the mountain.

Drumming his fingers on the hood of his pickup, Al waited impatiently for his hunting partner. Neither he nor Rose realized that, at that moment, they both had somewhat parallel thoughts. He was slightly drunk and wanted nothing more than to head back to their warm cabin and have a few more Buds.

Rose was also thinking about buds, but an entirely different variety—buds that you smoked rather than drank. *That was too close to our plants. Too close to us.*

This was not the first time that the girls had been accidentally shot at. Hunting season lasted for weeks and this part of the mountain was one of several locations where deer were usually spotted. The land was state-owned. The nearest private property was a mile away and belonged to Rose.

Hunters sometimes roamed near their growing areas, but so far the girls had been lucky. No one had come across their marijuana crops and, more importantly, they had not been hit by a stray bullet.

Rose knew that it wouldn't have taken much for Eddy to have spotted their plants. If he had walked a few more feet with his brain in gear, he would have easily noticed the pot. Some were over eight feet tall and all were a dark, healthy green—unlike the surrounding orange and yellow autumn leaves.

She had been concerned about the wind picking up. If it had been blowing in the wrong direction the so-called hunter would have smelled the plants before even seeing them. Cannabis gave off a strong and unique odour.

Several farmers in Fenton County grew marijuana. Her ex-husband's brother, Sheriff Gleason, had told her months earlier that he was annoyed with trying to bust them. There were simply too many. Besides, if he arrested any more growers, the economy around their small town would most likely collapse.

Beaswick's main source of income used to be from beekeeping. That had slowly evolved over the years into something slightly more lucrative—cabbage.

Now, one might say, the town's economy was still based on cabbage, but not the kind that grandma baked. On the street, this variety would bring in close to two thousand dollars a pound.

Sheriff Gleason understood why some of the farmers had changed crops. He had announced to Rose, with a pompous smile, "If I were them, I'd probably do it, too!"

She had secretly smiled, thinking, "Well, guess what? You *are* doing it, too. You're indirectly involved with growing pot. You're on the take. The take from me and God only knows how many other growers."

Her two friends scrambled up to her. Carla's face was flushed. "He could have killed us!" She said it accusingly with her hands on her hips, making it sound like it was Rose's fault that the hunter had fired shots in their direction.

Rose took a step back and raised her palms in defence. She understood that her partner was only releasing her tension. "Whoa! Take it easy. Everything's okay. Nobody got hurt."

Carla still needed to vent. "This is ridiculous. We're being hunted like animals. This has got to stop. This—"

"Auntie!" Jennifer was on the verge of tears. Carla's ranting wasn't helping. "Please. Let it go. I just want to forget about it."

She turned to her niece and grabbed her hand, knowing that Jen could easily be frightened. Trying to sound reassuring, she sputtered, "It's okay. I won't let that happen again." Carla had no idea how she could do that. They were playing a dangerous game of hiding in the woods while tending to their crops—especially with drunken hunters in the area.

With her free hand, Jen rubbed at the tattooed Japanese characters on her bicep for comfort, whispering, "Peace, love, happiness." She was not convinced with what her aunt was telling her.

Rose studied the marijuana plants several feet away as she picked at her red hair. Pulling out some of the larger pine splinters, she wondered how she could lighten the mood. Turning to the traumatized young woman, she confessed. "I was scared, too. Believe me. I almost wet my pants."

An anaemic smile slowly crossed Jen's face. She felt a little better knowing that she wasn't the only one who had been shaken by the hunters.

Rose looked in Al and Eddy's direction while reminding her partners again. "We knew what kind of risks we were taking when we went ahead with our plan."

She understood that her friends were questioning if what they were doing was worth it.

Smiling reassuringly, she spoke on a more positive note. "I never thought that our plants would be this healthy. We almost have *too* much."

Carla slowly nodded, knowing that her friend was right. The crop had turned out better than expected. However, there was still a lot of work to be done. They needed to harvest the marijuana—to remove the bud. That would keep them busy for weeks once they were safely transferred to Rose's barn.

Feeling a little more comfortable now that the hunters were gone, Jennifer nervously giggled, releasing some of her stress. "That Eddy guy had no idea we were even here."

They were experts at camouflaging and had gleaned information on how to become almost invisible from several sites on the internet. They had also learned how to cover their tracks and make it difficult for anyone to follow their trail. It was all part of the job. If they didn't pay attention to detail, they would find themselves in jail—or worse.

Her giggling was contagious. Rose and Carla chuckled along with her, loving the idea that they had once again gotten away with their grow operation without being spotted.

Chapter 2

The girls made their way to one of twenty marijuana gardens that were scattered in the woods. Being shot at by a drunken hunter was still very much on their minds as they tried to get back to the work that had to be done.

The locations had been carefully chosen. The plants were expertly hidden with branches and twigs, including camouflaged netting, but not at the expense of receiving enough sunlight. It was a tricky business that could reap a huge profit—if things went according to plan.

They constantly worried about the Drug Enforcement Agency who, on occasion, conducted surveillance from the air. To a certain degree Rose was pleased that she knew her ex brother-in-law, Sheriff Gleason, as well as she did. He would keep them informed of any planned flyovers—for a price, of course. Gleason always had a price.

Rose decided to have another talk with him. She hated to do that—to deal with the sheriff. He was becoming far too demanding about wanting more of her cash. She understood why.

He had a gambling habit and had tried to convince her that it was difficult for him to keep on top of things. That's why he had wanted the extra money. It was because of all the hard work that he was doing in looking the other way and keeping the law from her.

Rose knew that she was being scammed but had no other choice. It was far better to pay the sheriff a percentage from their crops than go to jail. She tried to think of it as just another business expense—some kind of security fee.

The three women crouched as they made their way single file through the barricade of sticks and branches that formed a crude fence around a growing area. It protected the cannabis from the deer.

This particular garden housed twenty-two plants and, once inside, Carla stood upright. She was still very much concerned about her niece. Jennifer could easily panic and act irrationally. It had happened many times before. *Who can blame her? Nobody wants to be shot at!*

Standing tall in the marijuana patch, Carla refocused. She was a large woman with a larger heart and almost took up as much room in the confined area as her two friends combined.

Peeking out from behind the barricade, she checked to make sure that there were no more hunters close by. Rose and Jen followed her lead. All three were on high alert.

Satisfied, Carla turned and faced the crop. It appeared almost ominous in the early evening light. The huge plants towered over them and she couldn't help but marvel at how well they were doing.

For a brief moment she had a disturbing thought. Were the plants dependant on them for survival, or was it the other way around? Were the women becoming slaves to the marijuana at the expense of risking their lives? She dismissed the idea, wanting to believe that it was more of a symbiotic relationship.

Back in early March they had cultivated the young shoots in Rose's barn. Later, they had transplanted the marijuana into larger pots and had hauled them to their final growing destination outdoors—a mile from her property.

A twig snapped from outside their barricade, making them drop to their knees. A dark figure moved in the bush no more than fifty feet away.

Rose's heart raced. If it was another hunter, she would yell out and let him know that she and her friends were close by and not to shoot. If it was an animal, it would bolt.

She raised her voice, her red hair whipping about in the strong breeze. "Who's there?"

The girls waited for an answer, their eyes riveted on the bush just beyond. The rasping sounds from the surrounding trees were their only reply.

Rose tried again, this time, louder. "Hello? Who's there?"

Carla's patience was running thin, especially after being shot at—twice. She pushed her way out of the barricade with Jen and Rose following closely behind.

They shouted out, hoping to either make a hunter aware that they were in the area or to scare off any animal.

A deer stood motionless in the shadows. Carla wondered when it would bolt and slowed her pace. Drawing closer, she was now only twenty feet from it. The animal had been shot in the neck. Turning away from her, it tried to flee, but collapsed on its front knees. Its hind quarters jutted up, making it appear to be in prayer.

Carla wanted to comfort it—to let it know that she meant it no harm. She wished that she could somehow explain that she wasn't like that Eddy who had probably shot it.

The thought of animals being hurt, especially by humans, made her ill. They were an annoyance, but she still loved the deer. Having part of their marijuana crop eaten by them didn't matter to her. What *did* matter was the animal's obvious trauma. Blood dripped from the neck wound, turning the dusty ground beneath a dark red.

The girls stood quietly as they watched the onset of death. There was an air of reverence to the scene. Mesmerized, they could not pull their eyes away from the suffering, young buck.

He broke the spell by attempting to stand, but his rear legs buckled and forced him on his side. The bullet hole in his neck made it difficult for him to pull in air. Panting hard, his laboured breathing took on an unnatural, raspy sound. He made several attempts at lifting his head, but it was futile.

For the moment, all thoughts of harvesting marijuana were gone—their hearts going out to the dying creature. They loved nature and hated to see something so beautiful die needlessly.

Rose thought about her dog, Kobi. The German shepherd had disappeared weeks earlier. It wasn't like him to go wandering off and not return. He was dedicated and fiercely protective of their property. They had searched her ten wooded acres with no success.

One afternoon Rose had opened the steel gate at the foot of her long driveway. She had planned on driving to Beaswick, ten miles away. A whiff of something rancid had assaulted her. Curious, she had followed the foul smell, thinking that it was a deer. No. It was Kobi, dead from a bullet wound. A hunter had probably mistaken him for game.

They missed him, his companionship and the security that he had provided. He had been a good deterrent for any unwanted visitors.

The deer made another attempt at standing, but failed. Still on its side, it wheezed several times before spastically kicking its rear legs once, twice and then … it was over.

They were shaken and wished that it was simply some kind of tragic mistake and that God would give the animal another chance. But, there would be no second chance. Eddy, the fearless hunter who had urinated and spat in the woods, had indeed killed a deer. He should be so very proud.

Ashamed with what the hunter had done, all three asked the same question. "Why?" The women were growers—not killers. They would never think of hurting another creature. They were gentle souls. How could shooting an animal and leaving it behind to die be called a sport? It was cruel and brutal. It was senseless to them.

Carla wiped away a tear as she lifted her head to the darkening sky. Struggling to get a grip on her emotions, she knew that it could easily have been her or one of her partners who now lay on the dusty ground, dead from a bullet wound.

A sniffle from behind made her turn. Jennifer was on her knees and trying to hold back tears. So far this had been their toughest day. Feeling helpless, Carla placed a hand on her niece's shoulder and whispered, "There is nothing that we can do." What they had experienced today was all part of their job. *That's right. That's why we're here—growing pot in the mountains. For money. Easy money.*

She questioned what she was thinking. *Easy money?* They had never worked so hard. Then there was the risk of being killed or going to jail. No. It wasn't easy money. Carla knew that they would earn every nickel.

Keeping her hand on Jen's shoulder, she waited patiently while her niece grieved for the animal, but they would soon have to get back to work. There was a lot that had to be done. More than a hundred plants needed to be brought down the deer trail to Rose's barn, a mile away, but not all of them tonight. It would have to be done very soon, though. It was late October. The growing season was over and the plants were ready for harvest.

Chapter 3

It was hard work for the three women as they tugged at the huge plant. The roots had grown through the plastic container into the surrounding soil, making it more difficult to pull out. No one spoke as they rocked the marijuana plant back and forth until it finally broke free from its bond with the earth.

Sitting on the dusty ground in the middle of their garden, they took a break. Rose's mind was on the slaughtered deer. She whispered, more to herself than to anyone else, "Why did they do that—shoot it?"

Her voice grew loud and now had an angry edge to it. "Shoot it and then be too lazy to carry it back with them. That Eddy guy shot it just for fun!" She usually kept things to herself, but sometimes she could snap, especially when she was stressed.

"It's okay." Carla tried to console her red headed friend. She knew that she was upset, but part of the reason had nothing to do with the deer being shot. Rose could carry a grudge—especially about men.

Her husband, Bernie, had left her for another woman over a year ago and she still loved him. His brother, Sheriff Gleason, had been involved and was partly to blame for their break-up.

In Rose's mind it was all Bernie's fault that their marriage had collapsed. It was his weakness that upset her the most—to take his brother's advice and leave their marriage. It was none of Gleason's business. He should never have meddled in their relationship.

She loathed the sheriff but still had to work with him. If she didn't, he could make things very difficult for her.

Rose also hated him for another reason. One night, over a bottle of wine, she had broken down and had told Jennifer and Carla the whole story. Feeling both disgusted and ashamed, it had been too much for her to carry. Her friends had listened on as she explained.

Gleason had come over and had insisted on more protection money. He had been drinking and wanted more than just her money. Rose had demanded that he leave. That's when he had grabbed her, forced himself on her and had raped her.

Her girlfriends had felt badly for her and hated the sheriff. There was nothing that she could have done to stop him. Rose couldn't go to the authorities. She would have been arrested for growing marijuana if she did.

For protection she had invited Carla to live with her. She could not be alone after what he had done. Besides, there was too much work for one person. Carla and, later, Jen, were the answer. Gleason never came by after Rose had explained that she had a girlfriend living with her.

Reliving the memory made her attack the next plant. Carla scolded her. "Don't hurt your back any more than you already have. Take a breather. Jen and I can pull this one out by ourselves."

The two women worked away while Rose tried to relax. Despite her sore back, at fifty years old she was still in good shape. She didn't even need to dye her long hair. There were a few gray streaks in it that some men found sexy.

Her plan was to make enough money so that she could move from nearby Beaswick. She had lived there most of her life and it was time for a change.

The small town had been founded back in the early eighteen hundreds by Samuel Wickins. The several square miles of open meadow had been an ideal location for raising his honey bees. As the community grew, the name Beeswickins was adopted in honour of Samuel. Years later it had been changed to Beaswick.

Rose knew too many people in the area and had felt awkward when Bernie and she had separated. There were rumours why her ex-husband had left her. Most were false. She suspected that Sheriff Gleason had spread his fair share.

A sharp pain stabbed at her lower back, making her wince. The effects of a car accident years earlier, before she had even met Bernie, still lingered. Rose had caught her then boyfriend with her best friend at a party. Feeling disgusted and hurt, she had wanted to walk home, but he had convinced her that it was too far. He would drive her back, instead.

Drunk, he had fumbled with excuses about what he had done—his mind not on the road. They had hit the ditch. He wasn't injured. She was.

God, I need a joint. No medication relieved her back pain more than marijuana. Her chiropractor had even recommended it. It also calmed her nerves. Rose needed it now more than ever.

That's why she had initially grown pot on her small farm—so that she could have her own supply for medicinal use. One thing had led to another and now here she was with her two friends involved in an outdoor grow operation.

She lit a joint and took a puff, holding the smoke in her lungs as long as possible. Almost instantly she could feel the calming effect as the drug took over, her pain slowly subsiding. Exhaling with a cough, she offered the cannabis to Carla.

"Uh, no thanks. I'll smoke some later. You relax." Carla eyed another monster plant, planning on how they could pull it free without too much effort.

"How 'bout you?" Rose studied Jen through watery eyes.

The younger woman hesitated—unsure if she should take it. Sometimes the pot had a mellowing effect on her. At other times it made her slightly paranoid.

"Uh, no. Not right now." Her emotions were running high with the events of the day and night was fast approaching. It was only five in the afternoon and already the pallor of an early winter's evening seemed to have closed in upon the hills and mountains.

Chapter 4

Sheriff Gleason stormed out of the Wells Fargo bank in downtown Beaswick. He did not want to remain in the loan officer's stuffy office any longer than he had to.

Standing on the sidewalk in front of the old two story building, he zipped up his police jacket, feeling the cold wind bite into him. He reflected on what the skinny banker had told him—that his financial resources were stretched to their limit and that he was 'maxed out'. They wouldn't lend him any more money.

The sheriff couldn't even re-mortgage his house because he had run out of equity. He had asked for a small loan—only forty thousand dollars—but the pimply faced kid had turned him down after explaining, with what Gleason thought was a sneer, "Cornelius. Your credit has run out."

He felt humiliated and was not used to being treated that way, especially by what he considered to be an insolent punk. He also did not like being called by his first name. Everyone in Beaswick addressed him as Sheriff Gleason. Not *Cornelius* Gleason. His classmates had used to call him 'Corny' and it brought back painful childhood memories.

For a moment he wondered how he could get even with the pasty-skinned clerk. *Maybe I could bust him on suspicion of trafficking.* It would be easy for Gleason to do. He'd simply plant an ounce or two of pot in the employee's car.

He dismissed the idea as he stood on the street, watching them lock the doors for the night. Chewing on a toothpick, he pondered on how he could get his hands on more quick cash. He would need to put the squeeze on some of the farmers and inform them that he was having trouble keeping things under wrap.

Before getting into his cruiser he glanced up and down Beaswick's main street. It was only four blocks long, but he didn't see any of it. His mind was on his serious financial issues. Sighing, he told himself to get a grip on his gambling. It was causing him too much grief.

A month earlier he had been up fifteen thousand. Not anymore. He knew that he should have taken some of that money and pay off a few bills, but he had felt lucky and had eventually gambled it away.

He needed to be careful. If he owed too much he could be disciplined. The California Justice Department had a dim view of any elected official who took advantage of their position—especially a sheriff.

That was why he would travel more than a hundred miles clear out of the county to the Nakusapee Casino complex. Outside of the card dealers, no one knew him there. He could gamble to his heart's content. Besides, he liked the feel of the place, being lucky at the tables many times before.

Thinking about the casino made his heart skip. He smiled as he got into his police car, reflecting on all the money that he had won in the past. *Yeah, when I win big, I usually toss the Indian dealers a few bucks.* He chuckled at the thought—about tossing the male Indians a few 'bucks'.

It was early Friday evening and the sheriff had planned on heading there this weekend. He had close to a thousand in cash. One of the so-called farmers had come through earlier.

Gleason put his financial woes behind him for the moment and dreamed about turning the thousand into ten times that amount at Blackjack.

Squeezing money out of the growers was easy for him. He was a bit of a salesman, telling them that he was doing his best in protecting them from the law. He would claim that he was their buddy, but he couldn't do more to help them unless, of course, he was given some … incentive. It usually worked.

If they gave him trouble he would go to stage two of his plan and drive to their farms in his patrol car with his red and blue lights flashing. Gleason would make sure that he was seen by the growers before heading back to town.

He loved the theatrics and that little display always worked for him. Within hours he would happily be counting wads of cash and everything in his world would be back to normal again.

On his way to the police station he pulled into a dark alley. Moments after rapping on the rear door of Fortune Liquors he heard Tommy Li's shuffling feet. The Chinese storekeeper peeked through the eyehole and exclaimed, "Ah! Shelliff Greason!" The old guy always got his l's and his r's mixed up when he addressed him. It made Gleason chuckle as he waited for Tommy to unlock the two deadbolts and remove the steel bar.

They had a deal. The sheriff would buy his booze at the rear of the store. He did not want anyone in the small community to see him sneak into the liquor store while on duty. Mister Li knew what he wanted and already had two bottles of Jack Daniel's wrapped in a plain paper bag before Gleason had his wallet out.

Minutes later, after stashing one of the bottles in his trunk and taking a much needed swig from the other, he was in his office with his feet on his desk, still angry with the banker turning him down.

Scarlett, his secretary, was on the phone with the deputy. Her shift had ended at five but Darwin kept her on the line. Her mood had changed from minutes earlier when she had been enjoying the *Hey Hey Song* on KRQY. She had even hummed a few of the lyrics that Tony Koenen had belted out. *Hey, hey, hey, hey, what a beautiful day. Everything, everything, is going my way.*

Things weren't going her way anymore. Now she was annoyed, especially having to tell Darwin everything twice.

Gleason chuckled, feeling a nice buzz from the recent swallow of Jack, as he listened in to the one-sided conversation. *Hey, hey, hey, hey, what a beautiful day.*

She called the deputy 'Gomer', behind his back. Gleason thought about the name. *He does look a little like a Gomer.* He had almost called him that on more than one occasion.

Darwin had severely screwed up since his arrival in Beaswick. The sheriff reflected on the recent drug bust. The grower had not cooperated and had owed him several thousands in protection money.

Gleason had given his deputy explicit directions where the drug raid would be taking place. Darwin, of course, knew nothing about any protection money. He was there at his boss's request, naively believing that he was enforcing the law.

The sheriff had wondered where he had gotten to and had waited several minutes before trying to contact him on the police radio. It was difficult to do. The reception could sometimes be poor in the mountains.

Somehow Darwin had gotten lost and had gone up a neighbour's driveway by mistake. He had pulled out his pistol and had arrested the wrong people.

The sheriff later learned that the new deputy had intended to yell, "Freeze! This is a drug bust," just like they did on TV. In his excitement, Darwin had instead sputtered, "Freeze! This is a bug rust!"

In spite of the circumstances the older couple couldn't help but nervously chuckle.

Gleason had needed to do some PR work and had finally convinced them of how sorry he and the police department were. He had explained that Darwin was new to the force and inexperienced. What he had really wanted to tell them was that Darwin was just plain stupid.

Whatever he *did* say, worked. The couple accepted his apology. Since the incident, he gave 'Gomer' the easy jobs and hoped that he wouldn't screw up again.

One of the skinny deputy's problems was women. Darwin was in his mid-forties and had been married several times. When a posting in Beaswick had come up, he had jumped on it to escape from his ex-wives. He simply loved women and flirted at the first opportunity.

Scarlett slammed the phone down after explaining to Darwin for the third time what needed to be done. She was clearly annoyed as Gleason made his way to the water cooler after eating a fortune cookie. Old Tommy always put one in the brown bag with the liquor. This one read, "Before you embark on a journey of revenge, dig two graves." He needed a cold drink, having difficulty swallowing it.

"Sheriff! I can't believe how stupid that man can be." She vigorously shook her head, making her earrings swing from side to side. Just yesterday she had purchased them at the local gift shop—the Bees N Stings. They were small, porcelain honey bees that hung from fine gold chains.

With an elevated voice, she continued. "Can you believe this one? I was telling him about a border town in Mexico and how a drug dealer had decapitated someone. Do you know what he said?" She turned to Gleason while trying to settle down.

He couldn't help but smile. "Uh, what, Scarlett? What did he say?" The sheriff braced himself, knowing that this was going to be good.

"He said, 'Gosh, that's usually fatal, isn't it?' Can you believe that?" She raised her eyebrows and waited for a reaction.

He didn't disappoint her. Chuckling, he shook his head at his deputy's stupidity. *Yes, Gomer. Being decapitated IS usually fatal.*

Looking out the window, she wrapped a scarf around her neck before putting on her coat. The wind had picked up and orange and yellow leaves swirled in the breeze from the trees that lined the dark street. A storm was brewing.

Still shaking his head at what she had told him, the sheriff followed her out the door before locking the station for the night.

Driving home, he was concerned about a few rumours. There were always rumours flying around Beaswick, especially when it involved illegal drugs.

Everyone knew that the governor of California was trying to cope with the rampant marijuana problem that seemed to only be getting worse. The more he tried to prevent the unlawful activities, the more resourceful people became.

A recent state-wide referendum for legalizing marijuana had narrowly been defeated. That concerned Gleason. Californians were beginning to take a more liberalized approach on pot. He didn't want that to happen and needed to keep his farmers on edge.

It might only be a matter of time before the state reconsidered and made the possession and even cultivation of the drug legal. California was heading for bankruptcy. State control would generate much needed tax dollars and eliminate a huge portion of the criminal element. Besides, the penitentiaries were overcrowded and there was no room for new offenders.

Not all of Beaswick's citizens were involved in growing—at least not directly. But, it was good for the local economy. The farmers were paying their bills on time and Gleason had been informed that sales in the latest iPhones had tripled in the past month at the computer store.

A few had foolishly threatened to squeal on him and not give him the protection money he demanded. But, it hadn't taken long for most to see things his way. Two had been busted and were now doing time. Gleason was not happy about that. There would be no more payoffs from them.

Some still refused to deal with him. One was Larry, Rose's neighbour. Months earlier he had promised the sheriff that he would 'shoot to kill' if he ever set foot on his property.

By nature, Larry was a peaceful man and loathed weapons and violence. Coming from a family of five boys, all were successful except for him. Even his younger brother, T-Bone, was doing all right—playing the system and using his auto parts business as a front for laundering drug money.

Larry was the exception. He was stubborn and continually made the wrong choices and annoyed the wrong people. He also talked too much.

Gleason bided his time and was determined to get money out of him one way or the other.

Chapter 5

Sitting in their makeshift garden, Rose took in another lungful of marijuana and rubbed at her lower back. She studied her two girlfriends as they worked at releasing one more giant plant.

Pulling her mind from the recent events—how they had come close to being killed by two hunters—her eyes wandered in the partial moonlight. She could barely make out the nearby polyurethane pipe that was fitted with a garden tap.

Months earlier they had trenched several hundred feet of black, flexible pipe that began in a pond near Jack Pine Road—the same road that the hunters, Eddy and Al, had been on earlier. A spring fed the small pool and was a constant source of water for their plants.

The girls had spent weeks installing the plumbing. They had also dug a small reservoir where they had mixed in the liquid fertilizer. From there, the water line branched into smaller pipes that were buried where possible. Some could not be hidden because of the rocky terrain. The girls had camouflaged what they could with branches and leaves.

With the natural slope of the land, no pump was necessary. All pipes were fitted with taps that a garden hose could attach to. They simply turned on the appropriate one when they needed to water and feed their gardens.

They had worked daily throughout the spring and long, hot summer, busily tending to their crops. Each had their assigned area and, by the time they had finished watering the last plant, they would begin all over again.

Rose took one more drag, her mind drifting as her friends struggled with another plant. Mumbling in the dim light, she reflected on how good their crop had turned out.

"Huh?"

"Nothing, Carla. I was just talking to myself. Here, let me help."

"No worries. Take it easy. We'll need you in a few minutes to help haul these babies down to the barn." Carla used brute force as she wrestled with the stubborn plant.

Rose took in one more drag, her back pain, forgotten. Her mind drifted to Bernie and how he had walked out on her. The only good thing about their separation was that the old two-storey farmhouse, along with its ten wooded acres, now belonged to her.

She was glad that Carla had accepted her offer and had moved in with her months earlier. Her long-time friend was happy to be out of the city. Kelowna had become too big for her.

They had reunited at the bus station in Beaswick. Both had been excited at seeing one another. There was a lot of catching up to do. Carla was elated with returning to the mountains. She had missed them.

Her husband had left for Kelowna three years earlier and had started a construction company. She soon followed. They had worked hard alongside one another—swinging hammers and digging foundations. Their business had flourished until the economic crunch. That's when they had lost everything, including their marriage. The timing was perfect for Carla when Rose had invited her to stay.

The two friends had first met years earlier as volunteers at the Buzzy Bee Summer Festival—a local farmer's market. Times had changed. The small festival had slowly evolved into an almost medieval and hippy-like affair, drawing in hundreds of tourists from across the state.

The girls had marveled at some of the outlandish and colourful costumes that many of the locals had garnished. Long hair and dreadlocks were the norm and live music played on throughout the three day event—from harpsichords to banjos—as residents mingled with tourists.

Someone on the planning committee had suggested changing the name from 'Buzzy Bee' to 'Bee-In', just like the hippies had done back in the Sixties.

The girls had volunteered at a booth selling different blends of honey. Rose had even sold some of her farm fresh eggs.

The smell of marijuana had filled the festive air—all under the watchful eye of the sheriff and his deputy. Gleason understood that it wouldn't have taken much for some of the farmers to sell their 'other' home-grown product—marijuana. There were always buyers in the crowd.

Darwin hadn't cared about any pot or smokers. He had been very much occupied with the many attractive women who had participated in the three days of merriment.

Rose and Carla talked excitedly about old times and how happy they were at seeing each other again as she drove to her farm in the mountains. It was at the end of McCulloch Road and wasn't a true, working farm. She only had a few chickens along with several rows of blueberries. Most of her ten acres were covered in trees.

Her nearest neighbour, Larry, had helped her on occasion before Carla's arrival. He had worked with her in planting both her blueberries and private supply of pot. Rose had made sure that he knew nothing about her additional marijuana that grew on the mountain, nearby.

It hadn't taken Carla long to fall in love with the place. Rose was pleased. Larry wasn't. He felt left out and wanted more than to just plant her blueberries. Rose knew very well what he wanted to plant.

Slowly, she had confided in Carla and had finally told her about her small grow-op. She had explained that she grew marijuana for her back pain and also a little extra to sell to a local dealer. With Bernie gone, the additional income helped her pay bills.

Carla had assured her that there were no worries. She understood and added that the whole state seemed to be growing it. Smiling, she had admitted that she also enjoyed a little cannabis. It went along quite nicely with her wine.

Before long she had settled in and had helped by watering their babies and making sure that the plants had enough nutrients and light. Rose had no problem selling the extra pot to her old school buddy, Phil, back in Beaswick.

Larry had stopped coming by once Carla had moved in. That was fine with Rose although she did feel sorry for him. He had his own problems. His seventeen-year-old son was a handful. She felt that the kid was a dysfunctional oaf. Rose wondered if it was because of all the illegal drugs that Larry had ingested before Mike had even been conceived. Perhaps it had altered the boy's genetic make-up. She wasn't sure.

Larry was a typical single parent who did all he could for his only child. From the day he was born, Mike had been a problem for his parents. His mother had been unable to cope—having had enough of him as well as Larry and his chronic pot smoking. She had left them when Mike was only three.

They had visited Rose on several occasions after Bernie had moved out. Larry would smoke a fat one in her kitchen while Mike watched cartoons on her satellite TV. Last year they had come over for Christmas, before Carla's arrival. After they had left, she had noticed things missing, a Christmas decoration, spoons—things of that nature.

She decided then and there that she wouldn't allow Larry or Mike over anymore. It wasn't Larry who had stolen the items. It was his son. She knew that he was a no-good thief that would only bring trouble.

Larry was shattered. He had taken her comments personally—not understanding that it was because of Mike that she wouldn't see him.

Carla and Jen yanked out the last plant and dropped it in a heap on top of the others. A cloud of dust briefly filled the small garden before the strong wind got at it.

Rose felt guilty. "Let me help you."

"It's okay. Auntie and I can do it."

She smiled at the younger woman and was pleased with how Jennifer had turned out as a partner. Even though she was small, that didn't stop her from working hard. She just needed love and understanding. *Thank God she has Carla.*

Chapter 6

She turned to the evening sky. Clouds had swept across the partial moon. The eerie light made Jen anxious to reach the safety of Rose's barn. "Are you ready?" She asked the question as she peered out from behind the barricade of sticks.

Rose had been running her fingers through her hair and shaking out more small particles of pine. Nodding, she said, "I'll lead the way." She felt much better after smoking the joint, the pain in her back now forgotten.

The wind whipped at them as the girls stepped out of the growing area. More leaves swirled in the air as they re-arranged the crude fence to prevent any deer from entering their garden. Eighteen plants had already been lost to them. That was nine thousand dollars worth of pot.

Quickly, they got underway and walked single file along one of the many deer paths in the area. Each struggled with two plants. Some of the leaves would fall off on their way down to Rose's barn. That was okay. The girls would return and clean up any evidence. Besides, the leaves had little value. What *did* have value were the buds—some the size of a small rose.

The sky grew darker, making Jennifer feel uncomfortable. She tried to think of something positive—how much money she could make. *Two plants per person multiplied by three. That's six plants to a load. It works out to one and a half pounds of bud.*

They could sell the marijuana for close to two thousand dollars a pound. What they were carrying had a street value of around three thousand dollars. That amount of money was far more than what she could have earned as a server at the local restaurant.

Jen had enjoyed the work and the tips at the Marmalade Cat Cafe had been good. On a busy day she could pull in thirty dollars. Now, that kind of money seemed like chicken feed to her.

Being involved in a grow-op certainly paid more, but she knew that her share wouldn't be one third. Rose had explained that there were expenses and risks.

She had far more to lose than her two friends. If they were busted, the state would seize her property. That's why Jen had agreed on her portion being twenty percent.

There were a lot of bills—the major one being electricity. They needed to be careful about using power. The utility company had been notified by the police to red flag any customers that consumed an abnormal amount. The list was emailed monthly to the Sheriff's Department. Gleason would inform Rose if her name was on it.

That was why the women had a gas powered generator—so that they could keep the grow lights on when they had nursed their babies in the barn, all four hundred of them. The plants needed enough light to grow the maximum amount of bud. Besides, the local power was unreliable, going down at least twice a month.

Another expense was Gleason. Rose met with him every few weeks, but certainly not on her farm. He knew that she lived with a girlfriend but had no idea that she had *two* friends staying with her.

They would meet in the small parking lot in front of the hardware store in Beaswick. Rose felt safer there. Gleason wouldn't try anything sexual in public. She never got out of her truck and always made sure that her doors were locked when she dealt with him.

Jen went through her calculations once more as she closely followed her aunt and friend down the dark trail. *Four hundred plants divided by four.* It took about four plants to produce one pound of marijuana. *One hundred pounds of crop at two thousand dollars per pound comes to two hundred thousand dollars—less expenses.*

Rose had lied to Gleason and had told him that she only had a hundred plants. After expenses he would get around five thousand dollars. That still wasn't a bad payday for doing nothing.

Jen double-checked her figures as she struggled with the large plants, trying to keep up to Carla and Rose who were now several yards ahead of her.

Pulling her mind from the dark, she calculated what her share would be. If Gleason got five thousand and expenses were fifteen thousand, she figured that she would end up with twenty per cent of one hundred and eighty thousand dollars. She smiled at the thought. *Thirty-six thousand dollars!* Carla would get the same. *Good for us. We deserve it.*

Rose was also thinking, but it had nothing to do with money. It was about the day's events. She could still smell the pine dust in her hair from the shattered branch. It made her relive the moment—how close she and her friends had come to being killed. The hunter had fired twice in their direction.

Then there was the deer. She wanted to believe that the poor thing hadn't suffered and had died peacefully. That wasn't true. It *had* suffered and had died painfully. *The young buck must have been behind us. That's what that hunter had been shooting at.*

Tall pine trees creaked in the distance as the wind increased. Jennifer felt a chill and picked up her pace, wanting to get closer to her aunt and friend. Looking over her shoulder, she worried that someone might be lurking nearby. Unaware that they had suddenly stopped, she bumped into them.

Chapter 7

A dark figure blocked their path a hundred feet away. Carla couldn't put it together. In a hushed voice she asked, "Who *is* that?"

Rose raised her hand to her chest, dumbfounded. "I … have no idea." *Somebody is trespassing on my friggin' property!*

The three women froze, wondering the same things. *Is it another hunter? Is it the law?*

"Row-Row-Rose! It's me, uh, Lair-ee." The wind swirled his voice through the trees and made him sound surreal.

"Larry? What …? What's going on?" *What's he doing here?* Rose dropped her two plants and hurriedly made her way toward him. Over her shoulder, she tried to explain at least part of the mystery. "It's our neighbour." Carla and Jen had never met him.

"Larry! What happened to your face? You're bleeding." Her voice was full of concern as she got closer to him.

Yelling his name out the way he did was painful for him. He hunched over and placed a hand on his chest for a small amount of comfort. A huge gash was above his right eye and another on the top of his head. A good portion of his blond hair was matted with blood.

Rose didn't give him a chance to explain. "Let me put my arm around you. We'll make our way to my house." It looked like he had been badly beaten. She wondered if there was someone waiting nearby, ready to attack her and her friends. The threat of being robbed was always on her mind. "Jen! Get the rifle." Turning to Carla, she commanded, "Come with me." If she needed muscle, Carla was the answer. For the moment, the large marijuana plants that they had been toting were forgotten.

Elm trees swayed in the strong wind as Jen hurriedly walked the several hundred feet to the barn. Orange and yellow leaves twirled in the air as chickens stirred nervously in the henhouse nearby.

A cold chill ran through her. It had nothing to do with the wind picking up or the temperature dropping. Jen was worried that someone would appear from nowhere and attack her and her friends at any moment—just like they had probably done to their neighbour, Larry.

Her hands shook as she fumbled with the combination lock on the old barn door. She had trouble unlocking it—momentarily forgetting the series of numbers. Taking in a deep breath, she told herself to slow down a notch as she looked over her shoulder at her aunt and friend. They each had an arm around Larry and were easing him toward the dark house.

She tried again and finally heard the satisfying click as the lock sprung open. The large door groaned on rusty hinges and the strong smell of marijuana assaulted her, overpowering the faint odour of hay and horse manure from years gone by.

Squinting in the dark, she could barely make out the many huge plants that hung from the ceiling as she entered the old clap-board building. It was far overdue for being repaired.

The barn had a lean to it that seemed to be getting worse with each passing year. Former owners had tried to reinforce the walls to prevent it from collapsing. That was forty years ago and the stubborn barn still remained standing.

Two small side windows were bordered up. Tiny cracks in the old roof filtered in only a little light from the partial moon, making it more frightening than comforting.

Jen zeroed in on the power generator in the corner. Behind it was a cluster of electrical wires that webbed outward toward the center of the old structure—crudely designed to deliver power to the array of grow lights that hung from the rafters. Leaning against a wall behind the generator was the Winchester. She snapped it up before locking the barn door.

Half walking and running, a vortex of autumn leaves twisted its way across her path as she hurried toward the house.

Carla and Rose were helping Larry up the three steps to the porch. The wind whipped at his shirt and flapped it open, exposing his lower back and skinny frame. He shuddered, partly from the cold, but mainly from the shock and fear that ran through him.

Reaching into her camouflaged jacket, Rose groped for her set of keys. She felt the furry, plastic honeybee with gangly legs that was clipped to the ring. Larry had purchased it for her months earlier at the Bees N Stings.

Inserting her house key into the deadbolt, she tried coaxing it to unlock. The tumblers were worn and rusty. Cursing, she made a mental note that, when she had time, she would spray penetrating oil into the lock so that it would operate more smoothly. There were a lot of things that needed attention in the old house but right now they were not her priority.

She silently cursed again, this time about Larry. The girls did not need any attention. *Is Mike behind this?* It wouldn't have surprised her if his son was involved.

Larry slouched against Rose as Carla stood next to him. He babbled on, attempting to explain what had happened. Rose told him to keep quiet. They would talk inside.

Looking over their shoulders, the girls listened for anything unusual while still on the porch—wanting to make sure that it was safe to enter the old house. Satisfied, Rose swung open the door and flicked on the kitchen light, anxious to get out of the dark.

The two women shuffled Larry to a kitchen chair and carefully sat him down. Carla was all business as she marched into the living room, checking that the windows and front door were secured.

They were three women living in the country at the end of a mountain road. Not only were they concerned for their safety, but now they were afraid for their neighbour who appeared to have been badly beaten.

Carla switched on the oil furnace as she made her way back to the dimly lit kitchen. A moment later Jen walked in, tightly gripping the rifle. "Everything okay?" She was surprised with how weak she sounded.

They nodded that yes, everything seemed to be fine, before turning back to Larry.

Jen turned off the light. She pushed the blinds aside and peeked through the narrow window next to the back door to make sure that nobody was out there spying on them. Satisfied, she flicked the sixty watt light back on. Months earlier they had changed out their bulbs with low-energy ones to reduce their power consumption.

Rose got busy dabbing at Larry's wound above his eye and on his scalp. She tried washing out some of the blood that had dried in his hair. Both of his eyes were swollen and an ugly bruise was developing around each.

Kneeling on the cold linoleum floor in front of him, she took a hard look at her neighbour as she held his hand. His other hand supported his rib cage. "Larry. Look at me."

She wondered if he was suffering from a concussion. He appeared to be drifting in and out of consciousness and his eyes were unfocused. Rose tried again and, this time, squeezed his hand tighter. "Larry. What happened to you? Who did this?" She was angry and concerned. *How could Mike do such a thing—especially to his own father?* It didn't surprise her. Larry and his son did have a volatile relationship.

Carla crossed her arms as she stood next to Rose, waiting for answers. Jen put the safety on and leaned the rifle in a corner—an older .243 Winchester.

"It was … uh." He was having trouble talking. His right hand was still on his upper body, protecting his side. Rose suspected that he had several broken ribs.

She remained on her knees as Carla dragged over a chair and plopped down next to her. Jen stood behind her and placed a hand on her aunt's shoulder for comfort as they studied him in the dim kitchen light, waiting for an explanation.

"You're safe with us, Larry." As an afterthought, Rose asked, "Do you want a couple of Tylenol?"

He nodded and took in a short breath. Pain tore through his chest.

"Jen. You know where they are. Go get some while we keep Larry company."

Jen grabbed the rifle, concerned that whoever had beaten Larry might have broken into their house. Feeling vulnerable, she entered the dark living room and did a quick scan, relieved that no one was there. Switching on the upstairs hall light, the low-energy bulb produced more shadows.

Hurrying up the stairs, she wondered about Larry. *Why would someone want to beat him up? Were they after money?* She leaned the Winchester against the bathroom vanity and pulled out the Tylenol 3's.

A sharp screech coming from outside made her drop the medicine bottle. Pills scattered across the bathroom floor as she spun around and faced the window.

Chapter 8

For a moment she crazily thought that the bizarre sound was coming from some sort of monster. It had clawed its way up the outside of their house and was intent on breaking through the bathroom window. It would rip her apart.

Jen knew that she was being foolish and over-reacting. It was simply a branch from a nearby tree that was rubbing against the house from the strong wind. She mentally scolded herself. *Pull yourself together. You just turned twenty-five years old. You're not some silly teenager!*

Turning back to the medicine cabinet, she studied her reflection in the mirror. Her shiny nose stud made a sharp contrast to her ghost-white face. *It's … it's because of the moonlight. That's why I'm so pale.* No. She knew better. It was because she was frightened and troubled.

Jeeze! What a day—being shot at by some drunken hunter and then, she gulped, *the poor deer dying in front of us. Now a neighbour shows up, beaten!* She felt defenceless. They had thousands of dollars worth of marijuana and all they had for protection was an old rifle. They didn't even have cell phones. There was no signal this far out from Beaswick—just a land line that seemed to go down more often than not.

"Jen?" Carla called up to her from the foot of the stairs. "Are you okay?"

"Uh, yeah." Her voice was faint. Taking in a deep breath she tried to compose herself. "I was just—" She swallowed hard. "I'll be right down."

"Looks like Larry needs those painkillers real bad." As an afterthought she added, "Bring down some scissors and a razor. The bandages are in the side drawer along with the iodine. Might as well bring those, too."

Jen got on her knees and scooped up the pills as the branch screeched again—this time sounding very much like fingernails on a blackboard. She grabbed what she needed and hurried down the stairs.

"Are you feeling better?" Rose had given him Tylenol 3's a few minutes earlier and wondered if it helped with his pain.

"Yeah, it doesn't hurt so much." He squirmed in the kitchen chair, obviously still in pain.

"Good. Let me have a look at your ribs." On her knees, she gently pried his hand from his chest. He winced.

"It's okay, Larry. I'll be careful." Slowly, she began unbuttoning his shirt while asking, "Are you ready to tell us what happened?"

He raised his voice and was close to tears. "Yeah, Rose. That's why I'm here. I can't go to the police!"

She opened his shirt a little more as he repeated, "That's why I came here. I had nowhere else to go."

"Everything is fine. You just take it easy."

He tried to relax as he explained what had happened. "I, uh, walked to your house along the trail between our properties. You weren't home but I saw your truck parked in the back. I wondered where you were." Taking in a short breath, he ploughed on. "I waited for an hour or so and then saw you and your friends coming down the deer path."

With his shirt now completely opened, Rose was appalled with what she saw. Angry black and blue marks covered his upper body. She put her hand to her chest and took a closer look. "Jeeze, Larry. What happened?" It looked painful. The dark bruises screamed out from his white, skinny frame.

He tried to take in a deep breath but couldn't. It hurt him too much. Grimacing, he gulped in a few shallow breaths instead and sputtered, "They came during the late afternoon. Three young fellas. I thought they were Mike's friends from school. They asked if Mike was home and I said no."

Rose's face paled. She had assumed that it was Mike who had been responsible for the beating.

"That's when they forced themselves into my house. That's when they made me sit in my kitchen just like I'm doin' here. That's when they said they would beat the shit out of me if I didn't give them my money."

Jennifer turned away, not wanting to hear any more. Rubbing at the Japanese characters on her tattooed bicep, she mumbled, "Peace, love, happiness."

"Who are they? Why did they think you had money?" Rose felt her stomach churn. This was not what she had expected. Three hoodlums had paid him a visit.

The girls waited for answers as the wind grew stronger, lashing out at the old farmhouse. It creaked and groaned in protest.

Rose tried again. "Uh, Larry? Why did they do it—beat you up?"

He took in another shallow breath before answering. "Uh, I think it was 'cause of Mike. I think he was braggin' 'bout having pot and how his dad grew it and made all kinds of money. They must a heard him yakkin' his fool head off at school. He's just like his mother."

Carla stood, unable to keep still. Shaking her head, she angrily whispered, "Those punks," saying it more to herself than to anyone else.

"Yeah." Larry looked up and carefully nodded in agreement. "Those punks." The effort was almost too much for him. Shuddering, he took in another painful breath.

Rose figured that he was a foolish man. He had exposed his only child to a life of growing and smoking dope. The kid was a jerk *and* a thief. But she knew that Larry was also partly to blame. People in town called him 'Canary' because he sang like a bird, having trouble keeping his mouth shut.

"I didn't think they would do it. There were three of them. I could a taken maybe two of them, but not *three*! I'd never seen them before. They held me down and kept asking where my money was. The bigger guy had a baseball bat, Rose—a *steel* baseball bat!" He had a tear in his eye and his bottom lip quivered.

"Jeeze, Larry. How much did they take?"

"All of it." He slowly shook his head as he said it while carefully guarding his rib cage. Repeating in a lower voice, he declared, "All my money." Disgusted, he looked down at the floor.

The basement furnace hummed and began to blow warm air into the kitchen, but it didn't help. They all felt a chill.

Angry with how callous and ruthless the punks could be, Carla asked, "Do you have any idea who they are? Maybe we could get those bastards—maybe put the police on their ass." She turned to Rose. "Maybe your ex brother-in-law could find out who they are and—"

Rose quickly cut her off. "No way! If we called Gleason, he and his deputy would do a search on Larry's property and, guess what? They'd find his grow operation and he'd go to jail."

They all knew how much she loathed the sheriff. The less she saw of him, the better it was for her. Rose tried to blank out what he had done to her in the kitchen months earlier. The thought made her skin crawl.

"She's right." Larry agreed. "There's nothin' I can do. I don't want the cops over—especially that fat ass." He shuddered as he gingerly held his chest. Looking down at the floor, he repeated, "There's nothin' I can do."

Still on her knees, Rose looked him squarely in the eye. "Yes, there is, Larry. There *is* something that you can do!" She was angry—not only with what the three creeps had done to him, but also with his son. Gripping his bony knees, she tried to talk some sense into him. "You can get rid of that kid of yours. Get him out of the house. He's nothing but trouble." Frustrated with him and his weakness, she spewed out, "Send him back to his mother. It's time you throw him out."

The last thing that she wanted was to be involved. *What if those goons decide to come over here? What if they force me into telling them where my money is?*

She had a lot to lose. Thousands of dollars were stashed away, but not in a bank. Rose couldn't afford to take that risk—to go up to a teller and deposit ten thousand dollars in cash.

People would wonder how a single woman living in the hills with no job could deposit that kind of money every few weeks. No. She hid the money on her property just like the other growers did.

She couldn't even use credit cards. If she did, she would need to make a deposit to pay them off. That would leave a paper trail. The only thing that she could do was hide her money and buy everything in cold, hard cash.

Jennifer placed a hand to her chest and stepped back from the group. She wanted to detach herself. This was too much for her. Being shot at earlier by two so-called hunters and then having to deal with the next door neighbour who had been badly beaten by ruthless thugs made her stomach twist. She hurried to the bathroom. Carla and Rose were unaware—their attention on Larry.

Rose got to her feet and inspected the top of his head before grabbing the scissors and bandages. Annoyed with both Larry and his son, she barked, "Keep still. I've got to cut some of your hair. If I don't, this bandage won't stick worth a damn." He had been shaking his head in despair.

She busily trimmed and shaved around his head wound and wondered what they could do to defend themselves if the punks came their way. The girls needed to keep a low profile. They could not get involved.

Larry, the 'Canary,' worried her as she dabbed iodine on his scalp and placed a bandage over the ugly gash. He knew that she grew a little pot for her back pain. He had even helped her. Now she was troubled that he might have told his son and prayed that nobody knew about her several gardens in the hills.

Rose delivered a pound or two of marijuana to Beaswick every week. Phil would meet her at the huge Exxon trucker station across town. He'd hand her the several thousands in cash and she'd hand him the goods.

She trusted him. They had grown up together and were close friends. And, he had never tried to sleep with her—unlike some of her other male friends. He was reliable even if he couldn't keep a job and, at fifty years old, still lived with his mother in a trailer park.

Rose had thousands of dollars in cash hidden on her property. With this new crop she would have several more briefcases full of money in no time.

He drifted in and out, dropping his head for a few seconds before coming to again. Rose got back on her knees and tried to get his attention one more time. "Larry." He was staring at the cold floor, dazed. She tried again. "Larry!"

"Huh?" He sat up a little. Pain shot across his gaunt face as he reached for his rib cage.

"Where—is—Mike?"

"Uh? I don't know." He winced as he turned to the kitchen clock. It was almost six. "He should a bin home by now for his supper." Close to tears, he shook his head, concerned about his son. *Did they beat him up, too? Is my son lying somewheres, bleedin'?*

Chapter 9

Mike was in the parking lot at the Beaswick Senior High School and gorging down on another hamburger. Eating two or more burgers at one time was no problem for him. He was a big kid for seventeen and took after his mother.

Sitting in his Toyota pickup with his head-banging music blaring, he waited for his three new buddies. They were a few years older than him and he thought that they were cool dudes. He liked the way they dressed and did crystal meth. Cramming in another mouthful before slurping his Coke, he wondered how they had made out with his old man. Did they get his money?

He hated Larry. He figured that he deserved a better dad. *The bastard always preaches to me 'bout doin' my chores.*

A few days earlier Mike had been hanging out in the school parking lot when Quincy had walked up and had asked where he could score some good grass. Mike had bragged to him that his dad grew some of the very best marijuana and to meet him back here the next day.

He saw Larry as a weak excuse for a father. He knew where he kept his cash. At least he thought he did. *Take the money and get the fuck out a Beaswick!* He had it all planned and figured that the old man had at least twenty thousand dollars stashed away.

His dad had surprised him by hiding it somewhere else. Larry was fed up with having his money stolen by his only child. Over the past year Mike had been taking a few dollars from him here and there and it was getting worse. His attitude toward his father was quickly deteriorating.

He was furious with Larry for hiding the money from him. *He doesn't even trust his own kid!* He figured that he should be halfway across the county by now with the cash. His cash! He deserved it. The old man could make plenty more. Larry had been broke many times before and would survive just fine. No problem.

After convincing them that his dad had money stashed and that Larry didn't have a weapon, they had made a deal. He and his new buddies would split it fifty-fifty. All they had to do was persuade Larry to give it up.

Mike didn't care *how* they got the money—as long as they did. Ten thousand was better than nothing. He opened his truck door and kicked out the hamburger wrappers and Coke container.

A minute later they pulled up behind him. All three jumped out of their car at the same time. He climbed out of his truck, stepping over his trash.

"You lied to us." The leader, Quincy, marched up to him and pointed an angry finger.

Mike was taken by surprise and tried not to stutter. "Wha-wha-what?" He couldn't figure it out. "Wha-wha-what are you talkin' 'bout?" They had left their high beams on and it made it difficult for him to see his new friends—only their silhouettes.

"He didn't have no twenty thou'." Karl spat it out.

Sal added, "We only pulled off six." They surrounded him, glaring accusingly.

"What? No. I mean, I saw the fa-fa-fuckin' cash just the other day when he went to his stash. He has a shoebox full of fif-fif-fifties, man. I seen it with my own fa-fa-fuckin' eyes." He lit a cigarette to help him remain calm. The more excited he got, the more he stuttered.

Although Mike was generally just plain stupid, sometimes he could be shrewd. He wondered if his new buddies were pulling a fast one—if they really *did* get the twenty thousand from the old man and were only going to give him a small share.

"We pumped him pretty good. You should a bin there. We took the baseball bat to him." Karl was talking excitedly. His black cap, with the words 'Mega Death' written on the front, bobbed up and down as he spoke.

"Yeah, yeah. Wha-wha-whatever." Mike didn't care what they did to his father. The old man was holding out. "He's screwing us over."

He tried to explain one more time as Quincy pulled out a meth pipe. "He's got more than six thousand duh-duh-dollars!" He said it to himself more than to anyone else. The old man pissed him off. His new buddies were also starting to piss him off.

"I don't think so. We worked him over pretty good." The bigger hood took a hit before passing the pipe to his partners.

Mike thought about how his dad was once again trying to screw up his plans. Three thousand dollars wouldn't get him very far. "No! He's got more money stashed. I know it. Where's the ca-ca-cash you already got?"

"Come on. Let's sit in Karl's car so we can talk about it."

Mike's three new 'friends' had already totalled it up on their way back from Larry's and had helped themselves to an extra thousand for their hard work in bat swinging.

Chapter 10

Rose tried getting his attention by gently shaking him. The Tylenol 3 was taking its toll and making him groggy. Slumped over, he groaned in pain. She tried again and, this time, softly called out his name. "Larry?"

"Uh?" He forced open an eye and was not exactly sure where he was.

"I'm going to take you back to your place." She was still on her knees in front of him. "I want you to listen carefully."

"Yeah. I'm listening." He tried to focus as he slowly nodded.

"It looks like you've got a few broken ribs and probably a concussion. You could see a doctor, but we've got to keep this whole thing quiet. Right?"

"Yeah, I understand." He sat up a little, his head beginning to clear. "He'd ask all kinds of questions and know right away I was beat up."

"Good. So, I'll drive you home." She paused and thought hard as she squeezed his hand. Talking slowly, as if to a child, she pushed on. "If Mike is home, he'll see me with you. He'll know that *I* know what happened. I don't want to get involved."

He looked at her with a blank expression.

Rose shook her head and raised her voice. "I … uh, *we* don't want to get involved." Studying him, she waited for a response. There was none.

Annoyed, she squeezed his hand tighter so that she could get her message across to the dazed man. "If he *is* home, then I'll …" She wanted to tell him that she would drop him off at the foot of his drive so that Mike wouldn't see her. She trailed off and realized that it didn't really matter. Mike would know that Larry had visited her. He would see the bandages on his dad's head and put it together.

Larry's eyes were glazed, not understanding. "What are you saying?"

What am I saying? What am I saying, you idiot? She was annoyed with him as she kept thinking about it. *I'm friggin' saying that we're screwed. Thanks to you and your boy, my friends and I are being pulled into your shit!*

She tried to calm down. "Uh, what I'm saying is that there is no need for you to tell Mike that we fixed you up. You just keep that part to yourself."

He carefully nodded while cradling his side.

Carla finally noticed that her niece wasn't in the kitchen and was relieved. She was very protective of Jen and didn't want her to be involved, but it was slowly becoming apparent to her. All three were caught up in Larry's predicament, whether they liked it or not.

"Now," Rose's voice grew lower, "my concern—" She stopped, carefully choosing her words. "*Our* concern is if Mike decides to do more talking and tells his friends that the neighbour next door is growing pot." She paused for effect before blurting, "He'd be making a big mistake."

"Huh? I'm not sure I'm following you."

"Larry! Listen. Please." She squeezed his hand tighter to make him understand.

He smiled stupidly back at her, loving her attention.

She again carefully chose her words. "We only have three plants and they are for our own personal use. We are *not* selling pot."

"Wha-at?"

Standing, she placed her hands on her hips as she looked down at him. "Let me give this to you, straight." Her fear of what could happen to her and her friends if the goons decided to return was escalating by the second. Rose pushed on with her lies. "I'm broke. I have no money. That bastard I used to call a husband stole it all."

"Jeeze. I'm sorry, Rose." He tried to shake his head with the news but stopped short, feeling dizzy. Instead, he took in a shallow breath and studied a spot on the floor to clear his brain. Moments passed before he mumbled, "Well, it doesn't matter. I won't tell nobody."

Wondering if she really was telling the truth, he added, "Why didn't you report it to the sheriff—that Bernie stole your money?"

"Think about it. Why would I do *that*? Bernie is his brother. The two of them were probably in on it when they robbed me. If I reported it I'd get tangled up with the authorities and uncomfortable questions would be asked. I can't have that. The best thing I could do was let it go."

He nodded and finally understood that getting the law involved would only make things worse for her.

"Anyhow, there's nothing to tell about me and my friends. Just make sure that if Mike ever asks, you tell him the truth. I'm broke and we don't grow marijuana!" She leaned into him and squeezed his upper arms, coming very close to shaking him. "Do you hear me?"

He did not like the way that she was talking to him. "Yeah. Sure, Rose. I hear you loud and clear. What do you think I am—a blabber mouth?"

That's exactly what she thought he was—a blabber mouth. "Of course not, Larry. Of course not. All I'm saying is that there is nothing here to steal and I would hate to have to send Gleason your way."

"Wha-at? You wouldn't send that fat-ass sheriff to *my* place?" He swallowed hard and sat up, momentarily forgetting the pain in his chest. Now she had his full attention.

He was worried that Gleason would bust him if he showed up at his door. There were several marijuana plants growing in his back yard and Larry had promised that he would shoot him dead if he ever set foot on his property. Still, if the sheriff wanted to play hardball, he could nail him in a flash.

"Of course I wouldn't send him over intentionally. You're my friend."

A cold sweat ran down his back as a thought occurred to him. *How would Mike survive if I went to jail? Who would look after him?*

Pushing on, she knew that she had struck a nerve. "We just need to be … careful. That's all. Things could get real ugly for *all* of us if we're not."

She gave Carla a wink before snapping out, "Get your handgun. From now on we're packing heat."

For a moment she didn't understand what her friend was talking about and almost blurted, "Handgun? What handgun?" She quickly caught on. Rose was saying it so that Larry would think they were armed. If he did say anything to Mike, he would probably end up blabbing that the girls also carried guns.

She hurried out the kitchen, pretending to get her pistol. The bathroom door was closed. Carla gently knocked. There was no answer. She knocked again before opening it a crack. The acrid smell of vomit filled the small room. Holding her breath, she peeked behind the door. Her niece was sitting on the floor with her hands covering her face, trembling.

Chapter 11

Seated in the rear of Karl's Honda, Quincy counted out the money that they had stolen from Larry—less the thousand dollars that was safely tucked away in his back pocket. Mike sat next to him.

"There, five thousand eight hundred and thirty-seven dollars. That's two thousand and …" He had trouble thinking straight. Scratching his shaved head, he hoped that it would somehow help his brain function better.

Sal was in the front and was the least stoned of the three. "It works out to two thousand, nine hundred and eighteen dollars and fifty cents, Quirk—, uh, Quincy." He caught himself. He had almost called him Quirky. His friend would not have liked that.

It didn't matter. He was too out of it to notice. "Uh, yeah. That's right. Two thousand and—" He stopped, needing to focus on counting the money. "Here, Mikie. I'll give you an extra dollar fifty to make it an even two thousand, nine hundred and twenty."

"That's bullshit!" He shouted it out as he glared at him.

"Whoa!" Quincy pulled back. "What are you trying to tell me? That you don't trust me?" He did not like being accused of anything, even if it was true.

"No. It's not that. He's got more money sta-sta-stashed."

"Oh?" He raised an eyebrow, perking up as he thought about having a bigger wad of cash in his jeans. "You sound real sure about that, Mikie." *Yeah, if we divide our share that's only …* He tried to figure it out while taking another hit from the meth pipe. *That's only … Aw, man. Is this shit ever good!* His mind drifted, enjoying the wonderful feelings that seemed to be touching every cell in his body.

Quincy had to admit that it *was* easy money. The old bastard had folded like a cheap suit once they had put the bat to him. He chuckled at the thought.

They were safe. Larry wouldn't call the cops. He couldn't. He would get busted if he did. The problem was that they had been promised more.

"I know he's got more money. He's screwing with you. You should go ba-ba-ba-ba-ba-ba—"

Sal couldn't hold back any longer. *The guy sounds like a fuckin' retarded sheep!* Mike's stuttering made him burst out in laughter.

Quincy ignored his buddy in the front seat. "Mikie. Are you *that* sure he's got more money stashed? We'd have to lay another beatin' on him. Maybe a lot worse than what he already got."

"Yeah, yeah. Whatever. You only took twenties. Like I said before, he's got a whole fa-fa-fuckin' shoebox stuffed with fif-fif-fif-fif-fifties."

Jerking his head back, Quincy tried to avoid the fine spray that Mike was delivering as he struggled with the word.

Mike leaned into his face, wanting to convince his new friend that his dad had more money for the taking. "I seen it!"

Now Karl was laughing along with Sal. The combination of meth and Mike's stuttering were too much for the punks.

Mike tuned them out, angry with his father. "You need to go back. Larry deserves what you give him. I hate him. He still has at least another tooah-tooah-tooah." He stopped, unable to continue.

Quincy kept his distance, afraid that this time Mike would throw up on him. *The kid's more screwed than I thought.*

The laughter in the front seat grew louder. Karl was in tears as Sal mimicked their new friend. "Ba-ba-ba-ba-ba. Tooah-tooah-tooah."

Mike was used to being made fun of and wished that he had his inhaler. It helped with his speaking. He cursed his old man for letting him forget it.

Swallowing hard, he tried again. "Too-ah-welve thousand stashed away somewheres. Too-ah-welve!" Just to make sure that Quincy understood what he was trying to tell him, he drew an imaginary number twelve in the air.

Satisfied that his new buddy had gotten the message, he inhaled deeply from his cigarette before flicking it out the window.

"Any idea where, Mike?" Quincy turned to his buddies and winked as he asked the question.

"I'm not sure." He was thinking hard. "There are a few places he could hide it, I suh-suh-suppose. I thought he would give it up real qui-quick. I didn't think the old man had much stomach for pain." *All I gotta do is convince my new buddies to go back and get every nickel. Then I'll be free—free from the stupid old man and free from Beaswick.*

His plan was to head up to Kelowna and hang out with a few guys that he knew. Maybe he could start his own grow-op. He knew how to do it. His old man had shown him. Larry wouldn't chase him. Mike figured that he was too weak to do that sort of thing.

He thought about how his dad had broken down not long ago when that woman from next door had dumped him. Larry had told him, in a whiney voice, "All Rose wants is to be friends." He had taken a hard look at his father, seeing how feeble and dumb the old man really was. *He can't even keep a girlfriend!*

Larry had wanted her to move in with them and had told his son that he was madly in love. It had made Mike sick. He had slapped his father across his face, letting him know that *he* was the boss—not his dad. He'd be damned if he would allow his old man to have someone live with them. *I'm seventeen for God's sake. I don't need some old broad in my house.*

He didn't have to worry. Rose wasn't interested, but Larry didn't see it that way. *The old man is stupid—and blind.*

"Mike. Mikie!"

"Huh?"

"I got an idea." Quincy paused while taking one more hit from the pipe. He was very stoned and loved the high, feeling like a king. There was nothing that he couldn't do. He was the man!

Blowing out a huge cloud of smoke, he carried on through watery eyes. "You come with us. You come back with us to Larry's. You don't need to walk in and see us beatin' on him. Just be an advisor. You know?" He was wound up and excited with the idea. "Like, we could threaten him again and maybe hit him once or twice. If he feeds us bullshit, then we can come back to you.

"You'd be waitin' outside. You could tell us if he was lyin'. You wouldn't even have to get out of your truck."

"Aw, fa-fa-fa-fa-fuck. I don't really want to duh-do that and don't call me Mikie." He was nervous with the whole idea.

Enjoying the moment, Quincy turned to his fellow hoods in the front seat. Karl had his baseball cap off and was scratching his greasy hair, chuckling. Two of his incisors and one bicuspid were missing. It made him look slightly demented. Sal was also chuckling as he picked at an open sore on his face.

Quincy could picture it—he and his gang beating the old man while the kid looked on. *It would be kind a interesting to see what Mikie's reaction would be. Maybe after we hit him a few times, I'll give him the bat. Yeah. That's what I'll do. I'll tell him to smack his old man hard. Tell him to hit him right here.* He put a finger to his temple and fantasized, surprised with how the idea was affecting him. He was getting an erection.

Pulling out of his reverie, he turned back to Mike and announced, "You can be there with us when we beat the old fuck."

He squirmed in his seat. "I ca-ca-can't do that."

"Wha-at?" Quincy jerked his head back, surprised. "What do you mean you can't do that? Come on, Mikie. Don't you want more money? It'll be over soon. Your old man will heal real fast. We ain't gonna kill him or nothin'. Just beat the livin' shit out of him."

"Yeah, I know. It's just that I …" He was struggling with what to say. "It's just that I don't want him to think that I'm …" He trailed off with the last part of his sentence before sputtering, "In-in-in-involved."

The three punks burst out in laughter, partly from the meth but mainly because of Mike's stuttering and stupidity.

Karl shook his head while glaring at Mike. "Are you that dumb? Think about it. He already knows you're in-in-in-involved."

Sal and Quincy were in tears, laughing at the way Karl was mimicking Mike's stutter. He was doing a good job.

His face turned a dark shade of red. "Da-da-don't call me stupid and da-da-don't call me Ma-Ma-Mikie!" His mother used to call him Mikie and he hated it.

Karl ignored him. "You told us that you're always home right after school is out. This time we suddenly show up at your place. He knows he's bin set up. He knows that you stayed away while we beat him up. He knows you've bin yakkin'. You can't keep your mouth shut!"

"Fa-fa-fuck you!" Mike's arm sprung up with a clenched fist.

Quincy grabbed his wrist, stopping him from doing anything stupid. "Whoa. Whoa. Whoa! Careful what you're doin'."

Scowling at Karl, Mike wondered if he could beat up the creepy bastard. He doubted it. Karl was almost as big as Quincy.

They were having fun with their new friend thinking that Mike was a loser. All three were enjoying themselves at his expense.

He jerked his arm free and glared at Karl. *I won't let that greasy bastard get away with what he just said. I'll get even—somehow, somewhere! I'll get even!*

Quincy's mood quickly changed. Now he was all business. With an icy tone he announced, "You're comin' back with us. No more bullshit. We only got the job half done. Get in your truck. We'll follow you." It was a command.

Mike was afraid of the big goon. He was also unhappy with where things were going. The situation was escalating. *If Larry would a played along the first time he wouldn't a had to get beat up again. The stupid old man.*

Chapter 12

Rose packed Larry into her truck as Jen and Carla looked on from the rear porch. They were worried that Mike could be home at any minute.

She turned over the engine several times before it started with a backfire. A blue cloud escaped from the rusty exhaust pipe.

Revving it a little, she turned to Larry and studied him for a moment before putting it into gear. He held his ribs as they headed down her long, narrow driveway that was lined with pine trees.

Stopping at the bottom, she unlocked the chain that secured the gate to a steel post. It was just wide enough for a single vehicle. A large, red and white 'No Trespassing' sign was strapped to the center of it.

Her dog, Kobi, was very much on her mind as she glanced at the 'Beware of Dog' sign nailed to a nearby tree. She could still smell the putrid stench in her mind when she had found him in the ditch several weeks earlier. *Maybe it's time to get another guard dog. We need better security.*

Larry was becoming a little more aware sitting next to her. He talked about this and that and tried to reassure her that there was nothing to worry about. That concerned Rose. The more he talked about not worrying, the more she did.

Leaving the gate open, she drove the half mile down McCulloch Road to Larry's home, trying to avoid the many pot holes that were scattered along the gravelled road. He didn't need any more aggravation to his ribs.

She cranked the steering wheel to her left and sped up his long, wooded driveway—anxious to drop him off and get back to her friends.

Her mind drifted to their marijuana crop as he rambled on, half listening to what he was saying. Tomorrow she planned on spending most of the day in the barn, cleaning the buds before Sunday's meeting with Phil.

She made a decision as they approached his house. They would take time to apply for a handgun. She and her girlfriends would each be required to provide the California Bureau of Firearms with a driver's license and thumb print. Ten days after the background checks, the girls would hopefully have the guns. There wouldn't be a problem. None of them had ever been in trouble with the law.

Hating weapons and violence, they still needed to protect themselves—especially now that Kobi was gone and three punks had paid Larry a visit.

"What? Sorry. I wasn't listening." She could easily become annoyed with him. He sometimes talked too much about nothing.

"I said that it looks like Mike's not home yet. I don't see his truck."

She breathed a sigh of relief. His kid bothered her. It wouldn't have taken much to get into it with him. That would only make matters worse. If she yelled and screamed at Mike, she knew that he would get back at her, somewhere, somehow. That was why she never told Larry about his son stealing things when they had come over last Christmas.

They pulled into a large, dusty parking area behind his A-frame log house. His property covered ten wooded acres and was part of his inheritance from his mother. Larry already had the truck's door open and one foot on the running board.

"Hold on. Let me help you."

He knew that he could probably walk on his own, but he loved her attention. He gingerly placed an arm around her shoulder as she helped him up the three steps to his porch. It brought back painful but wonderful memories for him. His mind drifted to the night, months earlier, when he had come over with a bottle of wine.

Even with his injuries and Mike on his mind, he wanted her. Her long, red hair and blue eyes made him crazy. Rose took the physical pain away from him. What hurt him the most was his emotional torment. She didn't want a relationship.

He could smell her hair and thought of how attractive and sexy she was. Larry could also smell the marijuana in her camouflaged clothing and knew why she had disguised her appearance. Of course he did. He was no dummy. He knew what the girls had been up to when they had been walking down the deer trail earlier. He had seen the huge plants that they had been carrying. They had an outdoor crop. It was as simple as that.

Larry also knew that Rose had been lying to him about the money. If they had an outdoor crop then they were making money. It was pretty easy to figure out. He wondered if he might be able to borrow a few dollars. They needed groceries. Mike also needed cigarettes. *Maybe she could lend me a hundred?*

He was glad that he had put twenty thousand away with his brother, T-Bone, a few days earlier. He didn't want Mike stealing from him anymore. It was becoming unbearable living with him. The boy was getting out of control.

Having had enough of him, he had wanted his son to move in with the mother. *Let her deal with the kid.* Mike had been threatening to do just that for months. Larry had hoped that it would have happened during the summer, but that hadn't worked out. She didn't want anything to do with Mike *or* with him.

The boy was becoming more aggressive and disrespectful. He was throwing his weight around and Larry found it almost impossible to reason with him.

And now this, having Mike's friends come over and beat him. He wanted to believe that his son hadn't been involved, that it had just been bad luck, but he knew better.

Larry was becoming increasingly afraid of his boy. Several months earlier he had woken to the sound of their stereo blaring. Mike had been asleep on the couch with a knife clutched in his hand while his crazy music played on. At first he had been concerned that his son was contemplating suicide but had reconsidered.

Worried for his safety, he had put a lock on his bedroom door thinking that his kid might try to kill him in his sleep. The next day it had been broken and several of his personal items had gone missing. Afraid of accusing Mike, he had decided to just let things go.

At his wits end, he didn't know how to deal with someone that he loved and yet hated.

"Easy, Larry. We're almost at your door." She figured that he must be in severe pain—the way that he was squeezing her.

"Uh, yeah, Rose. It hurts so much. Do you think—?" Stammering, he continued, now almost pleading. "Do you think you could stay for a while?"

Aw, shit. Here we go again. Now I know why he's holding me like that. She gently pushed him away and explained one more time. "Look, Larry. I can't. If Mike sees me, there might be trouble. You know how I feel about him. We've already talked about that."

"Yeah, I know. But, it's been so long and you know how I feel about *you*. I miss you."

The last thing that she wanted was to hurt him but knew that she had to be firm. "There would be too much trouble if we saw each other. I'm very … busy."

"I can see that—especially with your camouflaged clothing on." He was annoyed. Sometimes Larry could be capricious and quickly change his mood.

She paled, understanding what he was getting at. He knew that she had an outdoor crop. "What do you mean by that comment?"

"Uh, I just … well, you know. You're growing pot outdoors."

"Now you listen to me, mister! Make no mistake. There'll be hell to pay if you tell *anybody*!"

She decided to give it to him straight. "Sometimes you talk too much. You need to learn to keep quiet. That's why you got yourself into this mess." She jabbed a finger at her chest. "That's why you're getting *me* into this mess."

Fired up, she kept up her barrage. It had been one hell of a day for her and she needed to vent. "That's bullshit, Larry." She vigorously shook her head. "You keep your mouth shut about what I do."

"Yeah, it's just that I want to see you again." He opened his back door and reached for the light switch. *Hell. The power must be off. Again!*

Rose made out a broken chair in the dark kitchen as he shuffled his way in. She looked again. Blood was on the floor—his blood. Transfixed, she couldn't pull her eyes away. A moment later the moon came out and made the gelled mess look more like molten lead. The whole scene appeared surreal to her.

Larry fumbled with the kerosene lantern as she continued to gawk at the floor. His pool of blood now took on a gray, sickly look as the yellowish glow from the lamp filled the room. Swallowing hard, she tried not to think about what must have happened there earlier.

"Rose? Did you hear what I said? I want to see you again."

She looked up at him, surprised with what he was saying. *He's been beaten almost to unconsciousness and now he's talking about a relationship?* "I don't want that, Larry. I already told you."

Feeling foolish with her turning him down, he tried a different tactic. "I don't know how I'm going to get by with no money or nothin'. I'm not sure what to do."

He was hoping that, if Rose could lend him a couple of hundred, he and Mike would be fine for a week or so. Then he could get to see her again when he paid her back.

His only other source of income had been from Beaswick's grocery store. They had cut back his hours after Mike had stormed in and had demanded money from his father in front of customers. The scene had turned ugly and the owner had been forced into kicking the young bully out and banning him from the store. Larry's hours soon dwindled to nothing thanks to his son.

"What do you mean you don't know what to do?"

"Well, I got no money and you told me a little while ago that you got no money either. Like, how are *you* going to survive?"

She defended herself, annoyed with him once more. He was beginning to pry. "I meant that I was robbed of all my savings. I still have a *little* money." *What is he implying? That I should give him some cash? It's his own stupid-ass fault what happened to him—giving that kid of his whatever he wants!*

Softening a little, she stopped that way of thinking. Rose did have a temper and it sometimes got her into trouble. That was one of the reasons why her husband had left her.

Taking pity, she understood that Larry was only a lost soul with a big heart. That was the problem. He had too big a heart—too big a heart *and* mouth.

She saw the hurt cross his face in the soft glow of the lantern. It was more emotional than physical. A part of her wanted to hold her friend and help him. She hated to see Larry suffer.

Somehow the word 'advisor' sounded almost justifiable to Mike. He had heard the term on CNN a while back. A general or somebody important had been an advisor in some far-off country.

A part of him liked Quincy's idea—that he could advise his fellow goons on what to do if Larry didn't come up with more money. It made him feel important.

Mike figured that he would park near the rear of the A-frame log house, but not go in. He'd only be an 'advisor' and wait in his truck.

Quincy shoved the meth pipe in his face. Five minutes later, after his coughing spell, Mike drove up McCulloch Road toward home with his head-banging music cranked to the max. His three new buddies closely followed in Karl's Honda.

"Uh, can you at least get me a glass of water?" Even though she was annoyed with him, he still wanted her company.

"Yeah. Sure. But I can't stay long." Rose rinsed out one of several dirty glasses stockpiled on the counter. Placing it to his lips, he eagerly took a few sips, enjoying being pampered by her.

He rolled a joint at the kitchen table and lit it. A sharp pain stabbed at his chest as he leaned over and offered her the pot.

Rose took a hit and it felt like old times to him—when they used to smoke together. He missed it as he stared lovingly at her. She looked away, feeling uncomfortable. *What if Mike suddenly shows up? I've got to get back to my friends. I can't stay here much longer.*

"Uh, Rose? I've been running this through my mind the past couple a hours. Do you … do you think Mike did it deliberately?"

Blowing out the smoke, she turned to him, puzzled with the question. "Huh? That he sent the punks your way on purpose?" She was unsure of how to answer him without hurting his feelings. *Of course he did it deliberately, Larry. Give your head a shake!* She decided to lie. "Uh, I'm not sure."

"He wasn't always that bad, you know. When he was younger, sometimes he had a good heart." He knew that what he was saying wasn't true. His son had always had a mean streak.

Thinking back, he remembered catching him several years earlier with a squirrel. His boy had skinned it alive and had enjoyed watching it suffer. Larry shivered at the thought. *Who am I kidding? Mike doesn't have a good heart. He doesn't even have a heart!*

He tried to concentrate on the road and knew that he needed to be careful with his driving. Meth roared through his system making Mike feel euphoric. His mind drifted as he drove on, trying to keep an eye out for any deer that sometimes bolted in front of an inattentive driver.

A mile from home, he swerved. A tree had knocked down a utility pole in the windstorm. Slowing, he drove around the obstacle before getting back to thinking about how much money he would need to get out of Beaswick and, more importantly, away from his old man. The thought excited him. He would soon have a new start at life.

She studied him for a moment before saying, "Look, Larry. I've got to go." Rose was worried that Mike could be home at any minute. Besides, Carla and Jen would be wondering why she had been gone for so long.

"Yeah. I know, but hear me out." He passed the joint back to her, taking his sweet time talking about Mike and how he had raised him as a single parent. Now that his boy was older, things had gotten worse between them. He kept trying to explain and hoped that she would stay.

"Enough! I've got to go."

"Yeah. Sure. Can you …? Can you at least get me one more glass of water?"

Glancing at the battery powered clock on his wall, she was surprised with the time. It was just after seven. He had been rambling on about his son for close to half an hour.

She looked out his kitchen window for any sign of Mike, feeling a sudden chill. Rubbing her arms, she gave Larry a quick look before saying, "Good luck with your boy. It's time you get him out of your life."

He sputtered out a response as she zipped up her jacket, but she wasn't listening. She had had enough of his rambling and it was time for her to get home. "Good bye, Larry." She hurried to her truck.

Her emotions were mixed as she jumped into her Ford—angry with Larry and also angry with herself. *I should never have allowed him to get close to me. He still thinks that we have something going on between us.*

Rose turned the key. The old truck cranked over once, twice, before firing up. She pulled her mind away from Larry and his boy and wondered if it would snow tonight. It felt like it. The temperature had dropped and the wind was blowing hard.

They still needed to bring one hundred plants down from the mountain, but it wouldn't be tonight. The day had been far too stressful and crazy.

She sped down his long drive, thinking about Jennifer and if she was feeling better. Hopefully they could all get back to work tomorrow.

Halfway down, lights flickered through the trees. A vehicle, a quarter of a mile to her left, was fast approaching along the main road.

Is that Mike? She slowed her truck and had another look. *Two* sets of lights were coming her way. *Hardly anybody comes up here at this time of night! Are the cops following him? I've got to—*

Rose turned off her headlights, worried about being seen. Hitting the gas, her truck lurched forward in the dark. At the end of Larry's drive she pulled the steering wheel hard to her right and made the turn onto McCulloch Road and home.

Chapter 13

Larry held his side as he shifted on his chair, trying to get comfortable. It wasn't working for him. Even with the marijuana in his system, it hurt him too much to move. He decided to keep still.

His ribs were tightly bound by a towel and a large band-aid was on his partially shaved head. Another was above his eye.

He tried to think of something pleasant. *Rose! Will there ever be a chance at … what?* He was in love and planned on how he could see her again. *Maybe I'll go there tomorrow. I'll ask for more Tylenol. I'll tell her that I need her help and that the pain is too much for me.*

He was glad that Kobi was dead. The dog never liked him and he never liked the dog. That had made it difficult to go over for a visit. Not anymore.

Mesmerized by the dancing shadows that the kerosene lantern was giving off, he got back to his daydreaming. Now his mind was on his son. He knew that Mike had set him up. Larry also knew that Rose was right—that he should get rid of his boy. He hated Mike for the way that he had turned out.

Wanting to believe that things would get better, he tried to play it down. *The kid is only going through some temporary changes. That's all.* He caught himself and carefully shook his head, not convinced. *No. He's got to move out before things get out of hand. He might try to kill me when I'm sleep—*

He pulled out his bag of marijuana and rolled another fat one at the table. Taking in several shallow drags, his eyes filled with tears from both the smoke and the physical pain.

Feeling slightly better, his mind shifted back to Mike. *He should have been home two hours ago. It's already seven-thirty! Did he have supper? Did he take his puffer to school?* His son kept forgetting that he suffered from asthma.

Larry drifted, especially now that he was feeling a strong buzz from the pot. He recalled his visit to the drug store a few days earlier when he had gone in to buy a new inhaler and two packages of cigarettes for his boy.

The cashier had looked at him quizzically—two packs of smokes in one hand and an inhaler in the other? He had felt foolish, knowing what the clerk had probably been thinking.

He would have given his kid the money to buy the damn stuff but his son was banned from the store. Mike had been caught stealing a few weeks earlier so Larry had to do his shopping for him.

Headlights flickered through the living room window. *Mike is back! I hope he's happy with what his buddies did to me. The kid has got to learn to keep his big mouth shut. He's just like his mother. He talks too much. He just about got me killed for Christ's sake!*

Concerned about Rose, Carla stared out their living room window searching for her headlights. Her friend should have been back by now. *All she had to do was drop Larry off. Did something go wrong?* Trying not to worry, her mind drifted to happier times.

Last night they had celebrated Jennifer's twenty-fifth birthday. Carla had baked buns and a birthday cake using their farm fresh eggs. Later, they had had a glass or two of wine and had smoked a little pot while watching a movie on the satellite TV.

She chuckled at the recent memory. Jack Nicholson played the role of the devil as Cher and her girlfriends tried to teach him a lesson. The movie was called *The Witches of Eastwick*.

During a commercial, Jen had turned to Rose and, out of the blue, had asked if she had ever needed a man. Carla remembered the puzzled look on her friend's face.

Jen had explained a little more. With raised eyebrows, she pushed on. "Well, you know what I mean. Do you ever, ah, have a yen for a man?"

Rose had sputtered, trying to come up with some kind of answer, but Jen had had a little too much wine and kept at it. "What I mean is—do you ever have an *itch* for a man?" Jen had raised her eyebrows again as a devilish grin crept across her face.

Rose had spouted out, "I know exactly what you're talking about, young lady. Don't play sly with me!"

Carla stared out the window and thought about the question that Jen had asked her only yesterday. "Auntie. How about you?"

It seemed like years ago. She remembered saying something like, "Well, uh, hell yes! I'm only human you know."

They had all laughed, sharing the moment. That's when Jen had said, "Yeah, me, too. We should …" Her niece had hesitated, still thinking. "We should call ourselves, 'The Itches'." As an afterthought, thinking about the little town ten miles away, she had added, "The Itches of Beaswick." They had chuckled over that one as they poured more wine and got back to the movie.

Vehicle lights blinked from a mile away. There were two sets of them and they were heading her way.

Carla squinted to get a better view through the window. *Is it the police? Did Larry call the cops? Are they coming here?* She put a hand to her chest. They could not have the law snooping around on their property.

The kitchen light had been acting up for the last several minutes, finally giving up. That was normal, especially in a windstorm.

Jennifer mumbled something from the dark hallway.

"Huh? Sorry, what did you say?" Carla had her back to her and was preoccupied with the headlights.

"The power is out. Again."

She pulled her eyes away from the window for a moment and noticed that Jen had changed her top. Her complexion was almost as white as the sleeveless blouse that she now had on. Even in the dim moonlight, the Japanese characters for peace, love, and happiness that were tattooed on her left bicep stood out in sharp contrast to her pale skin.

Carla tried to speak in a calming voice, wanting to hide her concern about the approaching vehicle lights. "You know where the lamp is, dear. It's okay. The power's been out many times before."

That seemed to pacify her a little. Jen slipped back into the dark kitchen.

Worried, Carla did not want to tell her niece about the headlights—at least not just yet. There was no need to trouble her any more than she already was. She refocused on the two vehicles. They were getting closer.

Jen made an attempt at lighting the kerosene lamp. Finally, after the third try, a pale light began to fill the room.

Sitting in the flickering shadows of the kitchen, she decided to try harder at being strong. There was no way that she wanted to be a burden to her aunt and her friend.

With a queasy stomach she gave herself a pep talk. *Everything will work out.*

Chapter 14

Using her emergency brake, Rose came to a stop at the foot of her driveway. She did not want anybody to spot her brake lights.

Looking out her passenger window, she swallowed hard. The two sets of lights were fast approaching. *Why are they coming here—to my place? Did they see me? Is that Mike? Who's in the other vehicle? Is it the police?* Her mind raced as she searched for answers.

The lights grew larger as she kept staring, worried that it was the law. Blending together for several moments, they appeared to be one giant floodlight before they abruptly changed direction and veered up Larry's long drive.

She shut off her motor, worried that whoever it was might hear her engine and decide to investigate. Sitting in the dark, she waited for a few moments before stepping out into the wind. Curious, she made her way several feet toward a small clearing for a better view.

The cold wind whipped her long hair as she peered through the thick trees. The two vehicles were parked at Larry's and had also turned off their lights. From where she was standing, she still couldn't see much of anything.

The sound of loud music and vehicle doors slamming drifted toward her. Laughter and whooping sliced through the cool air. It sounded like there were several of them—all high and ready to party.

She tried to play it down. *It's Mike all right! Maybe it's not so bad. Maybe it's some of his friends.* Shaking her head, she knew that she was only kidding herself. *That spoiled creep doesn't have any friends. He never brings anybody home!*

The wind kept blowing her hair in her face. She tried to ignore it, preoccupied with who was at Larry's. *No. It's not some high school buddies coming over to play Monopoly. Larry is in trouble—deep trouble.*

His ears perked up. Another vehicle was coming up his driveway besides Mike's. *No! They're back. With my son!* Blood drained from his face as he tried to stand. A sharp pain sliced through his upper body and stopped him. Taking in a shallow breath, he gripped the table for support and tried again, this time slower.

Half on his feet, he questioned what he should do. There was no way that he could outrun them. They would be on him in a flash. Adrenalin pumped through his system as he wildly looked around his kitchen. *I … I need to defend myself. I can't let those bastards in! They'll kill me.*

Shuffling to the counter, he grabbed a knife covered in steak sauce from two days ago. He could hear the goons on his porch, laughing and having a great time. Shivers ran up his spine. *I … I've got to lock it!* Tightly gripping the knife, he hobbled toward the door.

Larry stopped in his tracks, dizzy. One hand held his chest. The other squeezed the knife. He was inches from the door when another stab of pain racked through his skinny frame. The room spun and his vision blurred.

He made a grab for the deadbolt, but it was too late. The door burst open and slammed into him, propelling the knife into the air as he fell on his back. Pain ripped through his upper torso, making him scream in agony as he hit the linoleum floor.

The bigger punk loomed in the doorway. The animal cry erupting from Larry momentarily surprised him. Tapping the steel bat in a threatening manner, Quincy studied the frail man beneath him with distaste, making Larry feel like a cockroach that needed to be squashed. "Okay, old man. We've had enough of your bullshit."

"Wha-what?" His voice was weak as he held his chest. Pulling in a shallow breath, he sputtered, "I … don't understand. Where's my son? Where's Mike?" He tried to sit up, but couldn't. Instead, he leaned back on his elbows and called out to the opened door. "Mike? Mike!" He prayed that his only child would miraculously save him from the beasts. "Mike! Please!"

The goon continued to pat the steel bat as he and his two buddies glared down at the helpless and terrified man.

Larry didn't understand and hoped that this was only a nightmare. *Why are they back? I gave them all my money.* His eyes were glazed with fear and pain as he gauged the distance between the creeps and the opened door. With considerable effort he got to his knees before making a feeble attempt at crawling past them to safety.

Quincy took a side-step, easily blocking his path. Looking down with contempt, he mimicked Mike's stutter. "Maw-Maw-Mike ain't gonna help you, old timer." He was having a great time as he hovered over his prey.

"Nobody's gonna help you. You had your chance but didn't play ball with us." Cocking the bat, Quincy looked like he was ready to hit a homerun clear out of the park. He swung hard as Larry scrambled under the kitchen table for cover. The bat narrowly missed him and smashed into a wooden leg. Splinters of hard maple flew into the air as he screamed out for mercy.

She heard the ungodly sound pierce the cold evening from a half mile away. *Is that him?* Rose wasn't sure. It seemed more animal than human. Besides, the howling wind that twisted through the trees was playing tricks.

Should I go let Jen and Carla know what's going on? Should I get the rifle and go back to Larry's?

She stood frozen next to her truck, undecided. Her anger began to take over. *No. It's Larry's own stupid ass fault that he got himself into this mess. He should have known better.* She was annoyed that he had allowed this to happen and decided not to get any more involved.

Larry's chilling scream cut through Carla like a knife as she stood on the front porch facing the wind. She worried about Rose as she wrapped her arms around her shoulders, trying to stop from shivering.

Turning to go back into the house, she glanced at the foot of their long driveway. In the dim moonlight she barely made out Rose's Ford through the thick trees. *Is that her? Standing by her truck? What is she doing?* Carla couldn't put it together.

"Okay, you skinny bastard. We can do this the hard way or we can go easy on you." Quincy had a crazed look in his eyes.

Sal and Karl yanked Larry to his feet and roughly shoved him in a chair. Standing guard behind him, they were more than ready to stop him if he tried to do anything stupid.

Karl wore a sickly grin, exposing his three missing teeth. He was clearly enjoying the terrified look on Larry's face and pulled his baseball cap tighter over his unwashed hair.

"Where's my son? Did you hurt him? Where is he? Please. Tell me." He sobbed it out as he held his ribs, fearing that the gang would end up murdering both him and his only child.

"Your son? You're worried about your *son*?" Quincy tossed the bat aside in disgust. Leaning into him, he grabbed the thin man by his blond hair and barked, "You stupid old fuck!"

A fine spray of spittle hit Larry's face. He closed his eyes to block out the demon that was only inches from him.

Quincy was infuriated. Nobody ignored him when he spoke. Nobody! Rattling Larry's head by his hair, he commanded, "Open your eyes, motherfucker!"

He decided that he had better open at least one eye. "Puh-puh-please. Maw-Maw-Mike? Help meh-meh-me. Where are—"

"Your son is the reason why we came back. He's been yakking to us sayin' you got a shoebox stuffed with fifties!" He was disgusted with Larry and how weak the so-called father was. *Daddy is whimpering for his stupid son.* The thug jerked Larry's head with every word that he barked out. "Where—is—the—money?"

"I-I-I told you. I don't *have* any more money." He squirmed in his chair, terrified of being beaten to death.

"Com' on. Hit him again. He deserves another good smack." Karl was excited as he stood behind Larry, ready to pull him down if he tried to stand.

Sal stood next to him, feeling slightly nauseous with the whole affair while Quincy smiled, pleased that Larry kept denying that he had money. He didn't want this to be too easy. He rather enjoyed the bat swinging.

Chapter 15

Rose heard it again—another sickening scream. *No!* Her stomach soured as she clinched her fists in anger and frustration. *Should I drive to my house and phone Gleason?* She opened her truck door and intended to do just that, but froze. *No. A bad idea. It would be like squealing on Larry. Gleason would put him in jail for growing pot. No, I can't do that. I can't phone the police.*

Taking in a few gulps of cool air, she turned in the direction of his house, anticipating another ungodly howl. *I need to do something, but what? Should I go back and try talking to Mike? Try to convince the stupid jerk to call off his punk friends?*

She nodded in agreement with her idea. *I'll drive to the foot of Larry's driveway with my lights off. Then, maybe I can get a better idea of what's going on—maybe reason with Mike.*

Wait a minute! She put her hand to her chest. *What if my engine backfires like it sometimes does when I start it? The punks will hear it. They might think that someone's shooting at them. That would draw attention to me.*

Rose felt helpless. She contemplated on simply walking to his place. It was only half a mile away. *And then what? Sneak up on them? Get a good look at what's going on?*

She was full of questions. *Why did they come back? Do they think Larry still has money? He told me that they took it all. Was he lying?*

"Come on, you old bastard. Come on!" Quincy was worked up and had a twisted look on his face. His buddies had witnessed it before. The adrenalin and meth were taking over and making him lose control.

His heavy gold chain dangled from his neck as he leaned into Larry's face. Foam dribbled from the corner of his mouth and a large blood vessel pulsed at his temple, creating a crooked, blue path along his shaved scalp. He looked like a rabid dog to Larry that was anxious to rip him to pieces.

Sal nervously picked away at his face. He was having doubts, worried that Quincy might be getting *too* carried away. It had happened before.

Not Karl. He was enjoying the moment and wore a goofy, toothless grin.

"One more time, Larry. Let's go through this one more time. Where—is—the—MONEY?"

"I told you." He raised his hands in front of him, trembling. "Please. Don't hit me. Believe me. There *is* no money. You took it all!" He tried to get on his feet. The two punks roughly shoved him down on the chair.

At that moment Quincy felt like he was on top of the world—a god at the center of the universe. He'd had a constant erection since swinging the bat the first time. There was no way that he would allow some old bastard to get the better of him—*especially* in front of his two partners.

No one spoke as he scooped up the bat. All wondered how far he would go. Sal winced, hoping that he was only going to threaten him with it.

Instead, Quincy wound up and swung hard. Fortunately for Larry, the bat slammed into the hard, maple wood and splintered a chair leg before continuing on its journey toward the soft tissue of his lower calf.

The chair slowed the bat's momentum only a little. Larry grabbed his lower leg. Hot tears ran down his cheeks as he and the now three legged chair toppled over and crashed to the floor.

He sat quietly in his pickup while listening to his father's tortured screams. Mike was becoming concerned—not about what they were doing to his father. No. He was worried that he and his buddies wouldn't get more money.

Damn him! I can't leave Beaswick with the cash I got. It's not enough. This is bullshit! Give them all your fuckin' money, Larry. Do it!

Another painful howl twisted its way through the neighbouring trees. Now furious, she was determined to storm up to his house. "Screw them. Screw them all!" Rose shook her head as she yelled it out, her red hair wildly flying about in the crazy wind. "How dare they beat him and steal his money. This has got to stop!"

She wondered about Mike. *What's he doing? Are they beating him, too? Was that him screaming?*

Again, doubt filled her mind. *Would I be doing the right thing—going over there?* She needed to be careful and was thankful that she had her camouflaged clothing on. *The important thing is that Jen and Carla are safe at home. Besides, they have the Winchester.*

Standing next to her truck, she reached for the door handle. *I've got to find out what's really going on. If the situation gets out of control, then I'll phone Gleason.*

Mike was distracted by an eddy of red and gold leaves that the strong wind had whipped up near the log house. The meth was doing its job and making him feel wonderful. The coloured leaves appeared magical to him.

Bored with his old man's screams for mercy, he amped up his truck stereo to ten notches beyond overload and sang along with the Blood Dawgs, his favourite group. "Never felt so disturbed. Wantin' to rip and shred. No end in sight. Should all be dead!"

She jumped into her Ford before losing her nerve. Wrestling with the wind, Rose slammed her door and gave herself a pep talk. *Come on, girl. Larry does not deserve to be treated like that. All you need to do is check things out and everything will be fine.*

She rubbed the furry bee that dangled from her key ring before starting her truck, praying that it wouldn't backfire.

"What's come over me? Feelin' sore. Need some help. Can't find the door." Mike sang the last two lines before jerking his head up.

Wha-at? What the fuck was that? A friggin' gunshot? He looked out his rear window. A thicket of trees rasped in the wind behind him. *Sounded like it came from the old lady's house next door.* He paused for a moment and thought hard.

More yelling and screaming from the A-frame distracted him. Annoyed with the racket that his father was making, Mike cranked up his music and got back to his dream about leaving Beaswick with a wad of cash.

Her nerves were already frayed when she heard the loud boom. Carla flinched, not believing what she was seeing. The Ford had backfired when Rose had started it and now her friend was turning her truck around. *She's heading back to Larry's with her lights off!*

She followed the truck with her eyes for a few moments before getting inside the house. Taking in a breath, she tried to collect her thoughts as both her heart and mind raced with fear.

"Jen?" She tentatively called out her name from the dark living room as she hurried toward the short hallway and kitchen. She did not want to alarm her niece any more than she already was, but there was nothing that she could do except tell her the truth.

She was sitting next to the rifle, anxiously squeezing her hands together while staring at the floor. Carla got down on her knees in front of her and carefully chose her words. "Uh, Jen? There's … something wrong."

Her niece mumbled incoherently, unable to meet her eyes.

Gently, she took her hand and tried to explain what was going on—that Rose was driving back to Larry's.

Jen snapped her head up in disbelief. "No! Rose needs to be here. With us! We've got to stay together." Her eyes bugged out as she scrambled for some sort of explanation. "Maybe … maybe she's going to get the sheriff."

"I don't think so. Not with her lights off. Besides, she could have phoned him from here. She's going to try and help Larry. I know it."

"They'll come *here*, Auntie! They'll come here and beat us! Damn her. Why can't she just leave things alone?"

Carla tried to calm her. "Everything is probably all right, but we need to know what's going on next door." She swallowed the lump in her throat. "Now, listen carefully. I'm going to take the rifle and head over to Larry's and see what—"

"Wha-at? You can't. You can't leave me here all alone—defenceless!"

Carla raised her voice. "All I'm going to do is check things out. Maybe Rose needs help."

Her niece was in tears and her nerves were shattered. *I'll be all by myself in this creepy old house while my aunt and friend are being murdered.* "Then I'll come with you. I … I need to come with you!"

"Jen! For God's sake! Get it together. You stay here. I'll be back in no time." Pulling a black cap over her short hair, Carla buttoned up her camouflaged jacket and picked up the old rifle, trying to remember when she had last fired it. Giving her niece one final look, she unlocked the back door and stepped out into the night.

Chapter 16

Squatting with his gold chain dangling from his neck, Quincy poked him with a splinter from the broken chair. Larry remained motionless, face down on the floor.

He sang out his name, still prodding. "Oh, Lair-ee. Come on, buddy. You're not helping things. You don't want me to hurt you again, do you?"

Sal wondered if they were wasting their time. He wanted to speak out but Quincy was in another one of his moods. No, it would be safer for him to keep quiet.

Now bored, Quincy stood and casually kicked him in the face. It wasn't a hard kick—just enough to get his attention. It worked.

Larry groaned, half conscious as he opened one eye.

The creep towered over him. A cross was stencilled on the front of his white tee shirt. Written on it in blood red were two words, *Judgement Day*. He had several tattoos on his arms and one that depicted a scorpion creeping up the side of his neck to his shaved head.

Larry snapped his eye shut, having seen enough. He prayed that the three punks would simply disappear.

Quincy flashed his buddies a wink before turning back to the beaten man on the floor. "I got a question for you. Tell me sumtin'." Now he examined Larry's bandaged head with interest—as if it were a choice cut of meat. "Larry. Oh, Lair-ee?"

Annoyed that he wasn't responding, Quincy barked, "Put 'em in another chair. I want to talk to him—face to face."

Sal and Karl jumped into action and roughly grabbed him by his arms, yanking him off the floor.

He screamed. The pain in his ribs and leg was unbearable. A stream of hot vomit spewed out of his mouth and splattered on the cold floor next to his pool of blood.

"Jeeze!" Quincy jumped back and was disgusted with the steamy mess. "Watch what you're doing. I almost got some on my boots!" He said it accusingly to his fellow goons and was very much concerned that he might get dirty. He added, "I don't want him passed out. At least not just yet."

Carla reached the foot of the driveway and looked down McCulloch Road. There was no sign of Rose or her truck. Another scream sliced through the wind making her jerk her head toward the sound. She pulled her jacket tighter. *What are they doing to him?* A lump formed in her throat as she answered her own question. *They're torturing him. That's what they're doing!*

Looking down at the rifle in her arms, she had unconsciously taken the safety off. She was being drawn into a situation that she wanted no part of and was going against her very fiber—her beliefs.

Holding the Winchester closer and almost cradling it, a strange mixture of comfort and excitement swept through her. She shook her head and tried to release the spell, puzzled with how she was feeling. Slowly, she found herself moving one foot and then the other in a zombie-like fashion, shuffling along the dusty road. She was being drawn into some kind of black hole by an inexplicable and powerful force. It was called survival.

Jen checked the front and back doors for the third time to make sure that they were locked. Her mind screamed out questions. *What if Rose and Carla are murdered and the thugs decide to come after me? Where could I be safe? Should I stay in the house or hide in the bush?*

She sat in the shadows of the kitchen with her back against the wall as the house creaked from the wind. Her nerves were raw from having one of the worst days of her life. In her mind she could still hear the gun blasts and whistling bullets as they tore through the bush only a few hours earlier and now … this?

An ashtray with a partially smoked joint sat next to her. She eyed it for a few moments before lighting it with shaky hands. Drawing in a huge toke, she hoped that the drug would help her relax.

Unable to sit still, she entered the living room and soon felt a strong buzz from the pot. It made her feel even more frightened and vulnerable. *I can't just sit here.*

I'll phone my mom. That's what I'll do. I'll tell her that I'm in trouble and if she doesn't hear back from me in an hour, to call the police.

She held the old phone to her ear and dialled, wondering if her mom would even bother to answer. *It's … not ringing. Something's wrong.* Pressing the heavy Bakelite handset tighter against her ear, she looked down at the floor, confused. *What's the matter with mom's phone?* Slowly, it came to her. It wasn't her mother's phone that was the problem. It was *their* phone. The line was dead.

Rose idled along the dark road with her headlights off and prayed that she wouldn't be seen or heard. She also prayed that she could talk some sense into Mike. Then, maybe together they could persuade the thugs into leaving.

An idea began to take shape. She would drop a bomb and tell them that the sheriff was her ex brother-in-law—that they had to leave immediately or the law would bust their sorry asses.

Using the emergency brake, she slowed to a stop at the foot of his long drive. She could barely make out the faint light in Larry's kitchen several hundred feet away. Carefully, she turned the old Ford around and faced it back toward her house. Her plan was to park by his mailbox, ensuring that she would have a quick getaway, just in case.

Taking in a deep breath, she cracked open her door. The dome light flashed on.

They had him in another chair. This one had all four legs intact and was a safe distance from the pool of blood and vomit. The kerosene lamp gave one finally sputter before running out of fuel.

Sal fumbled his way into the dark living room and rifled through drawers for candles. He had seen some earlier when they had been searching for money. Something caught his eye. It looked like a flicker of light. Curious, he moved closer to the window.

"Sal! Did you find anything? We need fuckin' light in here." Quincy did not like being interrupted with his interrogation. The dark was annoying him and he did not want to accidentally step into Larry's mess. But, more importantly, he wanted to continue seeing the fear on his victim's face.

Ignoring his buddy's question, Sal studied the foot of the long driveway through the thick trees.

Several moments passed before Quincy barked, "What are you doin' in there? Get a flashlight or somethin'. We can't see shit!"

No, there's nothing down there. Sometimes, if he took too much meth he would get a drug induced mental flash. It was happening too frequently with him.

"Sal?"

"I'm still looking. Gimme another second." Scratching his head, he told himself to go easy on his drug intake from now on as he rummaged through drawers before finding what he was looking for. He returned to the kitchen, forgetting about the flash of light that he thought he might have seen.

The candles produced giant, animated shadows. In his pain induced state, Larry believed that there were now six thugs beating on him instead of only three. He began to pray, knowing that his chances of surviving were probably next to none. "Please, God. I beg for your mercy. Make them leave. I didn't do nothin' to them. Make them leave me and my son alone."

The tattooed scorpion on Quincy's neck arched back as his head recoiled in disbelief. "Your son? You want us to leave you and your *son* alone?" Smirking, he turned to his partners. "Did you hear that, boys? Daddy here," he pointed at Larry, "is praying for us to leave him and his son …" He yelled out 'son' in a mocking tone. "To leave his 'son' and him alone."

He grabbed Larry's hair and ripped the bandage from his scalp. Shaking it in Larry's face, he screamed "What I want to know, fuck head, is *who* fixed you up?"

"Huh? Wha-at? What do you mean?" Larry knew very well what he meant. His bowels loosened, understanding that things were going to be getting a lot worse for him.

"You didn't shave your scalp by yourself now, did you?" He loved his self-appointed job of being the interrogator.

Worried that he might be drawing the girls next door into some very serious trouble if he said the wrong thing, Larry stuttered while trying to think fast. "Uh, yeah, I-I-I did. I feh-fixed myself up." *Be careful what you tell them. Don't blab your fool head off!*

Chapter 17

The strong wind lashed at her hair as she crept up his drive. Larry's property was filled with bush and thick trees. Keeping to the left, she used some of the growth for cover.

Rose reached into her pocket for a rubber band. Her hands shook as she tried to fashion her hair into a pony tail. It gave her time to think. *Am I doing the right thing—sneaking up on them?*

Two vehicles were parked near the back door next to Larry's pickup. One was Mike's Toyota. The other was a Honda sedan. She had no idea who it belonged to.

Inching closer, she made out a dark figure slouched in the Toyota. *Is that Mike? What's he doing? Why is he still in his truck?*

Twisted music blared from his cab. "Never felt so disturbed. Killin' would be good. They should be put to sleep. Drive the knife in, deep, deep, deep!"

She didn't know what to think. *Did he convince his buddies that his dad had more money stashed away? But, why is he sitting there and why did he come back with them?* She hoped that they had forced him to. Maybe they had threatened him. Crouching lower, she made her way toward his truck.

It's Mike all right. Should I talk to him? Walk up and tap on his window? Ask him what's going on? No, she couldn't do that just yet. She was too angry. It would be difficult for her to talk to him without yelling and, it would only make matters worse.

Rose tried to get her emotions in check and went through her questions again. *Why is he in his truck? Why isn't he protecting his father?* Mike had his chin on his chest. He looked stoned.

Keeping low, she managed to sneak past him to the rear of the yard. Larry's kitchen door swung open just as she slipped behind a large Ponderosa Pine.

A male with a shaved head and white tee shirt stepped out onto the porch.

Who the hell is that? Rose had no idea.

He stood there for a moment, his eyes adjusting to the dark. In his hand was a pipe.

The creep sauntered over to Mike's truck. Rose had a clear view of him and the rear of the house. He turned with his back to her only thirty feet away. Rapping on Mike's window, he yelled, "Turn that shit off!"

He snapped off his stereo before rolling down his window.

Quincy softened a little. "Why so glum?" *He's probably thinkin' we should go easy on his daddy.*

"Uh, I can't wait to get the fa-fa-fuck out a here. I'm movin' to Kelowna once we get the ca-ca-cash. I never wanna come back." Anxious, he bobbed his head up and down and asked, "Did you geh-geh-get it? Did you get more money from the oh-oh-old man?"

Quincy turned away, studying the rear of the house as he put the pipe to his lips. Finally lighting it in the blustery wind, the meth seeped deep into his lungs. He handed it to Mike.

He eagerly wrapped his hands around it and took in a lungful. Tears welled in his eyes as he blew out the smoke and drew in several gulps of air. He asked again. "Did you geh-geh-get it? Did you get more money from the oh-oh-old man?"

Ignoring Mike's question for the second time, several moments passed before Quincy finally spoke. "We gotta problem. A major problem." He studied the house as he said it, scratching his shaved head.

Rose leaned out from behind the large tree so she could hear more about this 'problem'.

"Wha-wha-what? What are you talkin' 'bout? I know the old man has maw-maw-money. I told you! Don't let him bullshit you. Don't let him bullshit *me*!" Stoned and panicky, Mike did not want to hear about any problem. He felt that his father was screwing him. Again! *Jeeze. Will this ever end?* Shifting in his seat, he squeezed the steering wheel, wanting to get things over with.

"Yeah, yeah. I know he's probably bullshitting us, but that's not what I'm sayin'." Quincy felt the dope rush through his body. It gave him energy. In his drug-addled mind he could no longer comprehend the moral difference between right and wrong.

She leaned out a little farther, annoyed by the grating sounds that the surrounding trees were making. It made it difficult for her to hear what the two jerks were saying. *What's he talking about? What problem?*

Mike was impatient with his father. He wanted justice. He wanted his old man's money. He figured that he deserved it. *The bastard's playin' games.* Wondering what Quincy was getting at, he asked, "Uh, wa-wa-what's the praw-praw—"

"We got bad shit happenin'." He turned and studied Mike, trying to suppress the urge to laugh at him. *What an idiot!* He thought about what he wanted to say, but it was hard for him to do. He was very stoned. The wind blowing through the trees distracted him. *Everything* at that moment distracted him—including Mike. Tired of looking at him, Quincy spun around in Rose's direction.

She jerked her head back. *Did he see me? He'll come after me. I've got to run.* Her heart was on overload and a rush of adrenalin filled her core.

Mike was talking to Quincy's back. "Wa-wa-what's the praw-praw-problem?" Not getting any response, he persisted. "You said tha-that there's a praw-praw problem?"

Quincy kept staring in her direction, having no idea that Rose was only thirty feet away. His mind drifted with the almost harmonic sounds that the trees were making. *It's like a sympathy.* He giggled. *No, I mean 'symphony'. Yeah. Symphony. It's nature's music. Cool and creepy.*

She waited with straining ears and pounding heart. *Did he see me? What's he doing?*

He pulled his mind away from his 'symphony' and turned to Mike. "We've got a huge issue goin' on."

She shuddered. *Is he talking about me?*

Mike tried to pay attention to what he was telling him. Things didn't make sense. "I-I don't un-un-under—"

"Looks like your daddy paid someone a visit and they fixed him up a little. They shaved part of his head and put a few bandages on him."

Sweat ran down her back. She was relieved that he hadn't spotted her, but now she wondered what the thug was getting at.

"What? Are you sure? Even if he did get help, he whoa-wouldn't a told nobody what happened."

Quincy shook his shaved head and chuckled dismissively at him. "Mikie. Mikie. Mikie! Sometimes you're so fuckin' dumb."

Angry, he wanted to quip back to his supposed friend but decided to hold his tongue. The bigger man made him nervous.

Talking down to him, Quincy continued in a mocking fashion. "He wouldn't a had to open his mouth. Anybody with half a brain can see he's been beat up! Come on, man. Use your friggin' head."

Mike didn't know how to respond to the bully.

"Now, where did he go to get fixed up? Huh? Where did he go?" He pondered his question while waiting for an answer.

Rose felt a new wave of panic sweep through her. *He's putting it together. It's only a matter of time before they come after me and my friends.*

"Uh, he might a gone to Beaswick." He added, "Maybe to the daw-daw-doctor 'cause—" He stopped and realized that it was a stupid thing to say.

Quincy shook his head. He felt like a teacher and that his dunce student had given him the wrong answer. Leaning through the truck window, he was in the kid's face. With total contempt, he barked, "Your daddy didn't go to no daw-daw-doctor."

Mike was livid. *You bastard! You're—*he tried to think of the right word—*mim-mimic? Yeah. You're mimicking me, you fat asshole.* He glared back with a burning face and gave him a warning. "I ta-told you before. Don't call me Mikie!"

Ignoring him, Quincy asked the question for the second time. "Now, where do you suppose good old Larry walked to, or crawled to, for help? Hmm?"

Rose had heard more than enough. The situation was getting terribly out of control and there was no longer any hope in reasoning with Larry's boy. He didn't care what they did to his dad and only wanted his money.

Chapter 18

Quincy stared through Mike—not seeing him. His meth brain was too busy trying to figure things out. *If Larry went to the neighbour for help, they would a called the police. Having a neighbour show up at their door badly beaten would a had most good folks worried. The cops would a bin here by now.*

He spoke mainly to himself as he did mental gymnastics. "Why didn't the neighbour take Larry to the hospital? 'Cause the dumb fuck can't go there. That's why. Good old Larry has lots to hide."

Scratching his shaved head, he kept up with his one-sided conversation. "The other reason might be 'cause the neighbour also has lots to hide and doesn't want to get involved."

Quincy relaxed a little and figured that they had nothing to worry about with the neighbour. *They probably didn't want any more to do with Larry except fix him up and get him back to his house. Good. Let's just keep this little party private.*

He was feeling wonderful and ready for more fun. It was time to put his plan into action. It was time to have some *real* fun.

"Never mind the neighbour, Mikie. He didn't call the cops so everything is cool."

Rose felt instant relief and hoped that he meant what he said.

Mike's eyes were glazed as he drifted away, escaping from the callous bastard that stood next to his truck. He tried to tune him out and looked on at the autumn leaves as they twirled in the strong wind.

"Mike. Mike! Listen to me."

"Uh? What? You were talking about the nuh-nuh—"

Tired of his stuttering, he cut him off. "Forget about the neighbour. We need your help." He shoved the pipe in his face and commanded, "Take another hit." He wanted to make sure that Mike was stoned.

"Ah, no. I'm already way too out of it."

"I said take it!" His words were hard and cold, daring Mike to refuse his offer.

Hesitating for only a moment, he grabbed the pipe and pulled in another puff.

Satisfied, Quincy changed his tone. "Tell me what it's like living with your dear old daddy. Tell me how good it's been."

He blew out the smoke and sputtered, "Good?" Surprised with the question, his mouth dropped. "I fa-fa-fuckin' hate it. I hate him and I hate livin' here!"

Pleased with the kid's reaction, he smiled. "Yeah. I know what you're talkin' 'bout." He had had a similar experience with his own father. Curious, he pressed on. "Uh … did he ever hit you? Did he ever beat up on you?"

"Oh yeah! He hit me ma-ma-many times." Mike angrily bounced his head up and down as he squeezed his steering wheel with both hands. Meth raced through his weak brain.

Perking up a little, Quincy asked, "Why did he hit you?" *This is getting interesting.*

He thought for a moment before explaining. "Well, I guess it's 'cause I punched him."

"You what? You punched him?" He stepped back, caught off guard. *That little prick just told me that his father abused him. Now he's sayin' that he punched him?* It was hard for Quincy to comprehend. He thought about how he would have come close to murdering Mike if he had done that sort of thing to him. Shaking his head, he wasn't sure who he was disgusted with the most—Larry or his idiot son.

Mike felt proud about how he had handled his father as he relived the memory. "Yeah. I punched him all right. I punched him right in the fuckin' face." He smiled with the thought and added, "I made his nose bleed 'cause he needed it."

"He … needed it? Why?"

His face darkened, remembering the sound of the hard smack and the sight of Larry's blood as it gushed from his nose. "He's always makin' me duh-duh-do my homework."

"Uh-huh." Quincy nodded and pretended to understand how Mike must have suffered having to do his homework. He thought back to how his own father had beaten the crap out of him many, many times for absolutely no reason. His old man terrified him and was now doing time in the state penitentiary. *Compared to me, Mikie has it real good. Yeah, too good! The spoiled bastard doesn't know* how *good he's got it.*

He focused back on his twisted plan. "It's time you make a break from all of this. You just need a little more cash. That's all that's keepin' you from livin' the good life."

"Yeah. You're right." He eagerly nodded, now happy that he and his new friend seemed to be on the same page. Still wanting an answer, he asked, "What happened in there? Did you guh-guh-get more money from him?"

Quincy's voice turned hard. "No. He told me that you were lyin'. He told me that you lied all along and that you're nothin' but a spoiled, little prick."

"Wha-wha-what?" Mike's mouth dropped as he glared at the A-frame through his dirty windshield. His grip tightened on his steering wheel, fantasizing that it was his father's throat that he was squeezing. *How could the old man say somethin' like that? He's made my life hell, always wantin' me to do this and to do that, and now he's tellin' my new buddy that I'm a spoiled, little prick?*

Quincy openly smiled, seeing the anger flash across his face. *This is getting too good to pass up.* He pretended to sigh as he pushed on with his plan. "Well, I guess we're done here. Larry tells me that he has no more money."

He was furious. *The old man is screwing me again! Just like he always does. He's got more money stashed! I seen it.*

"It's over, unless …" Quincy tried to sound serious. It was difficult for him to do. He was having too much fun and tried very hard at suppressing a smile.

"Unless wha-wha-what?" Mike turned to him with an opened mouth, having no idea what the bigger man was getting at.

His face broke into a malicious grin. He couldn't hold back any longer. "Unless you want to go in there with the bat and … talk to him."

He didn't hesitate. "Yeah, Quincy. I want to go in there and talk to him. I want to 'talk' to that piece of shit." His stuttering was momentarily forgotten. He was too angry.

Rose was only slightly relieved with what she had heard—that Quincy wanted to forget about the neighbour. *Maybe we won't get involved after all.*

What concerned her now was how Quincy had manipulated Mike into going back to the house and having a talk with his father. *He'll kill him!*

"Well then, come on boy. Let's go 'talk' to your daddy."

Chapter 19

He had an arm around Mike's shoulder as they walked toward the log house, pretending that they were the best of friends. Quincy silently chuckled at how easy it had been to dupe him. Mike couldn't wait to get at his father.

He was slumped in a chair and drifted in and out of consciousness as Karl and Sal stood guard over him.

"Larry? Oh Lair-ee! You got company." He sang it out and, grabbing him by his hair, roughly jerked his head up.

He winced in pain. Through tears, he barely made out his son standing next to the skin headed thug. "Mike? Is that you? Oh God. Tell them to stop. Please! Tell them to stop. They've been—"

"Shut up, old man!" His fists were clenched as he looked down at his father with contempt.

Even in the dim light of the candles Larry could clearly see the hatred in his son's eyes. "Please, Mike. You don't understand. Why are you helping them?" He sobbed it out. Somewhere in his heart he had hoped that his son would be there for him. His boy was there all right, but for the wrong reason—ready to beat him to a pulp.

Quincy grabbed Larry's hair and yanked his head up, enjoying the moment. He felt himself stir with the way Mike was talking to his father and had trouble understanding why he was feeling that way.

Karl wore a demented smile and eagerly waited to see what would happen next. *I bet he's gonna pound his old man with the fuckin' bat.*

Sal appeared ill and was repulsed with the whole scene—especially with the son ready to thrash his father. *He's going to kill him. I know it. This is bullshit.*

"Go ahead, Mikie." He wore a twisted smile as he handed him the bat. "Have a 'talk' with your daddy." Now he was very much aroused and anxious to see how far Mike would go.

Rose needed to get back to her friends. She had heard enough. *I'll phone Gleason and tell him what's going on. He has got to stop this! If I don't make the call, they'll kill him.*

Her stomach did flip-flops as she pushed away from the large tree. Stepping over several fallen branches, she was determined to get back to her truck that was parked at the foot of Larry's drive. Half running and scrambling, she made her way toward the parking area and Mike's vehicle as the moon momentarily slipped behind clouds.

Larry's back door swung open. She froze, totally exposed as Sal stood in the doorway with his head down and deep in thought.

"Where do you think you're going?" Quincy barked out the question from behind him.

Oh God! He sees me. What should I do? What should I say? She swallowed hard, her heart, racing.

His eyes were on Sal's back, unaware that she stood frozen in her camouflaged clothing in the middle of the parking area. He was concerned that his buddy would miss the show. Mike was about to start swinging. Why was he heading out the door?

With his head still down, Sal turned and faced his twisted friend. Fumbling with an excuse, he sputtered, "I gotta take a leak."

Rose seized the opportunity and bolted for cover toward Mike's truck.

"Yeah, sure, but hurry back. You don't wanna miss anything." He winked as he said it.

Sal couldn't wait to get outside. He was not enjoying this. The original plan was to beat the old man up a little and take his money. *Now we're back again and the kid is going to have a go at his father? With a bat?* No, Sal didn't like it at all. He needed a breath of fresh air.

Stepping out onto the porch, he faced Mike's truck. It was parked fifty feet away and Rose was crouched behind it.

Quincy ordered Mike to hold off with the bat until Sal returned.

"Buh-buh-but I wanna hit the mother—"

"I said hold off for a minute! You'll have plenty of time for that." He wanted to make sure that his friend wouldn't miss the show. He also thought that if Mike waited a few minutes then maybe the old guy would have a change of heart knowing that a beating was coming his way. Maybe then he would spill his guts and tell them where the rest of his money was. He smiled as he rubbed his hands together. There was no hurry. Quincy loved the anticipation.

In the dim moonlight, Sal slowly made his way toward Mike's truck. *This is going too far.*

Rose was on her knees near the tailgate.

He halted midway and wondered what he could do to stop the beating. *Maybe the kid won't take the bat to Larry. Maybe Quincy will stop him.* He shook his head and felt uneasy with the whole scene as he stepped closer toward the driver's side of Mike's vehicle.

Rose crawled on all fours to the passenger side—her mind, screaming. *What will they do to me if they catch me?*

Continuing down the road, Carla finally made out Rose's Ford. It was parked near Larry's mailbox and faced her. Her friend wasn't in it. *She shouldn't get involved. What is she thinking?*

A shallow ditch was at the corner of Larry's property. She stepped through it thinking that she could hide in the brush and still keep an eye out for Rose. A barbed wire fence blocked her way.

She struggled over the obstacle with the rifle in hand and got scratched in the process. Hiding behind a thicket, she studied Larry's house, several hundred feet from her, and wondered what was going on inside. *Is Rose with them? Did they get their claws into her?*

Sal stood next to the truck box and groped for a cigarette. He struck a match and cupped his hands, trying to shield the flame from the strong wind. At the same time he noticed something move near the foot of the driveway. The match momentarily blinded him. Squinting, he looked again in Carla's direction. *Another friggin' deer?*

He waited a few moments for his eyes to adjust to the dark while listening carefully. *Nothing. Just trees swaying in the wind.*

Satisfied that it was most likely a deer, he got back to the problem of how to diffuse the situation in Larry's kitchen. Sal picked at the open sores on his face, concerned. *This is bullshit. How can I take control? What can I do to stop the kid from beating his father to death? I can't reason with Quincy. He's too stoned.*

He gripped the truck box with one hand, taking in a long drag. Rose crouched on the other side, ready to bolt the moment he spotted her.

Unaware that she was there, he lifted his head to the night sky and speculated. *The old guy could get killed with a blow to the head. Then what? We'd need to—*

The backdoor of the A-frame swung open. Quincy stormed out to the porch, impatient. "What are you doin'?"

"Just havin' a smoke." Sal needed to talk to him privately. He knew that he had a better chance of making his point if it was only the two of them. "Come and join me."

Moments later Quincy stood beside him near the rear wheel. "What's the matter? Aren't you enjoying this?"

"Uh, I am, but I'm worried that he might kill his old man."

"Yeah. I gotta be careful about that. I'll let him play with him a little and we'll see what happens."

"I'm serious! If he hits him too hard, the old fucker will die. Did you see the look in his eyes? The kid absolutely hates his dad."

"Yeah, yeah. No worries. I'll hold him back." He kept talking. "Do you know *why* he hates him?"

Sal shrugged, not caring.

"He hates him 'cause …" He waited for a moment before taking in a breath. "Because Larry makes him do his homework."

Sal shook his head in disgust and looked down at his feet. *The kid is pathetic.*

Quincy put a hand on his partner's shoulder. "He also hates him 'cause … Are you ready for this?"

He looked up, waiting for more. This was getting too weird.

"He hates him 'cause his dad hits him. But, wait." Quincy held up a hand and paused for effect. "Do you know *why* Larry hits him?"

"Look, Quincy. I really don't want to hear any more of that stupid shit." He turned away.

That didn't stop his buddy from explaining. "His dad hits Mikie 'cause he needs to defend himself from his lil' boy beatin' on him!"

"That is so gross." Sal spun around and faced him. What Quincy was telling him was sick. "What kind of family is that? I mean, I thought *our* families were bad but not like *that!* This is shit, man. They're *both* disgusting. In fact, the kid is totally more disgusting than the old man. I almost feel sorry for Larry."

Quincy nodded. "I know. How would you like to have a boy like that?"

"I'd kill him if he were mine." He angrily flicked his cigarette butt into the air, feeling totally put off. The hot stub arched its way across the truck box before getting caught up in the wind. It landed on Rose.

She was on all fours. Burning embers rolled off her neck and down her front, getting trapped under her clothing. Panicking, she slapped at her chest.

"Come on. Let's get back in so I can keep an eye on him."

"Yeah, okay." That pacified Sal a little as they ambled back to the house, both preoccupied with the thought of Mike murdering his father.

Hot ash burned its way down her chest and mid-section. She was on her knees and frantically slapped at the embers while staring at the backs of the two goons as they made their way to the porch and house.

Mike had the bat tightly gripped over his head and was waiting to show off to his buddies. He swung hard as they entered the kitchen—determined to give his father the beating of his life.

Larry saw it coming and lurched forward, yanking a chair between him and his son. It worked to a certain degree. The bat smashed into the hard maple wood and slowed some of the momentum before glancing off his back. Slamming face first to the kitchen floor, the pain was too much for the frail man. He passed out.

Sal felt sick and turned away, having seen more than enough. He did not want to witness a murder. He was there to steal money, nothing more. Shocked by the scene, he looked out the opened door to escape from it all.

Quincy yanked the bat from Mike. He hadn't expected him to swing so hard. He was in his face yelling, "Jesus, Mike! Don't fuckin' kill him!"

"Quincy. Quincy!" Sal whispered it out in alarm.

Spinning around, he wondered what his friend wanted. His buddy was standing in the opened doorway with his back to him. "What? What is it?"

Sal was speechless as he kept looking out the door.

"Jeeze, Sal! What?"

He raised a finger and pointed. "I-I-I see a woman. By Mike's truck." Scrambling for words, he tried to make sense out of it. "It looks like she's …" He shook his head, hoping that it might help with what he considered an obvious vision problem. *I'm not really seeing this, am I?* "She's … dancing?"

"What?" Quincy tossed the bat to the floor. *He's way too stoned!*

"Yeah! She's …" He looked on in disbelief.

The bigger thug rushed to the door. Karl and Mike followed, wondering what Sal was talking about. Jammed together on the threshold, they could not believe what they were seeing.

Mike raised a finger and pointed at the gyrating figure only fifty feet away. "It's our neighbour! Row-Row-Row—"

II

Rose was performing a spastic dance in the parking area. The trapped cigarette embers under her clothing were burning her chest and midsection. She swatted at the hot ash, unaware that they had spotted her.

The four punks froze in Larry's doorway and had trouble believing what they were seeing. Some crazed, red haired woman was dancing and slapping at her chest in the partial moonlight. All wondered if they had overdone it with the meth—that they were experiencing a bizarre form of collective hallucination.

She pulled her eyes from her chest and looked up. They were gawking at her with open mouths. Goose bumps telegraphed down her arms and a chill ran up her spine. *I … I've got to get away! I've got to run!* Rose turned and bolted down the driveway. The hot embers that clung to her chest were the least of her worries.

The boys came to life. Finding their legs, all four scrambled down the porch stairs at the same time. They chased her, yelling and whooping. Sal trailed the group before deciding that he didn't want any part of it. He was worried about the way things were escalating. Turning, he made his way back to the house, concerned that Mike had murdered his father.

Rose was a hundred feet ahead of them and thankful for being in good shape. She felt like a hunted animal and knew that she was in some very serious trouble. Taking a chance, she glanced over her shoulder. There were three of them and they were gaining.

God, no! They'll rip me apart. She pumped her legs and focused on her truck at the foot of the driveway. Her thighs ached from the strain and her lungs were on fire. Unable to keep up the pace, she stumbled, falling hard on her side.

Pain tore through her right ankle. *No!* Rose struggled to her knees. *I've got to keep moving. I need to run!*

Stunned, she looked again as needles rushed up her side. There was no time to think about her ankle. What mattered was getting to the safety of her truck.

They could easily see her—even in her camouflaged clothing. Karl was a few steps behind Quincy as they raced down the driveway. Mike followed, trailing his buddies. His asthma was acting up and forcing him to slow down.

Quincy wondered why she was there. *Who the hell is she? Is she looking for trouble? I'll give her trouble. Big-time trouble.*

The punks were quickly closing in and Rose couldn't keep running at that pace. They were fifty feet from her when she reached the foot of Larry's driveway. Now she was hobbling—her truck seemingly miles away.

Carla was having trouble believing the crazy chase. Hiding behind a bush at the corner of Larry's property, she pointed the rifle at the thugs, worried about her friend. *Don't shoot just yet. She still might make it to her truck. If they touch her, then do it—start fucking shooting!*

Quincy was fired up. *The dumb bitch. Why did she have to go and meddle in our affairs?* He glanced behind him. Karl was several feet away and Mike was trailing with the bat. *Good!* He figured that it would come in handy. For a moment he wondered where Sal was.

Rose pushed her way along the dusty road, dragging her injured foot. *Please God. Help me make it to my truck.*

He tried running faster but couldn't. His lungs burned and his legs ached. Quincy was out of shape.

Rose grabbed for her door handle. Her hands shook as tears streamed down her face. Looking over her shoulder, the skin headed goon was almost at the rear of her pickup.

She yanked at the handle and threw herself in just as Quincy reached out, his fingers inches away. Pulling hard, she slammed it shut.

Furious, he wanted to wrench her out by her long hair, but Rose had already hammered down the lock button.

In her truck, she was safe for the moment and tried to catch her breath. Putting her hand on her bare chest, she could feel blisters forming. It was unbelievable to her—being hunted like an animal.

She stared at Quincy's angry face in disbelief as he slammed his opened hand on her side window. "You bitch! What were you doing? Snooping?" He kept crazily beating on the glass to draw her attention from Karl. She caught a glimpse of a shadowy figure in her mirror. *It's him—the other creep!* Lunging across her seat, she slammed the passenger lock button down just as Karl grabbed the handle.

He managed to open the door a fraction before the locking mechanism kicked in. Rattling the door, he tried to get it completely open. The clanking echoed throughout the steel cab.

Carla crouched behind the bush. She had a clear view of what was going on. Raising the rifle in the moonlight, she pointed it at the thug on the passenger side. He was on the running board and jiggling the door. She swallowed hard. *If he gets in, then what? He'll tear her apart!*

She was a mess, unable to keep the rifle trained on her target. *Can I actually shoot someone? No. I'll fire a warning shot over their heads. That will stop them.* She doubted if that would help.

What if they have a gun? What if they decided to circle around and shoot me instead? They're probably very capable of doing that sort of thing. They seem to have no problem in beating people up and terrorizing them.

Carla made her decision. She had had enough and would be damned if she and her girlfriends would be bullied. Living in the city, she had gotten her full share of crime. That was one of the reasons why she had moved to the country. Enough was enough. *I'll shoot first and ask questions later!*

Mike clambered into the truck box and raised the bat. Holding that position, he steadied his legs before bringing it down hard on her cab roof. His new buddies cheered him on.

With the bat held high above his head, he shook it in the air with one hand, pleased with their approval. His other hand formed a fist. He pumped it into the night sky before taking another downward swing.

The sound of steel striking her roof resonated throughout the cab. Rose shuddered. Her nerves were raw and she was being pushed far beyond her limit.

Mike stepped back and smiled as he examined his handiwork. Her rear window had a jagged crack running down the middle.

The punk that had been rattling her passenger door gave up trying to open it. Instead, he slithered onto her hood and glowered at her through the windshield. They were almost face to face when he yelled out something obscene. She found herself staring at his lips in morbid fascination, trying to read them. Several of his teeth were missing.

Her eyes shifted to his black cap. The words 'Mega Death' stood out in blood red. He looked wild and untamed, clearly gone bananas.

Frustrated that he couldn't get at her, he grabbed her wiper blade, trying to rip it from her truck.

She opened her mouth, waiting for words to form. Instead, an unintelligible gasp escaped from somewhere in her throat. It didn't matter. They wouldn't listen even if she did try to speak. They were feeding off one another and were out of control.

Another loud clang from the steel bat made her jump. Mike had clobbered her roof even harder. Cold chills shot up her back as the harsh, metallic sound rang throughout the cab one more time. The crack in her rear window grew tenfold.

Mike's pounding spurred the toothless goon on. With both hands, he hammered at her windshield as foam dribbled from his mouth. The wild pack would soon destroy her if she didn't do something fast.

I … I need to … She was confused and going into shock. *I need to drive away. I need to escape.* Rose reached into her coat pocket, searching for her keys. *Where …? Where are they! They're not here! Did I drop them? God, no!* With eyes fixated on the animal staring through her windshield at her, she fumbled through her pockets. *No! They must be somewhere on Larry's driveway. Maybe when I fell, they …*

She grabbed the steering wheel and tried to shake it, stupidly hoping that her truck would somehow start on its own. Through tears, she looked out her side window. The creep that had been at her door had disappeared.

Something soft brushed her knee. She jerked her feet off the floor, totally repulsed. *Oh God! He's groping my leg! How did he get in?*

Rose forced herself to look down, expecting to see a hand appear from under her dash. Her string of keys with the furry bee and its gangly legs dangled from the ignition. She had forgotten that she had left them in her truck in case she needed to make a quick get-away.

Taking in a huge swallow of air, she tried to slow her screaming heart. A small amount of relief swept through her. *Yes! I can still escape.* She chanced a closer look out her side window. There he was, the bigger thug with the shaved head. He was bent over, letting air out of her front tire.

An inner strength began to fill her core. Shaking her head clear, she was determined that she would not allow them to murder her. It was time to fight back. She turned the key. Her Ford surprised her by immediately coming to life. It seemed that her truck also had enough and wanted to escape the beating. Rose revved the motor. She and 'Ford' were now a team and would take care of this little problem together.

Carla took careful aim at the kid with the bat. He was the most threatening. She decided to shoot him first if the opportunity presented itself. He had to be a safe distance away from her friend if she did try a shot. She wondered how accurate the rifle was.

Still in the box, Mike backed away from the cab. Now was her chance. She aimed the Winchester at his legs and pulled the trigger. Nothing happened.

Puzzled, she held the rifle out in front of her and stared at it in disbelief before it slowly came to her. She had put the safety on when she had climbed over Larry's barbed wire fence.

This time there would be no mistake. She made sure that the safety was off before taking careful aim one more time. *Nice and easy, Carla. That's right. Breathe slowly and aim for his legs. Good! That's perfect. Here we go you mother fuck—*

Chapter 2

Adrenalin raced through her, numbing her pain as Rose hit the gas with her injured foot. Reading out her speed, she expertly shifted gears. *Ten … fifteen … twenty …* The creep with the missing teeth was sprawled on her hood, clinging to her wiper blades. Cranking the steering wheel to her left and then to her right, she concentrated on removing the scum from her truck. A cloud of dust billowed behind as the moon bathed the drama far below in a silvery sheen.

Mike had trouble keeping his balance and bounced around in the box. Leaning left and then right, he tried to compensate for her swerving. It was too much for him. He fell to his knees before scrambling back up, still clutching the bat.

Rose hit a large pothole dead-on. Her truck bounced into the air. Mike and the bat went flying, both landing hard on the dusty road.

In her rear-view mirror, she clearly saw him sprawled out across the road. He wasn't moving. "Good, you bastard. You're lucky I don't turn around and plough you into the friggin' dirt." For a moment that was what she planned on doing—spinning around and running him down. Her red hair bounced free from her ponytail as she shook her head in anger.

A hand slammed hard against her side window. Quincy was on her running board. Tightly gripping the framework of her outside mirror with one hand, he pounded on her window with the other. His eyes bulged with fear and panic as he screamed at her, threatening to get even if she didn't stop her truck.

Rose replied by ramming the gas pedal down and jerking the steering wheel to her left. Her truck clung to the edge of the road as she tried to shake off both creeps. 'Ford' bounced along for fifty feet before the underside got caught up in the soft shoulder. Her truck ground to a halt as the two remaining punks held on— their knuckles and faces white.

She stepped on the gas. Nothing happened. The motor had stalled. She turned the key but the engine refused to start. Rose tried again and this time pumped the pedal. The V8 sputtered once before roaring back to life. She released the clutch. 'Ford' wouldn't budge. A rear wheel spun uselessly in the soft shoulder, spewing out dust and gravel into the windy night.

The punks pounded on her side window and windshield, yelling out that she was whacko.

Rose was no longer frightened and crazily smiled at them. Now she was ready to kill. She took in a deep breath and switched into four-wheel drive. With a throaty voice full of passion she gave them the finger, shouting, "Here we go again, you motherfuckers!"

All four wheels gripped the soft gravel and her truck easily pulled free. Quincy and Karl held on and hoped that her pickup would sputter to a stop. It didn't. Her vehicle gained speed. Now they had passed the point of no return. The creeps could no longer jump. 'Ford' was moving too fast.

Rose cranked the steering wheel to her right. Her truck began to drift sideways. It was almost on two wheels before she regained control. Making a sharp left, she over-compensated and hit the shoulder once more before quickly recovering and getting back on the road.

The zigzagging had partially paid off. The punk on her hood had lost his grip and had bounced off, disappearing into the plume of thick dust behind her.

Looking out her side window, the one with the shaved head was no longer on her running board. Worried, she kept her eyes on her mirrors as she barrelled down the road, hoping and praying that he had also been thrown free.

It was difficult to see anything with the increasing dust in the air. She managed a final look. There he was—the second creep. The skinhead was crawling out of the ditch like an injured animal.

Rose wickedly smiled and felt very pleased with what she had done. *Good, you sons of bitches! I hope you've learned your friggin' lesson!* Pumped with another shot of adrenalin, she sped toward the end of McCulloch Road before turning up her driveway, anxious to reach her home and safety.

Carla crouched lower as the three creeps limped past her, up Larry's driveway. A few minutes earlier she had witnessed part of Rose's performance—the tires spinning and the gravel spewing. She hadn't seen all of what had happened, but had heard the screams from the punks, afraid of being thrown from the speeding vehicle. *Good for you, Rose. Good for you. You showed them not to screw with you. Sometimes you go crazy. I love that about you.*

"Son of a bitch. It's lucky she didn't kill us!" Karl was livid.

"Don't worry, my man. Don't worry. We'll get even." Quincy was doing his best at sounding calm. He was far from calm. He was shaken. That had been the wildest ride of his life. Placing his hand to his chest, he tried to catch his breath and slow his heart. *Holy shit! She's crazy!* Sweat glistened on his shaved scalp. Stopping for a moment, he turned and took a closer look at Karl. "You okay?"

"No! I'm *not* okay. That bitch hurt me real bad." A patch of skin was torn from his right knee. It looked painful. "I'm gonna get even with her. She almost killed me!" He had trouble believing how someone could do that to him.

"How about you, Mikie? You okay?" Quincy gave him a passing glance, not really caring how he felt.

"Uh, yeah, I guh-guess." He clutched the bat and whined, "She was goin' real fast when she threw me aw-aw-off."

Quincy nodded, still out of breath. He considered himself lucky—having only a few scratches—and thought back to when he had been hanging onto her mirror, worried for his life. She looked a lot like his Aunt Sylvia to him. He was confused. Aunt Sylvia had raised him.

We should just leave things alone. Maybe we scared her enough. He reconsidered. *No. Maybe she scared* us *enough! She even has Aunt Sylvia's hair—long, red and with streaks of gray in it.*

"I never li-liked her." Mike was brushing dust off his pants as he said it.

"Huh?"

"I seh-seh-said I never liked her. She's that woman that ma-ma-my dad fell in love with. Her name is Row-Row-Row—"

Quincy cut him off, having little patience with his stuttering. "Yeah? Why don't you like her?" He didn't care who Mike liked and was only half listening. His mind was still on what that crazy, red haired psycho had done to them.

"Well, 'cause she doesn't like me. That's why."

They slowly continued up Larry's drive as Quincy studied him. He understood full well why that woman didn't like him. He didn't care for Mike either. Nobody seemed to like Larry's son.

"Maybe she has some common sense. You know? Not like some of the idiots around here." Quincy was directing his comments at him.

It flew over his head. Mike nodded in agreement. "Yeah, you're right."

Quincy shook his head. *What a jerk.*

They walked a few more feet in silence. Mike thought hard before piping up. "We gaw-gaw-gotta go to her place. We gotta guh—"

"Why would we want to go there?"

"Well, 'cause she's got money. She grows paw-paw-pot, too!"

"Really?" Quincy was intrigued. "Does she live alone?"

"Yup. Only her. As far as I know, only her. She used to be married but her husband left her." Mike thought about it a little more. "Uh, I think maybe she's got a gir-gir-girlfriend that lives there, too."

Full of concern, Carla listened to the fading voices, especially with what Mike was telling his two buddies. She felt ill with the idea that they might come over to their place. *If they show up at Rose's, they'll …* She swallowed hard, knowing that she needed to make her way back to her friend and niece as fast as possible.

Chapter 3

She roared up the driveway to the safety of her house. Pain shot up her leg as she leaped out of the Ford. Trying to ignore it, Rose half limped and half ran to the rear door.

Jen had heard her coming and was waiting on the porch, clutching her hands. She was full of questions. "What's going on? What happened to your foot? Why are you rubbing your chest?"

Rose ignored her and hobbled into the kitchen. "Where's Carla?" She yelled out her name, wanting the three of them together so that she could explain what had happened. "Carla! Carla?"

Jen blurted, "She's not here."

"What?" Rose swung around. "What do you mean she's not here?"

"She took the rifle and headed down the driveway. She never came back."

"We … we don't have the rifle?" Rose felt weak and was quickly turning pale. She shook her head in disbelief. *How can we defend ourselves if the thugs show up? We won't stand a chance.*

"No," Jen was shaking her own head. "We don't have the rifle and I don't know *where* Carla is." She was on the verge of tears and asked again. "What's going on?"

"Okay." Rose took in a deep breath and limped into the dark living room. Picking up the phone, she told Jennifer a little of what had happened—how three punks had terrorized her and how she had managed to throw them from her truck. She dialled Gleason's number as she continued to explain.

Jen stared at her in disbelief. She was speechless and worried that the bullies would attack them here, in their house. What could she and her friends do to stop them if they did?

"Don't worry. Everything will be fine. They're shaken up. They won't give us any more trouble." Rose almost believed what she was telling her traumatized friend and was pleased with the way she had taken care of things with her truck.

She pressed the phone to her ear and waited a few moments before running out of what little patience she still had. "Come on. Come on! Answer your phone, damn you!" She pictured Gleason passed out on his couch with an empty bottle of booze between his legs. *Shit!* Breathing fast, her face was flushed. She hated to have to make the call to him.

Jerking the handset from her ear, she studied it. There was no sound on the other end of the line. Baffled, she tapped hard on the hook switch and waited for dial tone. There was none. Her mouth dropped as she slowly put the phone down. With vacant eyes she whispered, "No. This … can't be happening."

It was slowly sinking in. Carla and the rifle were gone. The phone was dead and the punks might be paying them a visit at any moment.

"Why? Why did she leave? Why did she take the rifle?" Rose shook her head, not understanding.

Jen burst into tears. It was too much for her. The marijuana that she had smoked earlier hadn't had the desired effect. Instead of calming her, it was creating the opposite—increasing her anxiety.

Rose had no time to comfort her. "Where the hell is Carla?" She studied Jen, waiting for an answer. "Where did she go? Tell me!" Things weren't going the way they were supposed to.

Jen shook her head and looked at the floor, feeling helpless.

Rose would have none of it. She grabbed her by her shoulders and shook her, repeating, "Where did she go? Answer me, damn you!"

"She … she walked out the door. She said that she wanted to check things out. They might have grabbed her and … she … they …" Jennifer was a mess.

Rose slowly released her grip and wondered where Carla was at that moment. *Do those animals have their claws in her?* Her mind was far from Larry. She didn't care about him anymore. Now she was only concerned about her friend.

The candles sputtered out. The only light in the kitchen was from the partial moon. It bathed Larry in a cold gloss as he lay motionless, face down on the floor.

Quincy loomed over the unconscious man and wondered how injured he really was. A part of him felt sorry and wanted to help. It wasn't Larry's fault that he had an idiot for a son.

Sal asked why they were scratched and covered in dust.

"That bitch just about killed us." Karl was furious. "If we hadn't a jumped off her truck she would a—" He shook his head, too angry to finish.

Noticing Karl's skinned knee, Sal was glad that he had decided to stay with Larry.

Mike was babbling and ignored his father who was passed out on the floor. Adrenalin was still in his system. He hoped to convince his new buddies how easy it would be to take money from Rose and her girlfriend. The more he talked, the more Karl agreed.

"He's right. We need to go over there. There are only two of them. It'll be easy."

Sal wasn't so sure. Now Mike and Karl wanted to go next door and steal money from two women? They would probably end up threatening them before getting any cash. He wondered how much money they had and if it was worth it.

Quincy wasn't so sure, either. He was still shaken by the crazy ride that she had given them and needed time to think. He squatted next to Larry. *He's still breathing. Good. We don't want to kill the poor bastard.*

Unsure of what to do, he went to the fridge and helped himself to a beer while Mike and Karl tried to persuade him into going over to the neighbour's. Quincy listened to them with half an ear as he looked down at Larry one more time. Wooden splinters surrounded the almost lifeless body.

They had beaten him to unconsciousness and yet he still hadn't told them where his money was. He couldn't help but have a begrudging respect for him, studying the skinny man on the cold, linoleum floor. He certainly had a lot more respect for Larry than he had for the man's deadbeat son.

Mike kept yakking, saying over and over how they could get easy money from next door.

Quincy raised his hand and cut him off. "Are you sure that there are only *two* women living there?"

He quickly answered his creepy friend thinking that there was still hope in taking the women's money. Then he could leave Beaswick with a good chunk of cash. "Yeah. There are oh-oh-only two of 'em."

Sal moved closer to him. "How do you know for sure?" *Is he bullshitting us again?*

He shook his head, lying. "Yeah. I ss-ss-seen her with Row-Row—"

Quincy knew he wasn't telling the truth. "What does she look like?"

He stammered, not knowing what to say.

Slamming his beer down, Quincy grabbed him by the collar and yanked him closer until their faces were only inches apart. "Look, you stupid bastard! I'm tired of your bullshit. You told us your old man had lots of money and he doesn't. We just about killed him 'cause a you!" He shoved him against a wall.

Mike had a stunned look on his face as Quincy pressed him hard against the kitchen panelling. He nervously tried to talk back. "I-I seen her and—"

"Shut your hole!" Quincy wouldn't have any of it. He didn't need to listen to the kid tell him lies. It was all because of Mike that things weren't going according to plan. They still didn't have the money that they had been promised. And, they had been thrown off that wild woman's truck and were almost killed.

Karl jumped in. "Mikie's not finished talkin'. He told me somethin' you should know."

Quincy pushed him harder against the wall. "Keep talking, but it better be good."

"Yeah. Sure. I understand. I-I-I just wanna give you the fa-fa-facts."

He released the pressure and Mike hungrily gulped in air. Taking a moment, he thought about what he should say. "Okay. I never met the other woman but I seen her from a distance."

The bigger man tried to be patient but the very sight of Mike annoyed him. He turned away and took a swig of beer as Larry's son continued with his jabbering.

"The two of them were dra-dra-driving into town when the old man and I pa-pa-passed them. They grow weed too and—"

Spinning around, Quincy bellowed, "The whole fuckin' county grows weed, Mikie. Tell me somethin' new." His mind was on that woman. She looked like his Aunt Sylvia to him and it made him feel uncomfortable.

Karl was also getting worked up. *How dare she sneak up on us! She was snoopin'. She was trespassin'. She was breakin' the law. And then, she had the nerve to try and kill us with her truck?* He shook his head in anger and disbelief.

Mike was thinking hard. Did his neighbour really have money stashed away? He had no idea.

Sal spoke up in a calm voice taking Mike off guard. "What do they do for a living? Where do they work?"

"Uh? Wha-at? They don't. They don't work. They don't have a jaw-jaw-job." He stepped away from the kitchen wall, still shaken with the way Quincy had shoved him.

Sal wasn't surprised. He knew that the women probably made their living by growing dope. If they did, then they would have money stashed away. They couldn't take large amounts of cash to the bank. They would do exactly what Larry did—stash it somewhere.

He carried on with his questioning. "How much pot do they grow? How much do they sell? How much money do they have?"

"Uh-uh-uh-uh?" Mike gave him a blank stare.

Karl had a few questions of his own. "What's their property like? I mean, do you think they have an indoor operation? Do they have an outside building where they grow? What?"

"Yeah. They got a barn. The old man helped her gra-gra—"

Karl pointed at Quincy. "See! There could be a pile of cash waitin' for us. We gotta go visit them."

Quincy turned away. He did not like being pressured and he also didn't like the idea of going over there.

He kept at it, now talking to his back. "Don't 'cha see? We gotta check things out!"

The bigger man didn't respond.

Karl persisted. "They must have a shitload of money stashed somewhere's. It's ours for the taking."

Quincy continued to ignore him, uncomfortable with going over there and facing that woman.

Frustrated, Karl shouted, "What's your problem?"

He spun around, annoyed with Karl's nagging. He was calling him a chicken and afraid of checking things out. A vein on his temple throbbed as he lashed out, "I ain't got no problem, buddy. What's *your* problem?" His face was inches from Karl's.

Neither knew each other that well. They had hung out a little, usually smoking meth. Sometimes Karl got on his nerves. He figured that the guy was a jerk and was always trying to take control.

Karl put his hands up and shook his head in a questioning manner. *What's with him?* "I just don't see no problem in all of us visitin' them old broads." He hated the way that his partner sometimes disregarded him.

Quincy paced the kitchen, avoiding the vomit and blood that lay next to the unconscious man. In his mind he didn't want to beat up his Aunt Sylvia. He also didn't want to let his partners know how he really felt. A part of him was concerned. He knew that Karl wanted to settle the score—angry that she had thrown him from her truck.

The blue vein on his temple throbbed harder as his fellow thugs silently waited for him to come up with some kind of plan.

Chapter 4

Speaking more to herself than to Jen, Rose announced, "We need to make sure that the doors are locked and the windows secured. Right?" She waited for a response from the younger woman.

Jen wasn't listening. Her nose was running and she was shivering, lost in another world. She rubbed at her tattooed Japanese characters for comfort. *Peace … love—*

"Jennifer! Get a grip." She tried to bring her out of her shock. "We need to work together!"

She looked down at the kitchen floor to avoid her friend's wild eyes. "Do you think we'll be killed? Do you think they'll break in and murder us?" Not waiting for an answer, she wailed, "I … I don't want to die, Rose." Shaking her head, she said it again. "I don't want to die!" All she wanted was to be safe at home with her mother.

"Jeeze!" Rose was beside herself. Yelling at her would only make things worse. Instead, she tried to calm both of them by putting her arms around her shaky partner and drawing her closer. The dark house groaned from the strong wind making Rose hug her tighter.

She made a pledge to protect her troubled friend if the hooligans paid them a visit. *Maybe I'm over-reacting. Maybe they won't even bother us.* Her pulse quickened as she replayed the recent events. *No! Don't kid yourself, Rosie. They acted like animals—the way they chased me.* She shuddered as she relived the nightmare. *The way they tried to get at me in my truck. They're crazy! They want money. They want blood!*

Mike probably told them that I grow pot and have money stashed. We need to be prepared. We need to defend ourselves. We … need a weapon.

The kerosene lamp provided little light as she opened the Tylenol bottle and gulped several pills for some badly needed relief. Her ankle throbbed and her back was beginning to flare up. She put the medicine in her pocket, knowing that it might come in handy later.

Placing a hand to her chest, she felt the blisters from Sal's cigarette. They were a shocking reminder of what she had been through earlier. The thought of how close she had come to being captured and possibly beaten sickened her.

She softly called out to her friend as she reached into the kitchen drawer and drew out a butcher's knife. "Jen?" Rose was determined to fight back if the hoods did show up. "I want you to take this."

"No!" Repulsed with the thought, she stepped back. Wanting nothing to do with the knife, she held her hands up in front of her as a shield.

"Please. You have got to protect yourself! You'll probably never have to use it, but ..." She let the sentence hang.

Jen crossed her arms and dropped her head, refusing to take the knife—refusing to even look at it.

Rose had hoped that her weak friend would at least try to protect herself but knew that Jen was beyond convincing. She was terrified and not capable of doing anything on her own.

I need to get her full attention. "Jen?" Grabbing her by her shoulders, she shook her, wanting to bring her out of her trance. "Jen!"

"Wha-what?" Tears freely flowed down her cheeks.

"I'm going to check the windows in the living room and make sure the front and back doors are locked. When I'm done, I'll check the windows upstairs."

"No. Don't leave me. Please. I don't want to be left here all alone in the dark."

"Take my hand. We'll do this together." She cursed under her breath. "Jeeze, I don't need this!" Rose wanted support and was frustrated that Jen was so fragile. She was also annoyed with herself, knowing that she had made a huge blunder in going over to Larry's. Now she felt responsible for putting her friends in danger.

But, I had to check things out. It's not all *my fault, is it?* Her thoughts turned to Larry. *It's because of him. If he wouldn't have ...* She softened a little knowing that her emotions were getting the best of her.

Holding the kerosene lamp in front of her, they slowly made their way through the dark house.

I'll run back. As an afterthought, Carla decided that she couldn't use the main road. *No. The punks will see me if they drive over to Rose's. I'll go through the bush instead.*

For a large woman, she could move fast. She pushed her way through several thickets. The terrain between the two properties was foreign to her. It was also tough going.

Looking over her shoulder, she could barely see Larry's dark house through the trees. She strained her ears and wondered what the punks were up to. Outside of the wind, everything seemed quiet—too quiet. A terrible thought crossed her mind. *Did they finally murder him?*

Chapter 5

Karl studied Sal. His friend was busily picking at scabs on his face. He wondered what he was thinking. "How 'bout you, Sal? Are you in?"

Quincy didn't like it. His partner was trying to take control. He stomped up between them. "You don't need to answer him, Sal," Spinning around, he let Karl know, by the way he glared at him, that *he* was the one in charge, no one else.

Karl yanked his 'Mega Death' cap tighter over his greasy hair. It wasn't supposed to be going that way. They should have had the rest of the skinny man's money by now. They did have some, but he wanted more, a lot more.

Karl figured that his so-called buddy was changing his tune. What was going on? He wondered if it would only be him and Mike that would pay those old broads a visit. Were Quincy and Sal getting cold feet? He stepped closer to both of them and asked, with an accusing tone, "What's with both of you?"

"Get outta my face!" Quincy shoved him back.

"Don't you tell me to—"

Sal jumped in between them, worried that the situation might get out of control. "Come on guys. Let's be cool, huh?"

Karl ignored Quincy for the moment and turned to Sal, asking him point blank, "Are you in or are you out?"

He did not like the position that he was being put into. Thinking about it a little more, Sal decided to go with his gut feeling. "Look. I don't think it's such a good idea, okay? I mean, we've got nothing to go on except for what *he* said." He jerked a finger at Mike. "He's screwed us around once already and—"

"I did naw-naw—"

"Shut up!" Quincy gave him a cold stare before turning back to Sal. "Keep talkin'." He was curious with what his friend had to say and knew that sometimes Sal could be right with his take on things.

Irked with the way things were turning out, he continued to pick at his face. The large amount of meth that Sal had consumed over the years had created several open sores. "I didn't come here to beat up on some old ladies. I came here 'cause," he pointed at Mike, "*that* prick told us his dad had all kinds of easy money."

Mike stormed up to him, ready to show him a thing or two. Quincy caught him by the scruff of the neck and yanked him back.

Feeling hurt and dejected, he vowed that he would get even with the bigger goon, one way or the other. *I'll get even with Sal, too! He better watch his back.*

Karl and Quincy ignored him, their attention on Sal. "You didn't answer me. Are you in or are you out?" Karl was in his face with the question.

"I'm not sure. I need to know if they have money stashed. I don't want to go beating them up if it's a waste of time." Sal looked at the floor, feeling uncomfortable with being put on the spot.

Karl turned to Quincy. "And … how 'bout you?" He asked the question with a sneer.

"Yeah. I'm in." He was apprehensive, thinking hard. "I'm in, providing …" He let it hang.

"Providing what?" Karl spat it out.

"Providing you, Mikie and Sal go in their house. I'll stay outside."

"You'll *what*?" Karl couldn't believe it. "No way! I ain't going in there without you. Why do you want to stay out of it? Huh? Why are you chickening out?"

"I'm *not* chickening out! Don't ever accuse me of that kind of shit." Quincy took a menacing step toward him.

Karl backed away and put up his hands. "Okay. Okay! Just relax." He waited for a moment before asking, "Do you even have a friggin' idea 'bout what we should do?"

Quincy did not want them to know that he was bothered by the red haired woman. She looked like his Aunt Sylvia to him. He also didn't want them to know that he had no stomach in beating up an old lady. He stammered as he tried to come up with some kind of plan. "Uh, Sal? You stay here with Larry. Make sure he doesn't give us any trouble. I'll head on over there with these guys."

"Just a minute." Karl glared at Sal and pointed a finger at him. "Don't you be expectin' to get a share of the money if you don't come with us."

Before Sal had a chance to reply, Quincy jumped in. "Okay. Fair enough." He turned to Mike and commanded, "*You* stay with your old man."

He vigorously wagged his head. "No way. I want a piece of the ah-ah—"

Quincy pointed at Karl. "Then *you* stay with him."

"Nobody needs to babysit Larry. He's out cold. We'll *all* go over there."

Thinking about having more money, Sal finally agreed. "I didn't come here for a few lousy dollars. If you're in, Quincy, I'm in, too." He added, "Those women could have thousands stashed away."

"Tha-tha-that's right! The-the-they could ha-ha—"

"Okay. It's settled." Quincy had made up his mind. The thought of more cash in his pocket quickly convinced him. *Forget that the red haired one looks like Aunt Sylvia. Just remember that she's nothing like her.* "Let's get going."

"Not so fast." Karl grabbed him by the arm. "If you're comin' with us then you're in *all* the way."

He jerked free knowing that Karl was right. If he wanted his share he would have to be totally involved. Still having doubts about what they were planning, he needed more time to think. "We'll have a little smoke first. Then … we'll go." He pulled out his pipe and passed it around. All four took a huge pull.

With the meth racing through his system, Quincy felt better about going over there. *We didn't start this shit. They did. The red haired one was snooping. She tried to kill us! We deserve to get paid.* After thinking about it a little more, he announced, "We'll take Mikie's truck."

"Buh-buh-but I don't want to take my …"

"Shut your stupid face! You owe it to us." Quincy did not want to leave any evidence that they had gone to pay Aunt Sylvia a visit in Karl's car. They would take Mike's truck instead. There would be no problem.

Chapter 6

After checking the upper windows, they slowly made their way down the stairs to the living room. Rose was in the lead with the kerosene lantern held out in front of her. Jennifer trailed closely behind. Everything seemed to be secure.

"No one can hurt us. We're safe here." Rose said it but wasn't convinced.

Jen felt trapped. "Why can't we just hide?" Her fear was turning into frustration. "Why can't we just go outdoors and hide? We can stay out of sight until Aunt Carla comes back."

"Honey, I really don't think they'll come here!"

"You don't know that for sure! Look what they've already done. They …" Jen began listing things off with her fingers. "They beat up Larry. They stole all of his money. They chased you down like a friggin' animal! They … they smashed your truck with the bat! They—"

"But don't forget that I scared them. I threw them off my truck. They wouldn't dare come—"

"If they can beat up Larry the way they did then what's stopping them from coming here?"

Rose slowly nodded. She knew that Jen was right. What her friend was suggesting wasn't such a bad idea. Not a bad idea at all. They didn't have to remain in the old farmhouse and wait to be terrorized. No sir. They could sneak out and head into the bush. Maybe they could find Carla. They just needed to be better prepared.

"Good idea. Very good idea!" She smiled as she patted her younger partner's hand. It looked like Jen was ready to fight back. "You get us a couple of bottles of water. I'll get my knapsack. We should also put on heavier jackets."

Jennifer thought about it some more. "Why don't we go into town? Why don't we just jump into your truck and head into Beaswick? We could get the sheriff. He'd fix things." She sounded hopeful.

Rose wondered about that. Should they go into town and leave Carla? *Maybe she's okay. She's got the rifle.* She was thankful that her ex-husband had left his Winchester with her when they had separated. Bernie's brother, Sheriff Gleason, had originally given the old rifle to him.

The more she ran it through her mind, the more she liked the idea. She knew that Carla was a bit of a mountain woman. *She should be able to take care of herself.* It seemed to her like the right thing to do.

Rose thought about the sheriff. She didn't want him involved unless it was absolutely necessary. *They haven't killed Larry, have they? Maybe they'll leave us alone.* She kept trying to play things down. *But, we need to be smart about it. They could still show up, here.*

"Come on, Jen. Let's lock up and head on down to Beaswick."

"Oh, thank you, Rose. Thank you! That's the best idea yet." She could hardly wait to get away from the creepy old house.

They stepped out into the wind and felt terribly exposed. Standing on the back porch, they waited for their eyes to adjust to the dark before Rose fumbled with her house key and lock. Hearing the satisfying click of the deadbolt, she turned and faced Larry's property, wondering what they were doing to him. Trees rustled in the wind.

Jennifer was near the truck when she saw the cracked rear window and damaged roof. She was unnerved. *Here is the physical evidence of what those animals are capable of doing!* Relief swept through her as they climbed into the old Ford.

Rose turned the key. The engine cranked over twice before starting. They were thankful that it hadn't backfired. They did not want any attention. 'Ford' was co-operating.

She was about to turn her headlights on but stopped. *No. A bad idea. I'll put them on once we get past Larry's.*

They were a third of the way down her long and narrow driveway when they spotted Mike's truck in the moonlight. It was on the main road and racing toward them. His headlights were also off.

Puzzled, Rose pulled to a stop, unsure of what to do. A thousand questions raced through her mind. *Why is Mike coming here? Is he alone? Does he need help? Is he trying to escape from those bastards? Did they finally kill Larry?*

She swallowed the lump in her throat as his vehicle rapidly closed the distance. Seconds later she made out two thugs standing in his truck box. They were at the foot of her driveway. *No!*

Jen rattled her door handle. "See! I told you! I knew they would come!" Terror was in her voice as she screamed it out, wanting to flee into the bush and safety.

Rose could only stare down at them, stunned with the turn of events. *Should I put my truck in reverse? No, it doesn't matter. The creeps will follow us back to the house. We're screwed no matter what.*

Frozen in her seat, Jen shouted, "They're getting closer!" Mike's truck was only a hundred feet away and speeding toward them. Now it was too late for her to jump out and hide.

Quincy was in the truck box next to Karl. He leaned out and bellowed into Mike's opened window. "Keep going! They got nowheres to go. We'll force them back to their house."

He stepped on the gas, unsure of where this was going. Thirty feet from Rose's truck, he slowed.

"Don't stop, dummy! Push her back!" Quincy pounded on the truck roof, yelling, "Go. Go. Go!"

He's gonna put dents in my roof if he keeps hittin' it like that! Pulling up to their truck, he nudged his Toyota against their Ford. He did not want to do any damage to his pickup and was concerned that his bumper might get scratched. Sal sat next to him, worried about what they were doing. *Maybe this is going too far.*

Someone in the box yelled, "Step on the gas! Push her back you fuckin' id-jet!"

The trees that lined the drive continued to groan and made it difficult for him to hear who had actually said it. It was either Quincy or Karl, but it didn't matter anymore. They *all* seemed to be making fun of him. Mike tried to block out their name-calling.

More banging on his roof echoed throughout the cab. His new friends were energized and impatient with the chase.

"Do it, damn you! Push her back! If you don't, I will!" This time there was no doubt who had yelled it out. It was Quincy and he was livid.

The Toyota's tires spun as Mike pressed down on his gas pedal in an attempt to push the heavier Ford backward to her house.

Rose kept her brakes on. The old Ford wouldn't budge as Mike revved his engine to near maximum. In desperation, she turned her headlights on and clicked the high beams.

Her truck was several inches higher than the Toyota. The goons raised their hands to shield their eyes from the powerful twin beams. It reminded Jen of creepy crawlers squirming when a rock was turned over.

Mike continued trying to shove the Ford back. It wasn't working. His tires kept spinning and churned up a cloud of dust in the swirling air.

Rose hammered on her horn with the hope that Carla would hear it and come to their rescue. It was pointless. The electrical connection had broken off months earlier.

They were at a stand-off.

Chapter 7

Karl gripped the baseball bat, yelling out over the wind, "We'll jump out and pull 'em out of their truck. They can't just sit there all night!" For one of the few times that evening, Quincy agreed with him.

Rose came to life and slammed her truck into first gear. She would not allow them to intimidate her and her friend any longer.

"What the—? What does that bitch think she's—?" Karl had one leg out of the box when she stepped on the gas. All four of her tires dug into the gravel. Slowly, her truck nudged Mike's smaller vehicle downhill toward her gate.

Quincy couldn't believe it. Frantic, he yelled out at Mike. "Do something!"

He froze, surprised with her nerve. *Shit! She's gonna scratch my truck!* Mike pressed down on his gas pedal. One of his rear wheels madly spun as he attempted to gain the upper hand.

Being bigger and heavier, the old Ford had the advantage and shoved them back, inch by inch.

His wheels churned up more gravel and the smell of rubber filled the October air. It was no contest. The Ford was in four-wheel drive and the Toyota was losing ground.

Rose shook her head and yelled out to no one in particular as she tightened her grip on her steering wheel. "Come on, you bastards! You want to play? I'll show you how to play!" She had a crazed look in her eyes.

"Jeeze!" Quincy was in a panic. They were being pushed farther down the drive and there was no stopping her. Over the din of screaming engines and spinning tires he yelled, "Put it in four-wheel drive or somethin'!"

Mike had one hand on his steering wheel. The other was busy wiping sweat from his brow. "The-the-there aint na-na-no four-wheel duh-duh-duh—"

They were nearing the bottom of her driveway when his truck began to slide sideways. One rear wheel and then the other spewed out loose gravel. The Toyota was being shoved toward the steel anchor post and the goons were helpless in stopping it.

She wouldn't let up. Her truck gained momentum as it bulldozed Mike's smaller vehicle toward her gate. The Toyota slammed into a tree a few feet from her steel post creating a large dent in his rear fender. Pine needles and cones showered down on both trucks along with several branches.

The boys were dazed by the impact and wondered what kind of crazed weirdo was behind the wheel of the old Ford. The front portion of Mike's vehicle remained on the driveway and completely blocked the girls from going into town.

Rose would not let up. Her truck ground against the corner of his front bumper as she kept her foot pressed on the gas. Metal screeched against metal. All she could think about was getting past the Toyota and escaping into town.

The Ford's tires dug deeper into the loose gravel, making her truck shudder. The Toyota refused to budge, now sandwiched between the swaying tree and her pickup.

Slamming it into reverse, she sped backward. *We can't go back to the house. They'll get us. My truck is our only hope!*

Stopping midway up her drive, her heart pounded and her breathing was fast and hard. She turned to Jennifer. Her young friend still had a grip on her door handle, frozen in fear and shock.

Rose's high beams were squarely aimed on the Toyota. The girls looked down at the punks, studying them in the bright headlights. The druggies were still in Mike's truck, stunned by the recent ramming.

She wrapped her fingers around her steering wheel and revved her engine.

Jennifer had been silent until then. "Rose? What are you doing?" She had a very bad feeling. "You're …? You're not going to ram them … *again*, are you?"

Her blue eyes sparkled and a wicked smile crossed her face as she stared through the windshield. "That's *exactly* what I'm going to do." The green dashboard light made her appear almost ghoulish.

The front portion of Mike's Toyota blocked their escape. She was bent on propelling it out of their way. Then, once they were in Beaswick, she made a promise that she would call Gleason. *Those bastards have crossed the line.*

"Put your seatbelt on, honey. Here we go-o-o!" She popped the clutch and 'Ford' leaped forward like a hungry lion, ready for the kill.

The roar of her engine made the druggies turn their heads in disbelief as they looked up at the fast approaching truck. Her yellowish headlights appeared as jungle eyes to the creeps down below, targeting them like wild game.

She picked up speed as she zeroed in on the demented gang. Quincy and Karl found their legs and leaped out of the box, scrambling for safety. Mike had his door partially opened and was about to jump out. Sal couldn't open his—the Ford was heading straight for it. He clambered across the seat and shoved Mike partway out.

The girls braced for the impact. Rose pressed down on the pedal harder, not caring. She was determined to smash Mike's truck into oblivion. *Those bastards need to be taught a hard lesson.*

Jennifer swallowed the lump in her throat, wondering if her friend had gone insane. She had wanted to jump out, but now it was too late. Nearby trees blurred past her.

Pandemonium filled the night as metal smashed against metal. The harsh sounds carried for more than a mile as dust and debris exploded into the air.

Sal and Mike were thrown out of the open door. Quincy and Karl cringed in the bush, witnessing the steel carnage from several feet away. The pine tree at the rear of Mike's truck madly rocked, flinging out more cones and branches, while the 'Beware of Dog' sign that was nailed to it shook violently.

Instead of creating an opening, the opposite had occurred. Mike's Toyota blocked their escape even more.

The women were stunned, coughing in the dust-filled cab. It didn't stop Rose from putting her truck into reverse and popping the clutch. All four tires bit into the loose gravel as she stormed back up her long drive once more. This time she drove even farther before stopping.

Adrenalin coursed through her veins. Shaking her head, she revved the old Ford, intending to ram the scum once again. She hoped that this time the Toyota would be pushed far enough out of their way so that they could get past it to safety.

One of her high beams was out, shattered by the impact. The other shot off at a crazy angle and illuminated the wind-blown tree tops behind Mike and his creepy buddies. The scene reminded her of Hollywood—the premier of a movie when bright flood lights searched the California sky. *No. This is no movie. This is for real!*

Quincy took several steps up the drive with the bat. His gold chain bounced on his chest as he shrieked out obscenities. It was almost comical to Rose.

Jen found nothing funny in it. She knew that her friend might have gone too far and had stirred up some very serious trouble.

Rose no longer cared. Yelling out, "Screw yo-ou-ou," she slammed her foot down on the gas pedal, oblivious to the pain in her ankle. The throaty sound of the engine roared out into the windy night as 'Ford' pounced once more.

Quincy stopped in his tracks, not believing what he was seeing. *What's that crazy, red haired psycho doin'? She's … she's coming straight for me! She's gonna—* Tossing the bat aside, he leaped behind a nearby tree.

Another deafening crash ripped through the night. Mike's Toyota reeled from the impact. So did the tree behind it. Karl and Sal ducked, afraid of being pummelled by more falling branches. The 'Beware of Dog' sign went flying into the night like a super-charged Frisbee. Sal stupidly wondered if it should have read 'Beware of OWNER' instead.

Mike cringed, witnessing the destruction of his pride and joy. Several bits of sharp gravel struck his face. He was unaware, staring open mouthed as his truck slid farther along the drive, continuing to block the girls' escape.

Chapter 8

C arla heard the tortured sounds for the second time—metal grating against metal. She charged through thick bush with the heavy rifle held out in front of her, wanting to be with her friends. *Rose and Jen tried to escape. That's what happened. The punks rammed them!*

Breaking through a thicket, she found herself on a narrow trail. It headed in the direction of the old house. *What will I do when I get there?* A shiver ran up her back. *Can I really shoot them?* She put a hand on her chest, worried that it might come to that. *If I need to, I will. I'm sure … I can do it.* She tried to convince herself as she puffed along the path.

Rose was in a daze and her nose was bleeding. They had slammed into Mike's truck much harder the second time. Her hands were clamped on her steering wheel as she vacantly stared through her windshield.

Jennifer's face was pure white. She had hit her head on the dashboard and her ears were ringing. Not quite sure where she was, she rubbed at her tattooed arm, looking for any kind of comfort. "Peace. Love. Happiness."

The Ford had bounced back several feet from the second impact and had stalled. A cloud of dust filled the air, surrounding the carnage for several moments before the wind got at it.

Rose shook her head and tried to pull out of her stupor. She cranked the engine, hoping to bring the old truck back to life. It sputtered and coughed before starting once again. Clanging from under the hood sounded very much like a damaged radiator fan scraping against metal.

She caught movement from her extreme left before her side window exploded. Quincy had hit it dead-on. Rose lurched to her right to escape from the blow, the bat narrowly missing her head. A spray of shattered glass filled the cab.

Leaping on the running board, he rammed his arm through the smashed window and grabbed for her collar. Rose's hair and shoulders were carpeted with glass as he jerked her, like a rag doll, into an upright position.

Jennifer shrank against her door, looking on in disbelief at his angry, red face. The monster was only inches away and the perverse scene reminded her of a slow motion horror movie, frame by crazy frame.

Karl was behind him with one foot on the running board and totally hyped. He kept shouting something about her being a psycho bitch. Rose couldn't quite make out what he was saying. Like Jen, her ears were also ringing.

He made an attempt at reaching into the cab through the pulverized window to get at her, but couldn't. Quincy blocked his way.

Karl's harsh voice brought Rose back to her senses. With a stupid grin, she nodded in silent agreement with him. *Yeah. You're right. I am psycho. But wait. Let me show you sick bastards how psycho I* really *am!*

With that promise and still grinning, she hit the gas. 'Ford' shot backward, making Quincy tightened his grip on both her collar and the outside mirror.

Karl jumped free as her vehicle crazily sped up the drive with his buddy still on the running board.

Her left hand squeezed the steering wheel. The other clamped down on his wrist. She was bent on not letting go and held him in a death grip.

Jennifer saw a side to her friend that she had never seen before. The bizarre scene made Rose's face appear twisted to her—a combination of hatred and craziness mixed in with an enormous amount of excitement. She looked past her friend, through the shattered window, at Quincy.

With an open mouth, blood had vanished from his face and his eyes were glazed in disbelief.

The Ford tore up her drive—the fan, clattering. She drove erratically with her left hand. The other squeezed his wrist as blood dripped from her injured nose.

He panicked as she gained speed, wanting nothing more than to leap to safety. Quincy tried pulling free from her steely clutch, but she held tight. Surprised by her strength, he couldn't help but wonder if his Aunt Sylvia had gone insane.

Now moving too fast to use only one hand, she released her grip on him, her eyes glued to her mirrors. The engine screamed. Both Rose and 'Ford' were stretched to their limit.

The scene was surreal to Quincy. He was unsure of what to do. Trees flew past him at an alarming rate.

They were doing close to twenty miles an hour when he saw an opening. He jumped.

Chapter 9

Carla could hear the high pitched whine and clanking of the engine over the wind. Rose's truck sounded close to its breaking point. She knew that the girls were in some very serious trouble.

The trail veered to the right and up into the hills away from their house. In a panic, she charged through thick brush. Ignoring the several scratches on her forehead, she pushed her way in the direction of their home, resolute in helping her friends.

Rose slowed her truck and pulled her eyes away from her mirror. Her one high beam was still on, partially illuminating Quincy on the shoulder of her driveway two hundred feet away. He was in a sitting position with a cloud of dust surrounding him, making the scene appear almost cartoonish. But, there was nothing funny about it. His toothless friend was limping up to him.

Feeling very pleased with what she had done, she smiled wickedly in their direction. "Don't screw with me, boys. Don't you dare screw with me!" Rose had every intention of putting her truck into first gear once she was at the top of her drive. This time she planned on knocking Mike's truck clear off the planet.

Her Ford had other ideas. It sputtered and coughed. The girls could smell antifreeze. Rose glanced at her temperature gauge. *Shit!* She pulled up near her house and turned off the motor.

Jen sat motionless and could not believe what had happened. She was far too frightened for words. Her right hand squeezed her door handle while the other picked out particles of glass that littered her hair and upper body.

They sat in silence, listening to the overheated engine snap and crackle as it cooled. Rose finally looked down at what she had been tightly clutching. It was Quincy's gold chain. Somehow she had ripped it off him in the chaos. Appalled, she flung it out her shattered window before wiping her hands on her pants to rid herself of the venom.

Slowly, she began to realize how carried away she had gotten. *Would I have killed them if I had the chance?* She squirmed uncomfortably with her question.

Over the past hour the moon had climbed higher into the night sky that was now free from clouds. The girls could easily make out Mike's truck at the bottom of her drive. Two of the hoodlums were attempting to get it running again. Quincy sat on the dusty shoulder in a daze as Karl shuffled his way toward him.

Rose turned to Jen. Defensively she said, "We gave them a chance. I blocked them from coming up to our house." Her voice took on a nasal tone from blood in her nose and her face was white.

Jennifer could only stare back at her, unable to respond. Her friend's tangled hair glittered from the hundreds of tiny glass particles and her deep blue eyes had a wild and crazy sparkle to them.

Rose swiped at the gelled blood on her upper lip as she tried to defend her actions. "They could have turned around but didn't. They had every intention of coming here and making our lives miserable—just like they did to Larry!" She was speaking fast, the adrenalin still raging through her system.

Open mouthed, Jennifer could only nod with glazed eyes, knowing that Rose was probably right. She had never seen that side of her friend and a part of her was afraid to disagree. *If I do, will Rose run me down, too?*

Seeing the trauma on Jen's face, Rose patted her friend's hand reassuringly. "I don't think we'll have any more trouble with those bastards." She forced a smile as she said it, wanting to believe that the punks had had enough. They would pick up their sorry asses and leave while they could.

Chapter 10

Sal and Mike worked hard at getting the Toyota back on the road. The passenger door was caved in along with the right front fender. It was a miracle that it still ran.

Mike kept muttering, "Low-low-look what they done to my tra-tra-truck. Look what they done!" He was shocked with the unbelievable turn of events. Stupidly, he contemplated on calling the police and telling that fat sheriff that he and his buddies had been rammed and were almost killed by some crazed woman.

Karl winced from the pain in his knee as he hobbled up to Quincy. Out of breath, he asked, "Are you okay?"

Quincy didn't answer. He sat dumbfounded on the shoulder of the driveway and wasn't quite sure where or even who he was.

He asked again as he pulled him to his feet. "Quincy! Are you okay?"

"Yeah. I … I think so." He rubbed the back of his leg and felt bits of gravel embedded in his skin. "Jeeze! That hurts."

"Let me have a look."

Karl stepped away and studied his buddy's back as Quincy turned on unsteady legs. He had a large tear in the rear of his pants with dirt and skin sticking to it.

In a daze, Quincy undid his belt and dropped his trousers. His right butt cheek was gouged and small pieces of sharp gravel were lodged in it. In a weak voice he mumbled, "Help me pull some of these friggin' boulders out."

Karl wanted no part of it, friend or no friend. He was not going to pull rocks out of anybody's ass. He pretended not to hear and asked, "What do we do now?"

Quincy was pre-occupied as he picked at his butt, his pants around his ankles.

Karl asked again. "What are we gonna do? We can't just leave. She tried to kill us! She totalled Mike's truck. She tried to kill you and me! She tried to kill *all* of us! That's bullshit." He was getting worked up. "And, what happened to your gold chain? They ripped it off!"

In a stupor, Quincy reached for it, surprised that it was missing.

"Her and her girlie friend are parked in their truck at the top of the driveway. They probably see you pickin' your pimply ass and are laughing at—"

Rose flicked on her one headlight for a second. Looking up, it appeared to them that the old Ford was winking and teasing them.

Quincy yanked up his jeans, feeling foolish. He wanted to leave—to head back to Beaswick. *Forget about more money. Forget about my chain!*

Karl kept at it, annoyed that the girls had the nerve to blink their headlight at them—especially with his stunned partner standing next to him in the driveway with his pants down.

"Quincy. We aint goin' to be beaten by some friggin' dykes! They tried to run us down. We need to get even. We need to go up there and take their money." As an afterthought he added, "Mike deserves to get paid for the damage to his truck."

"Wha-at?" Quincy looked at him incredulously as he buckled his belt. "Since when are you concerned about Mikie and his stupid truck?"

"Listen to me! We can use that on them. We can tell them that we'll leave them alone, but they owe us. They owe Mike. They owe him five thousand and then we'll leave. I don't give a shit about Mike. You know that."

Quincy paused for a moment with his hand on his buckle. "Yeah. Maybe you're right. We came this far, didn't we? We put ourselves out and, for what? For a few measly thou', that's for what!"

A part of him was afraid of Rose. Carrying on with his butt picking, he nervously looked at the top of her driveway and swallowed hard. *She's waiting, ready to run us down. Again! She's playin' with us. That's what she's doin'!*

"Uh, Karl? What if she starts it up and comes screaming down here again? She'll kill us. She won't stop." He was coming out of his shock.

"No. I heard her truck sputter. She had to turn it off."

Quincy shook his head, still not convinced.

Karl pressed on. "It smells like anti-freeze. She must a put a hole in the radiator or somethin'. They're screwed and they can't go nowhere's."

He doubted what Karl was telling him as they limped back to Mike's truck. Looking over his shoulder, he was worried that the crazed women might try to mow them down again.

Sal and Mike had the Toyota back on the road. The front tire continued to rub on the fender. They tried pulling on the metal to stop it from scraping the wheel. It helped only a little.

Mike whined, "Low-low-look what they done. Look what those bitches done to ma-ma—"

Karl cut him off. "We're going up there. Quincy and I both agree that they owe us money. Especially the way they treated us. We didn't deserve this. They're the ones that started it all. They even stole Quincy's gold chain!

"If that dyke hadn't a bin snoopin', none of this would a happened. We didn't hurt them. That …" He stopped, and, for a moment, didn't know what to call her. Searching for the right word, he finally settled on 'woman'. He shook his finger at the top of the driveway as he carried on with his ranting, "That *woman* threw us off her truck earlier and now," he paused for emphasis before raising his voice into a high-pitched whine, "this! She tried to mow us down and *kill* us!"

They nodded in unison. All four had difficulty believing how someone could treat them so badly and so disrespectfully.

"And, look what they done to Mike's truck." He pointed at it while shaking his finger. "There's no way you're *ever* gonna leave Beaswick with a wreck like that."

Mike's mouth dropped. It hadn't occurred to him until Karl pointed it out. *That truck will get me nowheres thanks to her.*

"Yeah. Maybe you're right." Sal reluctantly agreed with what Karl was saying. Still, a part of him wasn't sure if they were biting off more than they could chew.

Quincy wasn't so sure either. Literally getting his ass ripped made him think twice. No matter how hard Karl tried to convince them, he knew that he and his gang had it coming. *They* were the ones to blame, not the girls. He also knew that, if he had his way, he would drop everything and leave. But, he couldn't do that. He did not want to appear weak in front of them and decided to go along with whatever they agreed on—to a point. Still shaken, he picked at his rear.

Karl read what was printed on Quincy's dusty shirt. Raising his voice in a commanding fashion, he announced, "It's *Judgement Day*, boys!"

Quincy stopped his picking, not liking where this was going. He held his tongue as he climbed into Mike's cab from the driver's side. The passenger door was impossible to open.

He tried to sit. That didn't last long. His butt was too sore. He grabbed the meth pipe off the floor before clambering out. Finally lighting it in the nagging wind, he helped himself to a much needed lungful.

They grouped around him and, once the drug had taken effect, all complained about the two women, feeling justified that the girls owed them big-time.

Now filled with confidence, Quincy barked out the order. "We're goin' up there. They're not getting away with this." His buddies eagerly nodded, ready for action.

"Mike! If she starts up her truck and tries to block us, just keep drivin'. It's us or her, buddy." Quincy was giving him a pep talk. His plan was to ride in the box with his two pals. If that crazed woman decided to ram them, they could easily jump out. *Who cares about Mikie.*

Mike knew better than to argue with him. Full of apprehension, he got behind the wheel. Karl and Sal climbed into the box next to their leader. They felt far safer beside Quincy than being trapped in the cab with Mike.

The meth was doing its job and invigorating them. Quincy stood tall like a commander-in-chief. His body was charged with energy as he brandished the steel bat above his head like a sword. His shaved head glistened in the moonlight and the thought of being a pirate and ready to plunder excited him.

With a raised fist he yelled out the call to charge. "Let's give 'em he-llll!" He reached for his gold chain and realized once more that the red haired woman had stolen it.

They whooped and hollered, following Quincy's lead, as they shook their fists into the night sky. His three buccaneer goofballs were pumped and ready for action as Mike hit the gas. His truck, badly crippled from the recent 'accident', sputtered for a moment before slowly grinding its way up Rose's drive.

It was hardly the charge that they had hoped for. Instead, it was rather pitiful. The Toyota limped along at no more than five miles an hour. The sound of metal grinding against metal eerily mixed in with the creaking trees.

Mike turned on his headlights and hoped that it would add to their attack. They didn't work. Both had been shattered.

They quietly sat in her truck and waited for the goons to leave. A metallic screech made Rose jump to attention. *The scum are on the move!* She leaned forward and squinted, looking through the windshield. *Good! Get off my property you friggin'—*

Jen sputtered, "I … I think they're coming." Her voice filled with terror. "They're coming back! They're coming for us. I see them. They're swinging a bat." Panicking, she screamed, "Do something! Ram them, Rose. Start the fucking truck!"

Momentarily stunned, Rose could not believe that the idiots were still trying to attack them. *They should have turned around and gone home by now. They're … they're out of it. There's no stopping them. They're psycho!*

She turned the key. The engine cranked over, again and again, as the punks closed in.

Jennifer screamed at the truck, hammering the dash with both fists. "Start. Start. Start!" It didn't help. 'Ford' refused to listen.

Rose tried to get her attention. "Jen!"

She continued with her frantic babbling. "Please start. Oh my God, please, please, please …"

Frazzled, Rose turned on her one headlight.

Mike slammed on his brakes, worried that the twisted woman was going to charge them again. Her single headlight glared down at them at a crazy angle.

"What are you doin'? Keep going. She *can't* start the truck. She's just trying to scare us." Karl was screaming at his new buddy, impatient with the slow progress that they were making. He wondered if it would be quicker to jump out and charge ahead but dismissed the idea. *No. My knee is too sore for any serious runnin'.*

Unsure, Mike slowly pressed down on the gas. He was afraid and didn't want to die, especially in a vehicle accident.

His truck painfully ground and scraped its way up the driveway. With one hand on the steering wheel, the other gripped the door handle. His plan was to leap out the moment the deranged woman started up with her attack again. *To hell with my buddies. From now on I'm takin' care of myself!*

Chapter 11

Turning to her traumatized friend, she yelled, "Jen! We've got to get out of the truck. We need to get to the safety of the house. Now!"

She wasn't listening. Her eyes were glued to the approaching vehicle as it crawled up their driveway. In the moonlight, it appeared foreign and grotesque to her—an apparition that could only have been created in some far off solar system. Twisted metal seemed to shudder in pain as Mike's pickup ground its way closer to them.

Three silver figures in the truck box—one of them brandishing a bat—added to the bizarre scene. Shouting like demented creatures from hell, the animals pumped their fists into the night sky as they shrieked out expletive after expletive.

Mesmerized, the women sat frozen in the truck cab as the approaching horde grew louder. Now it was almost too late to make a run for their house and safety. Rose swallowed the mounting bile in her throat before yelling, "Jen. Get out. NOW!"

Tears streaked her friend's face. Absorbed in the thugs, she couldn't pull her eyes from them. Drool oozed from her mouth. "They … they're coming. They'll get us and—"

Rose slapped her face, this time screaming, "Get the fuck out of the truck and into the house!"

She raised a hand to her cheek, stunned with what the wild woman next to her had done. The slap burned, but did have the desired effect. In a daze, she pushed open her door.

Rose jumped out from the driver's side. Pain shot through her ankle. She tried to ignore it as she screamed out into the wind, "Hurry! For God's sake, hurry!" With blood on her nose and her glittery red hair wildly flying about, she appeared to be a crazed and witchy character to her traumatized friend.

Shaking her head to think clearly, Jen tried moving as fast as she could, having trouble finding her legs. In a flash Rose was behind her and roughly shoved her toward their house and safety.

The screeching from the driveway grew louder, further inflaming their shattered nerves. Now on the porch, Rose fumbled for her house keys. *No!* In the chaos she had forgotten to pull them out of her ignition. *Do I have time to go back and get them? Can I do it or should we just run into the bush and hide? No. They'll find us and—* She gauged the distance between her and the warped goons that were fast approaching. *I've got to do it!* Half racing and half hobbling, she scrambled back to the Ford.

What is she doing? Why is she running back to her truck? Has she lost her friggin' mind? Jen didn't understand. "Row-Row—?"

"Bitches! You'll pay for this!" They were almost at the top of the driveway.

They'll be on us in no time. Please Rose, hurry. Get back here and unlock the fucking door!

Rose leaned into the cab and grabbed at her keys. *Come on! Come on, damn you!* She was at a bad angle. The truck key remained lodged in the ignition. *I can't believe this is—*

"There's no escaping us. You're going to get what you deserve!"

She glanced over her shoulder. *No! They're almost here!* With chills racing up her spine, she clambered onto the running board and reached in deeper, finally pulling free the stubborn key.

"Hurry, Rose! Hurry!" Jen jumped up and down as she screamed it out. Mike's truck was now in plain view. *Should I run and hide in the bush?*

Rose didn't need to be told twice. Pumping her legs, she ran as fast as she dared back to the porch and Jen.

Karl bolted out of Mike's truck box, charged with energy. Quincy did the same and, for the moment, forgot about his sore butt and leg.

Rose scrambled up the porch steps and dropped her keys. She fell to her knees, groping for the key chain. Her hands were a mess. *She* was a mess.

Jen couldn't pull her eyes away from the approaching thugs. *I can't believe they have the nerve to come back. Haven't they had enough?*

Two of them were shuffling toward the girls like apparitions in the moonlight.

Looking down at Rose's back, she could not believe that her friend was still on her knees. "What are you doing? They're coming! They'll get us." Stomping her feet like a spoiled child, she screamed, "God damn it, Rose! Get on your feet and unlock the fucking door!"

Rose was pushed far beyond her limit. She bolted up with keys in hand. Turning to her demanding friend, she exploded with a mix of rage and fear. "Shut up! Just shut your stupid mouth! I don't need any of this. You're only making things—"

"You bitches!" Karl's icy voice sliced through the wind, cutting her off. He was closing in, shaking his fists.

God! Please. I need to calm down. I need to— Rose inserted her key. Using both hands, she jiggled the lock until the old door finally sprung open.

The two punks were only twenty feet from them when the girls stumbled into the house. Rose slammed the door and cranked the latch on the deadbolt. Jen's heart was in her throat. She gasped, "I … I think I'm having a heart—"

In a flash, Karl was at the door, turning the doorknob one way and then the other. The lock held fast. Pounding with both fists, he screamed, "You bitches! You tried to kill us!"

Quincy joined in, followed by Sal and Mike. The meth, mixed in with a healthy dose of adrenaline, ripped through their brains. Falling into the same mentality as wild dogs, the four fed off one another as they hammered on the old farmhouse door.

The girls pushed back, praying that it would hold and stop the pack from getting at them.

Frustrated, Karl rammed it with his shoulder. The impact bounced Rose and Jen several inches back and rattled the narrow window next to it.

They were relentless—the vibrations from their pounding carrying through to the women's very cores. "Bitches! Bitches! Bitches!"

Chapter 12

Carla crouched behind a small bush. She was on a knoll a hundred feet away and had wanted to be with her friends in the old farmhouse. The goons had beaten her to it.

The porch roof blocked her view of the freaks at the rear door, but she could hear them. Her stomach churned, hearing the rage in their voices as they screamed out obscenities to her friends.

A large kitchen window faced her, but she couldn't see inside. The house was too dark. She had looked out that very window only yesterday at the deer that frequently came to visit. Now she was on the outside and trying to look in.

The situation was escalating. The thugs were stoned and out of control. If they broke in, she knew that she would need to use the rifle. She was sick with the thought and hoped that things would end peacefully.

The girls pressed their backs against the door. The pounding and kicking carried on. The door vibrated. The side window shook.

Jen tried to be strong but it was too much for her. Tears streamed down her face as she whimpered uncontrollably.

The hammering slowly grew weaker and finally ended with an angry kick from Karl. "There's no escapin' us. We want money! We want revenge!"

Sal was having second thoughts about what they were doing. He was concerned with Karl talking about revenge and was worried that the situation was turning into something personal. Karl had an issue with the women and was obsessed with getting even.

That wasn't the way things were supposed to be. The original plan was to scare them a little until they gave up their money. Now Karl was yelling about revenge? *No, that's not right.* "Maybe we should cool it a little."

"Cool it?" Karl spun around, giving Sal a cold stare. "What are you talkin' 'bout? We're *not* gonna cool it! I say we go in there. That was our plan. Now you're backing down?" He was fired up—his face inches from Sal's. Pointing to his knee he demanded, "Look what they done to me!"

Quincy pushed his way between them. "Keep your mouth shut for a minute and listen to what Sal's got to say." He was also becoming concerned with where this was going and wondered if Karl was going to do something stupid.

He wasn't about to listen to either of them. Flustered, he limped toward the chicken coop and barn. *That fat bastard always needs to have things his own way.* Mike followed, showing his support for his new, creepy friend. Near the barn, Karl turned and gave his fellow thugs the finger.

It was too much for Quincy. He stormed up to him. "First of all, keep your big trap shut!"

"What are you going to do about it, huh? What are you going to do?" He poked his finger at the bigger man's chest, challenging him.

Sal tried to break it up. "You're acting like idiots! Back off. Both of you." They were angry with the way things were turning out with the two women, especially with Rose. She was making them think twice about how easy it would be to steal her money. They all took a moment to calm down.

Karl grumbled, "We need a plan." Before they could respond, he pressed on, getting worked up once more. "We … we need to bust in there. We need to make them pay for what they went and done." He touched his knee and winced. "The longer we hang out here, the tougher it'll be to get at 'em."

"He's ra-ra-right. Karl is ra-right. The longer we wa-wait the harder it'll be." Mike wanted very much to be a part of their discussion. His head bounced as he wildly nodded in agreement with his new buddy.

It reminded Quincy of a demented Jack-in-the-box. He had one when he was a kid and used to crank the handle to block out the yelling and fighting from his parents. He found himself mentally humming *Pop Goes the Weasel* as he glared at Mike.

A thought occurred to him. Shaking his head to rid himself of the song, he turned his attention on Karl. "Did you ever once figure they might have a gun or something?" He looked at the toothless goon as if he were a complete idiot.

"They would a used it by now." He said it defensively as he stepped back and crossed his arms.

"No, they wouldn't have. What if they have a gun? They never had a chance to use it. The red haired one had both hands on the steering wheel when she was trying to kill us with her truck and her girlfriend was sitting next to her, scared shitless! Maybe they left the gun in the house and are loading it while we're standing here arguing."

It hadn't occurred to them until now that the girls might be armed. They stepped away from the house and closer to the barn.

Mike got a powerful whiff of marijuana. He sniffed like a hound dog as he followed his nose.

"So, what do we do?" Sal waited for an answer, glad that Quincy and Karl were at least talking to one another.

Quincy tried to think things out with his meth brain. "We need to play it smart. We can't go bustin' in. They might shoot us."

"Yeah, I know, but—"

Ignoring Sal and his concerns, Quincy snapped out a command. "Mikie! Get over here."

"Uh, I smeh-smeh—"

"I said get over here!"

"Uh, ba-ba-but I smell—"

Having no patience, Quincy marched up to him, feeling the ache in his butt and leg.

"It's comin' from the barn." Mike cowered as he pointed to the old building, afraid of being slapped, or worse. "It smeh-smeh—"

Quincy was irked with Karl and was more than ready to take it out on Larry's stupid son. He raised a fist. *Pop goes the weasel. Pop goes the weasel!*

Mike put up his hands and cringed, waiting for the blow.

The pungent odour of marijuana grabbed Quincy's attention, his fist inches from Mike.

"Holy shit! I smell it, too!" Karl had his nose in a crack at the barn door.

Quincy smiled, his mood quickly changing. "If they got that much pot, then they must have a pile of dough hidden somewhere's."

The goofs all grinned, thinking that they just might have hit the jackpot.

Mike hurriedly made his way between the barn and chicken coop, wanting to scout things out and also keep a safe distance from Quincy.

Karl was on the other side of the barn. There were bars on two small windows that prevented them from breaking in. He shouted over the wind, "It smells like they got a friggin' ton of pot in there. They got lots of money. They can afford to give us a few thou for what they done. I'm gonna make 'em pay big-time." He was convinced that the women owed him money.

Sal grabbed Quincy by the arm. "I'm worried about Karl. We're getting deeper into this shit. We were supposed to come here for money—not revenge."

"Yeah. Yeah. Don't worry. I know how to handle him." Quincy dismissed his friend's concern. His mind was on the marijuana. They were definitely going to pay the girls a visit. "Mikie! Get over here."

"Uh, sure, Quincy. Wha-wha-what is it?" He was very eager to please his bully friend.

"Think hard about this one. Think real hard." He spoke slowly, looking him in the eye. "Did you ever see either woman with a gun?"

"Uh, no. I never." He vigorously shook his head.

"Okay, good. Now, did you ever hear gunshots coming from their place?"

"Nope. Nothing." He kept shaking his head.

"You're sure?"

"Yeah, I'm shu-sure. I never heard them fire one shaw-shaw-shaw—"

A satisfying smile crept over Karl's face. "That solves the little problem."

"Uh, maybe." Quincy thought hard while rubbing his buttock with one hand. The other fumbled in his pocket and pulled out the meth pipe.

Chapter 13

Holding hands in the dark, they sat with their backs tightly pressed against the kitchen door. The girls couldn't hear the punks but knew that they were out there.

Rose fidgeted, her curiosity getting the better of her. Now on her knees, she parted the venetian blinds on the narrow window next to the old door.

The thugs were at the barn, arguing. She knew that they could smell the pot curing inside and probably figured that she had money stashed or, at the very least, thousands of dollars worth of marijuana.

She tried to think like them. They were after money—her money. There was no way that she would allow that to happen.

How secure was the old house? She mentally went through the floor plan. *Three bedrooms and a bathroom are upstairs. There's the living room with stairs going up to the bedrooms. A bathroom and kitchen are on the main floor, and a hallway.*

The windows are old. So is the front and back door. They could easily break in. If they did, then … the game would be over. They'll torture us until I tell them where my money is.

Rose shook her head. *No. They wouldn't do that. They wouldn't torture us, would they?*

She reconsidered and thought about how they had beaten Larry and how they had chased her down his driveway. *How they tried to get at me in my truck. How they hunted me.* She felt sick and panicky.

"Jen? Jen! We need to get out."

"What?"

"I said we need to get out. We need to leave the house. Now's our chance. The punks are by the barn. They know that we've got a grow-op. They can smell the marijuana. They'll want either our money or our pot. We can't stay here any longer."

Rose racked her brain as she tried to come up with a plan. "We can sneak out the front door and hide in the bush. They wouldn't know we're gone. Maybe Carla's out there waiting for us. She's got the rifle."

Wound up, she chanced another look through the blinds. The jerks were still by the barn. She felt trapped. They were trespassing on her property and forcing her and Jen to flee from their home. She still couldn't believe they were here, especially after she had rammed them—twice!

Quincy noticed the venetian blinds move for the second time. Grabbing Mike by the arm, they made their way along the side of the house toward the front. He figured that he would use Larry's kid as a shield. If the women *did* have a gun, they would shoot him first. No worries.

Rose picked up the butcher's knife from the counter and stuck it in her belt. The girls half crouched and half crawled as they shuffled into the dark living room, ready to make a run for it out the front door.

It would be safer for them if they left the house. They knew the property far better than the thugs and it would be to their advantage if they were outside. They wouldn't be helplessly trapped when the punks broke in. Rose had her hand on the deadbolt.

"Uh, Rose? I think I saw something move. I saw a shadow ... or something."

"What?" She felt the hair on the nape of her neck stand.

Jen nodded as she peeked out the living room window. "Yeah. I think ... uh. I think I saw a shadow."

Rose hesitated, her hand on the lock. "You stay here. I'll crawl back and see if they're still by the barn." *What if they're standing outside our front door? We would have run right into them!*

Sneaking down the hall, she carefully opened the blind that was covering the narrow kitchen window—just a little. Still on her knees, she took a closer look and paled. They were no longer by the barn. They had disappeared into the night.

Raising the blind a little more, she moved closer to the window for a better view, wondering where they were. Her breath filmed the cold glass.

A hand slammed hard against the pane, aimed squarely at her face. Reeling back, she grabbed her chest.

"Oh, little gurr-url?" The punk was singing out the words as he pressed his face against the glass. "Oh, little gurr-url? I see-ee you. I'm gonna huff and puff and blow your house down." He crazily laughed, slapping his hand against the window.

She pushed away, her heart racing, as he examined her. *He's staring at me like I'm his prey. I need to close …*

His face contorted as he pressed it against the pane until his nose flattened. A splotch of mist from his hot breath formed on the cool glass. His tongue darted out like a lizard's, licking at the film.

Tiring of the game, he raised both hands above his head and pounded hard on the window, making it vibrate. The druggie's eyes were out of focus. He seemed more animal than human and was totally stoned, wanting to get at her.

She was repulsed by the sickening display and struggled with the tangled strings. The blind dropped, blocking his view.

But, it didn't stop him. He kept at it—slapping at the window while she remained frozen on her knees. The slapping grew harder as he yelled out his demented song. "I'm gonna huff and puff …" The old glass rattled from the pressure.

A silhouette appeared in the living room window. Another punk started beating on the pane behind Jennifer. She shivered as the large sheet pulsated, coming close to its breaking point. Now the scum were at both the front and back doors, hammering and kicking as they twisted the doorknobs one way and then the other, trying to get at the terrified girls.

Rose scrambled back to the living room and her friend. They faced the front door, tightly holding each another as the freaks continued with their hammering. She tried to reason with them. "Leave us alone! Please. Leave us alone. We didn't do anything to you." She felt drained and beaten.

"Oh yes you ha-have." The creep that had been at the back door sang out the words, this time from outside the front window. "Oh yes you ha-have!"

"What … what do you want? Why are you doing this?"

The pounding stopped. An ominous silence filled the old house. She waited for a response—feeling as if they were in the eye of a hurricane. Everything would be peaceful for a few minutes before the storm struck again. Then the vermin would carry on with their crazy yelling and pounding.

A vehicle door slammed, making the girls jump. Rose scrambled back to the narrow kitchen window and carefully parted the blinds. She was terrified that the punk was still out there and that he might slap at her face again. *What are they doing?*

Two of the creeps were in Mike's truck. The other two were near the driver's door passing around a pipe.

Jen needed to know what they were up to. She crept into the kitchen and squeezed her friend's shoulder. "Rose. Rose? What do you see?" She sounded like a frightened little girl—her voice high pitched and whiny.

"It's okay, sweetie. They probably think that it's time to leave. Everything will be fine." She didn't believe a word that she was saying. They hadn't left when Rose had rammed them twice. Why would they leave now?

Jen leaned over her friend's shoulder and peeked through the window, whispering. "Now's our chance to make a break for it."

Chapter 14

Rose considered the idea of her and Jen fleeing from the house. The more she thought about it, the more she didn't like it. She couldn't move very fast with her injured ankle and the only weapon that they had was the knife in her belt. They would be sitting ducks. She squeezed Jen's hand as she tried to explain. "We *can't* leave the house."

"What?" She shook her head, not understanding. "We *have* to leave. It's our only chance."

"No! They're setting us up. That's what they're doing. They're playing with us."

"Why would they do that? Why are they even here?" Jen raised her eyebrows with the questions and shook her head. It didn't make sense to her.

Rose thought hard for an answer. "They're here because … because Mike told them I have money. That's why. There's no other reason." She knew that there *was* another reason. There were several of them. It was because they had found her snooping at Larry's and she had thrown them from her truck. Then, there was the recent ramming in her driveway. *They want revenge.*

She felt guilty for pulling her friends into the mess. "They don't want to break in unless they absolutely have to. They could have easily busted down the kitchen door. They didn't because it would complicate things. They probably know that Gleason's my ex brother-in-law."

"But, if they know that the sheriff was related to you, then what are they doing here?"

"Good point." She placed her hands on Jen's shoulders and looked her in the eye as she asked the question. "Why aren't they worried about getting arrested?"

Jen was beginning to understand what she was getting at. "Do you think Gleason is in on this? Do you really think that?"

"Why else? They come over and beat the hell out of Larry. Who are these guys and why aren't they afraid of the law?" She tried to answer her own questions. "I'll tell you why. Because … because Gleason sent them over to Larry's so he could get a piece of the action. That's why."

"Well, it could be, but—" Jennifer was thinking hard.

"But, what?" Rose shook her head, waiting for an answer.

"Well, it could be that Mike blabbed that you grow pot. Maybe Gleason isn't even involved." She tried to think like them. "They … they figured you couldn't call the cops because you'd get busted for growing marijuana if you did."

Rose slowly nodded. "Yeah. That could be. Maybe Mike told them that I—"

"They're meth freaks, Rose. Do you know anything about meth freaks?" Before her friend could answer, Jen spouted out, "I do! My old boyfriend used meth all the time. They have no fear when they're stoned. No fear at all—especially with the law. They couldn't care less. And," she took in a breath, "they have absolutely *no* conscience between right and wrong. They become animals." She trembled as she repeated the last word. "Animals!"

Rose nodded in agreement with her friend and hoped that Gleason wasn't really in on it. They might need his help. It would only be a matter of time before the scum broke a window or door and made their way in. She tried to think clearly while planning on how they could defend themselves.

Jen wouldn't let up. "That's why we need to get out. We need to get out, *now*! They could murder us. They'll beat us just like they did to Larry. I'm sure." She thought for a moment before adding, "And, where is Carla?"

"Did you see that redheaded one freak out?" Karl laughed as he asked the question. Sal nervously laughed along with him. Mike let out a chuckle. He wanted very much to fit in with his newfound bad boys. "Especially when you started bangin' on the front window, Mikie." Karl slapped him hard on the back as he said it.

Mike was very pleased with his friend's display of camaraderie and, for the moment, forgot about his damaged truck.

Quincy ignored them. He was fixated on the farmhouse and wondered if the girls would run. Karl started to say something but he raised his hand and cut him off. "Get ready to move. I'm thinkin' they're going to make their escape real soon. Then we can hunt them down and bring 'em back in for some 'terror-gation."

He didn't want to forcibly break into their house. The less evidence, the better it was. But, they still needed to be careful. The women could bring in the law. Quincy knew that it was a fine line. If he and his buddies got too carried away, then the women would be forced into getting the police involved.

He wondered if they had friends that they could hire to get back at him and his gang. That happened at times—going above the law when a drug deal went sideways. There were a few guns for hire, even in the small town of Beaswick.

The original plan had been simple enough. Take Larry's money and lay low. Mike had told them that it would be easy and not to worry about his dad hiring any muscle to get back at them. The father was too weak to do that sort of thing. The kid had assured them that there was plenty of money for the taking.

The more Quincy thought about it, the more upset he became. Things weren't turning out the way he had planned.

Chapter 15

Rose wondered if she and Jen could fake it by opening and closing the front door and allowing it to slam shut. The punks might think that they were making a run for it.

Then … we could sneak out the back while they look for us in the front yard. And then, what? Where would we go? We could jump in my truck, but we wouldn't get very far. It would overheat unless we put water in it. It probably won't even start. We'd be an easy target. We can't just sit here. Where can we hide? Where can we go?

"Jen?"

"Huh?"

"Maybe I should try to talk to them—to the leader, that Quincy guy. Maybe I should try to negotiate with him."

"Negotiate?" Jen's mouth dropped. "Negotiate? You've got to be kidding me. How do you plan on negotiating?"

"Well," Rose was thinking out loud. "Maybe not really negotiate, but talk to him. Tell him that I'm related to Sheriff Gleason."

"It wouldn't matter to him. He doesn't care *who* you're related to. He wants money. That's what they all want." Jen shook her head at her friend. "Besides, you just about killed him. I don't think he or his buddies would be in any mood to 'negotiate'."

Rose was annoyed with the way she was talking to her. *Is she telling me that I went too far with those bastards?*

Jen could see what she was thinking so explained. "Look, Rose. I don't blame you. There was nothing more that we could have done, but you completely went over the top."

Rose sputtered in an attempt to defend herself. "I did not! They were going to attack us and I had to—"

Jen put a hand up and stopped her. "I know they deserved it. I know they should have been mowed down. You gave them a chance when you blocked the driveway with your truck—a chance for them to back away and leave. Those maggots could have easily turned around and headed back under the rock they crawled from. It wasn't your fault that they made the wrong choice, but—"

"But, what?" Rose took a step back, curious with what her friend had to say.

"Well, when you grabbed that skin headed guy by his wrist and raced back up the driveway, well—" A smile appeared on Jennifer's face as she replayed the scene. "Maybe you didn't go over the top after all. In fact, that was pretty cool. I've got to tell you that, at first, I thought you had lost it. But now, well, I'm proud of you. I'm glad we're friends." She leaned over and hugged the older woman, adding, "Good for you. Those bastards deserved it."

Surprised, Rose hugged her back. "Yeah, you're right. The best part was when that Quincy had his pants down around his ankles. He had such a stupid look on his face when he was picking rocks out of his hairy ass."

Jennifer giggled. "Especially when you flicked the one headlight on for a second or two. He … he looked like a stunned deer."

A moment later she was in tears, laughing along with Rose who pretended to be Quincy picking tiny stones out of his butt cheek. It was something that they both needed—to laugh and remove the stress that had been building. It was a release mechanism that was creating a stronger bond between them.

The laughter soon faded. They both came back to reality and realized once more how bad their situation really was. Standing in the middle of the dark living room, they were unsure of what to do.

Her anger grew, the more Rose thought about it. The instinct to fight back was returning with a vengeance. "They're not getting a nickel of our money, Jen. Nothing! We've worked too damned hard to give anybody, anything!"

Quincy took in another hit from the pipe and made a promise that this would be his last one for a while. He didn't want to get too stoned.

"I don't think they're gonna run."

"It's only been a few minutes, Sal. No need to rush into anything just yet."

They stood next to Mike's truck and tried to stop fidgeting. That was the one thing about meth—it was hard to keep still when the speed rushed through your system. They were all agitated with waiting and wanted action.

Mike took another puff and tried to suppress a cough. The smoke travelled deep into his lungs as he thought about his options. His truck was in bad shape. Now he would need more money before he could leave Beaswick. He grumbled, "Ya know? It's aw-aw-all 'cause a Larry."

Sal didn't understand. "Huh?"

"It's aw-all 'cause a Larry that my tru-truck got smashed."

"What are you talkin' 'bout?" Both Sal and Quincy shook their heads, wondering where the logic was.

"If he would a given us the money in the fir-first place this wouldn't a happened. My tra-truck would still be goo-goo-good."

The vein on Quincy's temple throbbed as *Pop Goes the Weasel* crazily played on in his head. He was fed up with Mike. "Hey, asshole! How did you get the money to buy your truck in the first place?"

He didn't answer. Instead, he reached into his shirt pocket for a cigarette. There were none. He had smoked the last one over an hour ago. Again, he cursed his father for not buying him more smokes when he last went into town.

Quincy glared at him. "I'll ask you again. How did you get the money to buy your truck?" Too agitated to wait for an answer, he blurted, "Larry gave it to you. Didn't he?" *How can he say something like that about his dad? My old man never gave me a nickel and this bastard in front of me has the nerve to blame everything on his father?*

Feeling cocky with the meth saturating his brain, Mike snapped back, "Aw, faw faw-fuck you! I deserved it."

"*This* is what you deserve!" Quincy slapped him hard across the face.

Everyone was taken by surprise. Even Quincy was astonished with what he had done and wondered why he had reacted so violently. Deep down, he understood that he was jealous. Mike was loved by his father—he wasn't.

With tears in his eyes, Mike backed away and rubbed his cheek, blaming his dad again for what had just happened.

Sal pushed his way between them. "Hey! Let's be cool. Relax a little. We've gotta work together."

Taking in a breath, Quincy tried to do just that—to relax, but it was difficult for him to do. His leg and butt cheek hurt. He wasn't sure what was going to happen with the two women and, to add to everything else, that selfish bastard named Mike was getting on his nerves.

A part of him wanted to talk to the one woman that looked like his Aunt Sylvia. He actually respected her for what she had done—grabbing him and throwing him from her truck.

Another part felt sorry for Larry. *He's a good father who loves his stupid son and his boy doesn't even appreciate it.* Quincy turned away from the group, his emotions taking over.

He told himself to get a grip. It was happening far too often. Sometimes he didn't like who he was—especially when he did meth. He felt he was going against his inner self in an attempt to prove something. Confused, he wasn't sure what he needed to prove. He lifted his head to the night sky, trying to clear his mind.

Staring at the moon, he thought about his Aunt Sylvia and how she had raised him. She used to bake bread. Coming home after school to the smell of baking made him feel good. It filled her house. He couldn't remember his mother doing that sort of thing. She had died of an overdose when he was only seven.

That's when his aunt had stepped in. He had never been so loved. In his mind he could still smell the fresh bread and apple pie and wondered if the lady in the house baked.

"Maybe we should bust into the barn." Karl studied the old building while thinking out loud. "It smells like tons of pot in there. We could help ourselves—sell what we don't need."

Quincy pulled away from his childhood memories. "We'll only take money from them. That's why we came here. I don't want to bother with selling pot on the street. Word would get around. Some of their dealer buddies would hear about it. No, we'll get cash and lay low."

"I think we should break into the house. I'm tired of waiting." The dope was making it difficult for Sal to keep still. His mood had changed because of the meth and now he wanted action. All four were more than ready to start moving again.

"We'll wait a few more minutes." Quincy was trying to follow his plan. He hoped that the women would flee from their house so that he and his gang could have a little fun with them. The boys would chase them down and the girls would be terrified and give them their money. There would be no problem.

He questioned that line of thinking. The red haired one would give them trouble. *Aunt Sylvia would stand up to us.* He didn't want to push the envelope too far. The last thing that he wanted was to hurt her.

They wouldn't really need to hit them. They would just rough them up a little until they found out where their money was. If the women were beaten, or if the house appeared to have been broken into, it could create some very serious problems with the law.

Again, it was a fine line. He knew that if he and his buddies went overboard the girls would phone either the cops or some of their friends. No. They had to be cool and only scare them so that they could get at their cash. That's all.

He still worried about the red haired one.

Chapter 16

Gleason was in his small house not far from his office. He brought his squad car home after his shift for two reasons. One was because he was required to. In case of an emergency he could jump into action. The other reason was because he was simply too fat and lazy and didn't want to walk the five short blocks to and from work.

His deputy, Darwin, had the other cruiser and was on duty patrolling the streets of Beaswick.

He was opening his fourth can of beer when his phone rang. Startled by such a late call, he spilled a little of the suds on his khaki coloured shirt. He hoped that the beer had landed on the spaghetti stain from lunch. *No worries. Alcohol is a good cleanser.* He chuckled at his little joke. "Sheriff Gleason, here."

"This is Frank Morgan from the California Justice Department. We've met before at your swearing in. Do you remember?"

"Uh, yes, Mr. Morgan. I remember." Gleason was instantly alert and totally sober. He knew who Morgan was. *He's that skinny guy that used to work for the Irvine Police Department a few years back.*

"There seems to be a problem with you and money." Morgan was all business.

He sputtered, "Uh, na-no problem, Mr. Morgan. No problem at all."

Frank Morgan shook his head on the other end of the line. He hated dealing with disciplinary issues, especially at this late hour, but knew that it was all part of his job. He had received several complaints about the sheriff and was being forced into getting involved before things got out of hand.

"Well, Sheriff, I'm sitting here with my laptop and reading a file that has your name on it from Internal Affairs. It's not pretty." He rapped on a notepad with a pencil for emphasis.

"Internal Affairs?" He almost yelled it out. "Uh, I'm not sure what you're talking about." Sweating, Gleason desperately needed a long pull from his can of beer. Was Morgan talking about the money that he was skimming from the marijuana growers?

Morgan leaned into his phone as he tapped harder on the notepad. "Look, Sheriff. I'll cut to the chase. You've got a big money problem and I don't like it." Stopping his pencil tapping for a moment, he drew a large dollar sign.

The sheriff's legs grew weak. He plopped down on his couch in a sweat. *What's he getting at? Who squealed on me?*

Annoyed with his subordinate, he underlined Gleason's name while saying, "You've got several unpaid bills and now I understand that you were at the bank late this afternoon wanting more money." He tried printing an 'X' over the dollar sign that he had doodled, but pressed too hard and broke the lead tip.

Gleason was instantly relieved. *It's not about the drug money!* He thought about the young loans officer who had turned him down at Wells Fargo. The relief quickly turned to anger. *I'll bet two to one the little punk squealed on me.*

Frank Morgan read his mind as he picked up another pencil. "Your application for a bank loan turned up on my laptop, Cornelius. You used me as a reference." Morgan called him by his first name, subtly implying that his title as Sheriff could be stripped if Gleason didn't follow the rules.

He was being watched and didn't like it. Closing his eyes, he rubbed his forehead while visualizing Morgan on the other end of the line. The guy had a pockmarked face and piercing blue eyes.

Turning back to the conversation, he worried about losing his job, but he also worried about not getting any more easy money from some of the farmers. *I've got to play it cool.* "Yeah, that's right, Mr. Morgan. I wanted to get my finances in order so I could pay off a few bills. It's been very hard for me."

With no response on the other end of the line, he cleared his throat and ploughed on with his lies. "I, uh, want to send my son to college and thought I could borrow some money." Reaching for his beer, he took a huge swallow and mentally patted his back, satisfied with his explanation.

"From what I'm reading in your file, you're son passed away over ten years ago."

"Er … yeah. You're right. But, it's my step-son and he's got cancer and—"

"Let's cut out the crap, Cornelius!"

Gleason winced.

Pausing so that the sheriff would sweat a little more, Morgan waited several seconds as he rapped the notepad with the new pencil. Finally, in a cold voice, he spoke slowly so that it would sink in. "You're forcing the Justice Department into giving you an ultimatum."

There was an audible gasp on the other end of the line.

Frank knew that he had struck a nerve and pushed on. "You still have a year left on your term as sheriff, but I also know that you have a serious cash flow problem. That is *not* what I want to hear—especially from an elected official."

"But—"

"Never mind the 'buts'. I'm giving you one last chance to get your finances in order. Do you understand?"

"Yeah, but—"

"I said never mind the 'buts'! My office will not tolerate having a public servant owe people all kinds of money. You're taking advantage of your position and I'm being forced to act. This is your first and last warning. Do you hear me?"

Gleason studied the floor and realized that he was in a very difficult position. He was not used to being given orders. He was the sheriff around these parts and *he* was the one who gave them out, no one else.

His mind rambled on how he could get his hands on some serious cash. All he needed was fifty thousand dollars. If he paid off bills rather than gamble it away, things would work out for him. He had no idea where he could get that kind of money.

"Cornelius? Are you there?" Normally Morgan would have set up a meeting with the sheriff rather than confront him on the phone this late in the evening, but there were budget constraints—especially in these tough financial times.

"Yes sir. I'm here. I was just thinking about what you were saying and you're right. I'm a little behind in my payments, but I promise to make it up."

Tired and with little patience, Morgan ended with, "It's all up to you, Cornelius." Without giving the sheriff a chance to reply, he hung up.

Chapter 17

Jen nervously asked the question as Rose peeked out the narrow window. "What are they doing?" The girls had turned off the kerosene lantern earlier so that they wouldn't easily be seen.

"They're coming back. They're walking back to the house."

"No! I can't do this. They'll kill us. I don't want to be murdered!"

"It's okay, honey." Rose turned and hugged her. She did not want her friend to emotionally collapse and knew that it wouldn't take much to push her over the edge. Trying to sound hopeful, she added, "Remember that Carla's out there watching over us." It didn't sound very convincing.

A knock on the door made them freeze in the middle of the kitchen. It repeated, this time on the side window.

Jennifer stupidly hoped that it was the mailman who was making a very late delivery. Maybe a gift—perfume perhaps? Was it the mailman? It sounded so non-threatening. *It's just a neighborly tap. That's all.*

She came out of her fantasy when she heard it again, now an angry rap. *That is not the mailman!*

"Open up!"

"Wha-at? What do you want?" Rose's voice was weak as they shuffled backward into the hallway. She clutched the butcher's knife and faced the kitchen door from twenty feet away. Jennifer cowered behind her.

"We just, uh … we just want to talk. That's all." Quincy tried to soften his tone.

Rose hesitated, wondering how to respond. "What do you want to talk about?"

He winked at Sal before continuing. "Look. We don't want to hurt anybody. Okay? We just need a little cash. That's what happened at Larry's. That's why we went over there. His son ripped us off. We thought Mike was home and we wanted our money back."

Mike could not believe his ears. His buddies were blaming *everything* on him. He opened his mouth to defend himself but Karl squeezed his shoulder, stopping him. Whispering, he explained that they would only use him a little so that they could get their hands on the women's money.

Rose took two steps toward the kitchen door with the knife held out in front of her. "Why did you have to go and beat up Larry?"

Jennifer followed closely behind, terrified of being alone. Gripping Rose's shoulder, she prayed that her friend would talk some sense into the punks and that they would simply go away. *Maybe … maybe we can still get out of this. Maybe we can reason with them.*

"Mike said he gave our money to his dad. We just wanted it back." As an afterthought, he added, "We need the money to pay some bills. It's only five hundred dollars."

Quincy winked at Sal again as he said the last part. He was very pleased with his story and they were both on the verge of laughter. Taking in a deep breath to try and compose himself, he carried on. "We loaned Mike the money to help him out."

Sal bent over. There were tears in his eyes as he shook his head to stop from chuckling. Helping out Larry's stupid son was the funniest thing that he had ever heard. His buddy was a master at bullshitting.

Rose stepped closer to the door and talked through it. "So, what do you want from us?"

"We want the five hundred that Larry owes us. You're his friend. *You* give us the money, uh, and my chain. It was uh, a gift from my … sister." He couldn't go on. It was too funny for him. The gold chain was stolen property and he didn't have a sister. He took in a breath to contain his laughter. Sal was giving him the giggles. "And then, of course, there's the damage to Mikie's truck."

Mike perked up with the last comment, annoyed with the way his buddies were behaving. *Quit your stupid laughing and what about my truck? Those bitches need to pay me a chunk a cash!*

Quincy wanted to convince her that they meant her and her girlfriend no harm—that he and his pals were simply innocent victims. It was the women who had attacked them, not the other way around. "All we wanted was to talk to you but you rammed us down the driveway." He said it accusingly, his mood darkening. Now he found it no longer funny and blamed everything on Rose.

She stood in a defensive stance in the moonlit kitchen with bright blue eyes and hair sticking out in all directions. Her ankle ached along with the blisters on her chest, but none of that mattered to her right now. What *did* matter was the nerve of those goons wanting money. Raising the knife, she jabbed it at the door. "I gave you a chance to back away. But, do you know what? You didn't take it, so screw you and screw your truck."

He stepped back, worried that her anger would somehow escape through the door and cause him some serious harm. His fellow goons also backed away. *Whoa! She's a bitch from hell.* "Okay. Okay! So we made a mistake. Can we at least talk about it?"

"What do you want?"

"Like I said, we only want the five hundred dollars that we're out and," he paused while searching for the right word, "uh, damages to Mike's truck. Then we'll leave." *Plus my gold chain, you bitch!*

"We had nothing to do with it. We shouldn't be involved. It's between Mike and his father. Just leave us alone!"

Quincy motioned for Mike and Karl to make their way to the front of the house. "If you don't give us the money, then we're going back and paying Larry another visit. Do you understand what I'm talkin' 'bout?" He spat the last few words out as the blue vein on the side of his head throbbed on. *Pop goes the weasel. Pop goes the—*

"Uh, I don't have that kind of money."

He slammed a fist at their door, skinning his knuckles. His other hand grabbed the handle and twisted it. "Don't you fuck with us, bitch! Don't you dare fuck with us. You got the money! We know you do. It smells like tons of pot in that barn. You guys are growin' it. You gotta have at least five hundred in cash!"

Sal was worried where things were going. He knew that Quincy could get crazy. *How can I stop him before he gets too carried away?*

Rose thrust the knife at the old door, yelling, "I've got a handgun. If you try to come in, I'll shoot! I swear. I'll shoot—all of you!"

"Okay, fair enough." He backed away and, for a moment, wondered how he should handle the situation. "I don't believe you got a gun. You don't got nothin'. You're setting yourselves up for a real beating."

Worked up far beyond reason, he barked, "Believe me. You saw what we did to your pal, Larry. You'll both get the same. Now, open—up—this—door!" He pounded and kicked at it. *How dare they grind my ass into the driveway and not pay for what they done.*

"Stop it! Stop it or I'll shoot!"

He stopped. "Why don't you open up the blind just a little so's I can see it? You know? Like, all you gotta do is show me the gun. A deal?"

"I don't have to show you *anything*!" She stepped closer to the door and shook the knife in his direction.

Quincy snickered. "You got no gun, bitch. You and your friend got nothin'. Now, I'm warning you for the last time. Open up this door and give us five hundred and, uh, damages, and then we'll leave."

He waited a moment to let it sink in before uttering, "If you don't, we're gonna make your lives … miserable." His voice dripped with contempt.

Between sobs, Jen tried to speak. She urgently tapped her friend's shoulder. "Rose! Listen to me. I … I've got five hundred stashed in the house. Maybe we should—"

She spun around and snapped out at her naive partner. "Don't be ridiculous! They won't leave if we only give them five hundred. They want more. Don't trust them. They're lying."

Quincy pounded on the kitchen door. Mike banged on the larger side window that faced the knoll. A moment later Sal and Karl were hammering on the living room window and door at the front of the house.

They yelled and screamed as their walloping grew louder. The bizarre sounds were in unison. All were perfectly timed as they bellowed out, "Bitches! Bitches! Bitches!"

The thudding blocked out the first part of what they were yelling, sounding more like, "Itches! Itches! Itches!"

The girls cowered in the dark hallway. Jen covered her ears as the yelling and hammering grew louder. The windows and doors vibrated. The air seemed thicker, the pressure, unbearable.

Rose grabbed Jen's hand. They bolted as fast as her sore ankle would allow up the stairs to the master bedroom near the front of the house. Huddling on the edge of the bed, they felt trapped and helpless.

Carla crouched lower in the moonlight and wondered how the bizarre situation would end. She could only see Mike. He was banging on the kitchen window with his back to her as their demented yelling carried on.

Can I shoot him? And, what if I do? The cops and ambulance will come. I'll go to jail. We'll all go to jail!

Chapter 18

Gleason stomped up to his fridge and was more than ready to open another cold one. The phone call from the Justice Department had shaken him. He reached for a can and stopped, deciding to have a shot of Jack Daniel's instead. Beer wasn't strong enough to help him deal with the problem. Jack would be the ticket.

He poured himself a stiff one over ice while contemplating how he could come up with enough money to get out of his financial jam. Spilling a little of it, he carried his drink with a shaky hand to his living room.

Flopping down on his couch, he took a noisy gulp, hardly tasting the smoky, oak flavour. His eyes fell on the framed photo on the wall across from him—shaking hands with the mayor of Beaswick when he had been elected sheriff. But, he didn't see any of it, his mind miles away.

Now what am I going to do? A warm glow crept through him as he mulled over his question. Taking another long swallow, he tried to recap his recent conversation with Morgan.

The greasy bastard got promoted real fast from the Irvine precinct. I guess that's what happens when you kiss somebody's ass. Not me. No way. Screw you, Captain Morgan!

The sheriff chuckled and figured that the guy might not be all that bad considering that he had the same name as Gleason's favourite brand of rum. He gulped down another slug and began to feel even better.

His eyes turned to the folder of unpaid bills that lay on the coffee table. Next to it was a deck of cards that he used for practicing Blackjack. He picked up the cards and shuffled them while staring at the bills, hoping that they would somehow magically disappear. However, the recent conversation with Morgan was forcing him to deal with them once more. Sighing, he put the cards down and went through the bills, one by one.

The power company wanted money for several months' worth of electricity. The cable company was threatening to disconnect him. His mortgage payments were falling behind. He owed ten thousand on his credit cards and his ex was suing him for alimony.

Shit! I'll need a decent lawyer—one that's not too expensive. Adding it up for the hundredth time, he hoped that he had somehow made a mistake with the total. No, there was no mistake. He needed around fifty thousand to stay above water. *Maybe if I had fifty thou', I could use forty of it to pay some of my bills. The rest, I could invest at the tables.* He caught himself, knowing that he had a serious gambling problem.

The whiskey was having the desired effect. His financial situation didn't seem half as bad as it had been only minutes earlier. He fantasized about making easy money at the casino when Darwin's voice pulled him out of his reverie. It came from the police radio that Gleason had set up in the kitchen.

The department had a small transmission tower near the station that covered most of the Beaswick area. But, there were several pockets with no coverage, particularly in the back roads. The mountains gave them reception problems from time to time.

He took another huge gulp, the booze burning its way down. Smacking his lips in satisfaction, he listened as Darwin yakked about nothing in particular.

Sheriff Gleason had the day shift, Tuesday to Saturday, from nine until six in the evening. Darwin took over from five until two in the morning. The one hour overlap gave them time to meet and compare notes. At the end of his day, Gleason would lock the office for the night and send his secretary, Scarlett, on her way home. Dispatch duties would then be turned over to the larger precinct in Kelowna, thirty miles away.

He poured himself another one while dreaming about how he could get out of his financial woes. Going on a budget and slowly paying down his bills wouldn't work for him. He had little self-discipline when it came to money.

The sheriff glanced at his watch. It was time to head to the pre-arranged meeting where he planned on picking up some much needed cash.

He was thankful that GPS units hadn't been installed in their police cars. There was no way that he would allow anyone to spy on him.

There had been a huge debate over what the state had planned on doing. The police union had claimed that it violated their civil rights. The department had insisted that it wanted the global positioning system installed in all patrol cars for safety reasons. The union went to court and lost. But, by then California was heading toward bankruptcy and had no money to implement the plan.

Gleason took another long swig, this time from the bottle. Sitting on his couch, he went over it one more time—the conversation that he recently had with Morgan.

"The bastard's snooping on me. That's what he's doin', shnoopin'." He noticed a slur in his voice. "Screw him! I don't need this job." He stopped that line of thinking. Gleason knew that he *did* need this job. From now on he would have to be careful.

He put the bottle back in the brown bag that Tommy Li had given him earlier and stepped out into the wind. A little tipsy, he made his way to his squad car—a Dodge Challenger. Before starting it he took another long pull. Seconds later his mind was no longer on his financial troubles. He felt wonderful and knew that he was well on his way to being drunk.

Firing up the engine, he revved it a few times before putting it into gear. He loved the car's throaty sound of power. It was almost sexual.

It didn't matter to him that he was now driving impaired to a pre-determined location to collect illegal drug money in a police car. He didn't give it much thought. What he *was* thinking, as the car veered off the road and onto the shoulder, was no longer about money. It was about Rose and their last encounter. He had been drunk then, too, when he had driven up to see her.

Gripping the bottle in one hand, he corrected his steering with the other as he roared down the quiet residential street. *Shit. I gotta back off on the gas a little.*

He remembered pounding on her door before a girlfriend had moved in. She wouldn't allow him in her house. He had threatened her by letting her know that if she didn't cooperate she would be in serious trouble. She had replied by telling him to screw off.

He smiled as he pulled into the vacant parking lot. He loved her spirit. *She knows I would never put her in jail. Not as long as she keeps paying me*. He wanted her money all right, but he wanted more than just her money. He wanted more of that loving—even if she didn't.

Parked in the rear of the gravelled lot, he tipped back the bottle and took one more long guzzle. Now there was nothing else for him to do except wait for his contact to show, hopefully with a pile of cash.

Chapter 19

They hammered incessantly on the farmhouse windows and doors, chanting, "Bitches! Bitches! Bitches!" The angry bellowing, mixed in with the eerie sounds from the rasping trees, created an almost supernatural presence.

Feeling trapped, the two women shuffled into the bedroom closet and huddled under a blanket, seeking any kind of comfort and security. Rose clutched the knife and wondered if she could ever use it.

A screech coming from the upstairs bathroom made her flinch. Through sobs, Jen explained that it was only a branch rubbing against the house.

The goons soon stopped their hammering. They had run out of energy. The only sound was the wind and the occasional scratching from the branch. That made things even worse. At least they knew where the creeps were when they had been pounding and yelling. Now, they could only speculate on what they were up to.

"Something's going on. They're too quiet. They're going to break in."

"I don't know, Jen. Maybe they're getting bored with the whole, stupid game. Maybe they'll leave." She wanted to believe what she was saying as she hugged her friend tighter.

"I say we go in there. Now!" Karl was pulling on his pant leg to try and get comfortable in Mike's truck. His knee was giving him trouble. The open wound was weeping and stuck to his pants. *Damn them.*

"Here, take a hit while we think about things." Quincy was in the passenger seat and shifted from one cheek to the other, adding, "But make it a small one." They hadn't planned on being gone for so long and now their supply of meth was running low.

Sal studied the barn in the moonlight. "It would be easy to break into that old building. We might find more than just pot in there."

"Nope. We're not gonna do that. We don't want to leave any evidence that we were here. Even with what we did to Larry. If we need to, we can blame his beating on Mikie." He chuckled, knowing that comment would upset him.

"What! Scra-scra-screw you and don't call me Mikie!"

Quincy raised his hand, threatening to slap him once more. "Shut up and listen to me. It's because of *you* that we got ourselves into this mess. It's because of the wrong information you gave us. You're the one who's to blame. You're lucky that we're letting you hang out with us. We should have left you back at Larry's."

"Fa-fa—"

"Shut the fuck up!" Quincy didn't like the brat. The more he thought about it, the more he saw how spoiled Mike was. When it came down to it, Larry was a good father—he was *too* good a father. That's what the problem was.

My dad wasn't a father—just a mean bastard that ended up in jail. At least Larry loves his kid. Mike doesn't know how lucky he is.

Quincy was aware that Sal and Karl had had similar experiences with their childhoods. He didn't know either of them that well, but did know that their parents couldn't care less about them. In fact, Karl's mother was doing time in the state pen for embezzlement.

He hung out with them on occasion but considered them losers, tolerating them to a certain degree. Karl was the biggest pain. He constantly challenged him, wanting to take control. He had an anger issue and always pushed the envelope. Sal was easier to get along with, but could also be annoying. At times he wouldn't follow their plans.

They got together when there was a job to do, like today. Otherwise they wouldn't see each other for weeks. That suited Quincy just fine.

"What are we gonna do? I've had it with waitin'. That woman needs to pay for what she done." Karl was picking at his knee through his torn jeans.

"Aw, screw you and you're knee. You ain't dyin'." Quincy was tired of his whining. He was also fed up with the whole scene.

"It's easy for you to say. You're not the one with the bum knee. That bitch is gonna pay for this." He pulled his pant leg up so that they could all have a better look in the moonlight. It did seem painful. "It's all her fault, how she threw me off the truck like that."

Mike piped up. "Mm-mm-me, too. Sh-sh-she threw mm—"

"For Christ's sake, we're not here to beat anybody up! You got it?" Quincy was concerned with Karl. He kept carrying on about getting even. "We're here for money. *Not* revenge." He didn't want them to lose their focus and take things personally with the women. That would only create more problems.

Sal readily agreed. "Yeah. You're right. So, what do we do next?"

Quincy studied his two partners for a moment, ignoring Mike. In a low voice he announced, "We're gonna' scare the livin' shit out of them."

Chapter 20

Gleason glanced at his watch for the third time and wondered again at why his contact was late. *Maybe the bastard took the money and ran.* It wouldn't have surprised him. He knew that he couldn't trust anybody— certainly not in this line of business. *It's a dog-eat-dog world.*

Taking another swallow of Jack, he leaned his head against his headrest, angry. Gleason usually got angry when he drank. He felt that he didn't deserve what life had dealt him and figured that he was better than that.

He rationalized that he was being forced into taking drug money to survive. *The county doesn't pay me enough.* The sheriff felt justified that he should make a decent living like everyone else around him. *Some of those bastards are pulling in six figures a year. If the friggin' growers can make that much, so can I!*

His police radio came to life. Darwin was yakking to Kelowna Dispatch about some kind of domestic altercation up on Verde Vista Road.

Sheriff Gleason closed his eyes and chuckled. He knew it was probably old Sammy acting up again. Either he or Darwin drove up that dusty road at least once a month. Sammy also had a temper when he drank.

He remembered the last time he had been sent out that way. Ella and Sam had been having another one of their 'disputes'.

They had once owned a restaurant, but nobody could remember its name. The joke around town was that it was probably called *Sam n' Ella's*.

He had managed to finally calm them. Ella had thanked him and had asked if he would like to take home a few buns that she had freshly baked.

Gleason smiled while thinking back. He had declined, but she had insisted. Before he could say another word, a hot, buttered bun had magically appeared in front of him. He had taken a bite and was impressed with how good a baker she really was.

He remembered happily chewing away when their dog, Charlie, had sauntered into their kitchen. Casually lifting its hind leg, the Great Dane had urinated on an opened bag of flour that had been leaning against the wall. With a mouth full of bun and butter, he was sick with what he had witnessed.

Neither Ella nor Sammy had paid the dog any attention and had acted as if that sort of thing happened all the time.

He shook his head at the thought and remembered bringing back six of her buns that she had proudly packed for him. Darwin had hungrily eaten two and had claimed, with a full mouth, that they were the best he'd ever tasted.

Sheriff Gleason debated about having one more drink. He eyed the bottle and decided against it. He was already drunk. Now it was time to sober up. He needed to be alert, at least a little when he met his contact. *Yeah, at least sober enough to count the money. I wonder how much they pulled off.*

His brother, Bernie, crept into his mind. A year earlier, Gleason had convinced him to leave Rose. Bernie had never been happy with her. The sheriff couldn't figure out why. She was hot. He figured that Bernie didn't like the idea that she grew marijuana. He also had trouble with her spirit. She was too fiery for him. *That's what it is. She's too damned fiery!*

Gleason had thought that he had it all figured out. The plan was simple. Wait for his brother to leave and then make his move. After all, Bernie *did* tell him that he wasn't in love with her anymore. That was perfect for Gleason. He planned on taking over as soon as his brother left the relationship, thinking that she had wanted him.

Begging for him to stop, Rose had pounded on his chest. It had only made him more aroused. He remembered lifting her onto the kitchen counter and loving the challenge. Feeling very smug, he knew that there was nothing that she could do to stop him.

Rose had pleaded with him not to do it and that it was wrong, telling him that she didn't want him.

Overpowering her, he had ripped off her pants. Obsessed, it had been much too long for him.

Very quickly it was over. He had mumbled an apology as she sobbed in anger and disgust.

Her red hair and blue eyes had turned him on. It had made him excited—too excited. He had wanted to do it again, very soon, and didn't care how she felt.

She was his for the taking, but things had changed. She had pulled a fast one by inviting a girlfriend to live with her. That had stopped him in his tracks.

Gleason fantasized that Rose was alone on her kitchen counter—this time lusting for him. A minute later he half heard someone snore. It was him.

Rubbing his eyes, he looked at his watch. It was time for him to get back to his house. He was drunk and tired. He also wondered what had happened to his contact.

Sheriff Gleason leaned his head back on the car headrest, intending to sleep for only five more minutes.

Chapter 21

Rose crept out of the bedroom closet, trying not to put too much weight on her injured ankle. She wondered what the thugs were up to. Limping along the dark upstairs hallway, she peeked out the second bedroom window at the rear of the house. They were near the barn in a heated discussion. She hurried back to Jennifer who was still huddled under the blanket.

"What? What's going on? What are they doing?"

"They're arguing. I bet they're fed up with all of this. I wouldn't be surprised if they're ready to leave."

"Really? You think so?" Her heart skipped as she prayed that Rose was right. She wanted to believe at least part of what her friend was telling her.

"Yeah, I'm sure of it. They would have broken in by now. Right?" Rose tried to sound convincing. "They could easily have busted a window and gotten in. They don't want to do that. They're already in enough trouble as it is with what they did to Larry.

"They figured they could scare us into giving them money and realized that we're stronger than they thought. They'll probably call it a night and head home. It's already close to midnight." Rose tried to make it sound like the delinquents were decent people who needed their sleep so that they could go to school or to their jobs or whatever, bright and early the next morning.

Jennifer thought that it did make a little sense. She rationalized as she rubbed at her bare arms. *The goons are from Beaswick. Not from some big city. They can't be as bad as the city gangs, can they?*

The pain in Rose's ankle and back was becoming unmanageable. She fished out two more Tylenol 3's and eagerly swallowed them while Jennifer thought about what she would do once the hoods were gone. Did she want to carry on with that kind of life? *No, not right now.* All she wanted was to go home to her mother. *No, maybe … maybe I should stay here. Maybe this is where I belong. My mom doesn't want me living with her.*

She also wasn't ready to give up the good money. Not just yet. Taking in a deep breath, she tried to be strong and stick with the program. *I'll help them grow pot, but from now on it will be with a gun.*

In her mind, the freaks were gone. She figured that Rose was right. They needed to go home. *They can't stay up all night, can they?*

She shook her head, realizing that what she was thinking was foolish. *Wait a minute.* A chill ran down her back. *They certainly* can *stay up all night!* Her ex-boyfriend kept awake for days when he did meth. He couldn't have slept even if he had wanted to.

They sat quietly in the dark, deep in their own thoughts.

Rose questioned if she should report the incident to Gleason. She knew that it all depended on what happened next. If the goons gave them any more trouble, *then* she would tell him. But, if they left within the next few minutes, she would try to forget about how they had terrorized her and her friend. The last thing that she wanted was to get the sheriff involved.

She knew that she would need to carry a gun from now on. All of them would. As soon as the mess they were in was over they would each apply for one. What they were doing for a living was far too dangerous and they needed protection.

"Rose?"

"Huh?" She had been drifting, feeling drowsy from the Tylenol.

"I … I want to tell you that, no matter what, I'm glad I'm here."

"I'm glad you're here, too." She tried to stifle a yawn.

"I love living out here. I've always wanted to be on a farm. I like the idea that we have blueberries, chickens and fresh eggs."

Rose nodded and gave her a reassuring hug. "I like it here, too. I'll miss the mountains, if I ever sell the place."

Jen tried to pull her mind from the thugs. "We need to collect the eggs tomorrow. Angel doesn't like it when I do that."

Rose understood what she was saying. Angel was one of their chickens that produced a lot of eggs. They named her that because she was pure white. It certainly wasn't because of her temperament. They still loved her even if she was a pain.

"She pecked at me the other—" Jen stopped, distracted by a light tap on the bedroom window. "What was that?" Goose bumps raced up her arms.

Rose's pulse quickened. "It could be the wind … blowing a branch?"

Jen pointed from the closet with a shaky finger. "Not on *that* window. There are no branches near it!"

The tapping continued, this time a little harder. *Tap-tap-tap* … They tried to ignore it, afraid to leave the security of their blanket and closet, but it was persistent and demanded their attention. *Tap-tap-tap* …

"Maybe it's Carla. Maybe she's trying to get into the house." Jen's heart pounded as she prayed that it was her aunt who was at the window.

Rose was thinking along the same lines, but it didn't make sense to her. *Why would she be on the porch roof, unless—?* She gulped. *Of course! The creeps are at the back door. Carla can't get into the house with them standing there. But, why doesn't she try the front door? Maybe she doesn't have her keys.* She could not envision her large friend climbing a trellis.

The tapping grew urgent. *Tap! Tap! Tap!*

Fidgeting, she could no longer keep still. "You stay here. I'll have a peek."

"Please. Rose. Don't leave—"

"It's okay. I'll be careful." Pulling the blanket off her, she crawled out of the closet, hoping that it was only something simple and non-threatening. *It could still be a branch blowing against the window. It's probably nothing to worry about.*

She tugged the strings on the Venetian blind, slowly raising it.

A dark figure was hunched over just outside their window holding something under his arm. He pressed his face against the pane, flashing a sick smile.

Carla had a partial view of the creep. Raising the rifle, her hands shook as she tried to take careful aim. *What's he doing?* She couldn't figure it out as she zeroed in on him with her finger on the trigger.

Pausing for a moment, she needed time to think. *Maybe I should just fire a warning shot over his head.* She slowly lowered the barrel.

No. If I do that, then they'll know where I'm hiding. They could easily circle around me. And then what?

Fast approaching her breaking point, Carla had enough of their stupid game. *I don't care anymore. Screw them. If that pervert tries to break in I'll shoot and ask questions later. That's what I'll do.*

Her rifle found its way back on the punk. With tears in her eyes, she aimed for his lower legs, praying for a miracle. *Please, God. Make them go away.*

He yanked out the object from under his arm, making sure that Rose had a good look. She did. So did Jen who stood behind her with an open mouth. They both swallowed hard.

It was one of their chickens and it was struggling to get free. He squeezed it against his torso, giving the girls a malevolent grin.

What is he doing?

Fishing in his pocket, he pulled out a knife with his free hand as the chicken panicked, its wings flapping crazily in the wind. Smiling, he gently placed the serrated blade against its exposed neck.

The girls shook their heads in disbelief as they stared out at the twisted scene. *No! Leave Angel alone.*

Carefully, like a surgeon, he slowly traced the knife across her throat.

What's he doing? Just having fun? Is that it? He's smiling while torturing our little Angel!

He barely cut into the soft tissue before a fine red line appeared across her white neck. More feathers flew as Angel flapped her wings, desperate to escape from the madman.

The creep wrestled with the squirming bird, struggling to keep her still. He succeeded by holding her firmly against his side, a hand gripping her head.

In a flash, Jen was at the window, pounding on it. "Leave her alone! Let her go, you punk!" Her sudden outburst made Angel squirm even more.

Now tiring of his game, in one clean swipe he took a hard and ruthless slash. Blood gushed and feathers flew in the moonlight.

The girls jerked away, repulsed by the macabre sight. But, the druggie wasn't finished with his grotesque performance. There was more craziness to follow. Now he was writing on the window—using Angel's blood as red ink and her severed head as a crude pen.

Has he lost his mind? What is he doing? He's trying to write something with her blood. It looks like an 'S'. Yes, that's what it is. What does it mean? No. Wait. There's more. They froze, unable to turn away from the morbid sight.

The bloody 'S' oozed down the window pane as he carried on with his scribbling. *What's he doing? What's he trying to say?*

It seemed to them like a deviant form of charades that they were being caught up in. *No. This is no game! This is not some kind of party.*

It slowly became clear what he was trying to write—the message that he was sending. It wasn't simply an 'S'. No, it was more than an 'S'. It was a dollar sign.

Angel was now fully decapitated, but still crazily flapped her wings. More feathers flew into the wind. The disgusting scene was too much for Jennifer. She bent over as stomach cramps assaulted her.

Rose was unable to pull her eyes from the warped performance. He was insane and would stop at nothing. Grabbing at her chest, she felt helpless and wondered what he would do next.

He ripped out a handful of feathers and made an attempt at pasting them on the blood-smeared window. Most stuck but some blew free. Holding the now headless chicken over his head, he shook it into the night sky as if it were some kind of bizarre trophy. Chicken blood dripped on his hands.

Rose continued to stare in horror, unaware that her traumatized friend had staggered out of the bedroom.

Jen was in the upstairs hallway, walking trancelike toward the stairs.

"Wait! Jen! What are you doing? Where are you going?"

She wasn't listening and was acting on pure adrenalin. What that monster had done to a poor, defenceless animal was despicable to her. She was halfway down the stairs and determined to confront the killer—to confront *all* of them—when Rose caught up to her.

Grabbing her by the arms, she violently shook her. "No! Don't go down there. Don't you see? That's what they want."

"I … I can't do this. I can't take it. They're … evil." Shaking her head, she pulled free from Rose's grip and covered her face.

"I know, dear. I know, but you can't let them get to you." She tried to put an arm around her but Jen wouldn't allow it. Her mind was filled with the gory image of Angel's feathers blowing in the wind and her blood oozing down the window pane. *Oh God. Please. Help us. Help me!*

"Come, let's go back upstairs."

She recoiled with the thought. The idea of returning to that room appalled her. "No!" She screamed it out. "I can't. Poor Angel. Her feathers are stuck to the window—with her blood!" Sobbing uncontrollably, she hated the way she was acting. Moments earlier she had been ready to confront the enemy. Now she had sunk to a new low.

Wiping at her tears, she took in a deep breath and, in what she thought was a convincing voice, declared, "I want to face them. I need to talk to them. Maybe … maybe then they'll leave. Then—" Jen stopped midway and knew that what she was saying made no sense. They wouldn't leave just because she talked to them. Who did she think she was?

Rose thought about their options. Where could they go? "Let's sit in Carla's room. We'll be safe there." She reached for her friend's hand to lead her to the second bedroom. It was upstairs and at the rear of the house.

"Uh. No. That's okay. I'll follow you." Feeling foolish with her weakness, she resolved to be strong and would not allow Rose to take her by the hand anymore. *I'm going to stand up to those jerks from now on!*

Entering Carla's bedroom, Rose realized that there was no lock on her door. She slipped her butcher's knife behind the wood casing. Not satisfied, she slid a chair against the door for extra security.

Chapter 22

He woke to a sharp rap on his side window. Darwin had spotted Gleason's car in the empty lot and was concerned. He wondered what his boss was doing there at this time of night. "Sheriff! Are you okay?"

"Uh, yeah." Gleason groggily rolled down his window.

He could instantly smell the booze. "What are you doing out here? It's close to two in the morning. Have you been drinking?"

"Uh, yeah. I had a couple of snorts." He was thinking fast and knew that the scrawny deputy could smell alcohol on him. It would be difficult to explain why he was in an empty parking lot and drunk at this time of night.

"Jeeze, Sheriff. You can't be doing that. What if somebody sees you?" He turned on his flashlight and studied him, totally disgusted.

"Turn that friggin' thing off!" Raising his hands, he tried to shield his eyes from the powerful beam. He did not like Darwin's questions, but, more importantly, he had waited all night for no money. Bill collectors were harassing him along with Frank Morgan.

"You're putting me in a very bad position. You've been drinking while driving." Darwin noticed the bottle of whiskey and added, "Not only drinking, but doing it in a police car." He said it accusingly.

"Don't you be self-righteous with me, boy!" The sheriff glared at him.

The deputy did not like that tone of voice. He would not be intimidated by his boss. He knew that he was right—not Gleason. The sheriff had broken the law and Darwin wondered how he should handle the situation.

Softening a little, Gleason scrambled for some sort of excuse. "Look. I was at home having a few drinks when I heard gunfire. I tried calling you on the radio but you were way up on Verde Vista Road dealing with Sammy again." He let out a chuckle in an attempt to lighten things up.

Stone-faced, Darwin looked down at him. He was not amused.

He ploughed on. "I decided to do some 'vestigatin' on my own. I parked here thinking that was where the shots were coming from." He tried to suppress a hiccup.

His deputy stepped away, repulsed by the smell. Breathing through his mouth, he tried to avoid the odour of sour whiskey and beer. "You did the wrong thing, Cornelius. Why did you bring booze with you?"

The sheriff stiffened. "I don't like your attitude. You better 'member who you're talkin' to!"

Darwin studied Gleason, annoyed with him. But, he was also upset that his plans for the evening hadn't worked out.

He hadn't been with a woman since his ex-wife. That was over a year ago. Stuck in Beaswick, the pickings in the small town for a decent girlfriend were slim. He had recently met Julie, a young Mexican with a to-die-for body, and had planned on paying her a visit that evening if he wasn't too busy. Well, that hadn't worked out. He *was* too busy. Old Sammy and the domestic dispute tied up the last part of his shift.

He was frustrated and now this—finding his boss drunk in a police car. "You head on home, Sheriff. We'll talk about it later." He wondered again why he was in the parking lot. There was no doubt to him that Gleason had been lying about the gunfire. *That's pure bullshit. Who was he waiting for?*

Gleason had his back up as he started the Challenger. He did not like the way Darwin was treating him. *I am not a criminal. I'm the sheriff for God's sake.*

He revved the souped up car close to its red line before shouting, "Screw you!" Gravel flew as he popped the clutch and fishtailed out of the empty lot.

Peppered by small rocks, Darwin turned his back, disgusted with the way his boss was acting.

The sound of squealing tires filled the night air as Sheriff Cornelius Gleason hit the pavement with the high-powered cruiser. Several residential lights came on as he raced down the normally quiet street.

The drunken bully has broken the law. Not only that, there's something funny going on. What was he doing out here at this time of night? Shaking his head, Darwin decided to write up a report on the incident when he returned to the office.

Chapter 23

Chicken blood covered Karl's hands as he led the way along the side of the old farmhouse. He couldn't wait to show Quincy what he had found. "You gotta to see this! We missed it the first time." Studying his partner in crime, Karl pointed and waited for his reaction.

Quincy took a good look, smiled and rubbed his hands together. Things were getting more interesting by the minute.

The house had cooled and the power was still off. The girls crawled under the blankets in Carla's bed to keep warm.

Rose glanced at the alarm clock as she swallowed more Tylenol. It was on battery back-up and, with each passing second, blinked its ghoulish-green display. It was after two in the morning.

Listening to the wind as it whipped through the trees, Rose recapped the day's events—how they had been shot at by the hunter and how she had been chased down Larry's driveway like an animal. Her right foot slammed hard on the phantom gas pedal as she relived trying to ram Mike's truck into oblivion.

Her mind echoed with the recent chanting by the goons. *Bitches! Bitches! Bitches!* The Tylenol was making her drowsy. She drifted. *Itches … Itches … Itches …*

Still too hyped to relax, Jennifer lay next to her and thought of years ago when she had visited her grandfather on his farm. He had several dozen chickens and had butchered one in front of her. It reminded her of what had happened to Angel.

She closed her eyes for several minutes before bolting up. Her hand flew to her chest. *Was that a squeak?* The sound came from downstairs. Facing Rose, she wondered if she had also heard it. No. Her friend had fallen into a fitful sleep.

Another squeak, sounding very much like rusty hinges, made her shiver. She began to pull the covers over her head but stopped. *No. I'm not going to hide anymore. It's time for me to be strong. It's time for me to take care of Rose for a change.*

Sitting on the edge of the bed, she rubbed her bare arms, full of questions. *Did the bullies break into the house? Are they downstairs?* Unable to remain still, she tiptoed to the bedroom door hoping that the sound had come from the upstairs bathroom. *Maybe that branch is still scratching on the outside wall. Maybe that's what I heard.*

Her stomach did flip-flops as she pressed her ear against a small crack in the old door. Holding her breath, she tried to slow her heart. All seemed quiet. Satisfied, she crept back toward Rose and safety, but froze midway. She heard it again. It was definitely a squeaky hinge. *It's coming from downstairs! Is it Aunt Carla? Did she sneak into the house?* Instinct told her to wake up Rose, but she had also made a personal pledge to take care of her friend.

Should I check it out? Should I open the bedroom door … just a little? I can do that on my own. I'll still have plenty of time if someone storms up the stairs.

Swallowing hard, she pulled the knife out of the wooden casing, not sure if what she was doing was the right thing. She gave herself a pep talk and pushed aside the chair that was jammed against the door handle. *It's time to be strong. I will not cower anymore.* Glancing over her shoulder, Rose fussed behind her with closed eyes.

With knife in hand, she pressed her ear against the crack in the door. All was quiet. Almost spellbound, she reached out for the old brass knob and slowly twisted it. The door opened a fraction. Her ears were on high alert as she peeked out, barely seeing the dark staircase several feet in front of her.

Afraid to move, she waited for another squeak so that she could pinpoint where the sound was coming from. There was none. Except for the wind, the house was deathly quiet.

Maybe … maybe I'm just imagining things. She swallowed hard before opening the door a few more inches and poking her head out. Everything seemed fine.

Opening it wider, she heard it again. It definitely came from downstairs.

With the butcher's knife held out in front of her, she crept to the top of the stairs. Peering through the shadows, she wondered if Carla had made the noise, but there was no sign of her aunt. There was no sign of anyone.

Another long, mournful groan filled the cold house, sounding as if the hinge was in terrible pain. Shivers shot up her back as she listened to the tortured metal.

It's coming from the downstairs hallway between the living room and kitchen. Is it the basement door?

Breathing hard, she rubbed her tattoo for comfort. *Peace. Love. Happiness.* She tried to yell out in a commanding voice. "Who's …? Who's down there?" It wasn't working for her. Her voice was feeble and the dark house swallowed up her question.

Rose moaned in her Tylenol induced sleep behind her. Jen turned and studied her friend through the open bedroom door. She was bathed in moonlight and didn't look at all like the tough, red headed, psycho that the creeps had called her only a few hours earlier. *Now she looks like an innocent little girl—a Raggedy Ann doll.*

Goose bumps crawled up her arms as she faced the dark stairs and living room below. *What if they're in the house?* The thought made her grip the knife even tighter, knowing that she was playing a very dangerous game.

Taking a step down the stairs, she called out in a quivering voice, "Auntie? Is that you?"

No answer.

Curious, she took another step. One hand was on the banister and the other clutched the knife. She still couldn't see much of anything.

Unsure of how far she should go, she glanced over her shoulder at Rose and gauged the distance. If she took one more step she might be *too* far from safety. She decided to sit so that she could get a better view.

Panning the living room through the banister spindles, she still couldn't see anything except shadows.

Waves of fear swept through her, overtaking her curiosity. *This is crazy. Carla's not there. I'm asking for trouble. What if they're waiting for me at the bottom of the stairs? No, it's time to get back to Rose—back to safety and the warm bed. This is getting too creepy.*

She stood and was about to turn back when she caught a glimpse of something hurling toward her from the living room. Raising her left shoulder as a shield, it slammed into her bare upper arm, making a wet smacking sound.

Jen winced as she dropped the knife and grabbed her bicep. Stunned, she peeled her fingers away. Blood covered most of her tattoo. *Wha-at?* She shook her head. *Why am I ... bleeding?* Things began to spin. *Was I stabbed? Why don't I feel pain?* Looking down at her feet, she screamed.

Rose bolted out of bed and hobbled to the hallway. Disorientated, she looked down the stairs at her friend. Jen was rubbing her arm. Drowsy from the Tylenol, she croaked, "Are ... are you okay?"

Jennifer couldn't speak. The blood on her arm wasn't hers. It was from Angel's severed head that lay next to her bare feet.

Gripping the banister for support, Rose tried again. "Jen? Jen! What? What is it?"

She turned to her groggy friend with disgust and fury. "Those motherfuckers. Those sick motherfuckers!"

Adrenaline flushed through Rose's system. She took three quick steps down the stairs and grabbed Jen by the hand. They needed to get to safety. Whoever was responsible for this grotesque act would attack them at any moment.

Moving as fast as she dared, she roughly jerked her friend up the stairs. Pain shot through her ankle. Rose ignored it. They had to get back to safety.

Jen had difficulty finding her feet as they scrambled into the bedroom. Rose slammed the old door and shoved a chair against the handle. Out of breath, she gasped, "Where is it—the knife?"

She wasn't listening. Her hand was covered with Angel's sticky blood and her mind was on the head that had been next to her bare feet.

"Where is it? The knife? We need to secure the—"

"They're inside! They're inside the house, Rose. One of them is in the living room!"

The bedroom door handle quietly turned. They were unaware. It turned again, in the opposite direction and this time, made a rattling sound. They stared at the brass knob as it menacingly twisted one way and then the other. Rose couldn't help but think of a coiled rattlesnake, ready to strike. They shuffled farther into the bedroom.

The gravity of their situation was quickly sinking in. There was nothing to prevent the punks from breaking in except for the chair that was wedged against the door. They no longer had the knife to defend themselves with. Jennifer had dropped it on the stairs.

They moved to the window to distance themselves from the scum. Tightly holding each other, they eyes were fixated on the handle as the old knob continued to turn one way and then the other. It took on a life of its own and now sounded like razor-sharp, metal teeth snapping at them.

Jen put a hand to her chest, unaware of the imprint that she was leaving from the chicken blood on her white blouse. *They're going to bust in at any moment.*

The handle stopped its crazy turning.

What are they doing? Why aren't they storming in? Are they playing with us? That's what they're—

Fists pounded on the thin door and the familiar chant started up again. "Bitches! Bitches! Bitches!"

Jennifer closed her eyes, wishing that she was in another galaxy, millions of light years away. Her hands flew to her ears to block out the ungodly sounds. In her terror, she had again forgotten about her blood-covered hand. Some of it streaked her hair and cheek.

Rose said a silent prayer, unable to pull her eyes from the vibrating door. It strained from the beating and a new crack appeared in one of its ancient panels. It was clear that it wouldn't hold out much longer.

The pounding and chanting continued as the animated handle crazily rattled.

They were trapped. There was no escape from the animals. Rose spun around and faced the window. She struggled to open it hoping that they could jump out if the thugs broke in. It didn't matter to her that they were on the second floor. She was more than willing to risk breaking a leg or arm as long as they could get away from the creeps.

It opened only a little and allowed in a blast of frigid air. The curtains slapped at her face, making her hair fly in all directions. Close to hysterics, she scanned the room for anything to break the glass with. The pounding on the door behind her was incessant and made it difficult to think.

Rose had been in a house fire when she was younger—trapped in an upstairs bedroom that had been engulfed in smoke. This was far more frightening. Back then she knew that help was on the way. Not now. There would be no rescue party coming to save them. They were on their own and would soon be ripped apart.

She grabbed a bedside lamp and was about to smash the window when the hammering stopped. Except for the flapping curtains, silence filled the dark room. She faced the door as she gripped her friend's bloody hand, waiting and fearing the worst.

Moments passed. She turned back to the window. *Please, Carla. Where are you? Oh God, Please! We need you!* Scanning the surrounding bush, she prayed that their friend would magically come to their rescue.

Movement directly below caught her eye. The meth freaks were leaving the house through the basement door.

Of course! There's an old trap door that leads to the basement. The wood is probably rotten and covered in weeds. They must have pulled it free.

"Rose. Duh-duh-do you see any-thu-thu-thing?" Jen was having trouble speaking. Her eyes were vacant and her nose was running. A strand of mucous clung to her chin and Angel's blood was smeared in her hair. With a bloody handprint on her white blouse, she looked a mess and appeared comatose.

Between sobs, her friend tried to answer. "They're … they're out of the house. They're standing by the truck. They … broke in through the basement."

Rose covered her face in despair. What she and her friend were being put through was too much for her. The goons had violated their home. They had violated her and Jen. "No. No. No!" With a face covered in tears, Rose wailed it out. The thugs had finally pushed her over the edge.

Jennifer had never seen that side of her. Rose used to be a pillar of strength—a fighter. Not anymore. Now her friend was breaking down in front of her. The horde had managed to snap her spirit and crush her very soul. She needed help.

Jen stared at her back. Rose was on her knees in front of the window, shuddering.

Rage began to replace Jen's fear and weakness. She was angry with the way she had cowered all evening. She was angry with Carla for not being there to help. But, most of all, she was angry with the goons. *It's time for me to take charge!*

III

Absorbed with confronting the meth freaks, Jennifer was no longer a frightened woman. Now she was determined to fight back. What they were doing to her and her friend was despicable to her. She shoved the chair aside that had been blocking the bedroom door and stormed down the stairs. Sidestepping Angel's severed head, she made her way into the kitchen.

It took Rose a few moments to realize that her friend had left the bedroom. Struggling to her feet, she hobbled after her. *What is she thinking?* In a weak voice she croaked, "Jen! Stop. Come back."

She wasn't having any of it. Intent on facing her enemy head-on, she unlocked the kitchen door and stomped out.

Two of them were on the porch, caught off guard.

"How could you? You killed Angel just for fun! You broke into our house! You … you … sleazed-out cockroaches!" She jabbed a finger at them.

Quincy and Sal stepped back, surprised with the outburst and also with her bloody appearance. It looked like she had been in a war zone.

Now far beyond fear, she lunged at the bald thug. He jerked away, putting out his hands in defence. Jen didn't let up. She pounded on his chest screaming, "You sick bastard! You sick bastard!"

Rose clung to the banister for support, hearing her friend yell at the thugs. *I've got to bring her back into the house. They'll kill her!* She limped out the kitchen door.

Jen was on the porch and attacking the bigger freak. Sal stood next to him. Rose had hoped that she could pull her back to safety. Now it was too late. There was no safety.

Having had enough of Jen's angry outburst, Quincy grabbed her fists. Rose tried pushing the big oaf from her friend. Sal jumped into action and roughly shoved her aside.

They dragged Jennifer into the dark kitchen as she struggled to get free. Rose followed, screaming for them to leave her friend alone.

Karl and Mike appeared out of nowhere. Karl grabbed Rose from behind and seized her hands. She tried to escape from his grip as he dragged her to a kitchen chair.

Mike rifled through drawers, searching for anything to tie the girls with. His eyes lit up as he pulled out a roll of duct tape.

Dropping to his knees on the cold linoleum floor, he planned on wrapping Rose's legs to the chair. She had other plans. Her injured ankle landed a blow to his face. They both grunted out in pain.

Furious, he made a second attempt. This time it worked. Overwhelmed, she knew that the situation was hopeless.

Mike strapped her upper body and hands to the chair as Karl held her down. Sal and Quincy did the same with Jennifer. The girls couldn't move. Both were tightly bound with tape.

Quincy slammed the door and lit the kerosene lamp, studying the women in the yellowish light.

Rose was unaware that her nose had started to bleed again. Her focus was on Mike. She tried to talk some sense into him. "I'm your friend. What are you doing?"

"Shaw-shaw-shut up, beh-beh-bitch!" He didn't want anything to do with her—incensed that she had destroyed his truck and had kicked him in the face.

"But, Mike. Do you know what you're doing? You'll go to jail—all four of you."

No one listened or cared.

She tried again. "You can stop it. I give you my word. I won't say a thing. I won't call the cops."

Karl snickered and sarcastically repeated what she said. "You give us your word? That you won't call the cops? You sure as hell *won't* call the cops! Not if you know what's good for you. *We* should be the ones calling the cops. Not you! Look what you done to me!" He lifted his pant and shoved his knee inches from her face. "We were attacked by *you*, you psycho bitch." He waited for her to say something—anything. Karl was looking for any excuse to hit her.

Rose closed her eyes, repulsed. She did not want to stare down the animal. The last thing that she wanted was to antagonize him.

Karl had been waiting for this moment. He glared at his partners, daring them to tell him to cool it. They looked away.

He turned to Jennifer—his face inches from hers. She noticed blood on his hands. Angel's blood! Her eyes filled with hate.

The kerosene lamp gave Carla a clear view of one punk through the large kitchen side window a hundred feet from her. He hovered in front of her niece who was strapped to a chair. *Is that blood in her hair? It looks like blood all over her!*

Swallowing hard, she raised the rifle and trained it on him. *What's his name? Karl? Yes, that's it. His bald buddy called him that when they were walking up Larry's driveway earlier. Guess what, Karl. I'm going to blow your fuckin' legs out!*

Forcing herself to remain calm, she tried to take careful aim, but he moved closer to her niece, making her lower the heavy rifle. Her anger was coming out in waves. *They're the ones who started this. We're the victims. We didn't want any of this to happen. It's because of them. They've got my friends tied up in our kitchen and my niece is covered in blood! That is bullshit.*

As if on cue, he moved out of her field of view. The guy with the shaved head took his place.

Carla pulled in a deep breath, now on a mission. Earlier she had made a pledge that, if the thugs ever set foot in their house, she would shoot them. Zeroing in on Quincy, she was more than ready to blow out one of his legs.

She had a clear shot. *That's it for you, motherfucker. Don't move. Just stay where you are.* Her finger slowly pulled back on the trigger just as her target moved out of her line of sight. *Shit!*

Carla worried about what would happen if she actually did shoot one of them. *It would be in self-defence. The law clearly states that I have every right in protecting myself and my home.*

The problem of course was that they would all go down. She and her friends would end up in jail for growing pot. The punks would do time for trespassing and theft and God only knew what else. Still, she couldn't just sit there. They were forcing her to shoot them.

She wondered if she should fire a warning shot. Would that stop them? Carla wasn't sure. They were very stoned and aggressive. If anything, it would give away her position and her advantage—surprise. Then, they might use Rose and Jen as hostages and torture them if she didn't give herself up. She swallowed hard.

Chapter 2

Rose gave up trying to reason with Mike. He wouldn't listen to her. Instead, she raised her voice for all of them to hear. "You're getting yourselves into some very serious trouble."

They all snickered—except for Quincy. He felt uncomfortable. Picking up the lantern, he held it near her face for a closer look.

She does look like my aunt. She even sounds like her, especially the way she's telling us that we're getting into trouble. He wanted to tell her to shut up but had difficulty doing that.

Rose stared back accusingly at him. He turned away, feeling awkward and somewhat ashamed. Mike noticed his reaction and wondered what was going on. Sal and Karl were too busy with Jennifer.

"You jerks!" Her chest heaved as she yelled it out. Wriggling in her chair, her face and blouse were matted in blood.

Rose was surprised with her friend—the inner strength that she was showing. *Just don't go too far with them. We don't know what they're capable of doing.*

Jen kept at it, targeting Karl. "Who do you think you are? Look at you. You're pathetic—killing a poor chicken and then smearing her blood on our window? You've got her blood all over your hands! And then," she shook her head, "having the nerve to break into our house and terrorize two defenceless *women*! You weak piece of shit!" She bristled with anger as she spat at him.

Karl brought up a fist, eager to hit her. Quincy grabbed his arm, stopping him.

Caught off guard, he yelled, "What are you doing? Get your hand off me." Karl yanked his arm free.

"Just cool it. Don't let her get to you." Quincy was trying to diffuse the situation as he struggled with how much Rose looked like his aunt. *The resemblance to Aunt Sylvia is … freaky! My aunt is Scottish with fiery red hair and blue eyes, just like—*

Karl turned back to Jennifer. He did not like the way that she was talking to him. He didn't like her attitude and he didn't like Quincy's, either.

Stepping closer, he had a better look at the defenceless woman bound to a chair in front of him. She had on a sleeveless, white blouse. The two top buttons had come undone revealing a hint of cleavage.

She's one hot little tamale. He wouldn't mind showing her who the boss was. Her nose stud and tattoo turned him on. He wondered what the Japanese characters meant and was becoming aroused.

Rose wriggled in her chair, trying to get free. It was hopeless. The duct tape held fast. She turned her attention on the bigger guy, feeling a strange connection between them. "Look, Quincy." She met his eyes. "This is going too far. You're going to be arrested. The sheriff is my brother-in-law."

He paled, turning as white as a paper plate. *Did we make a big mistake?* His mind reeled.

Mike piped up when he saw the look of concern on his face. "Tha-tha-that's not true. Tha-that's not true!" He shook his finger at her. "Sh-sh-she used to be his sister-in-law, but not any-moe-moe-more."

Quincy felt slightly relieved and tried to get back some composure. "Really? Tell me more."

"Sh-she was married to his bra-bra-brother, Buh-Buh-Buh—" Finally he spat out the name, saying, "Bernie." Gulping in a much needed breath he explained through his stuttering how Bernie had left her for another woman.

"How close are they? How close is the sheriff to her?" Quincy was still concerned and wondered what kind of a relationship they really had. Did they even have a relationship?

"Sh-she never see-sees him. The sh-sh-sheriff *never* comes here."

"That's not true!" Her hair wildly flew as she shook her head, denying what Mike was telling him. "Don't believe him. The sheriff and I are very close. He visits me … all the time."

Quincy had questions. "Uh-huh? So, he's in on the grow-op then, right? I mean, he must know you're growing pot. Right?" This was all getting very interesting to him. If she was lying about Gleason seeing her then Quincy and his buddies would have nothing to worry about. But, if she was telling the truth, then he and his gang could be in some very serious trouble.

He turned to Mike. "Think real hard. Is she close to him?"

"No. He's never beh-been here." He wagged his head. "Never!"

"How do you know for sure?" Quincy stepped closer, making Mike squirm.

"'Cause Larry nuh-knows. He was seein' her for awhile. He's in love." He kept thinking of how stupid his old man was. "She hasn't seen nobody 'cept for Lar-Lar-Larry. Besides, we can hear when a car drives up the road. Especially his. It's a high pow-pow-powered muscle car. The share-share-sheriff never comes here. We would a heard."

Quincy believed him. They all did. The sheriff would not want to get directly involved with her grow-op.

"He doesn't know *who* I sleep with!" Hatred flashed in her eyes as she tried to stand, forgetting that she was taped to a chair. "The sheriff and I are friends. We ..." She trailed off, knowing that she might have gone too far.

"Uh-huh? Sure you are. He visits you all the time, right? And then, what? Does he do the *two* of you?" Quincy turned to Jen as he said it, clearly enjoying their predicament.

"No. Really! We see each other. He'll make sure you all go to jail. We're ... in love." She felt sick with what she was saying. The mere thought of being in love with Gleason made her skin crawl.

"Yeah. Whatever." He knew that she was lying. What Mike was saying made far more sense than what she was trying to tell him.

Dismissing her, he lit the meth pipe and took in a huge lungful. Passing it around to his fellow goons, they all took a hit before it sputtered out. He dug into his pocket for more, realizing that their supply had run out. *Shit!* They hadn't planned on being gone for most of the night and now they were out of meth.

He grabbed a cloth from the kitchen sink and jabbed it in his pants, dabbing at his cuts and gouges. Both the pain and the lack of meth were making his temper rise. *We didn't deserve to be rammed like that, and*—he flinched as he plucked out another small, jagged stone—*she tried to kill me, throwing me off her truck the way she did.*

Rose dropped her head, not wanting to look at the disgusting creature in front of her who was picking at his rear. She had hoped to scare them off by telling them that the sheriff was her boyfriend. It was her ace in the hole and it hadn't worked.

Jen stared defiantly at Karl. He held her gaze and wolfishly grinned back. Curious, he pointed to her upper arm. "What does that mean? Uh, you know? Your tattoo. The stuff that's written on your arm. What does it mean?"

She gave him a sick smile. "It's a secret."

"You can tell me."

"It's three wise, Japanese words."

He stepped closer as she continued with her explanation. "It's an ancient proverb. It means …"

Leaning into her in anticipation and also to have a closer look at her cleavage, he eagerly whispered, "Yeah?"

"It means …"

He was inches from her, surprised that she was willing to share her secret with him, when she screamed out, "FUCK YOU, ASSHOLE!"

Karl jerked back, his curiosity turning to rage. Raising his hand, he brought it down hard across her face.

She recoiled from the blow. Hot tears streamed down her burning cheek as she glared up at him.

He felt stupid with the way that she had duped him and turned to his buddies, waiting for them to say something.

Quincy's blood pressure soared. The vein at his temple grew tenfold. He had a mix of feelings. *God damn her. She was asking for it, but he better not go too far. If he hits her again I'm gonna step in before it gets out of control.*

Taking in a few breaths to cool down, Karl decided to try something different. *That little bitch needs to be taught a hard lesson.* Her face was flushed and another one of her buttons had come undone. She turned him on.

Reaching out, he trailed his hand down her neck to her shoulder.

She winced from his touch, feeling disgusted. Hating to look at him, she dropped her head and stared at the floor.

Sal was behind her and grabbed her hair, roughly yanking her head up. "Take your medicine, little girl. You've been asking for it!"

Karl kept at it, loving the way that he was making her squirm. *I'll show you a thing or two, you little whore!* His fingers slowly slid across her chest, smearing more of Angel's gelled blood on her white blouse.

With an outstretched hand now firmly planted on one of her heaving breasts, he waited for her reaction. There was none. Disappointed that she was ignoring his groping, he wagged a finger in her face. "Let me tell you how it's gonna be from—"

She lunged forward, sinking her teeth into the soft tissue of his pointed finger. Both Sal and Karl were caught off guard as she gripped him like a junkyard dog.

He squealed, sounding like a stuck pig, before pulling free. Staring at his finger in disbelief, he raised a fist, screaming, "You dirty bitch! I'm gonna pound you senseless for what—"

Quincy was there in a flash and grabbed him. "Don't hit—"

"Let go of me. She bit me. Whose side are you on?" He was in the bigger man's face as he yelled it out. "Let me hit her, damn you!"

"You're not gonna hit nobody! She's going to co-operate." Quincy stood between Karl and Jennifer. In a threatening voice and racing heart, he repeated, "Believe me. She's gonna co-operate."

Chapter 3

Quincy pointed menacingly at Jen—making sure that his finger was a safe distance from her sharp teeth. "You see how this can get carried away? You see?" He swung around and faced Rose to make sure that she was also listening.

"I can't keep control much longer. These guys are ready to do some serious damage—to *both* of you! I'm only one man here. I'm trying my best to keep things cool, but it's up to you two."

Jen smirked through hot tears, no longer intimidated.

He shouted out a warning to her. "You can't get us all excited and worked up with your bad attitude or there'll be big trouble!"

Karl agreed with his bully friend as he squeezed his finger to stop the bleeding. "Fuckin' rights!"

Quincy tried to relax and not let the situation get out of hand. He forced a patronizing smile at Jen, hoping that she had gotten his message loud and clear. "Right, sweetie?"

"Screw you!"

Sal grabbed her hair and gave it a hard yank, tired of her attitude. "Listen to what he's saying!"

Rose tried to do damage control. "What do you want? If it's money, we have none."

Quincy turned to her, his face darkening. "Bad answer, lady. That is *not* what we want to hear."

Mike took Sal's lead and grabbed Rose's hair, jerking her head back.

"Please. Mike. Don't!" Her back ached from being strapped in the chair and now pain shot up her neck from Mike yanking her.

Quincy wondered how he could crack his Aunt Sylvia so that they could get at her money. He stopped that train of thought and realized that he was confused. *She is* not *my aunt!*

Karl focused on Jen's blood streaked face and blouse. He studied her cleavage. Four of her buttons were undone and five angry finger marks from the recent slap stood out high on her cheek. The top of her lace bra was in full view and he liked what he saw.

From a hundred feet away, Carla had a clear view of her niece. She could only see a portion of Rose and the creep with the shaved head. He was at the kitchen counter. The other two were standing in front and behind Jennifer. The one in the front was clearly the more threatening.

She checked again to make sure that the safety was off. *If he lays a hand on her again, I'll shoot. I swear. I'll shoot!*

Her aim was on the left foot of the thug that stood in front of her niece. She was more than ready to pull the trigger, but it was all up to Karl—her target. If he laid a hand on Jen one more time, she promised herself that she would do it. Then it would be over. The girls would notify the ambulance and police. Everyone would go to jail.

Mike jerked Rose's head by her hair again, imitating his new buddy, Sal.

"Mike. Please. You don't need to do that."

He gave it another hard yank. "Doe-doe-don't you be tellin' me what to—"

"Let go of her hair!" Quincy growled out the command.

"Buh-buh—"

"I said let go of her hair!"

Embarrassed and angry, he slowly released his grip. Quincy had slapped his face earlier and now he was yelling at him in front of everybody? *That is bullshit!*

Quincy ignored him and directed his attention on Rose. "You'll be good. Right, Sylvia?"

"What?" She shook her head, puzzled. "My … my name is Rose. Not Sylvia."

"Uh, yeah. I, uh … know. It's just that you, uh, look like a Sylvia to me."

She wondered what he was thinking. He looked very stoned.

Realizing his mistake, he tried to cover up by changing the subject. "I'm hungry." Quickly heading toward the fridge, he felt foolish with what he had called her. *Careful what you say. She's nothing like my aunt. Just remember that!*

The smell of homemade buns filled the air as he opened the dark fridge, reminding him very much of Aunt Sylvia's kitchen. He pulled them out along with left-over roast beef and Jen's birthday cake.

Karl was not interested in food. "Sal! Hold her by her hair real tight. I'm gonna have a little more fun with that bitch." Cautiously, he leaned closer to Jen.

Raising her pant leg, he caressed her exposed calf with his bloody hand. She squirmed, disgusted with what he was doing. Jen tried to kick out, but couldn't. Her legs were securely strapped to the chair. Hating him and what he was doing to her, she yelled, "You piece of dog shit!"

Karl straightened up and smiled his toothless grin before pulling his cap down tighter over his greasy hair. He was very much enjoying her reaction.

Quincy decided to put a stop to it. He needed to take command. "Karl!"

"Huh?" Raising his eyebrows, he wondered what his skin headed friend wanted.

"Go wash your hands." Turning to Sal with a pointed finger, Quincy snapped out, "You!"

Sal was all ears. "Yeah?"

"Go check out the rest of the house. See what you can find." He swung around to Mike. "And, you!"

Jumping to attention, he wondered what kind of important assignment he would be given.

"Make me some sandwiches!"

"Wha-wha-what?" He couldn't believe his ears.

Quincy had zero tolerance for the kid. "Do it! Get the mayo and mustard out of the fridge."

Mike shook his head. He'd be damned if he would make his so-called buddy a sandwich. Quincy was beginning to sound a lot like his old man to him. *I'm part of the team. Not his stupid maid!* "Bhu-bhu-but, I can check the place out with Sa-Sa—"

"I said get me some mayo and mustard. Now!" With little patience, he stormed up to him, frustrated with the way things were turning out. The childhood rhyme filled his head once again. *Pop goes the weasel. Pop goes the god damned weasel!* He raised a fist. *Yeah, I'll pop that weasel alright! Right between his eyes.*

Mike was frightened by the bigger man. Quincy had a crazed look in his eyes and was ready to snap. Deciding that he had better do what he was told, he reluctantly went to the fridge while planning on how he could get even.

Karl was in the bathroom washing away both the chicken blood and his blood. He studied the bite mark on his finger. *That hot little bitch! I got plans for her.*

Dabbing at his knee, he thought back to how he and Quincy had been thrown from that red head's truck. Mike had also been thrown but that didn't enter his mind. He was furious with her and wanted payback.

There was something else. He had been aroused with the small amount of blood that had been on Jennifer's lip after she had bit him. It was his blood and that somehow made him excited.

Quincy grabbed a large knife and sliced the roast beef at the counter while trying to reason with the two women behind him. "All we want is five hundred dollars. It's money that Mikie owes us. He screwed up."

Mike knew enough to keep his mouth shut. He was getting used to the idea of being blamed for everything. Feeling very much like Quincy's slave, he opened the mayonnaise and mustard.

Quincy pushed on with his attempt at negotiating. "You're Larry's friend. *You* pay us!" Hesitating for a moment, he added, "Plus, of course, the five thousand for damages to Mikie's truck." He hacked out a huge chunk of Jen's birthday cake as he tried to bargain with them. Taking a large mouthful, he mumbled, "And, my gold chain that you stole."

Rose ignored what he was saying and, instead, hoped that there might be a connection between them. *He thinks I look like Sylvia. Who the hell is Sylvia?* She wondered if she could use that to her advantage.

Knife in hand, he moved away from the counter and waved it in their faces, wanting to convince the women that the best thing that they could do was co-operate. He had no intention of threatening them. To him, the knife was merely an object being used to make his point—nothing more.

Carla saw it differently. She was in hyper-aware mode. The big thug was brandishing a butcher's knife in front of her niece and friend. Chills swept through her as she looked closer. There was more blood smeared on Jen's white blouse.

That's it! They must have cut her with the knife. They're fucking dead meat! She had a clear shot and was about to pull the trigger when the bald creep stepped away, back to the kitchen counter. *Shit!* She lowered the rifle.

"No. Don't mix the two together. I want my mayo on one half of the bun and the mustard on the other." He roughly shoved Mike aside. "Who makes the sandwiches in your house? Your poor daddy?"

Mike felt foolish. He didn't like being given orders. Quincy was taunting him and making fun. He fantasized about slipping rat poison in the sandwich.

Karl rummaged through drawers in the living room, looking for anything of value, but had trouble paying attention to what he was doing. He couldn't pull his mind from Jennifer and her lace bra.

Sal was upstairs checking out the bedrooms. It hadn't occurred to him that there might be *three* people living in the farmhouse rather than two. The closets were filled with women's clothing. He hadn't noticed that one of them held larger sized blouses and jeans.

Carla could only see a portion of Quincy's foot from her position on the knoll. Aiming carefully, she wondered how accurate the rifle really was. *What if the bullet deflects once it blasts through the window? It could go off target and kill him, or Rose.* She swallowed hard. *Or Jennifer!*

"Okay, girls." He was talking with his mouth full. "We need to figure out what to do. I'm telling you this while my buddies are out of the kitchen. They both have a short fuse. I don't think I'll be able to hold them off much longer. They want to do some serious damage to both of you." He tore free another bite from his sandwich. Mayonnaise clung to the corner of his mouth.

Jen was repulsed with the way he was eating. She was repulsed with everything about him. "You know what, you fat bastard? We're going to hunt you down. Don't think you're going to get away with this."

Rose jumped in and tried to negotiate. "What if I give you the five hundred dollars … tomorrow?"

He spat out a mixture of roast beef and bun as he shook his head. "Do you think I'm *that* stupid? Come on, lady. I wasn't born yesterday!"

Karl barged into the kitchen with Sal trailing behind. There was nothing of value in the house. He was fed up and wanted money. They *all* wanted money. Glaring at Quincy, he shook his head in disgust. His partner was at the table with a bottle of beer and cramming food into his mouth. *This is not a fuckin' picnic that we're on!*

In his mind, his fat, skin headed buddy was being far too patient with the women. *What's he doin'? This is pure bullshit! They owe us money and they owe it to us, now! We can't hang out here all friggin' night!* Karl was ready to do some serious damage to them.

Quincy wasn't paying attention to his incensed partner. His mind was on the homemade bread and roast beef. He took another huge bite.

Carla felt slightly relieved. It seemed that the situation had diffused itself a little. The one guy was eating. She figured that might be a good thing. Their minds were on food and not on her niece and friend.

She hoped that the snack might straighten them out. Maybe then they would head home. Glancing at her watch, she was surprised with the time. It was close to five in the morning.

Chapter 4

Rose wanted to believe that she could work out some kind of deal with them but knew that it was hopeless. She couldn't give them money. If she did, they would be back for more, again and again. "I guess you'll have to beat us up because we have no money. What are you going to use, the baseball bat? You're pretty good at that, aren't you?"

Karl stomped up to her. "Shut up, bitch. Just … shut up!"

It wasn't working for him anymore. She was no longer intimidated and was getting some of her strength back, partly because of Jen's attitude. Rose glared at his toothless face and shook her head defiantly.

Quincy turned to Karl and indicated with his head to meet him in the living room. They all knew that this couldn't continue. Something had to give. The girls were no longer frightened by them. It wasn't supposed to be that way. They should have had their money by now.

"It's time we hit them two bitches. I've had enough of this shit. We've screwed around all night and for what? A few thousand, that's for what!" Karl snarled it out as he squeezed his bitten finger.

Standing near the front door, Quincy tried to keep his voice down. "Yeah, yeah. I know, but we won't hurt 'em." He pulled out the meth pipe for another hit.

"Screw you! I saw you filling your face and drinking beer. What are you doin'? You're sending them the wrong message. They need to be shaken up and they need it, *now*!"

Quincy kept trying to light the pipe, forgetting that they had run out of meth earlier. Frustrated with the way things were going, he spun around and snapped, "Don't tell me that I'm playing this wrong. You're not going to beat them. You're just gonna scare them a little. That's all. Maybe break a chair with the bat. Nothing more! Do—you—hear—me?"

"I think you like 'em. That's what I think. I think you're goin' soft." He pointed a finger at Quincy, taunting him. "I saw the way you looked at that redheaded one. You think she looks like your aunt." He said it accusingly.

Quincy didn't know what to say. Karl was right. He was starting to warm up to her and had trouble hiding his feelings. Defensively he mumbled, "We'll scare them with the bat. Nothin' more."

He shook his head. "No. That's bullshit. They need a—"

Quincy jerked him close until their faces were inches apart. "Do you hear what I'm sayin'? Nothin' more! We'll just scare 'em."

He shook free from Quincy's hold. They glared at one another for several moments. Neither said a word before Karl finally turned and charged back into the kitchen.

Rose and Jennifer could feel the mood change as he stormed in. Quincy followed, worried with what his partner might do. Rose noticed how Karl wouldn't meet his eyes when Quincy stared at him. She felt the tension between them. The whole demented scene was escalating once more.

He tore out another bite from his sandwich and tried to calm down. Scowling, Quincy swallowed the mouthful of food. The wind had died and now the kitchen was deathly quiet. The only sound was from his agitated foot tapping on the linoleum floor.

He looked troubled and Rose had a very bad feeling. *This is it. They're going to do something stupid. I know it.*

Shoving his sandwich aside, he was no longer hungry. *God damn them!* He shook his finger in their direction. "I'm giving you one last chance. Where—is—the—money?"

The three hoods waited for an answer. There was none.

Fed up with the whole scenario, Quincy barked, "Karl!"

"Yeah?"

Quincy glared at Jen and then at Rose while thinking. *This is their last chance. I've had enough of this shit.*

The women stared back, full of hate and disgust.

With an angry face he snarled, "Get the bat!"

That was exactly what Karl wanted to hear. He was out the back door in a flash, marching toward Mike's truck with a smirk on his face.

Carla had been drifting to sleep when she heard the kitchen door slam. She swung the rifle toward the sound. Only part of Mike's truck was visible—the driver's side. She couldn't see Karl as he reached through the broken passenger window for the bat.

"Is that what you do to Sylvia?" Rose needed to connect with Quincy and stop where this was going. There was no doubt that they had reached their limit, ready to beat her and Jen. Why wouldn't they? They had eagerly done it to poor Larry.

He was taken off guard and didn't know how to respond.

She kept at it, hoping to ease the tension. "Tell me about her. You said that I look like her. Who is she?" *We might have a better chance of getting through this if I relate with him.* "Do you hit her with a baseball bat, too?"

He recoiled, insulted by her question. "Of course not!"

Rose waited for him to say more. He did. Softening a little, he explained. "I would never hurt her."

Okay. So Sylvia is either his mother, his sister or his girlfriend. "So, who is she? Who is this Syl—?"

He exploded with her probing. "Shut up! Just … shut up!" Clenching his fists, he kicked at her chair. *Pop goes the weasel. Pop goes the weasel! Pop goes the god damn weasel!*

Rose had struck a nerve. She knew that she was playing a dangerous game in provoking him. This 'Sylvia' was off limits. Quincy was fiercely protective of her.

He turned away and faced the kitchen cabinets, understanding that he was losing control of his emotions. *She knows how I feel about my aunt. Just don't listen to her.*

Jen sat defiant and was inspired by her friend—the spirit she exhibited and the fight that she had within. Seeing how vulnerable Quincy was, she picked up where Rose had left off. "This Sylvia, whoever she is, will find out. I'm going to make sure that she does. I'll track her down and tell her … *everything!*"

He gave Sal a weak smile, pretending that what Jennifer was saying didn't bother him.

Sal awkwardly smiled back and wondered why his friend was behaving so strangely. *What's with him and this 'Sylvia' shit?*

Rose had asked about his aunt and he had been surprised with his reaction. Having Rose mention her name made him feel guilty and ashamed. He knew that his aunt would be mortified that her nephew had sunk to such a new low if she were here right now. Beads of sweat rolled down his shaved head.

Could she do that? Could she track Aunt Sylvia down and tell her what we've done? Naw. There's no way. Don't worry about it. Don't let them get under your skin.

Despite his pep talk to himself, he *was* worried. *Maybe we've gone too far this time. It's one thing to beat up some bastard for his money.* He caught himself. *Larry's not a bastard. It's his son who's the bastard. But, it's a different thing when we hold two women hostage and terrorize them all night.*

He continued with his mental rambling and tried to justify what he and his accomplices were doing. *But, they deserved it. They tried to run us down. They tried to kill us! We had to do what we did because ...* Confused, he was having trouble understanding the difference between right and wrong.

Karl stomped in with the bat, ready to do some serious damage.

Worried that things could get too carried away, Quincy made a decision. *If we don't get their money after we scare them a little then, it's over. We'll leave. We will not hurt them!*

Jen's accusing stare was unnerving to him. Her piercing eyes made Quincy fidget. His hands trembled as he reached into the fridge for another bottle of beer. *Jeeze. You're acting stupid! Be cool and don't let them get to you.*

He tried to remain calm. "Okay, girls. Have it your way." Now he was behind them so that he wouldn't have to face the women. "If that's what you want for a lousy five thousand bucks then, that's what you'll get." He hoped that they would finally cave in and end the whole affair.

A twisted smile covered Karl's face. It exposed his missing teeth as he towered over the two helpless women while patting the bat.

Jennifer wickedly smiled back, challenging him. "Come on, you motherfucker! Give it to me."

Quincy stepped closer to Karl while glaring at Jen. *God damn, you little bitch. Don't be saying things like that to him.* He understood that his partner was unpredictable. If he swung the bat at her, Quincy knew that he would need to step in and stop him. Karl was only supposed to scare them a little. Nothing more.

Instead, he surprised all of them by dropping the bat to the floor. Karl had other plans. He rubbed Jen's shoulder, mindful of her sharp teeth.

She squirmed, hating his touch.

He kept at it as everyone looked on, wondering what he was thinking. Tiring of the game, he grabbed her blouse. Buttons flew as he ripped it open.

She tried lunging at him, screaming, "You pig!" The duct tape held fast.

Karl stepped back, worried that she could bite him again. Still smiling, he hungrily took in the view. Her breasts heaved with her rapid breathing and he liked what he saw.

Quincy wasn't sure how far he should let things go. *Maybe Karl can persuade them bitches with a little bit of touching.* He caught himself. If Karl *ever* touched his aunt, Quincy knew that he would stop him. He was repulsed with the idea.

Both women screamed out at them, telling the four perverts how disgusting they were.

"Yea-yeah! Touch her, Keh-Keh-Karl. Da-da-do it." Mike had come to life and couldn't take her eyes off her bra.

Quincy enjoyed their ranting—to a point. He took a swig of beer and smiled. *Good. We hit a nerve with them. Maybe now they'll give us what we deserve.*

The girls kept at it for several minutes, yelling and promising revenge as Karl loomed in front of Jen, his eyes mesmerized by Jen's heaving breasts.

Now fed up with listening to them, Quincy slammed his beer down. *God damn them. They had their chance. They could a given us their money. They had all night to do it! This is bullshit!* He had reached his boiling point. Foam spewed from the bottle.

His partners pulled their eyes away from Jennifer, wondering what he had in mind.

Bolting from his chair, he grabbed the butcher's knife on the counter.

Jen and Rose looked on, their faces, white. *Oh God, no! Now he's going to slit our throats?*

Carla squinted in the pre-dawn light, observing the disturbing scene unfold through the side window. The bigger creep was brandishing a large knife in front of her niece. *You son of a bitch!* Cold and calculating, she aimed the rifle, her hands no longer shaking.

He stepped away from the women and reached for the roll of duct tape on the table, cutting off two pieces. The girls relaxed, only a little, thankful that he wasn't planning on cutting their throats—at least not just yet.

He didn't want them to continue provoking Karl and, more importantly, he didn't want them to talk about his Aunt Sylvia anymore. It was too uncomfortable for him. It was time to shut them up. Standing behind them, he roughly slapped the tape over their mouths.

"There, that should solve the little problem. From now on this is gonna be a one-way conversation. I've heard enough of your bullshit. You're *both* gonna sit and take your friggin' medicine!"

Rose was nauseated by the tape and had trouble breathing through her bloody nose. If she threw up, she knew that they would probably let her choke.

The bullies had crossed the line one more time. Now the women couldn't even defend themselves by speaking out. The situation was worsening by the minute.

Karl's eyes went back to Jen's white bra and heaving chest. He decided to have a little more fun—especially now that she couldn't verbally lash out or bite him. With a sick grin, he reached out for her right breast.

"Yeah! Da-do it! Pull out a tittie so's we can all have a lo-lo-look." Mike stepped closer, totally excited.

She lunged forward, forgetting that her mouth was taped.

Surprised by her reaction, Karl jerked away. *That crazy little bitch. She's—*

Boom! The side window exploded. Shards of glass tore through the kitchen as Karl staggered backwards—his black 'Mega Death' cap catapulting across the floor.

Chapter 5

Quincy pressed his body against the wall. Sal ducked behind Jennifer and Mike dropped to the floor. Everyone's eyes were on Karl as he lay on his side at the foot of Jen's chair. The .243 hollow point slug had ripped a hole through his neck.

He clutched at his wound as he tried to speak. A wet, wheezing sound trickled from his throat.

Mike turned away, wanting to block out the sight of his new buddy who was twisting and bleeding on the floor. He found himself staring at the white kitchen cabinets in disbelief. A large splattering of blood and small bits of flesh stuck to them. Several of the globules were slowly sliding down the upper cupboards, painting a red, abstract mess.

Karl's legs spastically pumped as if he was trying to run for safety. But, it was too late. Slivers of glass surrounded his squirming body along with a quickly growing pool of his blood.

Quincy was unable to comprehend what had happened as Jennifer tried to scream. The group barely heard the muffled sounds coming through the duct tape. The anger that had been in her eyes moments earlier was no longer there. Now it was horror and disbelief.

Rose shook her head violently from side to side. *No! This can't be happening.*

Sal and Mike were in shock and could not believe what they were witnessing. *Everyone* was in shock as they stared down at Karl.

Tears blurred Carla's vision and her body shook. Feeling ill, she threw the rifle to the ground in disgust. She had been aiming for his legs and suspected that she had been far off target. Fumbling in her pockets for Kleenex, she dabbed at her eyes before taking a second look. Karl's hands were wrapped around his throat as he twisted and turned on the kitchen floor. She looked away, knowing that it was probably a fatal shot.

Sickening waves swept through her. She buried her face in her hands. Carla sobbed and prayed at the same time. *Why? Oh God, why? How could this have gotten so crazy? I didn't want to kill him! I … I only wanted to stop him. That's all. He was going to rape my Jenny. I … she …*

A sobering thought slammed into her. *Now they know where I am! What if they sneak out of the house? What if they attack me?* Her focus went back to the thugs, concerned for her own safety.

The idea of them hunting her down made her survival instincts kick in one more time. Now furious, she wanted to shout out and let them know that it was their own, stupid fault. *They* were the reason why their friend had been shot and was probably going to die.

The anger helped regain her composure. She scooped up the smoking Winchester and pumped in another round. The spent casing flipped into the air, landing near her feet.

Keeping a close eye on the house, she whispered words of encouragement to try and justify what she had done, hoping that she would feel better when she heard her voice. "Good going, girl. Good going. Don't screw with us, boys. Don't you dare screw with us!" It didn't help. She could not believe how weak she sounded.

Quincy's back was pressed tightly against the kitchen wall as cold air rushed in from the blasted-out window. Dazed, he slid to the floor, shaking his head. He still could not comprehend what had happened in front of him.

Karl had his hands wrapped around his neck and was trying to stem the bleeding. Everyone stared down at him, feeling helpless. Jets of hot, red blood squirted between his fingers before dripping to the linoleum floor.

He spastically kicked as he slid along on his back toward the kitchen cabinets. It appeared as if he was attempting some sort of weird break dance and it would have been comical if it wasn't so tragic. He tried to speak. Thick blood spewed out of his mouth.

Now near the foot of Rose's chair, their eyes locked. A look of disbelief was on his face as he struggled to breathe. He couldn't and was now turning a deathly shade of blue.

Rose had a fleeting thought of the deer several hours earlier. It had also been shot in the neck. She had felt sorry for the innocent animal. There was no way that she felt sorry for Karl. Instead, a small amount of relief crept through her.

She knew that Carla had been forced to shoot him. *If she hadn't, he would have raped Jennifer.* She could not imagine how her friend was feeling right now.

Quincy half crawled along the wall. He avoided Karl and was worried that he would be the next target. Raising a shaky hand, he groped for the lantern and turned it off. Early morning light streamed through the shattered side window and highlighted Karl with a deathly, blue tinge.

Even with fresh air blowing in, the atmosphere in the kitchen seemed heavy. Rose had difficulty breathing through her nose and could smell death with each shallow breath.

His partner gasped for air as Quincy shuddered. "Karl? Karl!" *Is he going to die? Are we all going to die?*

Karl tried to speak. It was impossible for him to do. Part of his windpipe had been blown out. Instead, he gargled up a frothy, crimson mix that bubbled from his mouth.

Quincy stretched out on his stomach and groped for an arm, worried about being in the line of fire. He dragged his partner toward the back door and away from the shattered window mumbling, "It's okay. It's okay."

He knew that it was a stupid thing to say. It was not 'okay'. In a panic, he squeezed his hands around Karl's neck and yelled, "Mike! Throw me a towel or somethin'. We've gotta stop the bleeding!"

Mike pulled his eyes from Karl and grabbed a kitchen towel. Haphazardly, he tossed it in Quincy's direction.

Blood oozed through his fingers as he wrapped it around the wound. A large, red pool was slowly making its way toward Rose. She lifted her feet thinking that she would be contaminated if any of his blood touched her.

Her mind turned to Jennifer. Her young friend had witnessed the event first hand. It had taken place only inches from her and reminded Rose of Jackie Kennedy and how her husband, JFK, had been hit by the assassin's first bullet. The president had also grabbed his throat. She was surprised with Jen's expression from behind the tape on her mouth. *Is that a smile?*

Karl's clouded eyes grew dim as he stared at the ceiling.

Quincy turned to Rose. "Please! We gotta do something! We gotta save him!" He hoped that his Aunt Sylvia could help. After all, she had in the past. She was always there for him with either a Band-Aid or a hug. *No.* Quincy was quickly figuring it out. *No Band-Aid or hug is going to help Karl now!*

Chapter 6

Sal's world was caving in. He slumped against the kitchen wall next to Mike and shook his head in disbelief, muttering, "I never thought he would do *that!*" He was pointing at Karl.

Quincy looked at him, puzzled with what he was saying. For a second *everyone* was wondering what he was talking about.

Sal kept trying to make sense out of what had happened. "We left him there, passed out on the floor. He said he didn't own a rifle." He shook his head, now angrily pointing at Mike as he raised his voice and repeated, "*He* said that he didn't own a rifle!"

Rose was quickly putting it together. *They think that Larry did the shooting.*

Mike cringed, feeling trapped. *Everybody is blaming this on me. It's not my fault. It's all 'cause a Larry. The stupid old man.*

"He said a lot of things that were bullshit." Quincy glared at Mike. "You bastard! You told us he had money and didn't own a weapon. Now look what you done!"

Quincy kept at it, his anger exploding. "It's all your fault. You lied to us. You've been lyin' all along."

Mike didn't know what to think. He could not believe that his father had kept a rifle from him for all those years and then … shoot somebody? No. That couldn't be true. "No way, Quincy! No way! The old man didn't daw-daw-do that. He doesn't even own a guh-guh-gun. He doesn't got the balls to do somethin' like tha-tha—"

"Screw you, Mikie. Who do you suppose did this? The tooth fairy? You've given us nothin' but bullshit all night long. Now," Quincy shook a bloody finger in his direction, "you get out there and talk to your old man. You tell him … you tell him that we gotta … we gotta get Karl to a hospital or somethin'! Walk out there and reason with him. He won't shoot you. You're his dummy son for Christ's sake. Do it. NOW!"

Quincy's pointed finger looked like a lethal weapon to him—ready to shoot if he didn't do what he was told. Mike pushed back harder against the wall and shuddered, wishing that he was with his mother.

Rose wasn't sure if she should talk to Carla and tell her to back off. *Would it help if they knew that it was Carla who did the shooting?* It didn't matter. She couldn't speak. Her mouth was tightly bound with tape.

Slowly, he released his grip on Karl's neck and shook his head in grief. Quincy knew that it was pointless. There was no longer any hope. His partner gave one final shudder—the bleeding finally over.

With tears clouding his vision, Quincy pushed away from him, now concerned for his own life. *Larry will shoot me next!* He felt trapped and wondered how he could get out of the terrible dilemma. *Mike needs to talk to his dad and tell him not to murder us.*

He cracked open the back door and took a tentative peek out the yard. Mike's truck glimmered in the early morning light. "Mike! Get out there and talk some sense into him!"

"Na-na-no way. He'll want me dead even more. He'll shoot me first. I beat him up!" For the first time in his life, Mike was afraid of his father. He squirmed against the wall and took several, short breathes. His asthma was flaring up and the last thing that he wanted was to negotiate with his father. And, he still wasn't convinced that Larry was responsible for the shooting. It just didn't seem like him to do that sort of thing. *My old man is too weak!*

Quincy thought about what Mike had said—that Larry would shoot his boy next. *Shit! I'm the one he wants to kill the most. I'm the leader in all of this.*

He turned to Rose. "Look. You gotta help us." Pointing at her, he hoped that she could negotiate with the crazed killer. "Why don't *you* talk to him? You're his friend."

Rose didn't know what to do. She wanted to at least explain to Quincy that … what? Trying to speak, she couldn't. The tape covered her mouth. She squirmed in her chair. *Take it off so that I can at least talk.*

Quincy was confused and didn't understand. He thought she was telling him, through her body language, that there was no way she would talk to Larry. He turned to intimidation. "Karl didn't deserve what he got! It's all 'cause of you bitches. You …" Close to tears, he dropped his head and trailed off, not knowing what else to say.

Rose thought about their situation. It seemed hopeless. *We're screwed. The cops will put the three jerks in jail. Jennifer and I will be charged with growing pot along with Carla. She'll also be charged with attempted murder.*

Looking down at Karl, she shuddered, correcting herself. *It won't be 'attempted' murder. He's friggin' dead!* Shaken, she thought about it a little more. *But, Carla had every right in shooting him. He was going to attack us. He was going to rape Jennifer.*

Seeing enough of the macabre scene on the floor, she squeezed her eyes shut as her mind reeled. *The law will probably put it down as self-defence. It doesn't matter. Our whole operation will be found out. The three of us will end up in jail. The three of them will be charged with assault and theft—maybe even attempted rape.*

Quincy tried again. "Please! Hear me out." Totally stressed, he wiped his bloody hands on his pants before continuing. "You gotta talk to Larry. He's you're friend. He won't shoot *you*."

With her eyes still closed, she vigorously shook her head, angry with him for terrorizing her and her friend throughout the night and destroying their lives.

Mike decided to try his hand at working things out. In a soft voice he called out her name. "Row-Row-Rose? Quincy's right. You ne-ne-need to talk to him." He felt foolish and fumbled in his pocket for a cigarette, forgetting that he had smoked the last one several hours earlier.

Now you're pleading with me? Minutes ago you were grabbing my hair, you sick bastard, and calling me 'bitch' with your new buddies.

Now you want me to save your miserable ass? You've all gotten yourselves into this mess, including your friend here who incidentally is dead. It wasn't our fault. It was your fault. We'll all go to jail because of YOU!

"Quincy?" Sal had been thinking hard.

His friend wasn't listening and was focused on Rose, wondering what he could do to convince her into working with them.

Backing into the hallway, Sal wanted to get as far away from Karl's body as possible. He was worried for his safety and spewed out the question. "Quincy! What if Larry busts in here and starts shooting?"

Quincy felt his bowels loosen. The thought hadn't occurred to him. He slammed the door and locked it. *Jeeze! That might just happen. What if he's out of it and has more killing on his mind? We did beat him senseless. Twice!* He swallowed hard with the thought. *If I were him, I'd probably do the same. I'd start shooting.*

"Quincy. Quincy!"

"Huh? What?" Sweat ran down his forehead.

Sal was in a panic as he crouched in the hallway. "We've got to get out of here. We've got to get out of this house. We're easy targets. We need to—" He stopped for a moment while trying to work out some kind of plan. Pointing at Mike, he sputtered, "You! Come with us." Sal figured that they could use Larry's son for cover if he tried to murder them.

"But, where could we go? Where could we hide?" Quincy looked down at Karl and felt sick. His friend was dead and he was sure that he would be next. Would he die from a gunshot wound? Would there be a lot of pain? He kept mentally rambling, knowing that Sal was probably right—Larry could show up at any moment.

"Quincy. Quincy!" He had backed into the living room. "We'll be next. That killer will break in." He pointed down the hallway toward the kitchen and added, "He'll come through that door and … and murder us." He shifted his finger to Quincy. "You'll be first. You were the one in charge. And then," he swallowed hard as he pointed to his own chest, "he'll come after me."

Pausing for only a moment, Sal made his decision. "I … I can't take this. I can't wait any longer. I'm heading out the front door. I'm going to make a run for it. We'll all be murdered if we stay here. Are you with me?"

"Wait!" He didn't want his friend to leave without him. He was thinking that maybe he could distract Larry while Sal made his way out the door. Then Sal could sneak up behind the crazed killer and—

"No. I *can't* wait! He's going to bust through that door. I know it!" He felt like a hunted animal, picturing Larry in a commando uniform kicking in the door with guns blazing. They wouldn't stand a chance. Larry would ruthlessly pick them off, one by one. He did not want to end up like his friend—a bloody mess on some stranger's cold floor.

Rose frantically shook her head so she could get Quincy's attention. *Please! Take the tape off my mouth so that I can explain.*

Quincy didn't notice. He was preoccupied with Sal. "Please! Stay here."

She tried yelling. A muffled sound escaped from her mouth. He turned to her and wondered what she was doing—why she was crazily shaking her head and now rattling her chair from side to side.

It was too late. Sal had the front door open and was pumped with fear and adrenalin.

"No, Sal. Don't! Let's think this—"

In a flash, he was gone, racing across the lawn toward brush just beyond. He zigged and zagged, trying to avoid being an easy target.

Sal was running for his life.

Chapter 7

Movement caught her eye at the front of their house. Carla swung the Winchester to her left. One of the punks was making a dash for it in the morning light.

She wasn't surprised and had suspected that they would try to sneak out and ambush her. *That's exactly what they plan on doing. One's running out the front door. The rest of the vermin will probably try to slink out the back. I will not allow them to get me.*

Having found out the hard way that the sights were inaccurate, she aimed just below his feet. The Winchester had a tendency to shoot high. Her plan was to hit him in the lower legs. She did not want to kill him. All she wanted was to stop him, fearing that if she didn't, he would circle behind her. If that happened, she knew that she would be in some very serious trouble.

Carla felt confident with what she was doing and knew that the law was on her side. The girls were being terrorized. Their home had been invaded and she had every right in protecting her friends and herself. She squeezed the trigger.

They winced at the gun blast. Quincy was in the doorway, witnessing his friend drop to the ground. He prayed that Sal hadn't been shot—that he had only decided to hit the dirt and lay low.

Rose squeezed her eyes shut to escape from it all. She could not believe what was happening. The situation was beyond crazy.

Mike pressed his back against the kitchen wall and covered his ears. Losing control, he urinated in his pants.

Quincy whimpered, "Sal?" His buddy was face down and motionless on the lawn. *No. This can't be.*

Bending over, he felt sick. *I just saw another one of my buddies get shot—right in front of me! That can't be happening. He didn't deserve that. Is he dead?*

Deep down, he felt responsible. He could have stopped it. No one else was to blame. He had made the wrong choices. Now he was sorry for what he had done—for what they had *all* done to Larry and the women. They were paying a huge price for their mistakes.

It didn't matter how he felt. It was too late. The thought that Larry could burst in at any moment made him lock the front door, terrified. *The killer is still out there. He'll murder us.* Quincy reconsidered. *No. Just a minute.* His mouth dropped as he pointed to himself. *He's after me! No one else.*

Falling to his knees, he crawled into a corner of the living room, dreading to return to the kitchen. Karl's lifeless body was in there and he also didn't want to face the girls. He drew in a deep breath, wishing for a huge hit of meth as he thought about his predicament.

Larry could easily shoot me if I'm alone. The hair on his neck bristled and shivers ran down his back. *I've got to stay close to Mike and the two women. Maybe they can talk some sense into him. It's my only chance.* Swallowing hard, he scrambled back to the kitchen.

Rose saw him slink past her on his hands and knees. She and Jen had crawled along that very same floor only a few hours earlier. *Oh, how things have changed.*

A large part of her felt sorry for him and she tried to get control of her feelings. *It's their fault. They're getting what they deserve. Carla was forced to shoot them. If she hadn't, we would have been raped.*

Still, it didn't sit well with her. *Is Sal dead?* She wished that it was only some kind of nightmare.

Quincy sat with his back against the kitchen door. Weeping openly, he looked very much like a lost child.

Mike sat in a pool of urine. His hands covered his face as he tried to block out the terrible night. Going over it again and again, he could not believe that his dad had shot his friends.

Carla's nerves were raw as she waited for the two remaining punks to make their move. Crouched on the knoll, she was midway between the front and rear of the farmhouse.

She didn't have time to think of where she had hit the second kid or if she had killed him. It no longer mattered to her. *There's no way I'm going to allow them to leave the house. They'd come after me in a flash.* She pumped another round into the hot chamber.

They all tried to come to terms with what had happened. No one could fully comprehend how the situation had gotten so crazy.

Rose thought about Karl and Sal—how their mothers would react once they heard the news. *Is Sal dead?* She also thought about the law. *They'll take us to jail. I'll need a lawyer. There won't be any money for one. The police will find my cash and keep it.*

She was emotionally and physically drained and tried not to look down at the body that was inches from her feet. Karl had died with his eyes open. Rose wondered what people saw at the moment of death. *Do they have some kind of spiritual insight?*

Rambling with her thoughts, she figured that the law would no doubt search her property and find her money. If Gleason found it first, Rose knew that he would steal it. He was nothing but a thief, even if he did wear a badge.

Squirming in her chair, she decided to hide her cash in a better spot once Quincy and Mike were gone and before the police arrived.

Rose thought about that. She had fifty thousand dollars stashed away. They would come with dogs and have them sniff through the barn. It wouldn't take long before they discovered her cash.

She was determined that no one would find her money. *As soon as the punks leave, I'll head up into the hills with the two briefcases and find a better hiding place.* A couple of spots crossed her mind.

Shaking her head, she knew that she was jumping to conclusions. *Forget about Mike and Quincy leaving. They can't. They're trapped.*

The more she thought about it, the more upset she became. *Things were going great until the goons showed up. We were making all kinds of money. We didn't ask for any of this. I should never have gone over to Larry's to see what was going on.* She blamed herself for getting her and her friends involved.

Jennifer tried to make sense out of everything. She secretly thanked Carla once more. *That Karl creep was groping me. He deserved what he got.*

Smiling from behind the tape, she felt proud that she had stood up to them. She had defied them. Jennifer hadn't realized until now how strong a person she could be.

It was almost six in the morning. The storm had passed and sunlight filtered through the cold kitchen. Mike and Quincy had been silent for over an hour, immersed in their own thoughts.

Mike sat on the floor with his back against the wall, afraid to move. He kept thinking about his father and couldn't believe that Larry owned a rifle and had never told him about it. *I would a seen it. Things just don't seem right.*

Quincy was also on the floor with his back against the kitchen door. His head was down and there were tears in his eyes. He kept wondering if Sal was dead and when Larry would storm in.

Karl lay still.

With the kitchen window blown out, the temperature in the house had dropped. Jennifer shivered. Her blouse had been torn open and her shoulders and upper chest were exposed.

Quincy had been thinking about his past—when he had been living with his Aunt Sylvia. She had been good to him. He had rarely gotten into trouble when she had been raising him. It was the anger that he had toward his parents that caused him to turn out the way that he did. He knew it. He also knew that he was to blame for his many poor decisions.

It was time for a change. He knew that his life was going nowhere. This whole shooting incident was forcing him to look at things differently. Did he want to end up dead, or spend the rest of his life in jail like his old man? No way.

This time he decided that he would quit taking meth. He didn't want that kind of life anymore. From now on he would be strong and not allow anyone to manipulate him, making a promise to go straight.

Quincy studied Rose's face in the sunlight, still believing that she was his aunt. *No! Get it through your skull. She's not Aunt Sylvia! She's Rose. She's a good lady. She and her friend both are.*

On cramped legs, he carefully made his way into the living room. Peeking out the front window, his friend lay still on the lawn. With tears in his eyes, Quincy made his way up the stairs while trying to avoid the windows. Larry was on his mind. *Will he bust in? Will he murder me?*

He thought about what he and his buddies had done to the women and Larry over the past several hours. Feeling dirty and shameful, he washed Karl's blood from his hands and pants, hoping that he could also wash away his guilt. It wasn't working for him.

Next, he wiped the tears from his face, studying his reflection in the mirror. "What can I say to the two women? I'm sorry that I terrorized you throughout the crazy night and now, before Larry kills me, I want your forgiveness?"

Five minutes later he was in the kitchen with four blankets. Stepping over Mike, he gently placed one over Jen's shoulders. He did the same for Rose. She looked up and tried to smile. The tape still covered her mouth. He smiled back, again feeling the strong connection between them.

Mike looked up expectantly, waiting for his blanket. Quincy ignored him and covered Karl, wanting to hide as much of the bloody mess as possible. Holding the last blanket, he sat in his spot and wrapped it around his shoulders.

He knew that it was time for him to explain why he did what he did. But, he couldn't. There was no explanation. Just excuses. Instead, he whispered, "You remind me so much of my Aunt Sylvia." He stopped and was unsure of how to continue.

Rose raised her eyebrows and blinked, waiting for more while Jennifer simply glared at him.

"She raised me. My parents … my parents were …" He thought long and hard as he held her gaze. Finally, he muttered, "My parents weren't parents."

His eyes were moist and he half chuckled as he wiped them with the back of his hand. "You know, I've never cried so much in my life until now. There are so many things to cry for—Karl and Sal, what happened to the two of you and … what happened to poor Larry."

Mike jerked his head up. *What's with this 'poor Larry' shit? And, where's my blanket?* It hadn't escaped him that Quincy had ignored him.

"Aunt Sylvia has long, red hair. Just like you. She also has blue eyes. She's Scottish. I bet you are, too. Right?"

She slowly nodded, exhausted and cramped from being strapped to the chair all night.

"She baked bread for me. She baked pies for me—apple and blueberry. Sometimes she would bake a cake for my birthday. When I got a scraped knee or cut my finger, my aunt would kiss it and make it better. My mom … she was never there. Aunt Sylvia always was." He wiped away another tear.

Jennifer's glare softened. She could identify with some of what he was saying. Her thoughts turned to her druggie mother who preferred to be with her friends rather than be with her own daughter.

"I know we did the wrong thing. We're bad asses. We got out of control. The meth and wanting money and, well, it was wrong. All wrong." He shook his head, trying to think clearly. "We … we got caught up in …" Faltering, he fell silent.

Jennifer's hard stare quickly returned. *Yeah, you got caught up all right. There was no stopping you punks when you killed Angel. When you terrorized us through the night. When your creepy friend was going to rape me! I hope Carla keeps shooting.*

He couldn't face the way that she was looking at him. *She hates me.* Covering his head with the blanket, he hoped that everything would simply disappear.

Jennifer realized that she had done that very same thing earlier. She had covered herself with a blanket in the upstairs closet and had prayed that it was only a bad dream.

Mike was angry with his so-called buddy. *The guy is a loser. What about the money? We could still get some.* He reconsidered. *No. We're screwed. I'll probably end up back with Larry. Shit! What if he really did shoot Karl and Sal? He'd go to jail.*

He wondered how he could survive if Larry did time. His dad always gave him what he wanted. If he didn't, Mike would simply take it. *What about my smokes? My medication? The stupid old man.*

Rose had a mix of feelings. She didn't trust Quincy and refused to fall into what could be a trap. *Is he trying to make us feel sorry for him?*

She reconsidered. *What he's saying is probably true—about having a bad childhood. But, it was a different story when his buddies were alive. We all have tough times, but we don't beat, rob and terrorize people!*

Rose decided that she couldn't carry it in her heart. It wasn't worth it. She had hated enough over the past. The negative energy had left a dark hole and had turned her into a different person—a bitter soul.

Looking over at Jen, she noticed the hatred in her young friend's eyes. Jen would need to deal with her feelings in her own way and in her own time. For Rose, it didn't matter anymore. The punks had all paid a huge price for what they had done.

An inner voice spoke out. *It's their fault. They started it all. We were innocent.* She caught herself. *No, we were not innocent. We were playing against the rules—against the law. We chose to take the risks. If we would have had regular jobs we wouldn't have needed to stash away our money. It would be in the bank. Not in a briefcase! We wouldn't have been targeted. Neither would Larry. We need to take at least some of the blame.*

Jennifer felt both troubled and torn. She had never hated anyone, at least not until now, and understood what Quincy was going through—how he must have suffered when he was a child. Even though her heart wanted to go out to him, she had difficulty doing that.

Her thoughts turned to Carla.

Chapter 8

Sheriff Gleason cracked open an eye. He was confused and not sure where he was. *I must have passed out on the couch.* His head throbbed and his mouth felt like the Sahara. Sitting up, he put a hand to his temple. *Was it only a bad dream?*

It was slowly coming back to him—his deputy finding him drunk in the squad car last night. *Shit!* He hoped he hadn't upset him. Darwin went by the book more often than not.

Gleason glanced at his watch. It was eight-thirty and he started his shift at nine. Slowly standing and still slightly drunk, he half tripped as he made his way to the coffee pot. A strong cup of java would hopefully shake off the effects from last night.

Darwin was on his mind and what he had said in the empty parking lot. It was something about them talking today. The last thing that he wanted was to deal with his deputy.

His mind drifted to his money problems as he shaved. *What happened to the contact last night? Did something go wrong?* He planned on driving by the punk's house later to see if he was home.

He cut his chin with the razor. "God damn!" Dabbing at the wound, he fumbled for a Band-Aid.

Minutes later he poured himself a coffee as he thought about Frank Morgan and their conversation. He didn't like being snooped on. The Justice Department could screw themselves as far as he was concerned.

He told himself to be careful. They were getting on to him. He knew that he had severely screwed up last night with his drinking and driving. That was not the kind of attention that he wanted and he knew that it was time for him to play it smart.

Hesitating for a moment, he picked up the phone and dialed Darwin's number. Gleason needed to smooth things over and apologize before it got out of hand. He was worried that his deputy might file a report on him. The phone rang only once before Darwin's voicemail kicked in. *Damn! He's probably still sleeping.*

"Uh. Hello? Darwin? It's me. Cornelius." He didn't want to leave a message, but it was too late. He was caught off guard. "Uh, listen—about last night, uh, well, I want to apologize. I, uh, was wrong." Pausing for a moment, he thought about what else he could say before mumbling, "I'm … under a lot of pressure."

Feeling uncomfortable, he hung up.

Scarlett was already on shift at the police station, reading the e-mail that Darwin had sent.

Attached is a report on an incident that happened at the end of my shift early this morning. Please forward it to the Justice Department. It concerns Sheriff Gleason. He has put me and the entire department in a very difficult position.

Deputy Sheriff Darwin Sanderson
Fenton County Sheriff's Office
Beaswick, California

She opened the attachment and got busy reading his statement when the sheriff walked in. They glanced at each other. Gleason wondered why she was looking at him like that. *Is it because of the Band-Aid on my chin or …?* They both nervously said good morning at the same time.

He asked her, as he always did the first thing in the morning, "Anything interesting happen last night?"

"Uh, no. I just checked in with Kelowna Dispatch. Darwin was up on Verde Vista Road again." She said it in a high pitched voice before looking away. It wasn't like her.

Gleason made an attempt at chuckling. "Yeah, I know. I heard a little of the conversation on my police radio last night. Sammy has got to stop getting drunk and hitting his wife." He mumbled, "Did he try any more of Ella's dog-piss buns?" Gleason was uncomfortable and again wondered why she had looked at him that way. Had Darwin already said something to her about what happened last night when he had found him drunk in the squad car?

She ignored his question. "Oh, and one other thing. The power and phone lines are down on McCulloch Road because of the windstorm last night. The utility crew will be repairing them this morning. A pole landed across the road."

"Anyone hurt?"

"No. No report of an accident."

"We need to make sure that the power crew has a flag person when they do the repair job." Gleason was thinking about the last time he had caught them working on the roadside with no cautionary signs or flag control. He had given them a warning.

"If they don't, *we'll* flag for them and charge double." As an afterthought, he added, "We'll fine them, too." He knew that the utility company was trying to save money by not using a full crew.

Gleason got busy with routine business, but his mind was not far from his contact and money. Finally tired of shuffling papers, he told Scarlett that he was going on patrol for a while and that he might stop off at the Marmalade Cat Cafe for a coffee.

It was always a good place to go. The 'Cat', as the locals liked to call it, was a quaint restaurant with an almost story-book appearance to it. It fit in perfectly with the community, selling exotic blends of teas, coffees and herbs. People loved to talk and would quickly forget that he was the sheriff as they sipped their brew. He had gleaned plenty of useful information over a cup of java the last couple of years.

He drove past the shabby house that the contact rented. There was no sign of him or his gang. *Did they take the money and skip town?* It didn't seem right to him. If they tried to make a run for it they knew that he'd put out an APB and have them apprehended. He could then trump up the charges and put them away for a long time. *No, something must have gone wrong.*

Scarlett busily read the deputy's report and was not at all surprised with Gleason's behaviour last night. He did like his alcohol. *Good for Darwin for standing up to him.*

Gleason would be furious when he found out about the internal police report. She hoped she wouldn't be around when he did, having witnessed Cornelius's anger many times before.

Just the other day he had been yelling into his phone, telling the caller that he could make his life miserable if he didn't back off. She figured that it might have been a bill collector. Over the past few weeks Scarlett had redirected several of their calls to his office.

Chapter 9

The forecast was for a clear and sunny day. The strong wind from the night before had left many trees stripped of their orange and yellow leaves. No one in the cold kitchen cared what the weather was like. All were preoccupied with their own problems.

Still in a daze, Quincy whispered, "Aunt Sylvia? Are you awake?" He was huddled under a blanket with his back against the door, thankful that Larry hadn't stormed in yet.

She slowly opened her eyes. Rose was exhausted. Her ankle throbbed and her chest hurt from the cigarette burns. She wanted the whole, degenerate affair to be over—back to the way it had been earlier, before Larry had stopped them on the deer path.

"I always liked your baking. I—" He caught himself, realizing what he was saying. "Uh, I'm sorry. I must have been dreaming."

Rose tried to nod. Her neck was stiff and she needed to stretch. She also needed to go to the bathroom.

Overwhelmed, he placed his hands over his face, still having trouble believing that his partners had been shot—at least one of them dead.

Rose noticed that Jennifer had also dozed off. Getting a whiff of something rancid, she turned her head. Mike was still against the wall in a pool of urine.

She tried not to gag as she looked down at Karl's blanketed body. He had been dead for several hours and the blood on the floor appeared sticky. Several flies had flown in through the shattered window and now buzzed around an uncovered hand. She noticed a ring on his finger. *Did he have a girlfriend?*

"Rose?"

She raised her head, wondering what he wanted.

"I'm sorry for all of this."

Her anger came back in waves. *Sorry? You're sorry? Sorry isn't going to cut it, pal. Too little, too late!*

"I … we didn't think it would get so … out of hand. We never thought someone would *shoot* us!" He shook his head as he tried to convince her that he and his partners weren't half as bad as she thought they were. It wasn't working.

"You're actually a nice person. You both are. I … we …" He took a deep breath and tried to compose himself, worried for his life. "I don't know how I'll ever get out of this." As an afterthought, he added, "*If* I ever get out of this, alive."

Rose closed her eyes. Her mind drifted to Carla. *How is she holding out? Especially after shooting two people!* She could not image what her friend was going through.

"Rose. Rose!" Quincy crawled up to her while keeping a wary eye on the shattered window. "Let me take the tape off your mouth. We don't need it anymore. Here, let me cut you both loose from the chair." His voice was elevated, now eager to please.

A minute later they were free and rubbing their arms. The girls slowly stood on unsteady legs. Pain shot up Rose's back and ankle.

Quincy remained on his knees. All night he had been in command and had barked out orders. Now, he was at their mercy. "Uh, what are we going to do?"

"Good question, Quincy. Good question." Jen stood over him as she arched her back and stretched.

He looked up at Rose. "Please. Talk to him. Tell him … tell him that I'm sorry. Tell him I didn't know it would turn out this way. Tell him that I'll leave and that I won't hurt you and that I'll never come back." He repeated the last part as he vigorously shook his head. "I'll never come back. Never!"

Jen looked down at him and smirked. "What do you mean you'll never come back? Are you *that* stupid? Of course you won't come back, you moron. Do you know why?" She hammered the words out as she answered her own question. "Because you're going to fucking jail. That's why! Do you think you can just leave and everything will be like it was?"

He turned away to avoid her barrage. "I don't know." He repeated it again, in a whimper, while looking anxiously at the door. "I … don't know! I just don't—" *Is Larry ready to bust in and murder me?*

"You're going to be locked up for life, buddy." She pointed at Mike, disgusted. "You and your pissy-pants friend."

Mike stupidly looked up, not fully comprehending what she was saying. "Wha-what?"

Ignoring him, she focused back on Quincy. "And, do you know what?" Jen's voice grew harder as she got worked up. "We're going to jail, too! Because of you. Yeah. Because of all four of you. You've ruined our lives you worthless piece of …" Close to tears, she was unable to finish and turned away. The very sight of him sickened her.

Quincy nodded at her back, still on his knees. "Yeah, you're right. You're totally right. We made a huge mistake. Now, things have … changed."

He pleaded once more with Rose. "Please. Talk to him. Tell him to stop shooting. Tell him I'll leave peacefully." Not getting a response, he pointed at her with a shaky finger. "Do *something*. You're his friend!"

Rose ignored him and grabbed Jennifer by the arm. "We need to talk—privately."

"In a minute, Rose. I've got to go to the bathroom. I need to wash off this disgusting blood." She looked down at the front of her white blouse. *Gross! Forget about ever wearing it again. It's covered in Angel's blood. I'll have to burn it!*

Minutes later, after they had freshened up, they met in the living room. Rose had taken Tylenol for her ankle and was beginning to feel a little better. Her mind reeled as she threw out the question. "How are we ever going to get out of this?" She was speaking more to herself.

Her friend gawked at her and could not believe what she was hearing. She took a step back, surprised with the way Rose was thinking. "Get out of this? Get *out* of this?" She shook her head in bewilderment. "What do you mean by 'get out of this'? We *can't* get out of this. We're in it, knee-fucking deep. We've got to—"

"Stop right there and listen to me!" Rose raised her hand, annoyed with how her friend could easily come undone. "There is no point in panicking."

"Panicking. Panicking? Are you out of it? There are two people who have been shot on our property—at least one of them fucking dead—and you're telling me not to panic?" Jennifer's eyes were wild and her face was pale. "There's no way out! We *have* to call the police." She was on the verge of hysterics.

Rose turned her back to the kitchen. She did not want Quincy or Mike to hear what she had to say. Taking in a breath to compose herself, she whispered, "The first thing that we need to do is talk to Carla. We've got to tell her to stop shooting. Right?"

Jennifer reluctantly nodded. She knew that Quincy and Mike were no longer a threat. Still, she wanted to teach them a lesson and let them know what it was like to be terrorized.

"Then what, Rose? Then what? They just drive out of here into the morning sun. Is that it? They just drive away and leave us with their two buddies? Bullshit!" She was close to yelling. "How can we explain all of this to the cops? You tell me." Her hands were on Rose's shoulders, shaking her. "Tell me!"

Rose stepped back, suddenly tired of her friend's ranting—tired of everything. "All we can do is let the police know the truth. We were well within our rights to defend ourselves. We didn't break the law." Shaking her finger at the kitchen, she muttered through clenched teeth, "They did!"

Chapter 10

While the girls argued in the living room, Quincy turned his attention on Mike. "You're our only hope. It's up to you to talk to your old man. Rose doesn't want to do it. You're the one who needs to do the talkin'. Larry won't shoot *you*."

Mike lifted his head and thought hard before asking, "Wha-what should I say?"

Good question, Mikie. What can you say after beating your old man with a baseball bat? That you're sorry? That it was a mistake? That you didn't mean to do it? Yeah, right.

"Tell him you were stoned. That's it! Tell him we were *all* stoned and things, well, things got out a hand. Yeah. Tell him you're sorry. We're both sorry."

Mike slowly stood and was half convinced. "You … you come with me."

"No way. He'll shoot me!" Quincy recoiled with the very idea of negotiating with Mike's father.

"If you don't go, then I won't either. It's you and me. Otherwise, I ain't goin' ow-ow-out there."

Quincy felt sick thinking about it—facing Larry and begging for his life. *Maybe he's not even there anymore. It's been a few hours since he shot Sal.* "Okay. We'll do it together. It's our only chance."

Mike made his way to the back door and grabbed the handle. Hesitating, he still wasn't sure if it was the right thing to do. It seemed so out of character for Larry to shoot somebody. *But, who else could a done it?* He paused and tried to come up with an answer. *It must a bin Larry, but where did he get the fuckin' rifle?* He shook his head, puzzled.

"Mike!"

"Huh?"

"We gotta go out there. That's the only way we'll find out what's goin' on. We can't stay here all day."

*   *   *

Carla caught movement from the corner of her eye in the thick bush behind her. She spun around, expecting a deer. They sometimes came out in the early morning.

It looked like a man a hundred feet from her. *What the*—? She pointed the rifle at the figure thinking that one of the hoodlums had somehow snuck out of the house and was going to attack her.

Shit. It's ... Larry? Relaxing a little, she motioned for him to keep down and come her way.

His face was puffed. Dried blood was on his chin and cheek. He looked stunned and unsure of where he was. Holding his rib cage, he limped toward her through the bush.

In a harsh whisper, she snapped, "Larry. Get down! Here, sit beside me." She wondered what was going on. "What are you doing here?"

"Uh, I ... Is Rose okay? What are *you* doing here?" Puzzled, he looked at the rifle.

She quickly explained, telling him that her friends had been terrorized all night and that she had shot two of the punks.

"Did you ... did you kill Mike?"

Chapter 11

The sleepy town of Beaswick disappeared behind Gleason as he made his way up McCulloch Road. His mind drifted. He had bided his time and had waited for the right opportunity to get some of Larry's cash—one way or the other.

When Mike had yakked about how much money his father had, it was the perfect opportunity to put Quincy to work for him once again.

He had busted the small-time hood only last week, but had dropped the charges, figuring that the thug could pay him back by doing a few odd jobs. This was one of them—going up to Larry's house and taking his money.

Gleason slowed his cruiser as he came around a sharp corner. A power pole lay across a portion of the road along with telephone lines. The utility crew hadn't arrived yet. He knew they would be at least another hour, having to come from Kelowna, thirty miles away.

He drove around several branches from the windstorm the night before when his police radio came to life. He was in an area where there was still some reception. "Yeah, this is the sheriff. What's up?"

"There's been a fender bender in town. Where are you?"

"I'm (crackle) (crackle)."

Scarlett tried again. "Hello, Sheriff. Can you hear me? Over." She drummed her fingers on her desk for a few moments. *Hmm, nothing. I'll try again in a couple of minutes. If I don't hear from him by then, I'll get Darwin to check things out. I know he could use the overtime.*

He drove past Jack Pine Road, the old logging road to his right. There were several cabins up that way. A few hunters, on occasion, spent a night or two there doing more drinking than hunting.

Frank Morgan had just sat down with a fresh cup of coffee when his secretary paged him. "Yes, Chynna?"

"There's someone on line three who would like to talk to you. I asked him what it was about but he didn't want to speak to me."

He wasn't surprised. Some people with anonymous tips needed to go straight to the top. "Put him on."

A moment later a male voice came on the line. "Uh, hello?"

"This is Frank Morgan from the Justice Department. How may I help you?"

"Uh, yeah. I … I got some information, but it needs to be kept confidential."

Morgan sat up, forgetting about his coffee. "Rest assured, sir, that whatever you say will be kept private. May I ask what this is about?" He grabbed a pencil and tapped it on his notepad as his ears played detective. The male caller had a slight accent. Puzzled, he tried to place it by visualizing the person on the other end of the line.

"Yeah, uh, that's why I'm callin'. I don't want to get into any shit with you guys. I … don't want you guys to fuck me up."

He sounds … Native American. "Go ahead, sir. We won't fuck you up. You don't need to give us your name or anything. There's no problem here." He doodled on his pad as he listened intently to what the caller had to say.

Morgan had been on the streets fighting crime for several years and understood that, if he used the same kind of language as the caller, things could go smoother. It seemed to work. The person on the other end of the line relaxed a little.

"Okay. That sounds fair enough. Uh, I'm phonin' you 'cause one of you guys is makin' me nervous."

"Go ahead. I'm listening."

"Well, uh, I'm a card dealer here at the Nakusapee casino."

"Yes, go on." Morgan was intrigued and wondered what this fellow had to say. He found himself doodling the Ace of spades on his notepad.

"There's this guy. He brags to me and my dealer buddies when he's drunk 'bout bein' a sheriff of some kind and …"

"Yes?" He busily drew a police badge along with a few question marks next to the Ace.

"Well, he's been comin' here often and he's been droppin' a fair amount of change at the tables."

"Yes. And ...?" He added a few dollar signs, his mind on what the caller was telling him.

"Well, I found out he's from Beaswick and so I called the police department there. The secretary gave me your number."

"Yes?"

"We was all wonderin' where he was gettin' that kind of cash. Know what I mean? Like, is he on the take or what? It just don't seem right to us."

This had been bothering Lewis George for some time. He saw the fat ass come in almost like clockwork and act like he owned the place. The guy would get belligerent if he lost and arrogant if he won. More often than not, he lost.

What upset Lewis the most was the last time the sheriff had visited the casino. He had won a few hundred and had tossed a one dollar chip at Lewis, telling him to put a down payment on a teepee. That comment had bothered him and his fellow dealers very much.

"Do you have his name—a description of him?"

"Nope." He paused for a moment before blurting, "I got sometin' better. Security video."

Chapter 12

The girls were in the living room and arguing about what they should do when Rose turned toward the kitchen. Mike and Quincy were walking out the back door.

She raced down the hallway as best she could while yelling over her shoulder, "Jen! We've got to stop them. Carla might keep shooting!"

Mike was in the lead as they stepped off the porch and faced the knoll. Quincy was half crouched behind him. They nervously scanned the brush, wondering if Larry would show himself. It was a beautiful sunny day and birds chirped in a nearby tree. Everything seemed peaceful.

Rose shattered the silence by storming out behind them, yelling, "Carla?" The birds took to the air.

Surprised, the boys spun around and faced her, not understanding. *Carla?*

She tried again as she limped past them toward the knoll. "Carla? Carla!"

A large woman in camouflaged clothing slowly stood. Waist deep in thick bush, her rifle was aimed at the two goons. At first they had trouble making her out and had no idea that Larry was crouched beside her.

Rose tried to calm her friend by waving her hands with palms out, feverishly shouting, "It's okay. Don't shoot. They want to leave. They said that they were …" She stammered, at a loss for words. "Uh, they said that they were … sorry." It sounded feeble.

Quincy and Mike were quickly putting things together. It wasn't Larry who had done the shootings. There was another woman involved.

Carla snorted, "Sorry? They said that they were *sorry*? That's a laugh."

Rose stepped closer to the knoll. "Please. We don't need any more shooting."

"I won't shoot if those motherfuckers leave in the next few seconds." She raised her voice as she shook the Winchester at them. "And then what? What do we do when they leave? What do we do for God's sake?"

Rose did not know how to reply and floundered. "Uh. Maybe we can—"

Carla didn't give her friend a chance to finish. Stressed beyond her breaking point she yelled, "What about the two that I shot? Are they … dead?" She prayed that she hadn't killed anyone.

"Carla, please. We can talk about that later. Right now we need to cut our losses. We need to get the police."

"Then we're all going to jail. It's not fair. We didn't do anything wrong. They did!" She took aim at them though the rifle sights.

Rose stepped out of her line of fire, worried that her friend might pull the trigger.

Quincy and Mike froze, knowing that the smart thing to do was to stay still and keep quiet—at least until the hyped-up woman calmed down.

"Carla. Please!"

She ignored her friend, her sights on Mike and Quincy. "What about you two bastards? Are you going to turn yourselves in?"

Quincy hadn't thought about that. For hours he had been worried about being murdered by Larry. Now things had changed.

"Answer me! Are you going to turn yourselves in?" She was more than ready to shoot both of them.

He gulped. *What else can I do? The cops will hunt me down if I run for it.* He had no other options. "Yeah, I'll turn myself in."

Mike stood next to him, trembling. His bladder was growing weaker by the second as he prattled out promises. "Yea-ah. Me ta-ta-ta-too! I-I-I'll be good from now on. I won't get into no more tru-tru—"

Rose begged her friend to listen to her. "Please. Put the rifle down. We need to talk before things get even more out of hand."

Carla knew she was right. Afraid that she might accidently pull the trigger, she reluctantly lowered the barrel, uttering a warning. "Don't fuck with me, boys."

Rose spun around and faced Quincy. She had been waiting for this moment all night. "I want you to leave. Right now! I want you both off my property. I don't care what you do after that. Just leave. Get going."

"But … what about Sal? We gotta find out if he's still alive!" Quincy hoped that he had only been wounded.

Mike wasn't thinking about Sal. He was thinking about himself. *Aw, shit! Now I gotta go back and live with Larry again. I don't even got a truck no more. Those bitches wrecked it. He's gonna have to buy me another one.*

Carla was far too stressed and agitated to remain still. She raised the Winchester and pointed it at them again, looking very much like she was ready to blow their brains out. In a cold voice she snarled, "Do what you're told. Get going. Now!"

Quincy tried to negotiate. "Okay. Mike and I will go." Shaking his hands out in front of him, he pleaded. "Just promise you won't shoot. Please. Put the rifle down."

"Not until you motherfuck—"

Frustrated and tired, Rose snapped out, "Carla! Listen to me. Put the rifle *down*. They want to leave. Two people have already been shot. We don't want any more bloodshed." All that she wanted was for the two punks to get off her property and never return.

Carla knew that Rose was right. She didn't want to shoot them, but she also didn't want them to do anything stupid. More importantly, *she* didn't want to do anything stupid. *I need to calm down.* "Okay, I'll do it. I won't shoot as long as you two get going." She dropped the Winchester to the ground.

Only slightly relieved, Quincy's thoughts turned to his two partners. "Uh, what about Sal? And … Karl?" He was confused. *Should I just leave them?*

Worried about Carla picking up the rifle again, Rose needed to keep an eye on her distraught friend. She gave Jen an order. "Check out Sal. See if he's injured or if he's …"

Jen made her way toward the front yard, wondering what she would find. *What if he's still alive? We'd need to bring him to the hospital. And, what about Karl? We can't just hide the body. We've got to get the cops.*

She was a few feet from him when she stopped. He lay face down on the lawn with a bullet hole near the top of his shoulder. A small patch of blood was on his shirt, surrounding the wound.

Studying him for a moment, she looked for any signs of life. There were none. She stepped closer and nudged him with her foot. He didn't move. Jen tried again, this time squatting and gently shaking him.

Carla took several steps through the bush in the direction of the front yard, closely following Jen with her eyes. She stared on as her niece prodded the body.

Seeing Jen poke at the lifeless young man sickened her. The realization of what she had done slammed into her core, overpowering her emotions. She bent over, her stomach churning. *I only wanted to wound him. That's all. But, I shot him, dead!* Having no control, she retched.

Jennifer hurriedly made her way back to Rose and the two remaining punks. She had seen more than enough. Facing Quincy, she barked at him with contempt and disgust. "Don't worry about your friend. Thanks to you, he's fucking dead!"

He's dead? He had hoped that Sal had only been wounded. He turned white with shock and disbelief. Needing to escape from it all, he mumbled, "I … I gotta get the keys. I need to get Karl's keys. His car is parked at Larry's. They're in his pocket. Mike's truck won't get me far." He took several steps toward the house.

"Stay where you are!" Jen yelled it out and was surprised with how she was taking charge. "I'll get the keys. You're not setting another foot in this house!"

Marching into the kitchen, she jerked the blanket off Karl. Turning her head, she concentrated on a spot on the floor while blindly sticking a hand into his jean pocket, groping for his keys. *Oh God. He's still warm!*

Jen was nauseated—being next to the corpse and having her hand in his pocket. She jerked out his keys. A wad of bills followed. Disgusted, she tried to stuff the money back in his jeans. *That's what caused all of this—Larry's friggin' money!*

The smell of blood filled her nostrils and the kitchen reminded her of a meat market. Gagging, she yanked the blanket over the body, not wanting to look at it any longer. Bile rose in her throat. *Jeeze!* Being assaulted once again by the would-be rapist angered her—even if he *was* dead. She hated to be near him—to touch his body and smell his putrid blood. *That bastard!*

She rushed out of the house and gulped in a breath before flinging Karl's keys in Quincy's direction.

Leaping up to catch them, a gun blast ripped through the morning air. He and Mike hit the dirt while Jennifer and Rose dropped to their knees.

Stunned, Quincy groped for a bullet wound, not sure if he was dead or alive. *What the ...?* On his stomach, he lifted his head and looked in Carla's direction, whimpering, "You promised you wouldn't shoot. You said ..."

A hundred feet to her right, a puff of blue smoke hung in the still air. Behind it stood Larry with the Winchester aimed squarely on him.

Chapter 13

His police radio crackled. Turning up the volume, he tried listening to Scarlett's garbled transmission but had difficulty making it out. It had something to do with Darwin and the fender bender. He only caught part of it—oblivious to the gun blast from Rose's property, two miles away.

Relieved that she wasn't trying to call him again, he continued speculating about Quincy and his buddies. *Are the punks still at Larry's?*

Five minutes later he cautiously rumbled up Larry's long drive in his Challenger. Karl's Honda was parked beside Larry's blue Chevy near the rear of the house. The sheriff's mind filled with questions. *Why are the boys still here? Is Larry here, too?*

Being shot at by Larry was very much on his mind, but he needed to find out what was going on. *Did the boys get his money?*

It seemed peaceful enough—too peaceful. He was on edge as he parked near the log house. Waiting for any signs of life from inside, he peeled the band-aid off his chin and dabbed at the razor cut before replacing it with a new one. Working up his nerve, he stepped out of his vehicle.

The kitchen door was ajar. That didn't seem right to him. He reached for his pistol before calling out. "Larry? Mike? Are you in there?"

No answer.

He stepped closer, now near the porch, as he tightly gripped his handgun. He tried again. "Hello? Anybody there?"

A squeak from behind made him spin around, his finger on the trigger. An old gate swayed in the gentle breeze.

Relieved that it wasn't Larry, he turned and carefully made his way up the steps to the backdoor.

Sunlight filtered through the kitchen illuminating wooden splinters on the linoleum floor. A sticky mix of what appeared to be blood and vomit lay near a broken chair. Flies buzzed over the mess and the kitchen reeked of marijuana and candle wax.

He tried to figure things out in Larry's doorway. *It was only supposed to be a simple beating. What happened?*

Gleason eased into the kitchen, worried that Larry was lurking nearby. He raised his voice as he tightened his grip on his pistol. "Larry! Mike! Are you there?"

The gate replied with another squeak.

Sweat ran down his brow as he walked through the kitchen, checking out the remainder of the house. *Larry should be home with a black eye or two. Nothing more. What's going on?*

Finishing his search, he felt both relieved and puzzled that no one was home. He studied the blood and vomit once more, worried that his goons had gone too far this time. *Maybe they murdered Larry and his boy and took the bodies into the woods. Shit. There'd be paperwork and explaining to do if that happened.*

It was strange that Larry wasn't around. What was even stranger was Karl's Honda parked in the driveway. *Why is it still here? Where is Mike's truck? Where is everybody?*

Chapter 14

Larry rammed another round into the chamber. Keeping the rifle aimed in their direction, he limped out of the thick bush.

Mike and Quincy stumbled to their feet while Jennifer and Rose looked on from the porch. Carla stood knee deep in bush with an opened mouth, not believing that Larry had actually picked up the rifle and had fired a shot. *What was he thinking?*

He stepped closer, completely focused on Quincy, and shook the Winchester menacingly at him.

Rose wanted to tell him to put the rifle down, but decided to let Mike do the talking. Maybe Larry would listen to his boy.

"Don't shoot. Please. I'm sorry that this all—" Quincy held his hands out in front of him and crazily hoped that it might help in stopping a bullet.

"Shut up!" He was only a few feet away when he snarled out the words. His fogged eyes shifted from Quincy, over to Mike, and then back to Quincy again. Motioning with the barrel he snapped out an order. "Move away from my boy."

Mike shook his head dismissively at him. "Lair-Lair-Larry. Put the fa-fa-fuckin' gun down. Who are you tryin' ta kid?"

He ignored his son and shouted out again. "Move away and put your hands above your bald head. Now!"

"Please. Don't shoot." Quincy knew that he didn't stand a chance in talking his way out of this one. Larry had murder in his eyes.

"I said move away and put your hands up. Do it!" He jabbed the heavy rifle at Quincy's chest, trying to ignore the pain that tore through his damaged ribs.

The bigger man took a step back and slowly raised his shaky hands. Tears streamed down his face.

"Good. That's real good, motherfucker." Larry let out a sick smile. "Now, get down on your knees, skinhead. Get down on your knees, real slow."

Rose shuddered, hearing the hatred in his voice. They were about to witness an execution in her driveway. She had to stop it. "Larry! Are you crazy? Leave him alone!"

He ignored her—his eyes on the big thug a few feet in front of him.

"Please. Don't kill me."

"I said get down on your knees, maggot fucker. Do it. Now!" He poked the rifle at his chest one more time.

Trembling, Quincy dropped to one knee and then the other, his hands held high above his sweat-drenched head.

Mike wondered what Larry had in mind. He had never seen his dad act that way. Slowly, a twisted smile crossed his face. He was beginning to enjoy what his father was doing—making his so-called buddy squirm. *Good. That bastard slapped my face. He forced me to make sandwiches for him! Scare him, Larry. Scare the shit out of him. He deserves it.*

Rose couldn't hold back any longer. Mike certainly wasn't helping. "Larry. Enough! He won't hurt anybody. Leave him alone. Let him go."

Ignoring her, he placed the tip of the barrel between Quincy's eyes. Larry was in another world and completely tuned out.

Quincy knew that he would be dead within the next few seconds. Things began to spin and he was close to fainting. Larry was pumped and had murder on his mind.

Carla took several steps down the knoll as Jen and Rose held their breath on the porch.

The tension was electric. Larry appeared demented. Rose questioned if he had suffered brain damage from the recent beating. He was not the Larry that she knew.

Mike wore a smirk as he looked down at his so-called buddy. "Don't worry. My da-da-dad doesn't have the fa-fa-fuckin' balls to pull the trigger."

Quincy winced. That was *not* what he wanted to hear. *Don't worry? Are you kidding me?* He made another mental note about the kid. *What does he think he's doing? He's provoking his old man. Shut your stupid trap, Mike! Just shut up!*

He glanced at his son while keeping the rifle pressed between Quincy's eyes. Larry didn't seem to know where he was or how he had gotten there. "Uh, what did you say? What did you just say?" He blinked several times as he tried to make sense out of Mike's comment.

He crossed his arms and glared at his father—his eyes full of hate and disrespect. "I said you don't got the balls to pull the trigger, old man. Tha-tha-that's what I said. You're too fa-fa-fuckin' weak!" He yelled out the last word.

Wanting everyone to know how he could handle his dad, he kept at it. "You can't do it, can you? I ta-ta-told them somethin' was wrong. I knew all along that it wasn't you who shaw-shaw-shot my friends. You don't gaw-gaw-got the guts!"

Shaking his head, he muttered, "You're wrong, Mike. You're wrong."

"Well th-th-then, do it! Shoot th-th-the motherfa-fa-fucker. Shoo-shoot him dead. Right between the eyes." He pointed at his own forehead to make it clear what he wanted his father to do. "I duh-duh-dare you." Dropping his hands to his hips, he taunted him, convinced that Larry couldn't do what he was asking. *He's just trying to show off to his stupid girlfriend.*

Quincy could not believe what he was hearing. Mike was daring his father to murder him. His mind filled with the old nursery rhyme. *Pop goes the weasel. Pop goes the weasel. Pop goes the god damn weasel! Shut your stupid trap, Mikie!* He couldn't stand the pressure and was having trouble catching his breath. Larry was about to blow his brains out.

"See. I toa-toa-told you! You're too weak to shoot anybody!"

"Nah-no. You're … you're wrong! I … I …" Larry took several steps back and tried to take careful aim at Quincy's head.

Mike shook his finger at his father, wanting to embarrass him in front of everybody. In a mocking tone he said, "You're just trying to show off to your gir-gir-girlfriend."

Quincy waited for the bullet as he mentally shifted from *Pop Goes the Weasel* to *The Lord's Prayer.* He had forgotten most of the words. A million things flew through his mind as he tried to prepare for his death. *Our father, up there in heaven. Hollow is your name. God bless me. God bless Aunt Sylvia. God …*

The rifle crazily shook in Larry's hands. Under enormous pressure, he knew that Mike was right. Tears streaked his face. *Look at me! I am too weak. I let the goons beat me and steal my money. I let my son take advantage of me time after time. I'm weak in front of Rose. I want her more than she wants me. I'm—*

Mike snickered. He enjoyed seeing his father break down and figured that he was probably only playing another one of his stupid games. *You sure are actin' stupid old man—'specially in front of your so-called girlfriend.*

Fed up and embarrassed with the way his dad was behaving, he took two quick steps and grabbed at the wavering rifle. "You stupid old—"

The deafening 'boom' made everyone recoil in horror.

Chapter 15

Sheriff Gleason was parked in Larry's back yard. He had been thinking about his financial woes and if the boys had gotten any of Larry's money when he heard the gun blast. *What the—? Is someone hunting on Rose's property?* It didn't make sense to him.

The last thing that he wanted was to drive up that way and check things out. *I shouldn't even be here—at Larry's! I will not get involved anymore than I—*

A woman's terrified scream a half mile away made him break out in a sweat. *It's Rose!* Racing down Larry's drive with his red and blue lights flashing, he tried to put things together.

Quincy was in another world and could barely hear her shrieks coming from the front porch. His ears had been deafened by the gun blast. *I'm … I'm still alive?* Open mouthed, he turned to Mike. Larry's boy was on his back and the front of his shirt was rapidly turning a deep red. Quincy still didn't understand.

Rose and Jennifer found their legs and raced toward Mike. "Oh, God, no! He's going to die. How—?"

"Stay where you are!" Larry swung the Winchester at them.

They froze, worried that he was out of control and would end up killing all of them.

He pumped in another round as Mike weakly raised his hand. "Da-da-dad?"

Larry was stunned and unsure of what to do. His rifle was aimed on the women, but his son was calling out for him.

"Da-ah-ad!" He was having trouble comprehending what had just happened and needed his father's help. Something was wrong—terribly wrong. Things were turning dark and now it was difficult for him to see. His hearing was faint and he felt a chill. Mike's shirt was soaked in blood and his vacant eyes fluttered at the blue sky. Too weak to hold his hand up any longer, he dropped it to his chest.

Larry's mind scrambled, looking for an explanation. *Mike grabbed the rifle. I accidently pulled the—* He shook his head in disbelief as the hard truth slammed into him. *No! It was no accident. I did it … deliberately.*

In a faltering voice, he groped for words. "Mike! Mike? I'm so sorry. I … I can't believe this happened." Forgetting about Quincy, he fell to one knee next to his dying son. "I-I-I … it wasn't my fault. It was an accident. I didn't want to shoot you, son." He shook his head, tears filling his eyes. "It will be ok. I'll call for an ambulance. I'll …" He stopped his blathering for a moment, knowing that it was a stupid thing to say. "I tried to be a good father. I really honest-to-goodness tried. I wanted you to be somebody. That's all. I wanted you to make something out of your life. Someone I could be proud of."

Scrambling for an excuse for what he had done, he grew defensive. "You turned on me, boy. You beat me up so bad—not only my body, but my heart and my soul. You killed me, Mike." He pointed at his own chest while dropping the rifle, repeating, "You killed … *me!*" Now he was on both knees, gripping Mike's cold hands.

Carla seized the moment and made a dash toward the dazed father a hundred feet from her.

Larry's attention was on his boy. Mike's eyes were closed and his heart was barely pumping. A moment later he stopped breathing.

"I'm … sorry. I'm sorry that it turned out the way it did." With a face tormented in grief, he looked down at his child as he tried to explain. "The more love I gave you, the more you took from me." He waited for any kind of response. There was none.

Now cradling his son, he continued to explain. "You wanted to kill *me*. I saw it in your eyes—the hatred. When you swung …" He swallowed hard as he relived the terrible night. "When you swung the bat, you planned on murdering … me!"

Carla scooped up the rifle. A deep rumbling coming from the foot of their driveway made her turn. A police car was roaring up with lights flashing.

Cops! Without thinking, she raced back into the bush with the Winchester in hand.

Seconds later Sheriff Gleason pulled up behind Mike's truck in a cloud of dust. He scrambled out of the high powered cruiser with his pistol drawn.

Carla anxiously watched from behind thick bush as Gleason yelled, "What's going on?" He zeroed in on Larry. The stunned father was holding what appeared to be his son. Next to them was Quincy. He was on his knees.

Rose made her way toward them as Gleason hurried to the father and son. With his gun in one hand, he turned and raised the other. "Stay where you are. All of you. Stay where you are!"

She stopped in her tracks.

Gleason approached Larry from behind and shouted, "Step away from Mike!"

His eyes were glued on his son, oblivious to the sheriff's command.

"I said move away from your boy."

Larry got to his feet and took several steps back, praying that the sheriff could somehow save his son as Gleason squatted and placed two fingers on Mike's neck, searching for a pulse. There was none. Swallowing hard, he turned to Larry in disbelief. "What happened?" He croaked it out.

"I shot him. I murdered my own child. God! It was an accident. No. Maybe not. Maybe I did it deliberately. I don't know. He deserved it." He rambled on. "No. I deserved it. I—he was going to kill me. He reached … and I shot … and he …"

Gleason turned to Rose, wanting answers. He raised his voice and tried again. "What happened?"

Larry's nervous chatter had given her time to think. She took in a deep breath while wringing her hands out in front of her. "Oh, God. This is so … terrible. I … Larry … he shot …

In a steely voice, Sheriff Gleason stood and waved his pistol at her. "God damn it! What happened?" *The kid's dead. I don't need that kind of shit. Now I'm being pulled into their mess!*

"Earlier, Larry show-showed up on our property. He told us that he—"

"He told who? Who did he tell?" *Damn it woman, I need answers!*

Her mind spun, unsure of how much she should tell him. Instinct told her to be careful. Gleason could not be trusted. She mumbled, "Jennifer and … I. He told us that he had been badly beaten." In a stronger voice, she added, "Hell, he didn't have to say anything. We could see for ourselves."

Carla listened on, not sure of what to do.

Chapter 16

Rose contemplated on how much she should tell the sheriff as he turned his back to her and studied Mike's damaged truck. *Just remember who you're dealing with. He's nothing but a thief and rapist.*

Getting a whiff of anti-freeze from her Ford, he wondered again what had happened. The front end was damaged and the roof appeared to have been hit several times by a blunt object. With little patience he spun around and barked, "Keep talking. Tell me the whole story."

Her survival instincts kicked into high gear. *Take in a deep breath and pull yourself together. Don't trust him and don't tell him everything.* "Well, uh, Larry came over and told us that there were three of them—three hoodlums that beat him up and stole his money."

She continued to half explain what had happened while Gleason studied Larry. *The boys did a good job beating him up. No wonder he's dazed.*

"We … we helped him out. We patched him up the best we could. I drove him back to his house." Her voice grew higher. "That's when they returned to his place. Then … they came here—the three of them along with Mike. That's when I rammed them with my truck to stop them. It didn't work. They tied us to chairs and terrorized us all night." She shuddered and rubbed her arms as she relived what had happened only hours earlier.

Gleason was full of questions. "Where are they—the other two?" He nervously scanned the area as he rubbed the Band-Aid on his chin.

"One of them is in the kitchen and the other one is in the front yard." In a lower voice she added, "They're … dead."

"They're what? Dead?" *Holy shit!* Gleason stared open-mouthed at her, stunned by the news. "How did they die? What happened?" Sweat ran down his back. *Jeeze! This whole scene is turning into a shit show!*

Annoyed that she wasn't answering him and also concerned that there were two more bodies to deal with, he raised his voice. "Answer me. How did they die?

She covered her face, pretending to sob.

He turned to Quincy. "You! Tell me! What happened?"

Still on his knees, he shook his head and looked away. *I'm not going to say nothing. Let him figure it out.*

Gleason hoped that Jennifer could explain things. He softened his tone. "You need to tell me young lady. What happened?"

"I … I … it … we …" She shuddered, making no sense as she babbled on. "It was … such a mess … and then it … I can't … please."

Shit! He marched back to Larry. He was on his knees and hugging his son, whispering apologies into his dead ear.

Squatting next to him, Gleason begged for an explanation. "Larry. Larry? Tell me what happened. Did you shoot those other guys, too?"

Hearing the sheriff's question—if Larry had shot the other punks—an idea began to take shape in Rose's mind.

Larry blocked out the sheriff and his question. He was absorbed in trying to remember happier times with Mike, but couldn't come up with any. He continued with his sobbing.

Gleason tried to put things together. Now there were *three* bodies to deal with. *A triple homicide! It was only supposed to be a simple beating. What went wrong?*

"All of you. Stay where you are. Don't move!" He backed toward his cruiser while keeping an eye on everyone. His main concern was Quincy. *Will he blab to the authorities? Tell them that it was me who sent him and his buddies to Larry's to extort money? That, because of me, there are three bodies to deal with?*

He tried to shrug it off. *So what if he does? It would be a small-time druggie's word against mine.*

Reaching in for the handcuffs in his trunk, he stopped. The bottle of Jack behind the spare tire poked out and beckoned him. He twisted off the cap and took three huge gulps from the jumbo sized bottle. *Damn! I shouldn't even be here.* Wiping his mouth with the back of his hand, he grabbed the cuffs.

The sheriff tried to sort out what had to be done as he pulled out a handkerchief and dabbed at his forehead. The first thing was to let his dispatcher, Scarlett, know where he was and what he had come across. He reached into his car for the police radio and paused, thinking hard. *She'll want to know why I'm even here.* Gripping the transmitter with one hand, he tried to get his story straight as he wiped his brow with the other.

I was, uh, checking things out. Yeah. I was concerned about the residents along McCulloch Road. That's right! They had no power last night because of the downed pole. I was only doing my job when I heard a gun blast and came across the gruesome murder scene.

His pulsed quickened as he pressed the transmit button. "Hello? Uh, Scarlett? Do you read me? Over." He waited for what seemed like an eternity, tightly gripping the hand-unit.

A crackle and hiss were his only reply.

Almost relieved that the radio signal was so poor, Sheriff Gleason planned on what needed to be done. He would secure the area and make sure that no one fled the scene before he checked out the other two bodies.

With cuffs in hand, he returned to the four suspects. "Rose. Take the cuffs. The rest of you, turn around and put your hands behind your back."

"But, Cornelius! We're not guilty." She was shocked with the idea of wearing handcuffs. "We shouldn't be arrested. We did nothing illegal. We were the victims in all of this."

"You're not getting arrested … just yet. I need to get control of the situation. Put the cuffs on everybody and then turn around so that I can handcuff you."

Moments later, with their hands now secured behind their backs, he turned toward the old farmhouse and swallowed hard—apprehensive with what he would soon find in the kitchen and front yard.

A body draped in a blanket greeted him. It lay in a pool of blood surrounded by shards of glass. *Shit.* The sight of it made him wince despite the strong buzz that he was feeling from the Tennessee whiskey.

In his fairly short career as a sheriff he had never come across a murder scene. That sort of thing just didn't happen in Beaswick.

He slipped on latex gloves and squatted next to the body for a closer look. Carefully peeling away the blanket, he examined the neck wound and shook his head. *It's torn pretty good. God damn!*

He pulled the blanket down farther and spotted a wad of bills poking out of the victim's pocket. Staring at the money for several seconds, he went through his options. *I shouldn't tamper with evidence, but I've got to take the cash. If Quincy blabbed that I sent the boys over to steal money from Larry, I could be in some serious trouble.*

But, if I take the cash, there would be no proof that Larry had even been robbed. It would make things look better for me. It would be the punk's word against mine.

He snatched up the bills and rolled the body on its side. Stuffing his hand into the other pocket, he pulled out more money.

Satisfied, he studied the blood splatter on the kitchen cabinets before turning toward the blasted-out kitchen window. Looking through it at the knoll, he speculated. *Larry must have been hiding up that way when he shot the kid.*

Carla remained frozen behind a bush.

Seeing enough of the grotesque scene, he made his way out the front door, spotting Sal on the lawn. He immediately noticed an entry wound on the top of the shoulder. Placing a finger on Sal's neck, he searched for a pulse. There was none. Gleason wasn't surprised. The body was already cool to the touch. Hesitating for only a moment, he pulled out another roll of money from the young man's pockets.

As the sheriff dug into Sal's pockets, Carla half-stood from behind the bush. She waved her hands, trying to get Rose's attention without Gleason spotting her. She needed to know if she should turn herself in.

Rose wagged her head and mouthed, "No! Get down. Stay hidden."

Unsure of what to do, she hesitated. *But, I've got to let the sheriff know that I'm here. I'm the one who shot two of them! I should be taking the rap, not my friends or anybody—*

"Get down!"

Carla slowly dropped to her knees, praying that it was the right thing to do.

"Shouldn't we tell the sheriff about Auntie?" Jen had a million questions as she pointed with her head in Carla's direction.

Quincy added, "He won't let up until we tell him *everything.*"

Rose's mind raced for a way out of their dilemma. A plan was beginning to take shape. Excited, she turned to Quincy. "You told us that you felt bad for what happened—for what you and your gang did. Right?"

"Yeah. I never thought that things would turn out like this! If I could do it again I would never—"

"If you want to help us then now's your chance. Just go along with my story. If you do, we can make it easy for you. We'll tell Gleason that you stopped your buddies from hurting us and you stopped Mike from trying to murder his father with a baseball—"

Too worked up to finish, she spun around to Larry. "Gleason already knows that you shot Mike, right?"

He had his head down and was in a daze. The only thing on his mind was his son.

"Larry! Listen to me."

Slowly, he looked up with glazed and teary eyes.

Rose needed to get her story straight before the sheriff returned. She repeated, in a loud whisper, "Gleason already knows that you shot Mike."

"Huh?"

She shook her head, annoyed that she was cuffed. She wanted to grab him so that she could get his full attention. Trying to calm her voice, she pressed on. "Remember? You half told the sheriff that you were the one who shot Mike when he pulled up our driveway."

He nodded stupidly, but couldn't remember what he had actually said.

"You need to tell him that … tell him that it was *you* who shot the other two punks."

"Wha-at?"

"Yes. That's right." She pulled her story together. "Tell Gleason that when you came out of your coma, after being beaten senseless, you …" She paused for a moment, thinking. "Yes! That would work. You heard screams coming from my place. You grabbed your rifle and came over here because you wanted to protect us. You wanted to protect *me*, Larry, because … you're my hero."

Rose knew that she shouldn't be talking like that. She was using her female influence and felt slightly ashamed. But, they were all in a very bad situation and for her story to work she would need Larry to go along with it.

He had been half listening to what she had been saying except for her last words. That got his complete attention. She had called him her hero!

Jennifer was excited with what Rose was saying. *Yes! That might work. We could still keep Auntie out of this if Larry takes the blame. She wouldn't need to go to jail. She* blurted, "That's right, Larry. You came over and hid in the bush. You saw how they were treating us and you shot them. We don't need to say *anything* about Carla. She was never here. You were the one who saved us. They were going to rape me!"

"Uh. Yeah. I … uh, saved you." He was beginning to warm up to their story. *I'm their hero and I saved them.* "But," he turned to Rose, "what about Mike?"

"You were stunned. You were beaten to within an inch of your life and mistook him for one of the thugs."

Wanting to believe at least part of what she was telling him, he nodded and repeated, "Yeah. I thought he was one of the thugs."

"That's right. You didn't shoot him deliberately. It was an accident."

"Yeah, Rose. It was an accident. That's all it was—a stupid accident. I didn't mean to do it. Honest. It was … it was just an …" He couldn't continue and turned away, shuddering with the thought.

"It's okay, Larry. It's okay." Rose wanted to put her arms around her friend and console him but couldn't because of the cuffs.

Jen and Rose prayed that the authorities would believe their story. So did Quincy. If they did, Carla wouldn't be involved and Larry might not even do jail time. He had every right in shooting Karl and Sal. And, Mike's death had simply been a terrible accident. All he had to do was stay in tune with what Rose and Jen were telling him.

Rose had another reason why the sheriff couldn't find out about Carla. It was money. She had a pile of cash hidden on her property. Once Gleason took them in, Carla could hide it somewhere far from the farm before the police did a full investigation. The girls had already talked about that months earlier.

Then Carla could hire a decent lawyer for us. At least we would be able to afford one. Otherwise she goes to jail along with the rest of us and the cops take all my money.

Larry interrupted her mental rambling. He had been thinking about her story. "But, I *didn't* shoot those two punks." Feeling manipulated, he turned to the knoll and yelled, "She did!"

Kneeling next to Sal, Gleason heard muffled voices coming from his cuffed suspects in the parking area at the rear of the house. He couldn't make out what was being said. Then he heard Larry yell out, "She did!" It was time for more questioning, but before he did that, he needed one more drink.

"Shhh. Keep it down." Rose nervously looked over her shoulder. There was no sign of Gleason. Sweat ran down her neck as she continued to try and convince Larry. "Carla doesn't need to be mentioned. Don't you see? Gleason already knows that *you* shot Mike. He also knows that you were beaten by the thugs and robbed. All you need to tell him is that you came over here to warn us because you heard them talking about paying us a visit.

"When you got here, they were in the middle of terrorizing us. You saved us, Larry. You saved *me!*" Rose leaned into him and batted her eyes.

His heart skipped a beat, loving the attention she was giving him.

Chapter 17

Shaken by the deaths of the three young men, Gleason's mind raced, worried about being implicated. *I need to be careful and think things out.* Figuring that a shot of Jack Daniel's would help, he made a promise that it would only be a small sip—nothing more.

Now next to the opened trunk, he quickly forgot his personal pledge and took a huge gulp as he went through his options. Feeling slightly drunk, he decided to play hardball.

"Who shot 'em?" He was in their faces as he barked it out. Before anyone could answer, he turned to Rose. "You better start telling me *everything.* No more bullshit! What *really* happened? And, where's the weapon?"

She tried not to gag from the strong smell of whiskey as he leaned into her and concentrated on getting her story straight. "Larry pushed his way through the bush and started shooting, wanting to save us. Thank God he did or we would have been raped." She looked hard into the sheriff's eyes when she said 'raped,' her hatred coming out like a cloud of poison.

He stepped back—feeling her anger and loathing pierce his thick skin.

Pulling her story together a little more, she carried on with her half truths. "They saw me snooping over at Larry's. I was worried about what they might do to him—if they were going to kill him. Two of them kept beating him. Especially Mike." Waiting for a moment, she added, "That's when Quincy tried to stop them."

Gleason smirked. *I've got three bodies to deal with along with a hoodlum that I hired to steal money from Larry. She's telling me that two of them beat Larry and that Quincy tried to stop them? That is pure bullshit! He's nothing but a two-bit punk.*

Turning his back to them, Gleason faced the barn, trying to think things out. Sniffing the air, he asked no one in particular, "What's that smell?" He knew full well what it was. Playing his game, he pretended he didn't know what was going on.

"Can you smell it? What is it? It's, jeeze, I don't know. It's on the tip of my tongue." Taking several steps toward the old building, his voice grew louder. "Oh, my God. It's the smell of marijuana, everybody. It's the smell of ... money. Hallelujah!" He raised his arms above his head and pretended that he was at some kind of religious revival meeting while doing a crazy, drunken jig.

She tried to reason with him. "Look, Sheriff. I don't know what you're getting at."

He spun around and faced her. The booze was hitting him hard—especially on an empty stomach and being drunk the night before. Everything was hitting him hard. Pointing at her, he snapped out, "Cut the goddamn crap. Don't tell me you don't know what I'm talking about. I'm no fool. You've all been lying to me since I got here."

Spittle ran down his chin as he continued with his ranting. "I've busted a lot of people for growing dope, but," he glared at the two women, "until now I *never* busted anybody for murder!"

"Murder?" Rose's mouth dropped and her stomach filled with acid. "No. You can't do that."

"Don't you be telling me what I can or can't do."

"Then you're goin' down with us."

"Huh?" Open mouthed, he turned to Quincy, waiting for more.

He repeated, "You're goin' down with us. You're the reason why my buddies beat up Larry. It was your idea. You sent us there so that you could get a share of his money."

"You what?" Jennifer could not believe what she was hearing. "You sent them over to Larry's—to steal his money?"

Ignoring her, the sheriff zeroed in on Quincy. *I knew he would blab on me sooner or later. He just can't keep his big mouth shut.* "Where's the rest of it?"

"Huh?" He was taken back by the cold question.

"God damn it. I said where's the rest of it—the money that you stole?" Gleason's patience was now long gone. Alcohol usually did that to him.

He stammered, not knowing what to say. "I ... uh, I ..."

Tired of waiting for an answer, he shoved his hands into Quincy's pockets and fished out close to two thousand dollars. Counting the cash, he growled, "That's it?

A few lousy bucks! You gotta be kidding." He was furious. "That's not all of it, is it? You kept some for yourself. You're trying to fuck with me. Right?"

Quincy shook his head. "No. That's it. Mike was wrong. Larry only had a few thou'." He stepped away, wanting to defend himself, but couldn't. His hands were cuffed behind his back.

Gleason took advantage and poked him hard in the chest, making him take several more steps back. He kept at it, jabbing his finger at him, still in his face. "Don't screw with me, boy. What about the shoebox stuffed with money? With fifties? Where is it? Where did you hide it?" *I gotta get all the cash. It's potential evidence against me. Besides, they owe it to me.*

The sheriff's blood pressure soared as he thought about how things had gone wrong. *The punks should never have gotten those women involved. The stupid bastards pulled me into this mess and now they're going to pay dearly for their mistake.*

Quincy mumbled something as he shook his head at the bully cop.

Gleason slapped his face. "I said don't fuck with me, boy!"

It was too much for him. Through tears he shouted, "I hate you! You're always screwing me. I tried to come clean. I even entered the drug rehab program, but guess what? You showed up with some free dope."

The sheriff opened his mouth to respond, but Quincy wouldn't let him. "Yeah. That's right! You knew I would take it. You don't want me clean. You want me to be your bum boy. Not anymore, Cornelius. Not anymore!" He glared at him, daring him to deny it.

What should I do with the skin headed fucker? Maybe I should shoot him so he doesn't yap his fool head off about me to anyone else. I could get away with it … maybe. It's his word against mine. He's got nothing on me. None of them have a thing on me.

Larry loathed him even more, now learning that it was Gleason who had been responsible for his beating. This whole situation was because of him and his greed, resulting in three deaths—including his son's.

At the same time he found himself feeling slightly sorry for Quincy. He was also one of the sheriff's victims. *At least the young man had wanted to go straight—to try drug rehab.*

Dismissing Quincy for the moment, Gleason focused on Mike. Looking down at the body, he held his breath. The kid's pants reeked of urine, but that didn't stop Cornelius. Squatting, he shoved a gloved hand deep inside a wet pocket and fumbled around before pulling out a damp pile of cash.

Larry couldn't believe how cold and calculating he was. It was finally sinking into him as he took several quick steps toward Gleason. "It's all because of you. You set it up. You had them come over and beat me to a pulp." He tried to jerk free from the cuffs.

Gleason jumped back. "Now hold on, Larry. It wasn't me. It was because of your son—the way he yakked his fool head off. News got around. I didn't know it would turn out like *this*!"

Larry knew that he was partly right. *Yes, it was Mike's fault. Yes, he hated me. I know that.* He tried to sort things out. *Still, the sheriff was in on it. He used the young guys to steal from me.* "How can you do that—to reach into my dead son's pockets and pull out money? My money!"

"It's my job. I need to, uh, extract all the evidence, uh, before it gets into the wrong hands." He tried to suppress a belch. It didn't work for him.

Rose momentarily put her anger for him aside, worried about her and her friends. "What are you going to do? What are you going to do with *us*?"

"Don't worry, sweetheart. I'll be taking you in. I'll be taking *all* of you in." He added with a grandiose smile, "On my own sweet time."

Gleason loved being in charge. With a fresh toothpick bouncing in his mouth and a wad of cash in his pockets, he looked them in the eye. "Let's get something straight. First of all, you've all been lying to me about what happened."

Jen tried to back up her friend's story. "No Sheriff! That's what really—"

He raised his hand and stopped her. Facing Rose, his voice grew hard. "You're telling me that Larry shot Mike along with the other two thugs, but the biggest punk of them all is still alive? Quincy would be the first guy I'd shoot if it were me." *Do they think I'm that stupid?*

Smiling self righteously, he kept at it. "I can't figure out why you're doing that—why you're protecting that scum bag. But, I *will* find out. I'll find out *everything*!"

Chapter 18

Loving the way that she was reacting to his threats, he stepped closer to her—his chest pressing hard against hers. With a sickly smile, he whispered, "Do you have *any* idea how you'll ever get out of your mess?"

She stepped back and tried to reason with him. "Do *you* know how we could get out of this," she added, "if … we made it worth your while?"

"Wha-at! Are you suggesting a bribe?" He put his hand to his chest implying that he was taken aback by the very thought of being offered money to cover things up. "I can't believe you would suggest that I go on the take to save your sorry asses unless, of course, it was a substantial amount."

He winked at her and knew that he had hit the jackpot. *They'll pay all right! They'll pay dearly for me to try and fix their screw-ups.* "How much do you have in mind if I could, uh, work things out?" His heart raced as he thought about the financial possibilities. *This could turn out to be a good day after all.*

Rose didn't want to go that route—to deal with him—but knew that she had no other choice. Gleason had them over a barrel.

Looking him in the eye, she demanded, "You tell *me* how you can get this thing cleared up before I ever tell *you* how much I'm willing to pay!" She had no idea how they could get away with everything and wondered how Gleason could help them.

"Whoa! Don't be talking to Mr. Sheriff like that." He didn't like her attitude.

"Okay, 'Mr. Sheriff.' Tell me how you can get us out of this and then … we'll talk cash." Her heart pounded with worry. *Can he do it? Will he work with us? I don't want to go to jail. We … don't want to go to jail!*

Carla heard every word from behind the bush and was surprised with Gleason's suggestion—that he could possibly help them. *Maybe it's going to work out after all. But, how can he help?*

He stepped back and took in the surrounding scene. Busily working the toothpick in his mouth, he glanced in Carla's direction.

She panicked. *He's looking right at me! Maybe I should give myself up.*

Oblivious to her hiding in the bush with camouflaged clothing on, his mind worked overtime. He pondered on how he could make some serious money. Still slooking at the knoll, he asked, "Where's the murder weapon?"

Rose's stomach twisted. She hadn't planned on him searching for the rifle. *He'll find Carla and—*

Jennifer piped up. "It's *not* a murder weapon. It's a rifle that was used in self-defence."

He turned to her, annoyed. "Yeah, yeah. Whatever, Princess." *She must be that friend that Rose invited to move in with her. She's the reason why I can't pay Rose anymore 'visits'.*

Trying to concentrate on what needed to be done, he explained, "First I have to find the rifle that was used in 'self-defence'. Okay? Where is it?" He stared at the group, waiting for an answer.

They all looked away.

"Come on, girls and boys. If you don't tell me I'm going to tear this place apart. We'll come in with police dogs. Maybe find more than just the rifle."

Squirming, Rose pointed with her head to where Larry had walked out of the bush and mumbled, "He did the shooting from over there." She paused for a moment before adding, "Then he dropped the rifle and came running down here, realizing that he had shot his son."

The sheriff turned to him. "Is that what *really* happened?"

Hating the man in front of him, Larry forced a nod.

"So the story will be that he shot the perpetrators and accidentally killed his son."

"That's the *true* story, Sheriff. The problem is that we'll all go to jail. The police will come searching for pot and money. That's where we *all* lose. None of us are going to jail. Do you hear me? None of us!" Rose gave him an icy glare as she tried to shake free from the cuffs.

Despite the situation, Gleason was aroused, loving the fire in her and the way that she tousled her red hair. He also loved the way that she shook her body.

"Okay. Just cool it a little, will you?" He was speaking more to himself and, for the moment, had forgotten about the rifle. Looking down at his feet, he rubbed his bandaged chin while thinking out loud. "So … what if we bring the bodies back to Larry's and claim that the shootings took place, there? Karl and Sal beat him and he gets a rifle and scrambles up the hill and starts shooting. Larry wouldn't do jail time for that. Maybe only house arrest."

Everyone was quiet for a moment, thinking about his idea. Would it work?

Gleason pushed on. "You girls wouldn't even need to be involved. Nor would your new buddy, Quincy. He was never there." He studied them for a moment before asking, "Sound good?"

Rose turned to Jen and Larry. "What do you think?"

Shrugging, all Jennifer wanted was for their lives to return to the way it used to be and prayed that her aunt wouldn't be involved. "Yeah, it might work." She said it with a sigh, exhausted. If they pulled this off, hopefully no one would go to jail.

Larry thought about what Rose had told him earlier—that he was her hero. *The sheriff's idea might work. I started shooting and saved everybody from the bad guys.*

"What about Mike? What about the fact that he was shot? How could you explain that?" Rose still had questions. They all did.

Gleason had always dreamed of being a lawyer. He fantasized as he spoke. In his mind he was pleading his case to the jury. With his head down, he slowly paced back and forth as he began his performance. "Well, you could say that Larry's vision was blurred because of the severe blows to his head."

Larry eagerly nodded. "Yeah. That's right. I couldn't see straight."

The sheriff pushed on, warming up to his fabrication. "So … he fired the rifle from the knoll near his house and didn't realize that it was his son who he was shooting at. Then he shot Karl through the kitchen window.

"The other victim fled the scene and Larry picked him off in the front yard, worried that the kid would double back and attack him. That would fly as an explanation." He crossed his arms in satisfaction, happy with his story.

Rose was only half convinced and needed to get things straight with him. "If this works, I want you to give me your word that there will be no more payoffs."

Gleason shrugged. "It depends on how much you're willing to put out for me to cover things up." He winked at her before glancing at his watch. *Yeah, she better put out for me alright!*

She picked up on him worried about the time. "How do you exactly plan on doing all of this? Aren't you supposed to be reporting in or something? Does anybody know you're even here?"

"No. No one knows where I am, but I will have to check in soon."

Gleason mentally went over what he would tell his superiors. They would question why he was in the area and how he had discovered the shootings.

I drove up McCulloch Road to check the downed power pole. Yeah. That's right. I kept driving to see if there were any more poles knocked down by the severe windstorm last night. I was concerned for the public's safety ... being the conscientious sheriff that I am. That's when I heard the gunshots. That's when I investigated.

Yes, that would work. I was on patrol doing my job, being at the right place at the right time and protecting the public.

He pulled away from his thoughts and got down to business. "We need to act fast if we want this to work." Smiling patronizingly at Rose, he rubbed his hands and added, "But, first ... I need a little incentive."

Chapter 19

Gleason carefully went over his plan in greater detail. He explained that he would drive back to Beaswick and report in while they delivered the three bodies to Larry's property. Within an hour he would return and, with their help, do some re-arranging to duplicate the original scene.

They would place Sal on Larry's front lawn. It would be in a similar position to where he had been shot at Rose's. They would do the same with both Mike and Karl, laying Karl's body in Larry's kitchen and Mike's body in his driveway.

Rose did not like it. There were far too many loose ends. "What you're planning is absolutely crazy! What about the lack of blood on the kitchen floor or on the lawn at Larry's and what about the spray pattern—the blood on the cabinets? And, one other thing. How do we duplicate the shot that went through my window at Larry's?"

Gleason shrugged in an attempt to dismiss her concerns. "From what I can remember, Larry has a similar window in his kitchen. We could fire a bullet through it, but we'll need to make sure that the slug doesn't get embedded in his floor. I'll bring back a few sandbags from the firing range. We'll lay them out and collect the lead after we shoot a hole through his window."

Larry eagerly nodded. "I got sandbags in the back yard. We could use those."

The sheriff ignored him. "Larry's house sits next to a hill, like yours. We'll make sure that the bullet enters the kitchen window at roughly the same angle as the one that killed Karl. He was stupid enough to step into the line of fire and was hit."

Larry kept thinking about what Rose had called him earlier—her hero. "It could work. I've got a window like yours, Rose. In my kitchen. I could save you from all of this." He nodded, agreeing with the sheriff's plan and liking the idea that Gleason would claim that his son had been shot by accident. *Yeah. I shot him in the dark when I was dazed. My name would be cleared because I didn't really … murder him.*

"I still think your plan is stupid! It will never work. How do we spray blood on Larry's floor and cabinets to make it look like Karl was shot there?" She shook her head in disbelief with what he was proposing.

Sheriff Gleason thought long and hard about her last question with a fresh toothpick in his mouth. Finally, he removed his sunglasses and, in a matter-of-fact tone, said, "We don't."

"What? What are you talking about?" Annoyed, Rose wanted him to take the handcuffs off. They were hurting her and her arms were aching.

"We get a bucket and some rags from Larry's place. We come back here and scrub your kitchen clean and rinse the rags in the bucket. We return the bucket back to Larry's along with the rags.

"When they do an analysis they'll discover that it was Karl's blood in the bucket mixed in with the soapy water and think that Larry, in a panic, tried to clean up his kitchen."

"What about Sal? What about *his* blood?" Rose shook her head. "This whole idea of yours is just … ridiculous!"

He carried on, trying to reassure all of them. "That won't be a problem, either. There was no spray pattern when the bullet entered him. He probably bled internally. We just need to place his body in the same position when he was shot, only in Larry's front yard instead of yours."

"What … what about footprints? What about fingerprints? What about Mike?" She was overwhelmed with what he was suggesting.

"Their foot and fingerprints are already there—at Larry's. Don't forget that the boys paid him a visit, earlier."

Gleason pressed on. "There would be no problem with Mike. There's no exit wound so there's no blood on the driveway. We can place the body on Larry's drive in the exact same position that it's in, here. They wouldn't know the difference, but the real problem is you, Larry." Turning to the skinny man, he looked him in the eye. "You've got to tell the police that you shot the punks in self-defence and then cleaned up."

"Yeah. Sure. If it means protecting everybody and I don't have to go—"

"Good. That's fine, Larry. Now …" He paused for a moment before continuing with his trumped-up story. "Most of what you'd be telling them would be true. The boys came back after beating you the first time. When you heard them coming up your driveway you hid in the bush with your rifle. You're not going to just sit there and take it."

Larry shook his head. "No sir! I was not going to take it anymore. I had enough of—"

"That's right. You were beaten to within an inch of your life, but you still had the smarts to hide from them. You were terrified."

"Yeah. It was dark out and I had to protect myself. I couldn't make out who was coming at me. It was an accident. I shot—"

Gleason placed a finger on Larry's lips to stop his gibbering. "Listen carefully. *This* is what we're going to tell them."

He took in a breath and studied them as he worked out what to say. "The punks pull up his driveway and storm into his kitchen and ..." Gleason pointed his finger at a phantom target. "Boom! Larry shoots Karl through the side window. The other kid sees this and panics. He makes a run for it. Larry picks him off in his front yard because he's worried that the punk will double back and get him.

"Mike races out the back door. Larry is confused. After all, he's suffered severe blows to the head. In a blur, all he sees is another crazed thug charging at him in the dark. He doesn't realize that it's his son and shoots again. Boom!"

"Yeah. That's right! That's what happened. Mike wanted to save me from the beatings. I didn't know it was him. I just kept shooting." Larry bobbed his head up and down, wanting to believe what the sheriff was saying.

Now very pleased with his story, Gleason pushed on. "So ... Larry doesn't know what to do. His first instinct is to cover up the shootings. In a daze, he mops up the kitchen. A few hours later it hits him. Poor Larry realizes that he needs to call the police. End of story."

All mulled over his idea, looking for cracks. It still seemed like too much of a long shot to them. The sheriff was yakking about some far-fetched plan and was trying to make it sound like it would be easy to pull off.

Rose wondered if Larry was agreeing so readily with the sheriff's story because he wanted to believe that he had shot Mike by accident. She still wasn't convinced. *But, what else can we do? We have no other options. We need to trust Gleason or we're going to jail.* She swallowed hard. *For a very long time!*

He kept at it, trying to sell them his plan. "If this works, you girls can move on with your lives. You wouldn't even be involved." He pointed at Quincy. "Neither would your new pal, and," he turned to Larry, "you'll probably do minimal time."

Troubled, Larry took a step toward him and mumbled, "There's something that you, ah, ought' ta know."

Gleason raised his eyebrows, curious with what the frail and beaten man wanted to tell him.

Rose's heart raced. She was ready to jump in and stop Larry if he mentioned anything about Carla.

Almost in a whisper, he confessed. "I got thirty marijuana plants in my back yard along with ten ounces of pot in the house."

Jennifer was relieved that he hadn't mentioned anything about her aunt and also excited that they might at least have a chance at getting out of their horrible situation. She blurted, "We can clean your house and yard up in no time. We'll bring the pot back here. We'll be careful about leaving any evidence. We're experts at covering things up. We'll … we'll wear gloves!" She was speaking fast and her face was flushed.

Sheriff Gleason studied them for a few moments while going over all the angles. "I'm not giving you any guarantees, but my plan might work depending on a couple of things."

"What? What are they? We can work something—"

"One is timing. You've all got to act fast. And," he paused for effect, "the second is money." His voice grew hard. "You need to pay me to get this thing covered, and you need to pay me, now!"

Rose shook her head. "First of all, why the hurry? Shouldn't we be careful and take our time?"

"The bodies will very quickly be missed. Not only that, the longer you wait, the better the chance there'll be glitches. We want to portray Larry as a disturbed victim who shot the intruders because he had every right in doing so.

"He's got to call the station and confess. If he waits too long, it'll look suspicious. And, we also need the investigation to be on Larry's turf. We don't want anyone roaming the neighbourhood and asking questions—especially here. The authorities have got to believe that he's up front with them.

"We need Larry to make it look like he only wanted to clean up the mess after he shot the perpetrators so that he could get it out of his mind. He was confused and the killings sickened him."

Larry bobbed his head, repeating in his mind what the sheriff had said. *Yes, I was sickened by it. That's true. I didn't know what to do.*

Gleason smiled inwardly and was very much impressed with his story. *Damn, I'm good. I should have gone to law school. I would have made a good lawyer. No. I would have made a GREAT lawyer!*

Jennifer kept thinking about his plan. "Uh, Sheriff? You're forgetting one very important detail."

"What?" He pulled out of his fantasy with a questioning look mixed in with a healthy dose of contempt. He did not like being told that he had missed anything, *especially* by a woman. "What do you mean that I've forgotten something?"

She figured that she and her friends would still be implicated. "What about Mike's truck? It's bashed up. It's got Rose's paint from her Ford on it. The cops will know that it was in a recent accident and it won't be long before they come looking."

Gleason shrugged, acting as if it were a stupid question. "It's simple. You'll need to hide it in your barn for now."

"What? Are you out of it?" Rose couldn't believe what she was hearing. "They'll find it. That would tie us to the scene."

Larry agreed. "Yeah. You're right. They'll come looking and then—"

Gleason raised his hand, trying to calm everyone. "Look. Stuff like that happens all the time." Taking in a breath, he ploughed on. "So, Mike's truck went missing. So what? The cops would figure that he hid it somewhere, maybe up in the bush, and then came back with his buddies to Larry's.

"They'll need a search warrant if they want to come looking at your place. Why would they want to do that? Why would they be suspicious of you or anybody else?" He added, "And, if they *did* get a search warrant, I'd be privy to it so I could let you know, firsthand. That way you could get rid of the truck before they even showed up."

He shook his head for emphasis. "Hell. You can't be so damn paranoid. There'd be nothing to link you to the shootings … *if* we do things right." He ended by folding his arms over his belly and saying, "That's the risk you're going to have to take."

Rose did not like it. She did not want Mike's truck on her property. Besides, she understood that there were far too many other things that could go wrong. Gleason was playing it down and making it sound easy.

She knew that he didn't care if they were caught. He would simply deny being involved. He'd be laughing all the way to the bank—with her money.

Taking in a deep breath, she tried to re-evaluate their options. There were none. *If we don't follow his plan we'll go to jail. It's as simple as that.*

Larry mumbled, "I could call T-Bone. He'd come and get the truck." His voice picked up a notch. "He's my kid brother and has an auto wrecking business. We could get him to crush it and sell it for scrap. All I gotta do is make a call and he'd be here in a flash." He turned hopefully to Rose.

She was jittery and felt sick with what they were planning. Could they really get away with it? They would definitely need to do something with Mike's truck.

"And what about *my* truck? They'll know that it's been in an accident."

"I can fix it. I've done that sort of thing before. You just need to keep it off the road for a day or two." Larry was excited with the whole idea and his voice grew louder as he tried to convince her. "It wouldn't take much to straighten out the bumper. I could fix your truck in … half a day."

Rose wondered if he had indeed suffered a brain injury. "Come on, Larry! Give me a break. My truck has got some serious damage to it. I rammed them pretty good."

Larry studied her Ford and realized that what he was saying was probably a little too optimistic. Snapping his fingers with his hands cuffed behind his back, he blurted, "I've got it!"

"Wha-at?" She shook her head. *Another stupid idea?*

"Why don't I ask T-Bone to haul your truck away with Mike's? It would probably cost you more than it's worth to fix. Besides, we don't need the connection. T-Bone could crush both vehicles and sell them for scrap. Then there would be no evidence. You can use my truck anytime you want 'til the heat cools off. It would be the easiest thing to do."

Now you're making sense. Rose knew that he was right. She would need to get rid of her truck and rely on Larry for a few weeks. That was the least of her worries.

Looking at his feet, Gleason kicked at the ground, saying, "There's also the post-mortem problem that we need to deal with. Time of death can be determined very accurately. We can't let this go on much longer."

Rose was still not convinced. A nagging thought kept creeping into her mind. *How much does he want?* Reaching the end of her patience, she snapped, "Take the handcuffs off so we can negotiate."

"Not so fast, Rose. We can negotiate very nicely with the handcuffs on."

His scheme will never work. They'll find some shred of evidence and figure out what really happened. We'll all end up in jail.

"I've got to report in real soon or they'll wonder what's going on." He nervously glanced at his watch again. "So? What will it be? How much will you pay me to make things easier for you?" He stepped back and smiled patronizingly at her.

"Forget it. You're idea has far too many holes in it. You'll end up with my money and we'll end up in jail!"

He shrugged. "Okay. No worries. I shouldn't even get involved with your stupid mess. Get in the car. All of you. I'm taking you in."

"No!" Jennifer was sick with the thought. "Please, Rose! Pay him what he wants. He can help us."

She ignored her friend and trudged toward the squad car with her head down. *That bastard. All he'll do is double-cross us!*

Jen trailed behind her, along with Larry and Quincy. "Rose?" Jen wouldn't let up. "Don't you see? We have no other choice."

Rose's mind raced. Gleason had offered to help them, but his plan would never work, would it?

Larry tried his hand at convincing her. "Uh, Rose? Maybe Jen is right. Maybe—"

"Just shut up. All of you!" She shook her head, feeling pressured.

Gleason barked, "Get in the car." He pointed at Quincy. "You. Sit in the front seat so I can keep my eye on you. The rest of you, get in the back." He swung open the rear door.

A sinking feeling swept through all of them. Jennifer sobbed uncontrollably as she slid next to Larry and Rose in the back seat. Quincy sat in the front, his mind rambling. *It's over. We're all going to jail.*

Rose looked out the car window in tears, feeling hopeless. *I can't give him money. His plan will never work.*

The sheriff slammed the doors and turned toward the knoll. *There's one more thing that needs to be done. I've got to find the murder weapon.*

Chapter 20

Gleason simmered as he pushed his way through thick brush. *God damn her! All she had to do was give me money. Then, maybe I could have made things easier for her and her stupid friends. But, oh no, she's too stubborn.* Unaware, he moved closer to Carla, his eyes on the ground as he searched for the rifle.

A flock of sparrows was perched in a small tree between them. Spooked by the sheriff, they took to the air. He lifted his head, looking in her direction.

He sees me! He's only fifty feet away. I need to stand—to give myself up. Carla wasn't sure what she should do.

Rose looked on, handcuffed in the rear seat of the police car, praying that somehow Gleason would stop his search.

"He'll find her. He'll find my auntie. It's only a matter of time and, when he does, he'll know that we've been lying to him." Jennifer kept up her nattering. "He's mean. He'll—"

"Shut up. For God's sake, just shut up!" Rose squirmed in her seat. Her nagging partner wasn't helping matters.

"No. I won't shut up!" The younger woman was defiant. "She's got a loaded rifle in her hands. What if she shoots him?" She gulped. "What if … he shoots *her*?"

Rose hadn't thought about that possibility. She knew that what Jen was saying could happen. Carla was stressed and unpredictable. So was Gleason. And, he was also drunk. Making a quick decision, she stuck her head out the window. "Gleason!"

He stopped in his tracks and turned—a sick smile on his face. *I knew she'd see things my way. She's got no other choice.*

She hesitated for a moment before blurting out, "How much do you want?"

How much do I want? All of it you hot little thing. That's what it all comes down to— money! Judging by the smell coming from the barn, he figured that the girls had several thousands of dollars worth of marijuana curing in the old building. *I bet she also has a ton of cash stashed away.*

He'd had a magic number stuck in his brain since last night. There was no way that he would settle for anything less.

Still smiling, he sauntered back to the squad car. Inches from her face he announced, "Fifty thousand dollars. That's what I want."

"What? Are you crazy? I don't have that kind of money. Forget it. We don't have a deal."

"Look! I'm putting my ass on the line to help you—*all* of you. We're talking murder. We're talking dope growing and trafficking." He counted out the items on his fingers as he continued. "We're also talking about theft, armed robbery, assault and the use of illegal drugs." Drawing in a deep breath, he finished with, "Fifty thousand is *nothing* for what I need to do to help you!" He made it sound like he was doing them a huge favour.

"No. I … I don't have that kind of money."

Jen lashed out at her. "Then it's all your fault that we're going to jail."

Rose hated the position that she was being forced into but knew that she had no other choice. Their only salvation was her making a deal with the sheriff. Ignoring Jen, she tried again. "How about twenty thousand? I can do that. Twenty thousand. Right now!"

Pausing for a moment, he thought about what he could do with twenty thousand dollars and shook his head. "No. What I have to do to cover your headache is worth way more."

"I can't do fifty. Please …" Rose knew that paying him money would still be better than going to jail.

He wondered what her bottom line really was. *Let's just see how much I can squeeze out of that bitch.* "Okay, how much *do* you have?"

"Forty thousand. I've got forty thousand in twenties. Think about it—tons of twenty dollar bills. Two thousand of them!" Sweat ran down her back as she tried her best to get him to visualize the money. Overwhelmed, she was close to breaking down. "You can have it. Just … help us cover this up!"

Rose had two briefcases hidden in the barn. Each contained twenty-five thousand dollars. "I've got fifty thousand put away, but we need ten thousand to live on. That's all we have."

Gleason's mind was on the thousands of twenty dollar bills. He had a brief fantasy—sitting on his couch with a bottle of Jack between his legs as he threw money into the air. It would be *raining* money. *I'd have more money than I'd know what to—*

A thought slammed into him. *That bitch! All this time she's been holding out on me and telling me that she's broke and can't afford to pay all of my protection money?*

She's got fifty thou' stashed away! Not only that, she's got a barn full of pot. She's been playing me for a sucker all along. How could she do that to me?

He couldn't let the opportunity pass. He would take the forty thousand. Of course he would. "Okay. Where's the money?"

Jen let out a sigh of relief. So did Larry and Quincy. *Good! We've got a deal. Maybe there's still hope for us. Maybe we won't go to—*

"I need your word." Rose tried to settle down. *Stay cool. Remember who you're dealing with.* "You'll take the forty thousand and nothing more, right?"

"Yeah, yeah. Where's the money?"

"Not only that. You'll cover this up and leave us alone from now on. Right?"

"Uh, no. Not for a measly forty thou'. I'll still want my protection money and you better be paying me my fair share every month from now on!" He pointed a finger in her face as he spat out the last part of his sentence.

Breathing through her mouth to avoid his whiskey smell, Rose thought about what he said. It sounded like Gleason was being sincere and was indirectly telling her that things would get back to normal—that he would still be on the take after this was over. *Besides, we're stuck. We need to work with him or else …*

Looking him in the eye, she made her decision. "Okay. We've got a deal."

Chapter 21

They were at the barn—Gleason and Rose. The others remained in the police car. "Take the cuffs off. I need my hands free so I can unlock the door."

"Sure, Rose. Sure. I'll take them off. But don't try anything funny."

She rubbed her wrists and tried to get the circulation back before spinning the combination on the lock. Her mind was full of doubt. *Is he really going to help?*

Wanting confirmation, she nervously looked over her shoulder at him. "You promise you'll cover the shootings and not incriminate any of us, right?"

He had his pistol out and nodded reassuringly, adding, "I have a lot to lose if this doesn't work."

She knew he was right. He had a lot at stake, but he also had a large amount of money to make if he went along with them.

The barn used to have its own unique odour of horses and hay. Not anymore. Pulling open the old door, the powerful smell of marijuana spilled out and enveloped them.

Rays of morning sunlight had found their way through the many cracks in the walls illuminating the suspended dust in the air. Giant marijuana plants hung from the rafters to cure. In a corner, an array of grow lights was fastened to the ceiling joists with electrical wires crudely strewn across them, culminating in a circuit box near the portable generator in the corner.

Rose slid out a bale of hay from an old stockpile near the rear of the barn. Gleason stiffened, watching her every move. Reaching in behind it, she pulled out one dusty briefcase and then another.

Excited, he dropped to his knees and tried to open one. It was locked. They both were. Frustrated, he barked, "Open them!"

She hesitated, close to tears. *We've worked so hard for this and now we're giving it away. All because of Mike and Larry. All because of the thugs.*

"I said open them!"

"I … I can't do it." She felt helpless. Their lives were now in Gleason's hands.

He bolted up, his face inches from hers. "Damn you! We had a deal. If you don't open them right now, you're all going to jail."

"Okay. Okay!" She forced herself to spin the cylinders and unlock a briefcase. Tears clouded her vision as she flipped it open.

Rows of neatly stacked twenty dollar bills, bundled in groups of fifty, filled the case. He grunted with pleasure as he rubbed his hands over the money in an almost erotic fashion, wanting to fondle each and every bill. "How much is in here?" He couldn't help but smile with eyes that were glued to the cash.

"Twenty … twenty-five thousand." She said it in a faltering voice while turning away, unable to look at the money—her money. *I should have given the five thousand to Quincy and his goons when they had asked for it hours earlier. They would have left and nobody would have been killed. I would still have most of my money.*

"Good. Very good. Now, open the other one." He was animated and almost drooled.

Rose unlocked the second case and stepped back, trying to put a positive twist on what was happening. *It's … it's still better than going to jail. At least we can get our lives back.*

Looking down at the greedy man in front of her, she was disgusted with what she saw. He groped a bundle of her cash in an almost sexual way, his eyes glazed with excitement. She felt violated.

Now satisfied, he slammed both briefcases shut before standing, firmly gripping one in each hand.

"Not so fast, Sheriff. I told you that I would pay you *forty* thousand. Give me back ten stacks. You've got fifty thousand there."

"Huh? Gosh Rosie. I must have counted wrong. My mistake." He smiled sarcastically at her.

She glared back, her anger quickly returning as she waited for her money.

"Turn around." He waved his pistol at her.

"What? What are you doing? We agreed on forty thousand dollars. We need the ten thousand to live on. Don't take all of it!"

He smirked as she pleaded.

"Please. That's all we have. You lied to us. We trusted you. We—"

"I said turn around. Now!" He made a threatening motion with his pistol.

"But, how could you—?"

"I'm telling you again. Turn around!"

Rose hated him more than ever. He had meddled in her married life. He had come over one night and had raped her. He had also taken money from her month after month and now … this? Gleason was double-crossing her again.

"I'm giving you one last chance. Turn around and put your hands behind your back. Do as I say or you're going to get hurt!" He jabbed the pistol at her chest.

A steady stream of tears ran down her face. She had no other choice. He was stealing all of her money. *The bastard. I knew it.* "You had no intention of helping us, did you?" Her body shook with anger and disgust.

"Of course I will." He wore a sanctimonious smile as he talked down to her. "It's just that I had my mind set on fifty thou', you know? And now that I've seen it, well," he shrugged, "that's the magic number. That kind of money will make me work even harder in fixing up your mess." His voice grew hard as he roughly snapped the cuffs on her. "Now, head out the barn."

With her head down, she trudged toward the old door, disgusted with what he was doing. Gleason gripped the two briefcases in his gloved hands and followed her into daylight.

Just outside, she turned and asked, "Now what? What are you planning on doing? I did what you wanted. I gave you the money."

Ignoring her, Sheriff Gleason put the briefcases down and holstered his pistol. He stuck another toothpick in his mouth and squinted in the morning sunlight before slowly putting his reflective sunglasses back on.

It was infuriating for her. *Who does he think he is? The pompous ass!* "Don't hide behind your stupid glasses. Look me in the eye! Answer the question. What are you planning on doing?"

He shrugged. "You know, sweetheart. I've been thinking and all and, well—"

"No. No. No! You lying, cheating son of a bitch. All you want is money." She screamed it out and knew that it was over for her and her friends. "You took all of it—all of our money. Fifty thousand dollars! You promised you would only take forty!"

They squirmed in the police car as they listened to what Rose as saying. They would be going to jail and Gleason would end up with the cash.

She decided to change her tune, now begging. "What about the protection money? What about all the marijuana in the barn? It's worth a lot. Please, Cornelius! We need you."

He shook his head. *I'll take them in and lock 'em up. Then I'll stash the money. No one will be able to prove that I took it. It will be their word against mine.*

They lied to me and owe me for all that I've put up with. Especially with the killings that they got me involved in. It's time that they pay me what I'm worth.

She tried again. "We can still make this work. Please! We can pay you more, once we—"

Tired of her whining, he snapped out, "Get back to the car."

Rose dropped her head. She had reached an all time low and felt both hopeless and betrayed as she headed back to the police car and her friends.

Halfway there, she turned and tried again. "Please, Cornelius! Don't do this. We'll all do years in jail. We'll lose everything! We'll—"

"I said get in the car. Now!" Impatient, he took a threatening step toward her. "I've got the power here. I've got the—"

"No you don't!" The hard voice came from the knoll.

Chapter 22

He spun around, not understanding and, for the moment, couldn't make anybody out. Squinting from behind his sunglasses, Gleason looked again.

A large woman in camouflaged clothing stood waist deep in brush a hundred feet away. She had a rifle zeroed in on him.

Blood drained from his face. Before he could say anything, she yelled, "Raise your hands. Put them up real slow or I'll blow you away."

"What? Who the hell are *you*?" Gleason looked from Rose, to Carla and then back at Rose in disbelief. "What's going on? Who is she?"

Rose could only shake her head, dumbfounded with the turn of events. *Oh God! Now what?*

"Now wait just a damn minute." Things didn't make sense to him. "How did you …? Who are you? Maybe we can—"

"Are you as deaf as you are stupid? I said put 'em up!" She jabbed the rifle in his direction.

Can this really be happening? She's not going to get away with this. She's threatening a police officer. He put the briefcases down and slowly raised his hands. "Who are you? Do you know what you're doing? Put the rifle down and we'll … talk."

"Oh no, Sheriff. I've been listening to you 'talk' for the last while and I don't like what I'm hearing. You're screwing with my friends and when you do that, guess what? You screw with *me*!"

She took several steps toward him with the raised rifle. "There will be no more talking." Her voice was hard as her mind worked overtime.

Carla knew that what she was doing was crazy, but that didn't matter to her anymore. Once again she and her friends were being used. It was time to put a stop to it. It was time for them to take charge of their lives.

Inch by inch, he lowered his hands. *Can I reach for my gun without her shooting me? And then—*

"I said keep 'em up! Do it!" *What if he tries something funny? I'd have to shoot him. Could I? Shoot a friggin' sheriff?* She was being pushed far beyond her limit. *I can't quit now! I need to be strong.*

Gleason's eyes were riveted on the burly woman. He wondered if she really would pull the trigger. *No. I can't chance it right now. She's pumped.* A cold sweat ran down his back.

"Rose? Could you …?" Carla had wanted to ask her to take his pistol from him but stopped. *No. I'd be putting her in too much danger. Quincy's bigger and dispensable.*

"Uh, Quincy?" *I need to trust him.* "Get out of the car and grab the sheriff's gun."

He froze with the idea. *Shit. What if he tries something stupid?*

"Get the pistol!" This time she yelled it out.

"I can't. My hands are cuffed behind my back."

"Yes you can. Do it!"

Struggling with the door handle, he stepped out of the police car and made his way toward Gleason. Jen and Larry looked on from the rear seat, not believing what was taking place.

The sheriff tried to reason with Carla as Quincy moved closer to him. "You won't get away with this. You know that. We can stop it right now. Put the rifle down and I'll pretend that none of this ever happened."

"Just keep those hands held high. Keep them real high." She turned her attention on Quincy. "Do it! Get his friggin' pistol."

He backed toward the sheriff and blindly searched with his cuffed hands. Fumbling for the holstered pistol, he uttered, "I know what you're thinkin', Gleason. Don't try nothin' stupid. She's more than ready to blow your brains out." He added, "She'll probably blow mine out too if you plan on using me as some sort of shield." Before he could respond, Quincy had the service pistol safely in hand and quickly stepped away, dropping it several feet from Gleason.

Carla relaxed a little. "Now, reach into your pocket, Sheriff, and pull out the keys for the cuffs. Take them out nice and slow."

Rose stood frozen next to the police car as her mind raced on. *We've got three bodies on my property and now a rifle is aimed at the sheriff? There is no way we'll get out of this one! Still, we've got nothing to lose. The bastard was going to steal my money and take us to jail.*

Jennifer looked on in disbelief. What her aunt was doing was beyond ridiculous to her. The situation was far too crazy. Leaning out the rear window she shouted, "Auntie! Please. We're getting deeper into trouble. We can't do this. We'll all go to jail. Maybe we should leave things—"

"Listen to me. All of you! Listen to me!" Carla snapped it out as she took several steps toward them, wanting to make her point. "We have no—other—choice. Do you hear me? He was going to take us in! We'd go to jail … for years, *if* we let him. And, he was stealing our money. *All* of it! This has got to stop."

Jen knew that her aunt was right. What else could they do? "I know but—"

"We don't stand a chance with him." Carla had their full attention as she made her case. "He sure as hell won't help. He'll only make things worse." She yelled it out as she shook the rifle at him—partly out of anger but mainly out of fear.

Gleason flinched—worried that she might shoot him. *Jesus! This is bullshit!* "Uh, look, lady. Just take your finger off that trigger before you—"

"But, Auntie …?" Jen interrupted him. Did Carla have some sort of master plan or was she simply running on adrenalin? Or was she so stressed that she was losing her mind? "Think about it. You can't just shoot him! We'll all—"

"I know what we *can't* do! We can't let that bastard get away with this. He's been taking advantage of us for months. We have no other choice. He forced us into a corner and now it's time to get our lives back. All night long we've been manipulated and terrorized. I'm sick of it. I … I just don't care anymore."

Determined that she and her friends would not be used by him any longer, she ended with, "We are not going to jail! Do you hear me? We are *not* going to jail!" She shouted it out.

Cold and calculating, she turned to Gleason. "Take the keys out of your pocket and throw them to me."

He hesitated. *Should I do it? Maybe I should take a stand. Maybe I should tell her to take them out. Then, when she does, I could grab her and—*

"Do it. Now!" Carla moved closer and this time aimed through the gun sights.

Forget it. I'm not taking any chances. She's ready to pull the trigger. I'll … I'll play it safe for now, but I'll hunt them down. I'll make sure that she pays—

"God damn it! DO IT!"

Slowly, he reached into his pocket and searched for his keys. It was difficult for him to do. His pants were stuffed with Larry's money. He snaked a hand around the wads of cash before finding the key ring. Tossing it in her direction, he silently promised that he would get even—one way or another. *Damn her!*

He turned to Rose. "I bet you wish they were still in my pants? You know? I bet you wish the keys were still in my pocket. Right? That would give you a thrill, wouldn't it? Reaching in and feeling me?"

Her mouth dropped in disgust.

Furious, he kept at it, knowing that he was only antagonizing everyone, but his anger was simply too intense. He felt humiliated. They had duped him. *How can I explain what happened when I file a police report? That I was ambushed because … because I didn't do a proper search of their property? I'll look stupid and end up losing my job.*

"Isn't that right, bitch? I know you liked it. It brings back hot memories—how I did you on your kitchen counter. How—"

"Do it, Carla! Blow that piece of crap all the way to hell!" There was pure hatred in Rose's eyes.

"I'm just waiting for one more reason. Just one more reason and then, boom!" Her finger itched on the trigger as she barked out, "Put 'em back up, Sheriff. Reach for the sky." Carla knew that she sounded like something out of a B-grade western, but she didn't care anymore. She was dead serious and shook the rifle at him to prove it.

He had no other choice and raised his hands above his head one more time.

"Quincy. Pick up the keys and un-cuff Rose."

Dropping to his knees, he scooped up the key ring and stood back to back with her. Moments later she was free. Quickly, she helped Larry and Jen out of the squad car.

"Rose," Jen tried to reason with her friend as she unlocked her cuffs. "This is going too far. My aunt has lost her friggin mind. You need to talk to her."

Larry had been unusually quiet as he went over the recent turn of events. But, it had nothing to do with them abducting a sheriff. No. He was brooding about what Cornelius had blatantly admitted to everyone.

It was far more painful to hear Gleason boast about his sexual encounter in the kitchen with Rose than the beatings he had been given earlier. The sheriff had bragged to everyone that he had raped the woman that Larry loved.

He couldn't keep it in. His hatred for the sheriff was no longer simmering. Now it was boiling over. "Let *me* blow him away. Let me kill him. He's the cause of all of this."

Turning to the sheriff, he ranted on. "It's because of you that I got beat up. It's because of you that those two boys were shot. It's because of you that Mike—" He halted, realizing that he might have gone too far and couldn't put all of the blame on Gleason.

Chapter 23

The harsh reality of what they were doing was quickly sinking in. They were abducting a sheriff and, once they were caught, the life that they had known would be gone forever.

Rose decided to remove Quincy's cuffs. If Gleason made the wrong move, Quincy might be able to overpower him. Larry and his damaged ribs wouldn't be much help. She had the key in the lock when Jennifer muttered, "Don't. I still don't trust him."

"We *need* to trust him. We have no other choice. What's Quincy going to do? He's got nowhere to go."

"It's just that ..." Jen still wasn't convinced. "He's been terrorizing us all night. He was the leader in all of this."

Rose knew that she was right. "Yes, but he also looked after us a little, too. He stopped Karl from beating us. He told us how sorry he was. He told us how Gleason used him and made sure he was still on drugs when he wanted to go straight."

The sheriff was furious with what they were saying about Quincy. "I know him. I've seen him in action. He's nothing but a meth freak."

Jennifer understood that it was probably true. *What will Quincy do if we release him?* She turned to her aunt with a questioning look.

Carla nodded in agreement with Rose. If they kept him cuffed, then what? What was the point?

Quincy made an attempt at pleading his case. He cleared his throat. "Look. What I did ... what *we* did, was wrong. I never thought that it would turn out like this! At least give me a chance."

"What about the money? There's fifty thou' in those briefcases. What about that? You've been after money all friggin' night. You could take it if we let our guard down, but if you did, you'd be hunted." Jen pointed to the sheriff, her anger taking over. "He thinks that it's *his* money. That makes it even worse. Mr. Sheriff will do what he can to steal it, with or without the law."

"Yeah. I know, but I don't want the money."

"What *do* you want?" Rose was trying to figure him out.

"I ... want a new start. I want to stop taking meth. And, I don't want to go to jail. The money doesn't mean a thing to me any—"

"That's bullshit! He's a drug freak. He'll take my—" Gleason quickly corrected himself. "He'll take *your* money. He'll steal it the first chance he gets."

Carla ignored him and turned back to Quincy. "Would you be willing to work with us?"

"To have him work with you?" The sheriff was incredulous. "What do you mean *work* with you? You're all going to jail. This is not some kind of family reunion. You've been doing too many drugs. You're crazy. That's it. You're all crazy!"

He wouldn't let up and kept trying to convince them that he could still help. "Get a grip. Get back to reality. I can get you out of this mess—*all* of you. Believe me!"

"Believe *you*? Yeah. Sure, Mr. Sheriff. We believe you all right." Carla shook her head with contempt.

Jen thought about her ex-boyfriend. He had never tried to stop doing drugs. Not like Quincy. He seemed genuine in wanting to change his life. Turning to Rose, she finally nodded. She had made her decision, but could not believe that she was putting her trust in a skin headed thug that had been terrorizing them all night.

With the cuffs now off, Quincy made a pledge to all of them. "I won't let you down. From now on I'll—"

"You son of a bitch." Gleason was livid. "You won't get away with this, boy. Let's work together. I'll see to it that no harm comes to you. We can share the money. You'll be free to go."

For a moment Quincy thought about that. *What if I did help him? What if I overpowered Carla and took the rifle? I could walk away from all of this and not do jail time.*

Thinking about it a little more, he mentally shook his head. *No. I'd still go to jail. Gleason would screw me one way or the other. I don't have a chance with him.*

Turning to his new friends, he announced, "I'll help you. We're in this together—the five of us."

Gleason was speechless. He had figured that he had half a chance if Quincy worked with him. Now that opportunity seemed to have evaporated into thin air.

Carla's shoulder ached from the heavy rifle. She wanted to lower it, but not just yet. There were still a few things that needed to be done. "Quincy. You and Larry cuff him."

"I … I can't believe that you're going to do that to me. I …" Gleason carried on with his huffing as the two men approached him. "Don't you dare lay a hand on me." He stepped back and made a promise. "I'll get you. Believe me, I'll—" They roughly pulled his arms behind his back and snapped on the cuffs.

"You're all in deep trouble. I'll make sure that you're arrested. I'll testify that I saw you commit murder. All of you!" Shaking his head, he threw out hard questions. "How do you think you'll get away with this? Huh? How? Where do you think you can run to? You *can't* run. You'll end up in jail. Hell no. You'll end up on death row!"

Now he had their full attention. There was no escaping it. They knew that he was right. They would go to jail—or worse.

Carla lowered the rifle and turned to the group. Exhausted, she said, "We need to talk."

The handcuffed sheriff stood alone in the parking area under the mid morning sun as they grouped on the rear porch, anxious to hear what Carla had to say. Rubbing at her shoulder, she whispered, "We've got to figure out what to do."

"What to do? What to do!" Jennifer panicked. Lowering her voice, she exclaimed, "There's nothing we *can* do. We're screwed. We've been screwed all night!" She pointed accusingly at her aunt. "I thought that *you* had some kind of plan figured out!"

If they released Gleason, he would arrest them and take them to jail. He would never work with them. Not anymore. Now, he was the enemy.

Carla had been thinking hard when she had been in the bush. Ignoring her niece's outburst she said, "Listen carefully to what I've got to say."

Chapter 24

Gleason was incensed as he stood alone with cuffed hands in the parking area. The group was huddled on the porch, whispering. *What are they planning?* He lashed out at Quincy. "I'm going to make sure you rot in jail, punk!"

Not getting a response, he directed his verbal assault on Rose. "You too, bitch. No wonder my brother left you. I think you're more of a dyke than anything else—living way up here with your girlie friends."

It was too much for her. "Shut up. Just—"

"It's okay." Carla put a hand on her friend's shoulder. "Don't get caught up with that kind of stuff. Don't listen to him."

The past fourteen hours was taking its toll on Rose. It was taking its toll on everyone. Tears welled in her eyes as she struggled to get control of both her hurt and her hate.

Carla tried to reason with him. "We've got a plan that might help *all* of us."

A sarcastic snort erupted from his throat. "Plan? You've got a plan? Yeah. Right! How do you think you'll ever get away with this? How? Tell me about your so-called 'plan'. Tell me!" He knew that they needed his help.

"We're going to keep you cuffed until we clean things up the way you suggested. We'll move the bodies to Larry's, but you won't get your money just yet. You'll only get it *if* you agree to work with us."

"I'm still going to make sure you rot in hell. All of you! You're kidnapping a sheriff. A sheriff!" His blood pressure rocketed to new heights as he screamed it out.

He understood that, if he played his cards right, he could still get his hands on their money. But, the problem was no longer about money. Gleason was indignant with the way that they were treating him and how they hadn't told him about Carla. *I'm a sheriff for Christ's sake! How dare they do this to me! They have absolutely no respect for the law!*

He already had a plan of his own worked out. *I'm going to tell Darwin and Scarlett exactly what happened.*

I was in the area when I came across the murder scene. Once I had them cuffed, I searched for the weapon. I was only doing my duty. That's when the bigger woman slithered out from her hiding place with a rifle aimed at me! At me! A sheriff for God's sake. I tried my best to negotiate but …

Carla turned to the group and nodded, giving everyone the signal. It was time to put her idea into action.

Rose gulped two Tylenol before hobbling to the barn. She was a mess as she stepped into the old building and retrieved latex gloves. They had a box of them stored near the marijuana clippings. It protected their hands from the residue that would leach into their bodies when harvesting the bud.

No one spoke as they rolled on the thin gloves. The girls knew that this was another turning point. So did Larry and Quincy. They had all agreed on some very tough choices.

The sheriff broke into a sweat when he saw them rolling on the gloves. *They're going to do something bad to me. Jesus! I need a drink.*

"Quincy." Carla barked out the order.

"Huh?"

"You and Larry put him in the trunk."

Gleason went into panic mode. "You won't get away with this. I'll get you. I promise. I'll hunt you down. All of you." His eyes bulged. "You can't do this to me! I'm the … I'm the law!" *They're nothing but low-life drug dealers and meth freaks. I can deal with them. I just need to scare them a little.*

He shouted over his shoulder as the two men jostled him toward his car. "Ya know what? I won't even get the law involved. No. That would be too sweet. I've got friends. I've got some real bad friends that owe me. I'm going to make sure that you all get the beating of your lives before I personally finish each one of you off." Spittle stuck to the corner of his mouth as he spewed out the last few words.

Carla had heard enough. They all had. "Lock the loudmouth in his trunk. Maybe *then* he'll shut up." They had hoped that Gleason would have cooled off and co-operate. Offering him money didn't seem to matter to him anymore.

He continued with his ranting. "They'll find out. The law will find out what you're doing. You won't get away with this. I don't care *how* much you give me. I won't cover for you!"

Everyone tried to ignore him as he kept it up. Fear was in his voice as Larry and Quincy shoved him closer to his trunk. "They'll ... they'll find out. They'll find fibers from my clothes in the trunk. They'll know that I was kidnapped. They'll—"

Jennifer jumped in. "He's right!" What he was saying was probably true. "They'll know we put him in the trunk."

Carla agreed. *We have got to be careful. There can't be any sign that we held him captive. We need to bind him in plastic so that there are no traces of fiber or hair. Then we can wrap some of that duct tape around the plastic to secure him.* She raised her hand. "Stop!"

Is she reconsidering what they are going to do to me? Gleason hoped that she had a change of heart.

She was in full control as she bellowed out orders. "Rose! Get some of that plastic out of the barn. Jen! Get the duct tape from the kitchen."

"What ...? What are you going to do? What are you going to do to ... *me*? Are you going to wrap me in plastic and ... shoot me?" He swallowed hard. *This is going too far.* He had a very bad feeling and realized that he may have underestimated them—that they would stop at nothing and could murder him if he didn't co-operate.

Carla responded in a matter-of-fact tone. "Sheriff. We're going to make sure that you're comfortable. Like I said, we'll get things cleaned up just the way you suggested. Then we'll have money for you, *if* you play along."

Moving closer, she gave him an ultimatum. "It's up to you. You can make it hard on yourself or easy for all of us."

Gleason slowly began to re-think his situation. *It might be better if I do go along with them—at least for now.* He understood that they were very capable of doing whatever it took to get out of their mess. *If I screw up, they'll shoot me. Hell, they've already murdered three people. They've got nothing to lose.*

Chapter 25

They enveloped the handcuffed sheriff in plastic. Several wraps of duct tape bound his legs and arms. They made a few holes near his mouth and nose so that he could breathe.

Larry helped Quincy lift him into his trunk. It was almost too much for Larry and he winced from the pain in his ribs. *Jeeze. He's gotta weigh at least three hundred friggin' pounds!*

There was a loud 'thunk' as Quincy slammed down the Challenger's trunk lid.

Carla focused on what needed to be done and tried not to think about the possible consequences. She had never known that side of her—of what she was capable of doing. *I've changed—going from a peaceful soul to a killer and now a … kidnapper?* Her mind was in shambles. *Are we doing the right thing? No. Of course not, but we—*

"Are you okay?" Jen saw her inner turmoil and was concerned for her aunt's emotional well-being.

"Am I okay? Am I okay? Of course not! I am *not* okay! We … we've got to get this done as fast as possible." She didn't want to lose her nerve. They had to keep busy.

Her pulse quickened as she threw out orders. "Quincy! You and Larry take some of that plastic and wrap the body on the front lawn." She didn't want to go near Sal.

"Rose! You and Jen do the same with the one in the kitchen. We'll put them in Mike's truck. I'll take care of Mike."

Larry turned away when she mentioned his son's name. So much had been going on in the last little while that he hadn't had a chance to think about him. He had been preoccupied with Carla's plan. He had also been thinking about Rose and their future together. *Was* there a future together?

The terrible situation that he and Rose were being drawn into was pulling them closer. *Now that Mike is gone, maybe she'll move in with me.*

Feeling guilty and somewhat ashamed with the way he was thinking, Larry grabbed the plastic and walked over to Sal's body, trying to block Rose out of his mind. *I just killed my son for God's sake and now I'm dreaming about a relationship?* He knew that it was his way of escaping from the terrible truth—what he had done to Mike. He also knew that he had to get a hold of his emotions.

Quincy trailed a few feet behind him, having difficulty coming to terms with all that had happened. *How did it get so carried away? All we wanted was to steal a little money and now three people are dead and we're kidnapping a sheriff!*

Larry winced as he got on his knees next to Sal. His ribs ached even more after he and Quincy had struggled with the heavy sheriff, lifting him into the trunk. So did his heart. He studied Sal's lifeless body. The morning sun highlighted his face. *He's gone. Dead!* Thoughts of Mike returned in a tsunami of pain, bringing tears to his eyes.

Standing behind him, Quincy was reluctant to get any closer. In a weak voice he muttered, "Could you, uh, do me a … favour?"

"Huh?" Surprised, Larry pulled away from his personal torment for a moment and looked up at Quincy. He wondered what he wanted.

"Could you at least, uh, cover his face with the plastic a little so that I, uh, don't have to look at him?" The bigger guy with the shaved head and scorpion tattoo also had tears.

Momentarily blocking his mind from Mike, Larry studied Quincy. *He does have a heart after all. He just kind a got caught up in the wrong direction.* He mumbled, "Yeah. Sure," before completely covering Sal with the black plastic.

With aching ribs, Larry got on his feet. "I need help with the bod—" He stopped short and tried to rephrase his sentence. "I mean, I need help with your friend, Sal." *This whole mess is forcing us to work together.*

Both got to work, uncomfortable with their momentary bonding. Quincy lifted the corpse by the arms while Larry struggled with the legs.

The sheriff's muffled obscenities broke everyone's concentration. Carla shook her head. *Here we go again. One minute he promises to work with us and the next minute he's making threats.*

She kept wondering how they could blackmail him. Accusing the sheriff of raping Rose wouldn't work. It would be his word against hers. They also had no hard evidence that he had been collecting protection money from them. It had always been in cash. Even if they *could* prove it, they would still end up in jail for growing pot and bribing a sheriff.

What about him hiring Quincy and his goons to beat up Larry? Could we nail him on that? She shook her head. *No. It would be Gleason's word against a meth freak's.*

Rose and Jennifer struggled with lifting Karl onto a sheet of black plastic while trying to avoid the pool of blood on the kitchen floor. Needing Quincy's help, they awkwardly shuttled it to Mike's truck.

Now working as a team, the five of them loaded both Sal and Karl into Mike's truck box.

Gleason anxiously listened to their every move, his mind racing. *They're doing just what I told them to do. They'll make it look like the murders happened at Larry's, but they're wasting their time. As soon as I'm free I'll let everybody know what really happened.*

Larry turned away when they temporarily moved his son and the two briefcases into Rose's barn. Moments later Rose closed the old door and snapped the lock. The sound made him shake with grief. *Poor Mike. He'll be all alone in there. Does he have his inhaler with him? Does he have enough cigarettes?* He prayed that his boy could somehow come back to life and that there would be better times ahead for both of them.

Carla rummaged in the bush and collected the spent shell casings before getting back to her friends. Worried that they might have second thoughts about what they were planning on doing, she asked, "Is everybody ready?"

They could only nod as they looked down at the ground. There was nothing left to say.

"Quincy?" Carla motioned with her head toward the Challenger.

Swallowing the lump in his throat, he made his way to the police car. Gleason's sunglasses and hat were on the seat. He put them on along with the sheriff's jacket. As an added touch, he stuck a straw in his mouth. From a distance, no one would be the wiser. He *did* look like the sheriff perched in his police cruiser.

Mike's passenger door was far too damaged to open so Rose climbed in from the driver's side and slid over. Larry sat next to her behind the wheel. Carla and Jen crawled into the truck box, keeping a safe distance from the bodies.

The two vehicles made their way down Rose's driveway. Larry drove at a slow speed because of Mike's tire. It continued to scrape the fender from the ramming hours earlier, making it difficult for him to steer, especially with his aching ribs. Quincy closely followed in the police muscle car with Gleason bound in the trunk.

It took several minutes before they reached the foot of Larry's property. The sight of his driveway made Rose relive the terrible night hours earlier. The goons had hunted her down it like wild animals. The sharp pain in her ankle made her replay the chase once more.

What would they have done if they had caught me? She swallowed hard and knew the answer. *They would have ripped me apart. Especially Karl!* It seemed like ages ago. *Now look at how things have changed. Mike is in my barn. Dead! Quincy is following us in Gleason's friggin' police car with the sheriff bound in the trunk and,* she shuddered in disbelief, *we've got two bodies in the back of Mike's truck?*

They pulled in behind Larry's A-frame, next to Karl's Honda. Still wearing gloves, Quincy and Larry did a switch with the bodies. They lifted Sal and Karl from Mike's truck and placed them in the box of Larry's blue, Chevy pick-up. Larry covered them with a tarp.

Carla had to ask the question. "Is everybody good so far?" They all needed to be on board with what they were planning on doing.

"Yeah. Let's just get this thing over with." Jennifer was beginning to lose her nerve as she trudged over to Karl's car. Sitting in the passenger seat, she tried to block out what they were planning.

Rose slid behind the wheel and turned the key with her gloved hand. Karl's Honda sputtered to life. Turning to Jen, she wondered how she was holding out. Her friend's face was white and she looked very close to having an emotional breakdown.

Jen stared out the windshield. The morning sun was shining through it at an oblique angle. "Wait a minute!" She yelled it out.

"What? What's wrong?"

"What's wrong? What's fucking wrong? Look at the windshield. Look at the dashboard. There are fingerprints are all over this car. Including Quincy's! The cops will know that he was in the Honda with his buddies." Having another panic attack, she gasped, "We've got to wipe everything clean. We've got to make sure that there's nothing that can link him to Sal or Karl!"

Rose shook her head, not believing how they could have overlooked something so important. "Yes. You're right. But, if we do that, the cops will be even more suspicious. They won't find *any* prints and it will only point to a cover up."

"We need to wipe off all the prints and then … and then …" Jen faltered for a moment before coming up with what she thought might be a good idea. "Then we need to pull the bodies from the truck and … plant their fingerprints on—"

"Stop right there! Don't be ridiculous." Rose put her hand up, interrupting her shaky friend. "You're saying that we wipe Karl's Honda down and then," she shook her head in disbelief, "we drag the bodies back here and plant their fingerprints all over the—" An idea slammed into her. "Quincy!" She yelled it out.

"Huh?"

"When you were in the car with your two buddies, where did you sit?" She squeezed the steering wheel, her emotions on overload.

"What?"

"I said where did you sit? Where did you put your hands? We need to get rid of your prints without removing Karl's or Sal's."

"Yeah. You're right. Of course!" He paused for a moment while thinking. "I was in the back seat. Yeah! I was in the back. So was Mike. We were counting out Larry's cash. I always sit in the back!"

"Ok. Good. All we need to do is wipe the rear door handles and back seat. We won't need to touch the front at all."

He added, "We've also got to wipe my prints from Larry's money." *Shit! And what else do we need to do? What have we missed?*

Minutes later Quincy rumbled up behind them in the Challenger, ready to follow them down the driveway. Sweat dripped from his shaved head and his hands were beginning to wrinkle from the latex gloves.

Larry carefully climbed into his truck and slammed his door. Carla was sitting next to him and had been drifting far away. The sharp metallic 'clang' made her jump.

He turned to her and tried to sound positive. "You know, uh, this plan of yours just might work."

She was shaken and unable to respond. Placing a hand to her chest, she was having trouble breathing. *What else have we missed?*

The three vehicles headed down Larry's drive, leaving Mike's Toyota behind. Their intent was to take Karl's Honda, the sheriff's cruiser and Larry's truck to a small clearing in the mountains just off Jack Pine Road.

Rose and Jennifer led the way in Karl's sedan as they drove along McCulloch Road. Quincy followed in the sheriff's cruiser. Larry and Carla brought up the rear in Larry's Chevy pickup with a tarp draped over the two bodies.

Gleason lay tightly bound in the trunk. *What's going on? What are they doing? They were supposed to set up the crime scene at Larry's. That's what we had talked about. Now we're on the move?* He twisted and turned as they made their way toward the logging road that hunters sometimes used.

He was angry and worried. *Where are they taking me?* His mind raced with possibilities. *Are they going to dump me in the woods? And then, what? Leave me to fend for myself while they try to make a run for it?*

Why are they taking three vehicles? I heard Larry's truck start. I thought I heard car doors slam from another vehicle. Was it Karl's?

For several moments he didn't understand. Then, it hit him. *Yes! Of course! That's what those bastards are going to do. They've got fifty thousand bucks. They'll leave the bodies in Karl's car and hide it in the bush somewhere. They'll leave me in the trunk and make a run for it with the money. Hell, I'd do it, too.*

Furious, he made a pledge. *I'm going to hunt them down. I'll rape that bitch again and again. I'll grab every nickel she's got.*

Quincy's going to jail. I'll make sure that he never sees daylight. He kept wriggling and twisting, trying to break free from the plastic and duct tape. *That little princess bitch, Jennifer! She'll be going to jail along with that dyke friend of hers. We'll get 'em. They won't get far.*

The tape held fast, forcing him to stop, at least for a few minutes. Hyped, he vowed that he would make them all pay dearly.

Making the turn onto Jack Pine Road, they slowly drove up the mountain. The small side trail that led to the clearing was several miles away.

Jen wanted Rose to drive faster so that they could get things over with but knew that an obvious dust cloud would be created and would only draw attention to their caravan.

Larry's mind drifted back to Mike and their stormy relationship as he and Carla followed the two vehicles in the noon sunlight. They soon trailed the group and were several car lengths behind.

Bill McPherson was in the bucket of the lift truck near the top of the new power pole that they had just put into place on McCulloch Road. In a day or two, when they weren't pressed for time, they would return and remove the old pole that had been pulled down by several trees in the windstorm the night before. Right now they could at least temporarily restore electrical service before moving on.

He had a partial view of Jack Pine Road as he lit a cigarette. The sound of a high powered engine from a half mile away caught his attention. Squinting for a better view, Bill saw two vehicles pass through a clearing. *Looks like a police car following a sedan. The cop is real close. I wonder what's up.* Moments later they disappeared behind a grove of trees.

His co-worker called out to him. "Huh?" If Cecil hadn't yelled out his name, Bill would have spotted another vehicle—a blue Chevy pickup trailing several car lengths behind the police car and sedan.

Rose had a rough idea of where the small side road should be. The last time she had been there was years ago. Looking through Karl's bug-streaked windshield, she did a double-take. A plume of dust drifted above the trees a quarter mile ahead of them. Another vehicle was speeding their way.

Jennifer saw it, too. "God, no! This can't be." They had prayed that there wouldn't be any traffic on the road.

Rose's knuckles turned white under her gloves as Jennifer's mind flashed back to her mother. *Will she visit me? When I'm in jail?*

Gunning the motor, Rose hoped that, if she drove fast enough, they could still make the turn onto the small side road without being seen. *Can we do it?* The dust cloud up ahead was quickly closing in on them.

Where is the friggin trail? We should be there by now! In a moment or two we'll be spotted and then what? Rose was sick with worry. *Whoever's coming our way will tell the police that he saw three vehicles, including the sheriff's. He'll give them a full description. How can we explain the bodies, the sheriff ... everything?*

Chapter 26

The two hunters barrelled down the washboard road after a night of serious drinking and poker playing. Al and Eddy usually had a late breakfast of bacon and eggs, but not today. It had been toast, and helped only a little in settling their stomachs.

Al was driving fast and his truck bounced over the many pot holes. They had managed to put away several cans of beer the night before at their cabin. Still a little drunk, he chuckled about last night. He had been teasing Eddy about drinking Bud Light instead of regular beer. "If you drink too many Bud Lights, guess what will happen? You'll get Bud lit!" He still thought it was all rather funny.

Eddy didn't share in his sense of humour and was getting sicker by the minute. "Pull over, fast! I'm gonna puke."

Rose swallowed hard, fixated with the oncoming vehicle just around the bend. She and her friends would have no reasonable explanation. Shaking her head, she tried to make sense of their situation. *I'm driving Karl's car. He just happened to have been shot dead in my kitchen! Quincy's driving a stolen police car with the sheriff kidnapped in the trunk, and Larry and Carla are behind him with two bodies in the back of his truck. Shit! We'll be caught red-handed.* She prayed that the narrow mountain road would magically appear on their right.

Staring at the cloud of dust ahead of them, it appeared to be settling. Rose didn't know what to make of it. *Did the vehicle stop? Why would they do that? Did they spot the sheriff's car? Are they poachers?*

Sunlight reflected off the chrome front bumper of the mystery vehicle just around the bend. For some reason it had pulled over. She still couldn't see all of it—there were too many trees in the way. That meant that whoever was up ahead might not be able to see them, either.

Rose could not believe their luck as she hugged the shoulder, trying to remain out of sight. The trail had to be close by.

Jen squeezed her door handle, full of questions. "What if they start again? What if whoever's up ahead decides to keep driving? What if he sees us? He'll see the sheriff's car and then ..." Too frightened about the possible consequences, she couldn't finish, unable to take her eyes off the glimmering bumper.

"There's nothing we can do!" Rose snapped it out, in no mood to listen to Jen spout out about 'what if's'. She was absorbed with finding the wooded lane. *It's got to be here. It's ... yes. There it is!* It was fifty feet in front of them and on their right.

The girls had unconsciously stopped breathing when they had spotted the dust cloud up ahead. Now they gulped in air as Rose made the turn.

Quincy closely followed and, several car lengths behind him, Larry pulled up the small trail with Carla clutching her chest.

The group was finally off the main road and had managed not to be seen. Everyone tried to relax. It was impossible to do.

The entourage continued up the one-lane road that was lined with thick maple and birch trees. It was just wide enough for a single vehicle. They manoeuvred their way around several downed branches from the windstorm the night before and pulled into a clearing.

Rose spotted the mountain stream fifty feet to their right. It was exactly the way she had remembered it years ago when she used to party in that very same location. The hard-packed ground was littered with broken glass, beer bottle caps and numerous foot and tire marks from the many bush parties—one as recently as a few days ago.

Stepping out of their vehicles, they grouped in a circle under the blue sky. They were shaken by the mystery vehicle that had stopped for no apparent reason. Looking back at the narrow trail, they knew that someone could drive up it at any moment.

They were in the back country near a bubbling stream. Things should have been peaceful. Gleason thought differently. He tried his best to thump and kick. *They're going to leave me here and make a getaway. Once they figure they're someplace safe they'll make an anonymous call to the station and let them know where I'm at. I'm on to them and their sick plan.*

Wanting to ignore him, they hoped that he would settle down. But, it wasn't working for them. They were very much stuck with his ranting.

Eddy staggered out of the ditch and climbed into Al's truck. He wiped a string of vomit from his mouth before slumping next to the Browning Mark II and Marlin 336C. Both .30-30 rifles were loaded and ready for action.

His friend studied his pale face and chuckled, thinking that it was all very funny.

"What are you laughing at? Haven't you been sick before?"

"Whatever. Do you want me to drive real slow so your poor tummy doesn't get too upset?"

Eddy only grunted as he reached into the glove box for the Tums.

Al put the truck in gear and drove slower, taking pity on his friend as they came around the bend. They passed the narrow roadway that the group had driven up only minutes earlier. He put on his brakes and sniffed the air.

"Eddy? Do you smell it? Do you smell the dust?" He looked out his side window, speculating. "Someone must have just pulled up that trail."

The group stopped breathing when they heard brakes screech a hundred yards from them.

"No. Please don't come up here. Whoever you are, please, just go." Jennifer prayed that the driver would somehow hear her and take her advice. The pressure was too much for her as she carried on, now almost out of control. "Please God. Make them go away. We don't need this. If they come here, we're screwed!" Tears streaked her face. "They'll find us and then—"

"Just shut up for a minute, will you? We don't need you falling apart!" Carla was furious with the way her niece was behaving and had little tolerance for her. *I can't deal with her stupid babbling anymore. I can't deal with anything anymore.*

Al put his truck into reverse and slowly backed up to the intersection, curious. Earlier they had planned on checking things out that way to see if any deer were in the area. Now someone had beaten them to it.

They listened intently as an engine idled not much farther than a stone's throw away. It would only be a matter of seconds before they would be found out.

Jennifer fell to her knees, sputtering. "Wha-what if the sheriff starts banging and pounding again. What if they hear—?"

"Quiet!" It was Rose's turn to snap out at her. Straining her ears, her mind raced. *If they come our way we'll have to make a run for it. They'll spot the sheriff's car. They'll hear his ranting from the trunk. We'll be caught for sure.*

Eddy whined, "Shit, Al. They're hunting in our spot." He wiped his mouth—this time with a cheese stained napkin that had been on the truck floor for eons.

"Could be kids," his partner mused as he studied the narrow lane from his driver's window. "They sometimes go up that way to party and smoke their Mary Jew Anna."

"Yeah. Could be." He shrugged while trying to hold back a burp.

Hesitating for a few moments, Al finally put the truck into gear. *There's no point going up that way right now. Those kids probably scared away any game. Forget about hunting there for a few hours.*

Driving down the mountain road, they were oblivious to the nearby group that was collectively holding its breath.

They were carefully listening to the vehicle as it meandered down the road when Gleason's police radio burst out in loud crackling and fizzling.

Surprised and under enormous stress, Rose grabbed her chest. *Dear Jesus!* Chills shot through her. They were in a pocket that still had radio reception.

"Sheriff, (crackle)? Are you (crackle) (crackle)? Over." The signal was poor and the voice, full of static.

Scarlett was concerned. Sheriff Gleason had been out of contact for close to three hours. She wondered what was wrong. He had never been that late reporting in.

The group shuffled closer to the police car, hearing the urgency in the dispatcher's voice.

She tried again. "Sheriff! (crackle) you there? Where (crackle) you? Can you (crackle) (crackle)? Over."

More static snapped and hissed, making it hard for them to understand what she was saying. They leaned into the open window to hear every word.

Instead, Gleason yelled, "See! I told you. They're coming. They'll get you. All of you. There'll be no escaping. You won't—"

Scarlett's voice interrupted him. This time it was crystal clear and her tone sent shivers up everyone's spine. "Darwin! The sheriff's not responding. Are *you* there?"

"Go ahead. I can (crackle) (crackle) you." A few more snaps and crackles followed and then, silence.

Carla motioned for the group to step away from the cruiser. She needed to speak to them without Gleason listening in. They made their way to the small creek. It was no more than ten feet across and bubbled peacefully in the early afternoon light.

Anxiously squeezing her hands out in front of her, she turned to them. "This is it. We've got to act fast. They'll come looking for him very soon."

Everyone felt they were in the middle of a nightmare. The unbelievable events that had taken place over the past several hours, coupled with the lack of sleep, was surreal to them. They simply nodded in robotic fashion to what Carla was saying.

Rose's mind was on the close encounter with the mystery vehicle only minutes earlier. *What if the radio had squawked when whoever had stopped near the trail? They would have heard it. Then they would certainly have driven up here to check things out. They would have seen us. We'd be like sitting ducks. There would be nothing we could—*

Carla took in a deep breath. "We're going to cross the line and get deeper into this shit." She paused for a moment to let it sink in. "More than we could have ever imagined. It's either him," she pointed at the police cruiser, "or us. Don't forget that. *We* are the ones that are being forced into this." She almost made her plan sound justified.

Rose had doubts. They *all* had doubts. *One minute we're law abiding citizens and the next—? No, we're not law abiding. We're friggin' grow operators. All of us, except for Quincy, and he's certainly no angel.*

Carla was amazed with who she had become over the past several hours. *Transformed from being a gentle soul to becoming a … what?* Trying not to think about it she announced, "We can't afford to stay here much longer. We need to get this done. Now!"

They flinched with her words as she pushed on. "Someone might drive up like they almost did a few minutes ago." She looked in the direction of the main road, adding, "We have got to act fast!"

Jennifer's stomach flipped. In her mind she could hear police cars speeding toward them. Her hands were soaked in sweat from both the latex gloves and nerves. Her pulse rate was now far exceeding its safe limit.

In silence, they grouped into a tight circle seeking comfort from each other. Even Gleason had quit his ranting—the only sounds coming from the creek.

A faint, insect-like droning began to fill the air. They looked up at the blue sky. It was getting louder, the unmistakable sound of a single engine airplane and it appeared to be flying toward them.

Jen pointed to it, claiming, "It's the police! I know it. It's a search plane from Kelowna. It's coming our way." Her eyes grew large as she shook her finger at it.

"Just shut up! Just shut your stupid trap." Carla was livid. "Use your brain! Why would they suddenly send a friggin' airplane to search for the sheriff when he hasn't even been reported missing yet?"

"But, I see it. It looks like—"

"You don't see shit! It's probably just some guy having a leisurely Saturday morning flight." She grabbed her niece's shoulders and shook her. "I don't need *you* or anyone else to panic right now. Do you hear me? It will only make things worse!" Carla glared at her before turning away, fed up with the way her niece had been frightening everyone with her weakness and stupidity.

The droning slowly faded as they continued to look up at the cloudless sky.

Larry jolted everyone back to the moment by blurting out, "I'll do it. I've got nothing to lose."

"That's not going to happen." Carla's voice bit into all of them. "We'll do it the way we talked about. That way we'll *all* take the blame." It was now or never. She whispered, "Quincy?"

He broke into a sweat, knowing what she was about to ask.

"Get his … pistol."

On weak legs he made his way to the police car, his mind trying to block out what they were about to do. Moments later he handed the sheriff's gun to her by the tips of his gloved fingers.

Their eyes locked for a second before Carla reached out for it. At the same time she held out her other hand. In it were five sticks.

Chapter 27

Eddy and Al carried on with their journey, hunting for game along a logging road a mile from the group. They pulled over and, with rifles in hand, walked for several minutes through thick bush.

It was too much for Eddy. He needed to sit and was still not feeling well from the many Bud Lights that he had eagerly consumed the night before.

Al pushed on, scanning the area for deer. Disappointed, he trudged back to his buddy. "There's nothing here. We might have to—" A sharp 'crack' split the air, interrupting him in mid-sentence.

"What the—?" It sounded like a gunshot, but not from a high calibre rifle. It was more like a firecracker. "Sounds like kids. Just like we figured." Al pointed in the direction where they had come from. "They're probably on that trail goofing around and settin' off fireworks." He added, "Halloween *is* just around the corner."

"Yeah." Eddy agreed, not really caring. All he was concerned about was his stomach.

Sitting on a large boulder, they took in the view of the sleepy valley down below. A small plane grabbed their attention as it flew toward Beaswick, several miles away.

They drove down the dusty road in Larry's Chevy. He kept the speed to a minimum even though they wanted to get out of the area as fast as possible. Rose sat next to him. Quincy, Jennifer and Carla were in the truck box with a tarp covering them.

"I, uh, feel terrible." Larry glanced over at her as he gripped the wheel, needing to unload his guilt.

Is he talking about what we just did or is he talking about Mike? Her heart pounded as she prayed for all of this to be over.

"Things were getting real bad around the house. He hated me. I still don't know why. Maybe it's 'cause I raised him as a single parent. Maybe it's 'cause I was too good to him." He tried to forget about Mike but couldn't. Close to tears, he searched for answers. "Maybe it's because ... he was rotten to the core. I don't know." He looked at Rose for support.

Sitting stone-faced, she was unable to respond. The last thing that she wanted to think about was his son. Her mind was on what they had done only minutes earlier. It was unbelievable to her.

He tried changing the subject. "That Quincy seems to be coming around. He's really not a bad kid. Maybe just a little off track. That's all. His parents—did he talk about them?"

She squirmed, wishing he would step on the gas. This was not a date that they were on. Instead, she told herself to remain calm, understanding that they had to be careful. They couldn't drive too fast. It would only draw attention to them if they did.

"Rose?"

"Huh?" She was preoccupied with thinking about the police. Were they on their way—coming to arrest her and her friends? It took an enormous amount of will power to focus back on Larry.

He tried again. "Did Quincy talk about his parents?"

"Pull over. I'm going to be sick." She pushed open the door before he came to a full stop and leaned out. Retching, she tried to empty her stomach but hadn't eaten anything except for Tylenol 3's over the past twenty hours.

Minutes later they were back on the road, anxious to get to the security of her house.

Larry waited for her to settle down before trying again. "Did Quincy talk about his parents?"

"Yeah. When we were in the kitchen." It seemed like ages ago as she reached over and turned on the truck heater. Shivering, she could not believe how weak she sounded. She dabbed at her eyes as she looked over her shoulder, expecting to see a police car trailing them.

"What ...? What did you talk about?"

"Huh?"

"I said what did you talk about?"

Shit! Larry! Just shut up. I don't want to talk about anything. Not now! She forced herself to answer. "We talked about his aunt. He said that she looks a lot like me. He loves his Aunt Sylvia very much. She raised him."

That seemed to satisfy Larry for the moment. He tightly gripped the steering wheel as they ambled along the dusty road.

It seemed to take forever before they reached McCulloch Road. So far they had been lucky. They hadn't met any traffic and there were only three more miles to go.

"We've got a lot of work to do, Rose."

Hearing her name made her jump. She had been daydreaming about the police interrogating her.

Larry took a nervous glance her way. "Do you think we'll ever get out of this?" Not waiting for an answer, he carried on with his jabbering. "It's just come to such a … head. You know? Mike and all, well, it just doesn't seem real to me."

Pressing on, he tried to make sense out of what had happened with him and his son. "It's as if … it was meant to be. Like, I didn't know *what* to do with him anymore. I was afraid. He had a mean streak and was ready to do me some real harm and, well, I guess he did."

"I don't give a damn about Mike!" She snapped it out, tired of listening to him prattling on about his son. "I'm worried about *us!*" Rose was exhausted and her ankle and back ached. So did her chest from the cigarette burns. All she wanted was to get back to the safety of her farm. Looking in the truck mirror one more time, she needed to make sure that nobody was following them. Her reflection surprised her. She looked horribly stressed.

"He was going to kill me. You know that, don't you?" He wouldn't let it go and turned to her for confirmation.

"Rose?"

She was in another world, unable to reply.

That didn't stop Larry. He had to get things out. "He was going to kill me! He was going to beat me to a pulp. What saved me was Quincy. He stopped my son from murdering me." He squeezed the steering wheel tighter as he relived the past evening.

She pulled herself back to the moment. Speaking hurriedly, she hoped that the quicker she talked, the faster he would drive. "Mike was a rotten apple. He brought it on himself. There's no one else to blame. He wanted you to blow Quincy away. He was taunting you in front of all of us to murder him!" She swallowed hard with the thought.

Waiting for a moment to let it sink into him, she caught her breath before pushing on. "Quincy seems to be genuine. He just needs to stay off drugs."

Larry slowed his vehicle, nodding in agreement. "If this works out, what do you think we should do with him? I mean, how does Quincy fit in? Will he just move away from Beaswick?"

Shit! Aren't we home yet? Come on, Larry. Step on the friggin' gas! "No. We can't have him move. We've got to do things slowly. The glitch is the connection that he had with Sal and Karl. The police might come knocking on his door. He could break down and spill his guts. He'll have to stay in town for a while so that nobody gets … suspicious." She shook her head, overwhelmed.

Rose understood that there was one other glitch. It was Larry. He talked too much. *How long can he keep his mouth shut before he starts yapping his fool head off?* In her mind, there were far too many loose ends. They would get caught.

Squinting through the rear window for the fifth time, all she saw was dust. "If the cops pay him a visit, Quincy has got to tell them that he and his buddies had a falling out—that he wanted to go straight. He was finished doing drugs and had stopped hanging out with them."

"Yeah. That might work. He could claim that he had nothing to do with them if they ask. Besides, he told me he wasn't that close to Sal or Karl in the first place."

"Really?" Her interest perked up.

"Yeah. They weren't buddies like he first let on. He only saw them once in a while."

Rose wondered if the police would even question Quincy as Larry kept on talking. "At least we've got it figured out with Mike. If the cops come looking, I'll tell them that he took off to go live with his mother. I'll call the school and let them know that Mike is … gone." He trailed off with the last part of his sentence and realized once more that his son was indeed gone—this time for good.

"What about his truck? I had to do it, Larry. I wouldn't let them come up my drive. Mike's truck is smashed pretty bad."

Despite their horrid situation, Larry pulled his eyes off the road for a moment and smiled lovingly at her. "That's the least of our worries. I'll call my brother, T-Bone. He'll take care of it. He'll take care of your truck, too. He's got a huge flat deck. Two vehicles can easily fit on it. He'll cover them and haul them away for scrap. No worries."

"Yeah, but still … what if the cops come our way?"

"Why should they? We covered our asses pretty good. We wore gloves. We just need to get rid of any tire marks in your driveway. And," he added, "footprints."

A disturbing thought made her shift in her seat. "He … must have heard the gunshot from your place. He must have—"

"Huh? Who?"

"Think about it. Why did Gleason suddenly pull up *my* driveway when you shot Mike? He must have been at your place checking to see why his goons for hire hadn't paid him yet."

Larry swallowed the lump in his throat as he thought about all the covering up that they had to do, not only at her place but now also at his. "And, what else do we have to do? What have we missed?" He tightly gripped the steering wheel while deep in thought. "There's too much that we could have easily overlooked. They'll find—"

Rose jumped in. "We need to retrace our every step. We can't let anything slip by."

His mind scrambled with the full scope of what needed to be done. A sense of urgency came over him, making him step on the gas—no longer concerned about the dust cloud that they were creating.

Tired of talking about it, Rose fell silent for several moments before turning back to him. Now she felt sorry for her friend. "I hope you're okay about Mike and what we need to do." She pushed on. "It might be better this way. At least he'll always be near you." Fidgeting, she turned and looked back for the sixth time to make sure that they still weren't being followed.

Larry stared out his windshield, reflecting on what she had said. "He'll always be near me. Whether I want that, well, I just don't know."

She wondered how he was *really* feeling. He had been through hell—being beaten with a baseball bat, passing out and then killing his only child. *And then, what we did to Gleason.* She swallowed hard.

So far he seemed to be holding up and, at times, looked almost relieved—as if he had gotten rid of a cancerous growth.

Finally, they turned up her driveway. She would need to repair the gate and clean the post. Some of Mike's paint from his truck was on it. She kept worrying. *What else do we have to do?*

Again she relived how close they had come to being caught. They had almost left their prints behind.

An empty shell casing had remained in the breech of the Winchester after Larry had shot Mike. The fingerprints on the casing belonged to Rose. She had loaded the rifle months earlier.

They had needed to remove all prints from the rifle and spent shell casings before planting Gleason's fingers on them. That way they hoped that the police would assume that it was the sheriff who had loaded the rifle and had done the shootings.

She went over it again. *Yes. That should work. After shooting his first victim in the creek, he pumped in another round, ejecting the cartridge. Pulling the trigger once more, he murdered the second young man and left the empty cartridge in the chamber. We covered everything, haven't we?*

Chapter 28

Larry drove the ten miles into Beaswick and phoned his brother, T-Bone, from a pay phone at the Exxon station while Jennifer and Rose worked at cleaning the blood from her floor and kitchen cabinets. Most of it had dried and made it difficult to do. But, a few of the larger pools were still wet and needed to be blotted. The dark, stringy globs clung like red mucous to the white, paper towels.

Carla and Quincy struggled with covering the blown-out kitchen window. Using plastic, it was impossible for them to concentrate on what they were doing. They kept thinking about the police and if they were on their way. The temporary repair seemed to take forever.

Everyone went over it again, wondering if they had been spotted on Jack Pine Road. How could they explain why they had been there? What if they had left evidence—hadn't wiped a fingerprint?

Two hours later T-Bone had come and gone. He hadn't asked any questions and the issue with the two trucks seemed to have been taken care of.

Rose felt a chill. *Still, what if T-Bone is pulled over by the police? What if he says something? What if—?*

The power was back on and they had their radio tuned to the local AM station. They could at least get a signal from KRQY. It was four in the afternoon when the news filled the kitchen.

Earlier this afternoon, two hunters stumbled across what police are calling a double murder and suicide attempt. Beaswick's fifty-one year old sheriff, Cornelius Gleason, was found in his cruiser with what appeared to have been a self inflicted gunshot wound to the head. The incident occurred in a heavily wooded area just south of our community.

Two bodies were also discovered in the vicinity. The sheriff was rushed to Saint Francis hospital in serious but stable condition. The crime unit from Kelowna is now on the scene. Police aren't saying much more at this time. More details to follow.

This is KRQY news in Beaswick, California.

Blood drained from Rose's face as she gripped the back of the kitchen chair. *Hunters found him and he's in serious but stable condition? That can't be.*

She felt faint, her head spinning. *We … we killed him. He can't be alive! Please God, don't do this. Give us a break. We've been dragged through hell and now he's still … alive?* With an open mouth, she gawked in disbelief at the radio, waiting for more information. Instead, the DJ came back on.

Hey, hey, hey! We gotta brand new song by Tony Koenen called *Promise Land*. Have a listen.

"It's a long way back, runnin' down New Mexico

Thinkin' of the world and where I stand

In the middle of it all, talking to myself again

Sometimes I know, I think too mu—"

Rose switched it off, in no mood to listen to music. She had to think things out. *He's still alive? That can't—*

Jen rubbed her tattoo, sputtering, "Row-Row-Rose! Do you think … do you think he'll—?"

"Don't go there." Her voice sounded frail. "Let's just say a prayer and hope that he dies." Releasing her hold on the chair, she needed to sit.

Carla paced the kitchen—her mind running wild. Her stomach burned with acid as she went through it again. *They found him … still alive? Can the police track us down? They can't with the rifle. Rose told me that Gleason gave it to his brother, Bernie, a few years ago. It's still registered in the sheriff's name. No. They can't tie us to the shootings with the Winchester.* Her mind searched for anything that they might have missed.

It was impossible for them to remain calm. They had far too many nagging questions. *Will he pull through? Will he talk? Will we do life in jail?*

Carla peeked out the living room window. Greasy handprints from one of the goons glared back at her. *Shit! We've got to get that cleaned.* On shaky legs she scanned the living room, looking for anything else that could incriminate her and her friends.

Larry kept staring at the silent radio in disbelief, hoping for more information. For the first time in his life he was speechless as his mind reeled with the news.

They had prayed that their plan would work thanks to Carla's quick thinking. There was no way that they could have negotiated with him. Gleason would have dragged them under and their lives would have been ruined.

They had offered him more booze when they had pulled him out of his trunk. He had taken several huge swigs while trying to negotiate with them, worried for his life.

Promising that they would only cuff him to the steering wheel before letting the authorities know where he was made him feel a little better. The whiskey had also helped.

Carla could not believe that he was still alive. *There was blood and gore splattered all over the friggin' inside of his windshield! We planted his pistol in his hand to make it look like a suicide. He was shot in the head for God's sake. He can't be alive!* She closed her eyes, reliving the horrid scene. *He … he did scare the hell out of me.*

Playing it over, she remembered climbing into the Challenger from the passenger side just after he had been shot. The strong smell of gunpowder, coupled with the blue smoke, had forced her to breathe through her mouth as she held the rifle in her gloved hands, trying to place his prints on it.

She could still picture him—his head slumped forward with dark blood dripping on his uniform from what was left of his shattered face. Carla knew that she would carry that gruesome scene for the rest of her life.

It had been unbelievable to her. *He was still breathing after the gunshot to the head. No,* she reflected, *it was more like a wheezing and gurgling sound.* She shook her head. *The bastard should have died within a few minutes!*

Carla continued to play back the moment—when she had unlocked the handcuffs and had reached for his left hand. They needed both hands on the rifle for prints.

That's when it had happened. While trying to grab his hand, it had spastically lurched forward, taking her by surprise. Flaying out as if it had a life of its own, it had half slapped at the dashboard with its blood-smeared fingers. She had recoiled with surprise and disgust.

Returning to the kitchen, Carla could not believe the news. *He's still alive?* She mentally shrieked those three words out again as she shook her head. *HE'S—STILL—ALIVE!*

There had been blood on his left hand. They had needed to wipe it clean before planting his prints on the rifle. They could not have any of his blood on the Winchester. If there had been even a trace of his blood on the rifle then that would have indicated that he had shot himself first before shooting the two punks. That wouldn't have made sense.

Carla remembered Jen standing next to Quincy near the driver's door. She had yelled out at her niece to open the door and help. Jen had been comatose, unable to move. Close to panicking, Carla had turned to Quincy. "I need help. Open the fucking door!"

In a stupor, Quincy had come to life and had pulled open the door, grabbing the errant hand and holding it tight while she wiped it clean.

Carla replayed how she had somehow managed to place the sheriff's prints from his right hand on his pistol and the shell casings. Being that close to the blood and gore had made her gag.

She could not believe what they had done, but more importantly, that he was still alive.

Chapter 29

Larry squeezed the edge of the kitchen table and vacantly stared at the wall across from him, shocked by the radio report. His knuckles were as white as his face and his mind spun with questions. *They must have found him minutes after we did it. Was it that mystery vehicle? Did it come back?* He kept playing over the scene.

He and Quincy had carried Karl to the creek, partly submerging him. Repeating the procedure, they had done the same with Sal, placing his body in the knee deep water several feet downstream from Karl.

They all prayed that the authorities would believe that the two victims had been murdered in the creek as they tried to flee from Gleason.

The group had been lucky because of the wind the night before. Numerous large maple and birch leaves covered the ground. Still, they had needed to use their camouflage skills to their fullest to remove any evidence of unwanted footprints and Larry's tire tracks.

They had also dropped a shell casing near Gleason's car and had hoped that the investigative team would assume that was where the sheriff had been standing when he had murdered his first victim. Then, he had pumped in another bullet and continued with his shooting spree, killing the second young man farther down the creek.

No one felt guilty. They all believed that he deserved to die and were angry that he was still alive. Was he doing it intentionally—staying alive so that he could somehow get even with them like he had promised?

Detective Noah Trites, along with two veteran officers from the Kelowna precinct, was on the scene. This was his first murder/suicide case. That's what the police were calling it at this time—an M/S.

Officers Rene Dussault and Vic Little spent several hours combing the area. They searched the sheriff's vehicle, as well as Karl's Honda, for evidence.

Noah was well aware of their last names and what their colleagues called them behind their backs—Do So Little. That wasn't quite true. They were meticulous and had a high degree of success in clearing cases.

Frank Morgan, from the Justice Department, had informed them that the sheriff had a serious gambling problem. The police had paid a visit to a casino and had viewed incriminating security video. Cornelius Gleason had been betting large amounts of money—far more than what he could have earned as a sheriff.

Morgan had added that he had recently received a report from the sheriff's deputy in Beaswick. Gleason had been parked in an empty lot at one in the morning and Darwin had wondered why he was there, drunk in his patrol car. He had suspected that the sheriff had been waiting for someone.

The deputy had also received a voicemail from him just this morning—that he was sorry about what had happened last night. The sheriff had sounded stressed and had explained that he had been under a lot of pressure.

Detective Trites closely examined the two bodies in the creek and paid particular attention to the gunshot wounds and the angles of entry. One victim had been shot in the neck. The other had possibly tried to flee and had been shot farther downstream.

The entry wounds were puzzling to the novice detective. They didn't correlate with the slope of the land. Both slugs had struck the victims at a high angle. For that to have occurred, the shooter would have had to have been at least fifty feet above his target.

Officer Dussault came up with a possible explanation and suggested that the two victims could very well have slipped in the creek when they struggled to escape. That could explain the angle of entry.

After the killings, Noah figured that the sheriff must have had some kind of emotional breakdown and couldn't live with what he had done. Crumpled on the passenger seat next to an almost empty bottle of whiskey was a sliver of paper from a fortune cookie. The detective plucked it up with gloved fingers. *Before you embark on a journey of revenge, dig two graves.*

Detective Trites closed his eyes and tried to place himself in Gleason's mental and emotional state. The sheriff had been behind in his alimony payments and had several outstanding bills. He also had a gambling problem coupled with his drinking. Just yesterday the bank had turned him down for a loan. Desperate, he needed fast money.

His thoughts turned to the two victims. *What about the bigger guy? He had an ugly gash on his knee. Small bits of what look like gravel were embedded in his jeans. Did he stumble at another location?* Noah kept mentally asking questions. *Had there been a previous altercation? The other victim had grass stains on his sneakers and shoulder. How did he get those?*

They found a pipe in the Honda and knew what it was before doing an analysis. There was little doubt that the two victims had been high at the time of their deaths and that the sheriff had been drunk.

The department was doing a background check and slowly getting a rough character profile on each of the young men. Both were small-time drug users. An autopsy was scheduled within the next few hours.

Detective Trites shook his head as he tried to reconstruct the tragedy. He knew that the toxicology report would be positive. There were far too many lost lives because of drugs and alcohol.

Dussault and Little continued to search the area while Noah questioned the two hunters who had come across the scene. They stated that there had been dust in the air at the foot of the narrow lane earlier and had figured that it was kids who were fooling around.

Later, from a mile away, they had heard what they thought was a firecracker. They had waited for close to an hour before deciding to go back, hoping to hunt in the area. That's when they had found the sheriff and the two young men.

Both hunters were visibly shaken as they described in morbid detail the disturbing scene. At first they had assumed that the sheriff was dead until they noticed one of his hands. It had twitched. Immediately, one of them had headed into Beaswick to call the police and ambulance while the other stayed behind and tried his best at keeping the sheriff alive.

Detective Trites interviewed the crew from the power company. Bill McPherson stated that he had seen two vehicles on Jack Pine Road while working near the top of a power pole. One was a police car and it had been tailing what looked like a Honda sedan. He added that the cruiser was almost on the other vehicle's rear bumper.

"There were two people in the first car. I'm sure."

"Can you describe what they looked like?"

McPherson had pondered the question for several moments before shaking his head. "I only saw the two cars for a few seconds before they slipped behind some trees."

He had also interviewed Darwin, along with the dispatcher, Scarlett. Both had been stunned by the news and had no idea that the sheriff had been so troubled.

Scarlett did admit that she had noticed alcohol on his breath on more than one occasion. She had added that recently he had been plagued by calls from bill collectors.

Darwin had explained that the sheriff had been extremely agitated and intoxicated the previous night, squealing his tires and shouting obscenities as he roared out of an empty lot.

Had the sheriff been involved in a drug deal that had gone wrong? Did he have an emotional breakdown caused by alcohol and financial worries? And, did he end up murdering two small-time hoods before attempting to take his own life?

Did that really happen? Noah still wasn't convinced. *There's something else. He had marks on his wrists. How did he get those? Was he tied up?*

It was already late afternoon when they finished cleaning Rose's property. They had scrubbed down the windows and doors of all prints before raking Mike's and Gleason's tire tracks from the driveway and parking area.

Next, they had tackled the last thing that needed to be done. They had removed Mike's body from the barn and had placed it in the back of Larry's truck. Larry remained in the kitchen, unable to go near his boy.

Within two hours they had dug a grave in a small clearing at the rear of Larry's acreage. He stood next to it in silence as they gently slipped his son into the earth. Everyone felt a mixture of grief for Larry and also relief. They had finished dealing with the last body.

Rose placed an arm around Larry's shoulders as they stood over the shallow grave in the early evening. They wanted to reassure him that it had been an accident. Mike should never have reached out for the rifle. Especially with the way Larry had been hyped and dazed. It was his son's fault that he had been shot.

Larry tried to remain strong. It was difficult for him to do and several times he broke down, feeling a terrible loss and an enormous amount of guilt.

They knew that Mike's absence would probably go unnoticed. He didn't have any friends and the school would accept Larry's explanation that he had gone to live with his mother. His teachers would probably be glad to be rid of him.

There was one final chore that had to be done. They needed to drive Quincy home to his small rental house in Beaswick. The police might want to pay him a visit. That could be a possibility. Had someone seen him and his two buddies hanging out together yesterday? The cops could have some uncomfortable questions for him.

They went over their story one more time. If the police did pay him a visit Quincy would claim that he hadn't seen his two acquaintances for several days. He was trying to go straight and had had enough of the drug scene. He was home last night.

Once it was dark, Larry dropped him off several blocks from his house. Everyone wondered if the police would be there, waiting. Would the cops find a shred of evidence that would lead them to Rose and her friends? If they did, it would mean jail for life. Thankfully for them the death penalty in California had been declared unconstitutional.

Chapter 30

The autopsy and toxicology reports were completed the following morning. As expected, methamphetamine was found in both young men. The reports also confirmed that the sheriff had been intoxicated.

Detective Trites was having breakfast at the Marmalade Cat Cafe with officers Dussault and Little when his phone chirped. Forensics had found bruises on Gleason's wrists, the result of handcuffs.

"The way I see it," Vic Little paused before swallowing the last of his eggs, "the sheriff follows the two punks up the mountain road because he's suspicious and happens to be in the area. Right? I mean, he might have been on patrol for poachers."

Dussault nodded. "Sounds plausible. Pass me the ketchup."

"We know that Cornelius has a money problem. He follows them to a clearing and—"

Detective Trites interrupted him. "Wrong. Why are the two victims driving to some secluded clearing with the sheriff following them? Not only following, but actually tailing them? That doesn't make sense to me. It had to have been pre-arranged. He knows the two druggies and plans to meet them in the woods for a possible money transaction. Maybe some sort of payoff. Otherwise, he would have pulled them over immediately." He took a sip of coffee and added, "Why else would they want to drive out there?"

Dussault waved his fork. "True. Good point. Maybe the sheriff ordered them to meet him in the clearing so that they wouldn't be seen together. And, when they get there, he tells them to hand over the money—the seven thou' that we found on him. He needs it because of his gambling problem. The punks don't like it and …"

Trites helped him fill in the rest of the story. "So, they overpower him. That Karl guy was a big guy. Between the two of them they could have taken Gleason by surprise and handcuffed him. Both punks looked like they had been scuffed up a little. Maybe that's what happened. Things didn't go according to plan for the sheriff."

"Maybe." Dussault was warming up to the story. "So … what do you figure happened next?"

"They end up having a discussion—the three of them. The sheriff tells them to take the cuffs off or they're going to jail. The two young men have second thoughts about what they've done and realize that maybe they should let him go, knowing that they would never get away with it.

"When they do, the sheriff pulls out his rifle and … boom! He's angry and drunk." Noah leaned back in his chair, thinking hard. "But, why would he actually want to kill them? Was he trying to cover something up?"

"Could be that he was working with them, scamming money. Maybe they threatened to expose him." Dussault chewed on another forkful of egg.

Vic Little carried on where they left off. "Then the hunters show up and find the sheriff and the two dead guys in the creek. One of them notifies the police while the other stays with Gleason and keeps him alive."

The detectives felt that most of their story seemed to fit, but there were several things that they still had trouble with. They had found Karl partially submerged and yet there were traces of dried blood on his hand and pants that hadn't completely washed away. The lab report indicated that the blood was from fowl, possibly a chicken.

Did he work on a farm? How many are in the Beaswick area and how many raise chickens?

There was something else that the three of them found even more puzzling—Karl's index finger. It had been bitten, but not by the sheriff.

Once he dropped Quincy off at his house, Larry hurried back to the girls and told them not to worry—that everything would be fine. There had been no sign of the police.

They remained unconvinced and were deeply concerned that the authorities had found a shred of evidence that would implicate them. The cops would show up at any moment.

Though they were exhausted, sleep did not come easy. The thought of Gleason raping her kept creeping into Rose's subconscious. Tossing and turning, she tried pushing him away. It was impossible for her to do. Part of his face was missing as he kissed her, his blood dripping on her hands and chest. She could smell him in her dream—the odour of sour whiskey and beer.

Carla dreamt that the police were on their way. They had finished a detailed search of the crime scene and had found her prints. They would be coming for her at any moment. They knew that she was guilty. She was a killer and there was no getting around it. It was as simple as that.

In her dream, lights flashed red and blue as they roared up her driveway. There wasn't only one police car. The entire population of Beaswick was in a fleet of squad cars speeding toward her. She thrashed her legs, trying to flee, but there was nowhere to hide. The town was out to get her.

She couldn't breathe as she fell deeper into her nightmare, smelling something peculiar in the air—thick and heavy. It was a strange and acrid smell that enveloped her. She couldn't put her finger on it. It was recent and nagged at her sub-conscious, making her choke. Gasping for air, she bolted upright shouting, "Gunpowder!"

Jennifer's nightmare was similar to Carla's. He was still alive—the beast that tried to rape her. Karl's hands were ice cold and his face was blue as he fondled her breasts. She could feel his frigid fingers on her bare nipples and tried to escape but couldn't move.

In her sleep, she looked hard at the shady figure that was only inches from her. No. She had been wrong. It wasn't Karl who was fondling her. The face that loomed in front of her was …? She wasn't sure. Most of it was missing, reduced to a bloody pulp. Some of the red mess dripped on her white blouse.

She screamed out in her sleep, but it didn't matter how loud she yelled. There was no escape.

Quincy lurched in his sleep as he tried to avoid the steel bat that the police were using during their interrogation. He kicked at his dirty sheets and mumbled that he was sorry, so very sorry.

No one cared or listened as the bat came down hard, smashing into his ribs. Screaming for mercy, he couldn't make out who was swinging it. At first he thought it was Gleason. He tossed and turned, trying to escape as the dark figure raised the bat once more, wanting to beat him to a wet and slippery pulp.

Taking another look, he was wrong. It wasn't a policeman swinging the bat. It was far worse than a policeman. It was his Aunt Sylvia.

He bolted out of bed, his hand on his heaving chest. *It's okay. I'm safe. I'm at home.* It was coming back to him, fast and hard—the shooting deaths of his partners and what he and his new friends had done to Gleason. Overwhelmed, he fumbled through his small house in search of a meth hit.

The girls were up early the next morning and exhausted—physically, mentally and emotionally. All wondered when the police would show up. Carla kept looking down their driveway, listening and closely watching for any sign of the law. *Did they already question Quincy? Did he break down and tell them … everything?*

Larry wanted to visit them, especially Rose. He needed to know if they had heard more news about the sheriff. He had convinced himself that Mike had simply gone to live with his mother. It was her turn to deal with the kid. *Yes. That's what happened. It was time for my boy to leave.*

The three women broke into a sweat at the sound of a vehicle coming up their driveway. It was Larry's truck. They did not want to see him but knew that they needed to stay in touch—at least for a little while.

He talked about this and that as they nervously sipped their coffees, waiting for the latest news on KRQY. Larry tried catching Rose's eye and hoped that she would at least smile at him, wanting to confirm that he was still her hero. She ignored him.

The smell of vinegar and several cleaning products hung in the kitchen air from the cleanup the day before. Jen was at the table facing the white cabinets—her mind reliving the gory scene. *Did we wipe it all off?* She could still visualize Karl's blood oozing down the cupboard door. Shaking her head, she tried to break free from the grotesque image.

Unable to remain still, she squirmed while asking no one in particular, "Why don't we just leave? Why don't we take the money and disappear? They'll never find us."

Carla placed a hand on her niece's shoulder and tried to answer her in a calming voice. It didn't come out that way. It sounded strained and weak. "You know that wouldn't work. They *would* find us. It would be an admission of guilt. We have got to wait it out. We need to lay low. We can't just run off."

On edge, the younger woman jumped up from the table. She needed to vent. "We can't just sit here and do nothing. They'll be here any minute. I know it. We have got to do *something*!" She stared down at her aunt, clearly frustrated.

"Yes. You're right. We need to …" Carla turned to Rose, trying to ignore her niece and another one of her outbursts. Thinking that the police could be lurking nearby, she whispered, "Rose?"

"Huh?"

Carla studied her for a moment from across the table before forging on with her idea. "There's something that you, uh, need to do."

"Wha-at? Need to do? What are you talking about?" Her face paled and her hands shook as she clutched at her coffee cup.

"You have to visit him. You have got to go to the hospital and … visit him."

Jennifer's mouth dropped. She had trouble believing what her aunt was suggesting. Quickly in her face she shouted, "Are you crazy, Auntie? Why should we get more involved? Leave it alone. Let it go." The idea sounded absurd to her.

Before Carla could respond, Jen explained what she thought was the right thing for them to do. "We need to leave Beaswick. We'll take the money and get away from here as fast and as far as possible. We can't go *near* him!"

"No! You're wrong." Carla barked it out, annoyed that her niece seemed to always be arguing with her. "Think about it. Rose is Gleason's ex sister-in-law. She *is* still kind of family. If she doesn't make an effort to visit him, the police might become suspicious. We … we need to cover *all* of our bases."

Larry threw in his support. "Yeah! Carla's right. The cops will start digging deeper. They'll look at every angle. To shoot somebody is one thing, but a *sheriff*? That's one of their own! He's like a brother to them. They won't let up until they find us. They'll keep looking and looking, hunting down every lead until—"

"Shut up, Larry. Just shut up! You're not helping matters." Rose was on the verge of tears. *Sometimes he just doesn't know when to quit.*

Larry felt foolish. Rose didn't care *how* he felt. Her mind was on what Carla was suggesting. She knew that her friend could be right. *But, isn't that a bit of overkill? The last thing that I want to do is see that creep—the bastard who forced me and my friends into trying to kill him.*

Carla continued. "What you need to do is visit him as soon as possible."

Rose put her coffee down, spilling most of it. She could not stop trembling and was amazed with her friend's suggestion. "There is no way on this green earth that I could ever go near him!" *What is she thinking? Has she lost it?*

Squeezing Rose's hand to comfort her, Carla forged on. "He's probably in a coma, but we've got to find out what his condition really is. We can't live like this. He might still be able to talk. And, if he does, he'll tell them … everything." She gulped, "And then what?"

Rose gave her a blank stare, not knowing what to say.

Carla pushed on, trying to convince her that it was the right thing to do. "If he does talk, then we'll have to do what Jen said—be on the run. Our lives would be ruined. We'd have to start all over again and constantly keep looking over our shoulders."

Rose shook her head. "We're going to be constantly looking over our shoulders for the rest of our lives, regardless of what we do. Our lives are ruined if he lives or if he dies! It doesn't matter anymore."

Carla leaned forward and squeezed her friend's hand tighter. She lowered her voice. "Before we panic and do something stupid we need to find out what's going on with him. You could ask one of the hospital staff—just a simple question out of concern. Something like, 'Oh, the poor man. Will he ever recover? What a shame'. Stuff like that."

"But, I … I can't. I can't do it. I …" She faltered and was sick with the thought of being near him. "I … uh, excuse me. I … need to …" She bolted for the bathroom.

Jennifer had been thinking about Carla's idea a little more. She had to agree that it was a good plan after all and, outside of making a run for it, it was the only logical thing that they could do. They had to know how bad Gleason's condition really was. It made sense. *At least we'd be doing something besides sitting around and feeling trapped. Maybe then we can move on with our lives.*

Rose struggled back to her friends a few minutes later and gripped the back of her chair. Her red hair made a sharp contrast to her almost flour-white face.

Jen's heart went out to her. In a soft voice she whispered, "Rose?"

"Uh?" Slowly, she turned to her before sitting down, not trusting her legs.

"You don't even need to see him." Jen leaned over and gently took her by the hand. "Like Carla said, you could bring a card. Yeah, you could bring a card saying how sorry you are about hearing the terrible news. You could give it to the nurse. She could take it to his room for you. They probably won't even allow visitors."

Rose felt pressured and pulled her hand away. "Just leave me alone." Her friends were pushing her into checking things out while they stayed safely away from him. "Why me? Damn it! I don't want to look at him! I—"

"You've *got* to visit him! It will help *all* of us."

She snapped back at Jen, taking everyone by surprise. "And then what?" She shook her head, blurting, "Sign the friggin' card with 'Love from the Itches of Beaswick?' It just doesn't seem—"

Jen burst into laughter. She couldn't stop. The absurdity of their situation, coupled with exhaustion, made her laugh at Rose's sarcastic suggestion even harder. "Yeah. That's right. That's what we'll do. We'll sign the card with … with, *The Itches of* …" In tears, she couldn't continue.

Baffled by her reaction, Rose slowly let out a weak smile. It was contagious. A moment later she was chuckling along with her over-strung friend.

Larry stupidly looked at Carla for an explanation. He wondered if the two women were having an emotional breakdown. *What the—?*

Carla couldn't hold back, either. The puzzled look on Larry's face made her giggle. A moment later she joined her friends, having a much needed belly laugh as she wiped away at tears. It was a well deserved stress reliever.

Larry gawked at them, shaking his head, dumbfounded by their reaction.

Rose dabbed at her tears and took in a deep breath, reflecting on how quickly things had changed. It had only been two days since Jen had suggested calling their group 'The Itches of Beaswick'. So much had happened since then that now it seemed like light years ago.

Pulling back to the cold reality, Rose knew that her friends were right. Gleason was probably in intensive care and wouldn't be allowed visitors.

She hoped that he was also under a police guard. That would prove that the authorities believed he had murdered the two thugs before trying to kill himself. He would be under arrest.

It was all up to her to do a little investigating. If she and her friends wanted to live any kind of normal life, she would need to find out how bad his condition really was and, more importantly, if he would ever recover.

She would bring a small token to the hospital, perhaps what Jen had suggested—a card. It had to be something that the police could read. It would send out the right message and show the authorities that Cornelius's former sister-in-law was concerned about him. That would hopefully take away some, if not all, suspicion.

Have other members in the community or family delivered flowers or cards to him? What about his brother, Bernie? He might be there at his bedside. The thought made her stomach churn. Rose did not want to see her ex-husband.

Carla hurried into the living room, thinking that she had heard something at the foot of their driveway. *Is it a car?* She peeked out the front window. *No. There's nothing there. At least not just yet, but …*

Rose held her coffee cup with shaky hands, thinking about it a little longer before announcing, "I'll take Larry's truck. I'll stop at the gift shop and buy a card." She was talking fast to no one in particular.

"I won't go to his room. I'll drop the card and gift off at the nurses' station and ask them what his condition is." She squirmed in her chair, wanting to convince herself that it would be an easy thing for her to do.

Chapter 31

She had trouble applying her make-up. Her hands were too shaky. Rose tossed her kit to the side with nerves that were stretched to their limit. Instead, she focused on what she should wear and chose a blouse that covered most of her burns on her chest. Some were now angry sores.

She stared in the mirror as she ran a brush through her long, red hair. Several small pieces of pine were still lodged in it from two days ago.

Gripping her brush tighter, she questioned if she could do it. Could she drive into town and enquire about Gleason's condition?

But, we need to know how he is. Will he live? Will he talk? Will he die? Bile rose in her throat, making her drop the brush. She stared at her image in the mirror and scolded herself. *It not a question of if I can do it. I have got to do it!*

Her friends gave her one final hug and reassured her that she looked great and that everything would be fine. Larry squeezed her a little too hard. She pushed him away.

Swallowing more Tylenol, she started down her driveway. Her mind rambled as she ground the gears in Larry's truck, unable to concentrate on her driving.

The news on the radio hadn't given out much more information except that he was in stable condition at Saint Francis Hospital. Rose wanted to believe that they had everything covered—they would not be found out and Gleason would die.

She glanced at the tree near her gate where she had sandwiched Mike's truck with her Ford two nights earlier. Pieces of bark had been chipped away from the impact. She worried if the police would investigate her property.

Anxious to get it over with, she found herself speeding down McCulloch Road toward town. A huge plume of dust followed her. She wasn't paying attention. Instead, she went through the events from the previous day one more time.

We were forced to shoot him. Gleason is nothing but a bastard. It's his fault that we tried to kill him. He was going to take us in and book us. He was going to steal our money. We would be in jail right now thanks to him.

Red and blue lights flashed up ahead. She stomach flipped and her heart felt like it was about to explode. *Oh God! Is it the cops?* Squinting, she looked again. *Yes! It's a police car parked across the friggin' road! It's … a road block!*

Sweat rolled down her back. *This is it—the end of the line. I can't turn back, now! They've already seen my dust.* Bile filled her throat.

Rose was convinced that they had a dragnet set up. They were hunting down the killers and hadn't been fooled by what had appeared to have been a double murder and attempted suicide. No. They had found hard evidence indicating otherwise. She would be questioned and would break down and admit to everything.

The lone officer stood in the middle of the road several hundred feet in front of her. His cruiser was parked behind him and partially blocked her route.

A crazy urge to step on the gas and make a run for it came over her. She caught herself and knew that it would be a ridiculous thing to do. Swallowing hard, she wanted to rid herself of the mounting acid in her throat.

She pulled closer. There was no escape. A utility truck was parked behind the patrol car and wires stretched across the road. The policeman held up his hand for her to stop.

With a racing heart she put on her brakes. Stunned, she had no idea what to say or do as the officer sauntered up to her, seemingly in slow motion. Blood drained from her face and she felt light-headed. Trying to slow her breathing, she gave herself a mental pep talk. *This is it, Rosie. You'd better perform perfectly or it's all over. Look him in the eye! Don't turn away.*

"Good morning, Ma'am." He studied her with interest. *Why is she gripping the steering wheel so tightly?*

She nervously smiled while staring through her windshield. *Oh God. I can't do this.*

An inner voice screamed back, *You've got to do this or you and your friends are going to jail! For life! Look at him, damn you. Pull your eyes off the god damned road and LOOK AT HIM!*

"The power crew is still working on the pole that fell over the other night. They needed to come back to finish the—"

She took her own advice and met his eyes, blubbering, "Oh. Tha-that's okay by me. I … I'm in no hurry." *What a stupid thing to say! He knows by the way I'm acting that I'm a killer. I can see it in his eyes.*

"Do you live up that way?" Deputy Darwin nodded in the direction where she had come from. *I'm making her uncomfortable. What's going on?*

"Uh-huh."

"I see." He paused for a moment. *This is getting weird. I felt something strange when she looked at me.* His pulsed quickened.

What's he waiting for? Why doesn't he say something?

He pulled in his stomach and placed his hands on his hips as he took a step back from her vehicle. Two of his fingers nervously flicked his holstered sidearm.

Things started to spin for her. *This is it. It's all over for me and my—*

"Uh, how long have you lived there? I mean, up that way. Uh, in the hills." *I think … I think that …* For a moment Deputy Darwin had difficulty understanding her behaviour. Then, in a flash of what he thought was brilliance, it came to him. *That's it! That's what it is. I think she's attracted to me!* He re-assessed her. *She's not a bad looking woman. There aren't that many in these parts.*

Rose was falling to pieces. *I need to let him know that …*

She's got real nice cleavage. Mmmm, I wouldn't mind playing with— He blinked, taking another look. *Are those marks on her chest?* He quickly dismissed them, his eyes returning to her breasts as he speculated about a possible relationship. *Is she married? I don't see a ring. Forget it. She's probably too old. Still …*

She wanted to be relieved of her guilt. It was too difficult for her to carry any longer. At that moment she didn't care if she was found out and was more than ready to blurt out a confession. Rose turned her head away from his prying eyes, mumbling, "I need to let you know that—"

"Ma'am?" He had been half listening, his eyes on her cleavage.

"Huh?" She faced the deputy once again.

"I asked you how long you've lived up there." He pointed with his head to somewhere behind her and smiled inwardly. *Yup. She's hot for me, alright. She can't take her eyes off me or my uniform.*

"Uh, for several years. I live alone. My husband left me." *Shut up! Now you're babbling. Don't confess and don't give out any more information than you need to.*

"Uh, Miss? Uh, I was wonderin' if, uh, would you ..."

Oh God, no! He wants me to step out of the truck. He's going to handcuff me!

A horn honked from behind him, interrupting Darwin. *Dang! I was going to ask her out for a coffee.* The driver in the utility truck had moved off the road and the crew was ready to allow traffic through again.

The deputy sheriff tipped his hat with an officious smile while making sure that his stomach was still pulled in. He also stuck out his chest, convinced that women loved men in uniform.

Hmm, maybe she's a little too old for me. Still ... "Uh, you have a nice day." Reluctantly, he waved her through and hoped that he would run into her again. *Maybe I can find out her name. We could still go for that coffee or ...* He fantasized, wondering what she looked like naked. *How long has it been since she's been with a man. A real man!* He puffed out his chest.

Rose had trouble breathing. She tightly held on to the steering wheel with a sweaty hand. The other ground the truck gears as she continued along the dusty road. Taking a chance, she looked in her mirror. He was staring back at her. *Oh my God. Oh my God! I can't do this. He's ... he's going to hunt me down.*

She drove a little farther before chancing another look. Now he was busy writing something. *He's taking down my licence number. Wait a minute. It's not my license number. It's Larry's! He'll call Larry and ...* She trembled with worry. If he phoned Larry, she knew that their game would be over. Her neighbour would quickly spill his guts.

I'll run a check on her plates and get her name and number. She did say that she lived alone and that her husband left her. I just might give her a call. He smiled with the thought. *Coffee with her could turn out to be very ... delightful.*

Taking in several gulps of air, she tried to relax as she drove toward Beaswick. *It's okay. He would have pulled me over by now. Things are still good. Just don't do anything stupid!*

She thought about it some more. *No! It's not okay! He wrote down Larry's plate number. He'll call him. He'll—*

Cranking the wheel to her right, she pulled over and swung open her door, vomiting coffee. Rose couldn't stop her retching. Her stomach was a mess. *She* was a mess.

The Bees N Stings was to her right as she pulled into town. It was filled with all kinds of bee trinkets and local art including a selection of drug paraphernalia tucked away in a back corner of the store.

A few tourists were still in town, even in late October. Several glanced her way as she entered. *God! They know what I've done. It's written all over my face.*

Keeping her head down, Rose hustled to the rear of the store. She was on a mission. Rifling through the greeting card display, she tried to settle down. Her hands trembled and tears filled her eyes. It made it difficult for her to read any of them. Finally, she picked out one that she thought might be appropriate.

Appropriate? How can I find an appropriate card under these circumstances? She almost burst out in laughter, more than ready to once again release her tension.

What would be the right card? Mmmm, 'Sorry about shooting you in the head. I hope you never recover' or, 'A bullet to the head wasn't good enough to kill you'? Or, how about, 'Please die, you thieving rapist'. No. Hallmark doesn't make cards like that.

Her mind wasn't on what she was doing. She kept thinking about the policeman and how he had been studying her. Concentrating harder, she found a card and gift that she hoped would make it look like she truly cared about Gleason. The gift was perfect—a small glass vase with a single red rose in it.

Her old friend, Anne, was behind the cash register. "Rose! What a surprise. I'm sorry to hear about the sheriff. The whole town is 'buzzing' with the news."

Please, Anne! I don't need your 'bee' humour right now. She stuttered out a reply. "Yea-yea-yes. It's … terrible."

Anne loved to gossip. "The police figure that he owes lots of money. It looked like a drug deal gone bad. I can't believe it. What's this world coming to? Our own sheriff involved in illegal drugs?" She shook her head in disgust, making her long honey-bee ear rings swing from side to side.

Rose smiled inwardly. Her friend sounded so self-righteous. Everyone knew that she and her husband had their own grow-op in the hills.

She pulled out cash for the card, vase and rose, anxious to get things over with.

Chapter 32

She parked in the small lot. Saint Francis was on the edge of town and only had twenty beds. Rose opened the get-well card and, with a shaky hand, wrote, "I'm sorry about what happened to you, Cornelius. I wish you a speedy recovery. Hugs, Rose."

She took in a deep breath. *There, that should do it. I'll make my way to the reception area and let them know that I'm his former sister-in-law. I'll ask what his condition is and if he'll ever recover. Then, I'll leave the card and gift. They can bring them to his room.* Her stomach churned as she went through the main doors to the admitting area.

Hazel was on duty behind the main counter. They had gone to school together. "Rose! What a surprise!" She hurried over and hugged her friend, noticing the stress on her face. "I'm so sorry about the sheriff. How are *you* holding out?" *The poor thing. She must be going through hell. It's hard to lose family, even if he was a bastard.*

"Uh, I'm okay. I'm … still in shock. I can't believe what, uh, happened."

Hazel put her arm around her old school chum. "There, there, there! It's going to be just fine."

She shuddered when she heard those words—that it was going to be just fine. *What does she mean by that? Is he getting better?*

Hazel turned to her co-worker. "Cadence? Take over for me at the front desk. I want to spend a few minutes with my friend."

The young nurse looked up at her with a phone in her ear and nodded.

Hazel marched Rose down the hallway with her arm tightly wrapped around her waist. "He'll be glad to see you."

Rose stopped in her tracks and almost dropped the glass vase and rose. "Wha-at? What do you mean? He … he's okay? He's getting better?" She felt faint.

"No, no, silly. It's just a figure of speech. The sheriff is in a coma, but I'm sure he'll know that you're at his side." She added, "He'll feel you."

She was terribly disturbed with what her friend was telling her—that Gleason would 'feel' her. The very thought made her want to throw up again.

Halfway down the hallway, Hazel stopped in her tracks and studied her. She knew that she shouldn't have said what she did. She was giving Rose false hope and so changed the subject. "What happened to your ankle? You've got a limp."

Stunned and also overwhelmed, she mumbled, "Uh, nothing. Nothing at all." *Damn. I answered too quickly. She'll know that I'm lying.* "Uh, I just … slipped … a few days ago. I'll … I'll be okay."

Her feet moved robotically along the polished floor as they continued toward his room. She had no control over her actions and was afraid that if she stopped walking, Hazel would become suspicious. She was being forced to his room just like she and her friends had been forced into shooting him.

They were at his door and Rose was surprised. There was no police guard. Did that mean that the authorities thought Gleason was innocent—that it had been a setup?

She had mixed feelings and had hoped to see a policeman standing by his door. But, she would have been terrified if one were actually there. If an officer *was* there, she knew that she could easily blurt out what she and her accomplices had done—that they had tried to murder a sheriff after killing three young men. Then it would be all over for them.

A morbid curiosity swept over her as Hazel slowly opened Gleason's door. Still in the hallway, Rose felt a strong urge to look at him first-hand.

The room was empty except for what could only have been Cornelius. His head and face were completely bandaged with bands of white gauze. An opening was left for his one eye and another for where his mouth had once been. He was partially propped up and faced a window. Several clear tubes protruded from his head and his heart monitor emitted a steady *beep, beep, beep.*

Rose took a few tentative steps into his room and froze.

Hazel had a tear in her eye, noticing the emotional shock on her friend's face. *The poor thing. I never knew they were that close. She seems so … out of it.*

It was too much for her. Trembling, Rose hurried past him to his window—having seen more than enough. Through tears, she spotted a small portion of McCulloch Road in the distance. Her eyes shifted to the right—to a grove of thick trees miles away where Jack Pine Road would be. *That's where it … that's where we did it. That's—*

Gargling noises made her spin around. She found herself staring at his bandaged head. Hazel had cranked up his bed a little more and now he was looking straight at her with his one eye. "Raw-Raw-Raw …?" The beeping from his heart monitor increased.

He's trying to say something. I don't … I can't … She trembled as needles shot up her spine. *What if he lurches out of bed and attacks me. I … I've got to—*

"Rose? Here, let me take those." Hazel hustled to her side, worried that her friend might drop her gift and card. *She's acting like she's just seen a ghost!*

Reaching out for the vase, she studied her long-time school friend. *Rose looks stunned. Who can blame her? His face has been destroyed. He's been linked to a drug deal and double murder. No wonder she is so … shocked! And, are those burn marks on her chest?*

Acid gurgled in her throat. Rose jammed her gift and card in Hazel's hand before rushing to the door, needing to escape.

"The washroom is over here, dear. Let me help you." *Poor Rose. It's one thing to hear the news on the radio, but it's another entirely different matter to actually see the victim first-hand.*

She bolted into his bathroom and retched in the sink. Turning on the water, Rose splashed at her face and studied herself in the mirror. *Oh God. I should never have come here. It's too much. I … I need to be strong!* She took in a breath, trying to settle down, and gave herself another talk. *Hold in there, girl. There's only one more thing that has to be done and then … it's over.*

Hazel read the card and smiled before placing it on Gleason's bedside table. It stood alone—the only one that he had received. No one else seemed to care about the sheriff. Besides the police, Rose was the only person who had paid him a visit. *She is so sweet to come by and see him.* She placed a hand on her patient's brow, trying to slow his now racing heart. *Beep! Beep! Beep!*

Rose staggered out of his bathroom, her face as white as a paper plate. "I've seen enough. It's … it's time for me to go."

Hazel took her by the hand and led her to his doorway. She felt sorry for her distraught friend. *It looks like she's been through hell and back.*

Pausing at the threshold with her back to him, Rose felt his one eye burn its way through her soul. The hair on the nape of her neck bristled as she hurriedly escaped into the hallway.

Hazel caught up to her and tightly clasped her arm, concerned that she might faint.

Stopping at a water fountain near the main entrance, Rose took several huge swallows, beginning to feel a little better. The hospital exit was only a few feet from her and her 'visit' was now over. She could leave at any time.

"Uh, Hazel?"

"Yes? What is it, dear?"

Rose looked her in the eye. "Will ...? Will he ever ...?" She hesitated, not knowing how to ask the question.

Her sympathetic friend read her mind. "I'm not sure. He's got a very good doctor taking care of him—a Doctor Klein from Irvine. He's new here and is a specialist in that sort of thing. Would you like to speak with him? He's in his office."

"Yes. I would like that very much. I want to know—"

"Yes. Yes. Of course. Let me call him."

He answered on the third ring.

"Hello, Doctor. It's Hazel in Admitting. I have a family member here that would like more information on the sheriff's condition. Do you have a minute?"

"I vill be vight there, yeah?"

Moments later Doctor Joseph Klein stepped out of his office to meet with Rose. He had moved to Beaswick six months earlier. Rumour had it that he had been involved with a company called Bosch Research and had been forced to leave. At the time there had been a cloud of controversy with what the research company had been involved in.

He was a thin man in his mid-fifties and partially bald. To compensate for some of his hair loss he sported a salt and pepper beard. He had moved from Germany years earlier but still carried a thick accent.

Briskly, he walked over and introduced himself as he pushed back his horn-rimmed glasses. "Please, come widt me. I am sure dat you have a lot of questions, yeah?" He had a clipboard under his arm as Rose followed him.

They entered his office so that they could talk privately. It was more than what Rose had hoped for. She would get the news of the sheriff's condition first-hand. Sitting across from him, she tried to get comfortable. Slowly, she began to relax. The worst of the ordeal seemed to finally be over and now she would get some much needed answers.

"Doctor? Do you think that the sheriff could ever be … somewhat normal again?"

Doctor Klein took off his glasses and cleaned them as he thought of the best way to answer the difficult question. He slowly put them back on and studied his clipboard.

Rose noticed a photo of him and his family on his desk. He looked much younger in the picture, posing with his wife and what could only have been his young daughter.

"Do you vant me to give you a general overview or, because you are immediate family, a detailed description?"

"Tell me. Please. Is there any hope?" She was surprised that he had said 'immediate family'. Obviously he was unaware that she was only an ex sister-in-law.

He understood that the poor woman was concerned with the sheriff's outcome. *Of course she would be. She is family. She loves him.*

"Dee sheriff suffered severe trauma to his face and head—dee result of a .38 calibre bullet dat had been self-inflicted."

She let out a small gasp when he said 'self-inflicted'.

Unnoticed, he was absorbed with giving a professional and detailed description. "It entered dee head under dee chin." He pointed to the underside of his own chin to illustrate.

His actions made Rose relive the moment—hearing the gun blast and seeing the spray of blood and gory pulp explode from his face. She could almost smell the acrid gun powder as she sat across from the skinny doctor in his sterile office.

He pushed on. "Dee bullet shattered dee jaw and severed most of dee tongue."

Doctor Klein studied her with the last part of his sentence before making a decision. He would give her all the facts. She was the only person who had visited his patient. *Perhaps she could relay the difficult news to the rest of his family.*

"Dee bullet removed part of dee nose and dee left eye. In dee process—"

Rose flinched as she listened to his detailed description of the gruesome damage that she and her friends had inflicted on him.

He stopped for a moment, noticing her reaction. *Am I saying too much?* Doctor Klein decided to press on. *She needs to know dee facts.* "In dee process, dee bullet caused serious injury to dee brain. Vee can attempt to mitigate some of dee damage, but ..." He trailed off, implying that to repair the brain would be difficult, if not impossible, to do.

He shifted his attention to the sheriff's other medical issues. "Part of dee face could be reconstructed, but it depends on how much you vould be villing to spend to have that take place."

She was surprised with what the doctor was suggesting—that she would pay for Gleason's facial reconstruction. "But, will he live?" She tried not to sound desperate, but she and her friends had been anxiously waiting for an answer for what seemed like years. *Will he fucking talk again?* She squeezed her hands as she nervously sat on the edge of her chair, waiting for his diagnosis.

He shifted in his seat and felt uncomfortable with the question. *She seems to be very attached to dee sheriff.* Clearing his throat, he pushed on. "Vell, dat is a difficult question. At dis time he is in stable condition, but, again, vee do not know if he vill live or if ... uh, perhaps ... perhaps it would be best if ..."

He trailed off, not knowing how to explain to her in a delicate fashion that it might be better if Gleason *did* die.

If he lived, he would be faced with first degree murder charges and would probably end up doing life in the penitentiary. With a shattered face and prison to look forward to, well, it certainly wouldn't be pleasant for him—especially being an ex-sheriff.

Rose nodded, understanding what he was implying. "Thank you, Doctor, for all that you've done."

He stood and took her hand, concerned that he might have said too much—that the sheriff would be better off dead.

Chapter 33

The following morning Doctor Klein made the call to Detective Trites. Noah wanted know if the patient showed any signs of consciousness.

Gleason did have some moments of lucidity. They were infrequent, but there had been several occasions when he had opened his one eye, seeming to be rational.

Klein questioned if he really *was* capable of becoming somewhat normal. It was difficult to tell. His jaw and tongue were severely damaged and he had limited motor skills, at times having no control over his arms and legs. *Still, there is hope. The human body sometimes performs miraculous things—especially dee brain.*

The few times that Gleason had been aware, he had pounded on the hospital bed with his fists and feet. He could become very violent and irrational, going into an uncontrollable fit of rage. It was another sign of brain damage.

Today he was apparently at peace. Doctor Klein made the call and, ten minutes later, Detective Trites was at his bedside.

"Please. Vee don't vant to disturb him anymore than necessary. Speak softly and keep your questions to a minimum. And, remember dat brain damaged patients sometimes have an acute sense of hearing. Be careful what you mutter under your breath, yeah?"

Nodding his understanding, Noah spoke in a whisper, worried that a loud voice might set the sheriff off once again. "Can you hear me?"

Gleason was propped up with a drainage tube embedded somewhere in his shattered face. Another was in his upper arm. Gauze bandages covered most of his head as he stared out his hospital window with his one glazed eye.

Waiting for several moments, Noah tried again, uncertain if the patient had understood his question. Leaning closer, he cleared his throat before asking, "Can you explain … what happened?"

Laboured breathing, along with the steady beep from the heart monitor, was the only reply. Raising his voice, he tried again. "Why did you do it? Was it a drug deal gone wrong?" The detective was anxious to put closure to the case. He studied the shattered man that lay before him, hoping for some kind of explanation. Instead, the heart monitor filled the room with its regular beeping.

He can't hear me or he doesn't understand my questions. Noah shook his head and turned away, ready to leave the room. "Thank you, Doctor, for at least allowing me to ask him a few—"

Thump! Thump!

The detective spun around and faced the patient once again, puzzled.

Using both hands, Gleason's slapping grew louder. Thump! Thump! Thump! Thump! The beeping from the heart monitor increased in frequency.

Alarmed, Doctor Klein closely observed his patient. *The sheriff is once again exhibiting signs of irrationality and profound emotional disorder!*

Noah could feel the frustration emanate from Gleason and wondered if the sheriff was attempting to communicate. He tried again, keeping his question short and to the point. "What happened out there—in the woods?"

Gleason's medication was quickly wearing off and he was becoming more aware of his surroundings. Pausing his slapping for a moment, he raised a hand and pointed at the window.

Noah was confused as the sheriff shook a finger at the distant hills and tried to speak. "R-rr-rrr-rrr ..."

The detective was mesmerized by the clear, plastic drainage tube that was attached to somewhere in the patient's head. It had bounced when Gleason had gargled, quickly filling with a crimson froth. He followed the mess with his eyes as the disgusting fluid continued on its journey, ending in a container strapped somewhere next to the hospital bed. Noah was fast becoming ill.

With his eye glazed over, Cornelius dropped his arm. Now his bed slapping grew vigorous. It appeared as if he was slipping into delusional irrationality. The heart monitor chanted out a warning. Beep! Beep! Beep!

Doctor Klein left the room and hailed the floor nurse down the hall. "Vee need to administer more medication. He is out of control vonce again." His patient would be given another strong sedative.

Noah stared in fascination as the brain damaged man raised his hand and again pointed at the window. *What is he trying to tell me?*

An unintelligible sound escaped from the hole in his face, followed by a pink mist that hung in the air. He continued with his urgent slapping.

Doctor Klein hurried back to the room and gripped Noah's shoulder, ready to pull him from Gleason's bedside. He was concerned that the questioning was damaging his patient even further.

Ignoring the doctor, Noah leaned closer to him. "What? What is it? Tell me?" Now he was only inches from the shattered face.

The sheriff made another attempt. "Rr-rr-rr-rr ..." Blood soaked the surrounding gauze where his mouth had once been as his eye widened. Somewhere in his traumatized brain he had finally noticed Rose's gift—the single red rose in the vase on his window sill. He lowered his finger and took careful aim while his other hand carried on with its vigorous bed slapping. Thump! Thump! Thump!

Now too agitated, he bolted upright. "Row-Row-Row ..." Out of control, he twisted and turned, struggling to escape from his bed as his heart monitor screamed out a warning.

Doctor Klein grabbed a flailing arm, trying to restrain his patient while yelling out at Noah, "Dee poor man has had enough!"

He nodded his understanding. Gleason wasn't making any sense. He almost felt sorry for the maniacal man. In a soothing voice, he tried to calm him. "It's okay. The doctor is here. He'll take the pain away. I'm sorry that I've upset you." He had never seen anything like it in his short career as a detective and was unprepared with what was taking place.

"Nah-naw. Row! Row! Row!" Gleason gurgled it out. He hadn't killed *anybody. It wasn't me! It was that redheaded bitch, Rose! She tried to murder me—an innocent police officer who was only doing his job!*

In a flash, he reached out and grabbed Noah by his bicep. Squeezing hard, Cornelius was determined not to let him go. *I've got to tell you what really happened!* His blood pressure soared as his heart monitor wildly beeped.

Noah tried to pull free but Cornelius held fast. His crazed fingers squeezed tighter as his sharp nails pierced through the detective's sleeve and into the flesh just beneath.

Klein and Noah pried at Gleason's biting fingers in an attempt to release his steely grip from the detective's upper arm. But Cornelius was demonstrating unbelievable strength. He was relentless. His yellow nails clawed deeper. *He needs to know the truth. I can't let him leave until he knows what really happened.*

Noah finally broke free from the wild man and stumbled back. His sleeve was shredded and blood ran down his arm.

The floor nurse burst in to administer the medication as Klein continued to try and subdue his patient. It was difficult for the doctor to do. Gleason easily overpowered the skinny man and twisted and turned to escape from his bed. An intern bolted in to assist. It wasn't enough. Very quickly another one appeared.

The sheriff was on his feet as the medical staff tried to control the crazed patient. A high pitched whine screamed out as the heart monitor tore free from his body. Blood and medical waste splashed to the floor from the ripped-out tubes and the smell of urine quickly filled the room.

With superhuman strength, Gleason took a slippery step toward the rose and vase on the window sill. "Row! Row! Row!"

"Inject him!" Klein yelled it out over the din as he tried to bring his demented patient under control.

Struggling with the two interns and doctor, he took another step, chanting. "Row-Row-Row." *That bitch! I'll find her. I'll find them. I'll make them all pay!* Stitches tore free from his ravaged face as more blood soaked through the white gauze that enveloped his head.

The doctor and interns tried to hold him back as he pushed his way toward the window. Making a desperate lunge, he managed to grab the small vase and rose just as the staff overpowered him. The vase slipped through his fingers and shattered on the grisly floor, but he managed to hold fast to the rose.

The nurse expertly injected the powerful sedative into his left buttock. His ranting slowed as the drug quickly took over. "Row … Row … Row …" He sputtered it out as he clutched his trophy.

Weak from both the sedative and his exertions, they easily shuffled him back to his bed before inserting the tubes and reattaching the monitor.

Detective Trites took in a deep breath through his mouth. The rancid smell of the hospital room was too much for him and he felt ill. Shaking his head in sympathy and bewilderment, he had trouble dealing with the pitiful display that he had just witnessed.

Taking a few guarded steps toward the sheriff's bedside, Noah needed to speak to the drugged man one more time. He felt sorry for Gleason and wanted to let him know that he finally understood. He understood everything. What the sheriff had been trying to explain to him had been in his face the whole time. But, he hadn't seen it until now. *How stupid could I have been?*

Now on his back, Cornelius drifted into a dreamlike trance while still clutching the rose. "Row … row … row …"

Noah whispered, "Sheriff? Can you hear me?" Not expecting an answer, he gently pressed on. "Don't worry about a thing. I finally figured it out—what you've been trying to tell me. Now I understand."

Gleason stopped his muttering. His body stiffened, hearing every word the detective had said. *You … you understand? You … understand what … what really …?* Fighting the potent sedative, he gripped his gift by the stem and shook it in Noah's face. *You … you … under …*

"I understand completely what you were trying to tell me. You said, Rose. Right?"

Relief swept through him. *Yes. Yes. Yes! That's right! Finally, you know. It was Rose and her stupid …* Now too weak to hold it any longer, the rose fell from his grip, landing on his pillow next to his shattered head. A tear slowly formed in his only eye. It stubbornly clung to his eyelid for several moments before spilling over and falling on Rose's gift.

One of the petals took on a darker shade of red as the young detective looked on in fascination. *The sheriff's tear and … the rose petal. They've become one—blending together. Why is that somehow bothering me?*

They were alone in the hospital room—just the two of them. The only sound was the slow and steady beeping from the heart monitor. The sheriff seemed at peace, as if a huge weight had been lifted from him.

Slowly standing, Noah made his way to the door and paused before turning back to the drugged patient one more time. Speaking softly, more to himself than to Gleason, he whispered, "Yes, that *was* a rose that you were clutching, Sheriff. A beautiful, red … rose."

Beep! Beep! Beep!

ABOUT THE AUTHOR

Gerald Deshayes lives in Kelowna, British Columbia and has three daughters, three grandchildren, and a great granddaughter. Writing, along with music, has always been a passion of his. *The Itches of Beaswick* combines both. The song, *The Itch of a Rose*, written by Tony Koenen, beautifully captures the story in musical detail and features Rose, the lead character. For a **free** download and lyrics, please visit **geralddeshayes/music.com**

This is Gerald's second novel. If you enjoyed *The Itches of Beaswick*, please check out his web site at **geralddeshayes.com** for more information about his first novel, *GENE*.

TONY KOENEN …

Gerald Deshayes is a 'word wizard', author and friend whom I admire.

I was first introduced to *Gene*, at a music session. This was his first full length medical fiction novel. I would not consider myself an avid reader, but found myself engrossed in this fascinating story and finished it in only three days. My high school teacher would have been proud of me. I couldn't put the book down, totally captivated by the intriguing and twisting plot.

It was at that same location where Gerry later invited me to read a rough draft of another book he had been working on … *The Itches of Beaswick*. I felt honored to be asked to read this draft because of how my respect has grown for Gerry's talent since the *Gene* affair.

I took the draft (in a big blue binder) up to my motor home in the mountains of British Columbia—a special place for me that inspires my creativity. Eagerly opening the first page, I had no clue what his latest novel would be about. I thought that there had to be a semblance to *Gene* in some shape or form. I was dead wrong. Finishing the three hundred and some pages in only two days, I could not put it down! It drove me crazy, wanting to know what next, what now!

It's funny how things turn out. When I was in Southern Florida a few months earlier, I had written a composition on the acoustic guitar, but the lyrics just weren't coming to me. I liked the music and felt it deserved a good story. But, it was waiting for a good lyrical content to come through me.

The day I finished *The Itches of Beaswick*, my song now had a story!

Recorded and produced by Tim Ford, (Mclaren Studios), Tim is not only a talented musical artist but also my co-writer. Many thanks go out to him for helping me make *The Itch of a Rose* come to life.

EXCERPT FROM GERALD'S FIRST NOVEL—*GENE*

He suspected he was having a nervous breakdown. Why else would one of the hospital counselors show up in his room? Gene wasn't quite sure. His mind was elsewhere. He knew that Doctor Klein had made the appointment soon after he'd left his bedside. He wondered what the good doctor had told the counselor; that his young patient was on the verge of—losing it? Perhaps he was.

The counselor introduced himself as Bruce somebody-or-other and looked to be in his mid-fifties. It was hard to tell. The shaved head and small diamond earring appeared to make him look younger. He had an easy manner, nothing what Gene would have expected in a shrink. He was also short.

He smiled as he casually pulled a chair up beside Gene's bed.

Gene smiled back. "Sorry I can't shake your hand, Bruce."

"Yeah, I know. You've suffered a terrible accident. I can only imagine how you feel, my man."

Gene tried to nod as Bruce continued, still standing beside the chair he had pulled up.

"You know, Gene, I've talked to a lot of patients who are in the same situation as you. It's never easy. I do want you to know that I have a lot of experience with this sort of thing."

"How many?"

"Pardon?"

"How many people have you talked to that are like me?"

He slowly sat down, giving the question some thought. "Well, no one is like you, Gene, but … there are many similarities." He leaned back, looking up at the ceiling. "You know, I'm guessing maybe one hundred people. I've never really counted until you asked."

Gene liked him. He was honest, short and answered questions with facts. He smiled, noticing how Bruce waved his hands while speaking.

"There have been some unique cases, some worse than others. The bottom line is I truly feel I've helped them help themselves."

Gene was becoming angry. He could feel his cheeks flush. He couldn't help but think, "*Yeah, you're just another one of those doctors with a healthy body who's preaching to me.*" He decided not to go in that direction. He knew that he was angry and frustrated. He'd had enough for now. He was going to try and keep an open mind instead.

Bruce sensed what was going on and was ready for it. He wanted Gene to talk as well. He wanted some feedback. He quickly stood up. Gene noticed the guy couldn't keep still. He decided to nickname him 'Warp' as in 'Warp Speed.'

"So, you must be wondering how I do it, right? How do I, Bruce Whitman, help people—people like you?" He waved his hands, palms out.

Gene was wondering the same thing. He tried to stay positive. It was hard to do.

"The answer is we do it together. You and me." He pointed toward Gene and then to himself. "Let me take some of the pain away, Gene. I mean, why not? I'm your friend. I know we've just met but I'm not here to hurt you. I like you. I was eighteen once. Yeah, I know it's hard to believe, looking at me now." He smiled. Gene couldn't help himself. He smiled back, now listening intently.

"I used to think I could do anything." He paused, trying to think of the right word. "I was, hmmm, invincible. Yes, that's what I thought I was, invincible! I've got some crazy stories to tell you." Bruce looked up at the ceiling, thinking back to a time years ago. He was also waiting for Gene to respond. He had given him a hook, waiting to see if he'd take it. He sat back down, crossing his short legs.

"Uh, like what?"

Bruce smiled to himself, pretending he was still far away. "What? Oh yeah. Well, the time I was playing in this blues band. Yeah, I used to play bass guitar in this blues band. Know what it was called?" He stood up again, leaning over toward Gene as he asked the question, not expecting an answer. "The 'Strange Movies.' That was the name that we called ourselves." His face broke into a broad grin. Now he was really thinking of the past.

"The *what*?"

Bruce shook his head and chuckled, straightening. "Yeah, I know. Stupid name, huh?" He was having fun. He hadn't thought of those days in years.

"Hey, no, that's kinda cool! So like, what happened?" Gene had momentarily forgotten his problems. He wanted to hear everything Bruce had to say about the band. He loved that sort of stuff.

"We wanted to enhance the show a little, you know? We wanted to perform with a strobe light so our stage presence would be better. We'd seen a few acts that had done that sort of thing so we thought, well, it would be cool to do. Know what I'm talking about?" He raised his eyebrows.

"Uh, I guess so." Gene trailed off, not quite sure, waiting for more of an explanation.

"Well, back then there was this movement, this"—he held up his hands once more—"thing called a 'Psychedelic' movement." He had two fingers extended, indicting he was quoting as he spoke. "That's what it was. Yeah …." He was lost in his own thoughts for a second or two but then came back, seeing the confused looked on Gene's face. He smiled, knowing Gene had no idea what he was talking about. He needed to have been there to fully understand the movement back in the sixties.

"Yeah." He was getting excited as he spoke. "People wanted to be free and expressive. It was an era that was very visual, right?" He nodded, agreeing with himself, walking around the chair as he continued. "Yeah. So, in the music business somehow someone had thought of combining color with music, creating a light show." He again quoted with his fingers. He couldn't keep still, walking back and forth from Gene's bed to the window, sometimes circling the chair as he spoke.

Gene was mesmerized. *Yes, the guy's name should have been 'Warp.'*

"What a lot of bands were using for the visual experience was a backdrop with colored lights. There weren't any giant video screens back then, only projectors and two or three bed sheets sewn together. Different colored plasma gels or whatever would be displayed behind the band on the sheets resulting in an explosion of … color!"

Bruce smiled at the thought. He visualized an old bed sheet stretched out behind the band with lights projected onto it, knowing how archaic it was compared to today's technology. He looked at Gene, thinking that if the kid could jump out of bed so he could hear him better, he would. Gene was all ears.

"So … one of the things introduced in the light show was the strobe light. It was made up of a very bright light that flashed on and off several times a second producing a visual effect that was very cool. Very cool indeed! When it was on, you could see people in the crowd moving, appearing to be in slow motion. The movements seemed … choppy, because you'd only see the crowd when the light was on. The problem was it cost too much to buy. One of our buddies told us he'd built a strobe light and wanted to know if we would use it."

"Yeah, so … what happened?"

Bruce looked at the young man lying on the bed paralyzed from the neck down. He thought Doctor Klein was wrong; he wasn't having a nervous breakdown. He needed to get his mind off his problems, even for a few minutes. The kid would be all right.

"Well, it was nothing more than an electric motor with a fan belt that turned this plywood wheel, see? The wheel was about three feet in diameter. It had a hole cut out near the edge. The hole was around six inches across. As the motor turned the plywood wheel, a light would shine through the hole with every revolution of the wheel. It was like turning the light switch off and on about ten times a second. It did have the strobe effect so … we set it up on stage and started playing songs to about two hundred people. That's when all hell broke loose."

He paused, relishing the moment, seeing the look of anticipation on Gene's face. He liked the kid. He thought, *"Good. It's working."* He figured the last thing Gene was thinking about at that moment was his hopeless situation.

"What happened?" Gene wanted to shake the answer out of him.

Bruce pretended he was in deep thought. "Huh …? Oh yeah. We were playing like crazy, playing the blues and grooving, man, enjoying the strobe effect." He was getting great pleasure in bringing back the old jargon. Words he no longer used. "Yeah, the crowd was grooving too, man. They were really getting into it. They loved it. They thought we were cool. C-O-O-L!" He spelt the word out. "The problem was—" He smiled at the thought. "The problem was the plywood wheel. It would make a bit of a 'flap-flap' sound as it spun around at a high speed. We knew how to handle the noise it made. All we had to do was turn up the volume on our amplifiers. That was our solution to everything back then." He smiled again, thinking about the high decibels he had subjected himself to in his younger years.

Gene was smiling too, thinking about the old technology. He imagined being there, taking in the scene.

Bruce continued. "So, we're in the middle of our tenth song. I think it was 'Satisfaction' by the Rolling Stones when we heard this crashing noise. All four of us—Don, Jim, Bill and myself—looked over to the side of the stage where this marvelous

Piece of equipment was positioned. The plywood wheel had come loose, flying across the stage, barely missing us. Several people in the audience screamed as the wheel spun out of control, racing across the dance floor."

His hands were held up high, reaching for the ceiling to illustrate. "By the way, that was the *only* time fans ever screamed at us while we were on stage." He winked as he said it.

Gene was laughing. He could see the band standing on stage with stunned looks on their faces, the crowd looking on in disbelief, all wondering what the hell was going on. Was this part of the act? He kept on laughing. This Bruce guy was C-O-O-L!

Bruce laughed with him. It was funny indeed. They stopped after a few minutes, Bruce pretending he was playing the guitar, humming a few notes to 'Satisfaction' as he danced around the chair. This set them both off into another fit of laughter.

After a minute or so they stopped and looked at each other. Both took in a deep breath. Bruce knew the bond had been made. He liked Gene. He had to choose the next few sentences very carefully. "So … what about you, Gene? Have you ever played in a band?"

"Naw. I wanted to, but—" His cheeks were sore from laughing. It had been a long time since that had happened.

"But what?"

"My dad and mom, they—"

"They, what?" Bruce came closer to him, this time sitting still on the edge of the bed.

"They never supported me. I—they—well, it just didn't work out."

"Yeah, I hear you. My mom and dad were like that, too."

"Really?" Gene was surprised. He hadn't given much thought to other people's problems.

Bruce was drawing Gene out of his shell as he kept on talking. "I couldn't stand being with them in the same house. They were so un-cool, man. I had nothing in common with them, even the music. They didn't even know who the Rolling Stones were."

"Yeah, I know what you mean." Even though he was only eighteen, Gene knew who the Stones were. He and his buddy Dan were mostly into rap but did like some of the older music. "I was never close to Mom *or* Dad. I wanted to be, but—" He stumbled with what he was trying to say. Bruce sat there, patiently waiting for him to continue. He smiled and nodded, encouraging him to go on.

"I loved them both. They didn't love me back!" He spoke with defiance, no longer smiling.

Bruce wanted to reassure him both parents probably loved him but stopped short, letting Gene continue.

"Anyhow, no, Doctor. I never played in a band."

He could sense Gene was shutting down, not wanting to talk. He tried changing the subject.

"So, what *did* you do for fun, and please, my name isn't 'Doctor.' Call me Bruce, okay?"

"Yeah. Okay, Bruce. Hmm, what did I do for fun? Good question. Nothing really. I hung out with some of the guys down at the gym."

"Did you want to build up your body?"

"Yeah, I wanted to be a muscle man."

"Why?"

Gene was staring at the ceiling, thinking about the question. He felt like he was squirming. He knew that was impossible. He couldn't move from the neck down. "Why? I dunno. I guess I wanted to be popular."

They talked for over an hour, Gene opening up a little more, telling Bruce how he wanted to be a hero. Bruce would nod and encourage him, sensing the disappointment and anger below the surface. He tried coaxing him into talking about his social life. In particular, he wanted him to talk about girlfriends but sensed a strong reluctance on Gene's part.

Doctor Klein had been right in arranging the interview. Bruce was starting to build a pretty good profile of Gene. He saw two immediate issues. One was

Gene's hurt and anger with his parents. The other was his frustration with the opposite sex.

As he talked, Bruce wondered about the parents. They certainly sounded dysfunctional. He wasn't sure if they cared about their son. The hospital could call the parents once more, asking them to come and visit, but they couldn't force them to.

The other issue was more intriguing, the issue on how he handled the opposite sex. He knew that a young man such as Gene would have problems with girls, no matter if his parents were supportive or not. That was normal. What wasn't normal was his anger toward them, not only his anger toward females but also his anger toward himself.

He tried to get the interview on to a more positive note but it was proving too difficult. In the end, Bruce told him how much fun he'd had. He really meant it, saying he'd be back again soon. He started to walk away, stopped, turned and faced Gene, pretending to play the bass guitar, humming 'Satisfaction' one more time while dancing.

It didn't take long for Gene to break up and laugh again. He had tears in his eyes, especially when, unbeknownst to Bruce, Doctor Klein entered the room behind him, witnessing the crazy performance.

Bruce looked at Gene, wondering why he was laughing so hard. Surely, what he was doing wasn't that funny, was it? He continued to dance while pretending to play the guitar. He finally turned, bumping into Klein.

He blurted out, "Oops! Sorry, Doctor."

Gene thought he was going to pee the bed. Bruce had a sheepish look on his face as he quickly left the room.

Doctor Klein couldn't help but chuckle, a rarity for him. He was glad he had called Bruce. He was one of the best. He was anxious to read the counselor's report.

GENE—AVAILABLE AT BOOKS STORES ON LINE OR AT TRAFFORD.COM
ISBN 978-1-4251-5627-5